# DRAGON LEGACY

# DRAGON LEGACY

## DRAGONS OF BOSTON BOOK THREE

### CHRIS A. JACKSON

FALSTAFF
BOOKS
WWW.FALSTAFFBOOKS.COM

*We are all in a state of recovery, constantly, from the trauma of our lives and the world around us. This novel deals with a lot of traumatic psychological trauma, including PTSD, Social Anxiety Disorder, survivor's guilt, paranoia, and psychosis. As a writer, I take these disorders seriously. As a sufferer of some of them, I treat them with all the empathy in my soul. This novel is dedicated to all of us who suffer invisibly. You are not alone.*

---

*She flies through dense trees, a forest of green, a million scents a riot in her mind, colors muted in the darkness, but details were sharper than she's ever known. The wind and leaves caress her smooth, sensitive scales like the brush of a lover's fingers.* A lover... *One scent leaps out from ahead, a shape moving in the gray and green foliage, darting, running, fleeing in blind panic, its heartbeat a rising cadence in her ears. That scent plagues her—so familiar, it sparked warm memories—but the flight of the shape flips a switch in her mind:* Prey. *She wheels in, closing fast, jaws gaping to drink in that scent, meat, muscle, bone, sweat... Her prey—two legs, agile, naked, beautiful—darts and dodges but cannot evade her. Her neck flexes, jaws opening for the kill...and Charlie turns to look back at her in terror. He opens his mouth, and his scream ignites her every nerve.*

Charlie!" Lori Watkins lurched up in bed, *her* bed, her sheets, her pillows, and her stuffed animals. *A dream, a nightmare...* But as she reached out to Charlie's side of the bed, she realized that only half of her nightmare had been a dream. And reality was far worse.

This wasn't her bedroom. The things were hers, the furniture, the pictures on the walls, even her familiar flannel pajamas, the Hello

Kitty nightlight, and the squeaky queen-sized mattress that she and Charlie bought at an estate sale when they moved in together. But the room wasn't their bedroom. This wasn't their apartment. The walls were the wrong color, the windows and doors in the wrong places, the shades different, the scene outside fake. The room was part of her prison, though her keepers insisted that it wasn't that. She was sick, that much was true. She'd sweated through days of fever, doctors and nurses with face shields and rubber gloves, needles and biopsies, and a lot of medical talk. She was sick.

And Charlie was dead.

"Oh, Charlie..." Lori fell back and reached out to draw his pillow close. His scent, still on the fabric beneath the case, sparked a million memories of him. Walking, talking, eating Cheerios, making love... The other memories were dim, fogged with pain and anguish, his screams echoing in her mind with the smell of blood. A wracking sob tore at her chest, and she wailed into his pillow.

"Lori? Are you all right?"

The voice—not Charlie, but one of her keepers, Doctor Price—tore her from her misery to find the room lights on low. There was no one there, of course, just a voice from the intercom speakers. They were watching and listening to her day and night, and the thought of it creeped her out like ants crawling on her skin. The thought of voyeurs spying on her every move, monitoring her, invading her privacy, her misery, set off an uncharacteristic flare of anger.

"No!" Lori flung the sheets aside and lurched out of bed. "No, I'm *not* all right!" She stalked into the bathroom—not her bathroom, even though her toothbrush stood in her toothbrush stand, her towels hung on the racks, and her hairbrush lay beside the sink—and slammed the door.

The lights came on low automatically, though she didn't need them; the nightlights were more than bright enough for her to see. She turned on the water and stared at her reflection until steam rose from the sink. Puffy red eyes stared back from beneath disheveled brown hair, her face flushed. Her irises seemed wrong, jaundiced, sickly. She looked like shit. Of course, she hadn't been sleeping, and she kind of felt like shit, too. Not as bad as the days of fever, but she ached all over, especially her hands, and she had a dull background headache.

"Can we get you anything?" Price's disembodied voice asked.

"No!" They said they didn't watch her in the bathroom, but she doubted that. The water was hot, so she washed her face, relishing the warmth. Leaning on the sink, she tried to breathe deeply, to let go of the anger, the pain, the loss. "Just leave me alone!"

"All right, Lori. If you need something to calm you down, just say so."

*Something to calm me down...* Lori clenched her hands, her nails biting her palms painfully. That seemed to be their answer to everything: more drugs, more psychotherapy, more invasion of her privacy, her body, her life. *My life...good food, school, the dream of owning a restaurant, and Charlie...goofy, kind, smart, silly, tender Charlie. All gone.*

Another sob tore at her. Her life was over, Charlie was dead and she was in this...this *zoo*, infected with some freaky virus they couldn't cure. Her teeth clenched so hard that her pulse pounded in her ears. Pain flared in her palms, sharp and piercing, wrenching a startled gasp from her throat.

The water in the sink ran red.

"What the *fuck*?" Lori opened her hands to find four lacerations in each palm. They weren't deep, but enough to bleed, and they were from her own nails—her sharp, curved nails. She flexed her fingers, and the claws slid out half a centimeter. She screamed, "What the *fuck* is happening to me?"

"What's wrong, Lori?" the Price voice asked.

"What the fuck is *happening* to me?" Lori stared at her hands, her nails, her *claws*. Blood dripped into the sink and roared in her ears.

She heard a door open, not the bathroom door, not her bedroom door, but the apartment door. Metal clicked on metal, the guards, but there were more than only those two. Lori didn't know how she could tell, but there were four people, two of them guards, an attendant, and Doctor Price. The information seemed to bounce around inside her skull unasked for. She stared at her hands and staggered back from

3

the sink, blood dripping bright and slow to spatter on the smooth tile floor. It smelled like meat, like food. The bedroom door opened, and Price called her name.

Lori's back hit the wall, and she slid down, staring at her hands, her claws, her blood. She flexed her fingers, and the claws slid out from her cuticles again. She relaxed, and they retracted. A shuddering moan of horror tore at her throat.

"Lori?" A knock sounded on the bathroom door, and it opened. Price crept in, cautious, fearful. The two female guards stood behind her, their weapons held low, but ready. An attendant behind them held a first aid kit in trembling hands.

"Get out!" Lori raged, clenching her hands into fists again, drawing the pain in like a drug, letting it fill her. "I don't *want* you! I don't want *this*!" She shook a bloody fist at Price.

"Lori, let me give you something to calm you down." Price reached for the pocket of her lab coat and withdrew a small syringe. "You're upset. We told you the infection would cause some changes. Stop hurting yourself and relax. We're trying to help you."

"*Help* me?" Lori drew another shuddering sob and tried to unclench her bleeding fists. The sight of the needle, the guards with their weapons, the fear in their eyes—especially the fear—electrified every nerve in her body. The primal urge to lash out, to tear flesh from bone, to bury her teeth in their throats surged up her throat like sour vomit. "What the *fuck* is happening to me?!"

"We don't know, Lori, but we're trying to help you." Price edged closer.

Something in Lori's strange new suite of senses twisted in her mind; something wrong about what Price had said. A single thought congealed: *Liar!*

Price took another step closer. "Let me give you this medicine. It'll calm you down."

Lori unclenched her hands, forcing calm, denying the visceral urge to kill. She drew her claws from the palms of her bleeding hands and nodded, trying to breathe, to think through the blood and horror.

"Good. Okay, just hold still." Price crouched and popped the cap off the needle. The cap clattered to the tile floor. The shiny metal of the needle glowed in the low light. "Just a little stick."

Lori nodded, dragging a ragged breath into her lungs. The needle slipped into her arm with barely a prick, and the syringe's plunger pushed the drug into her. It stung, but only for a second. Lori hugged her knees, blood smearing her pajamas. Tears, anguish, loss, memories, and pain vied with the urge to rip, tear, bite, and kill. Lori had never been a violent person, until now, and the urges horrified her as much as her mutated nails. When the drug dimmed her vision and fogged her mind, she welcomed it.

---

I'm *really* starting to hate needles." Aleksi watched Reggie pull a murky mixture from a red-labeled vial into a three-cc syringe and suppressed a shiver. This would be her third treatment in her new regimen to reverse the changes in her genome brought on by the *Homo draconis* infection. She'd received one each day since she'd returned to Persephone's family mansion and the Sanctum.

"I could leave a hep-lock in if you'd prefer." Reggie put the vial down, tapped the syringe, and expressed a tiny bubble.

"No thanks. I'd probably tear it out in my sleep." *If I could sleep.* The first two treatments—multiple CRISPR therapies targeting specific segments of her altered genome mixed with protein-altering transfer RNA phages that would speed along the phenotypic changes—had left her itchy and uneasy. She forced tense muscles to relax, laid back on the comfortable recliner, and pulled the soft cotton poncho she wore around the Sanctum for a modicum of modesty up to her shoulder.

"Suit yourself. Now make a fist." He applied a C-shaped spring clamp to her bicep since her wings made tourniquets impossible.

Aleksi complied, curling her claws to keep them from piercing her palms. Reggie slipped the needle into her vein with a pinch of pain and pulled up a tiny amount of blood to make sure he was in. Loosening the pressure clamp, Reggie injected the mix. It tingled up her arm, and her heart skipped a beat.

He pulled the needle and pressed a cotton swab to the puncture. "There you go. Let me know if you feel any nausea or anything."

"Thanks." Aleksi forced a deep calming breath and nodded, resisting the reflex, as always, to draw away, lash out, flee, strike, kill. The urges were so much a part of her now that she didn't have to think about suppressing them. These people were her new family; they had given her an irreplaceable gift, allowing her to touch the man she loved without the fear of turning him into a monster, and they were giving her more with every injection. *Anything to be human again...* But this wasn't going to happen overnight.

The complete therapy would take a long time. They didn't fully understand everything that the *Homo draconis* infection had done to her, and undoing it would be like disassembling a house of cards in reverse order. They had mapped most of the cascade of changes. Tens of thousands of gene alterations, insertions, expressions, deletions, had to be undone, and they couldn't just start anywhere. Fully half of the changes coded for RNA expressions that made more changes. If they made a change downstream in the cascade without first fixing the upstream alteration, they would be wasting time. The upstream change would simply re-express, and they'd be right back where they started from.

"How's the patient?" Persephone entered the treatment room with her usual smile and bounce, the persona she used when she was playing her part as the wealthy socialite.

"*Impatient.*" Aleksi rose from the reclining chair and rubbed her arms under the poncho, rustling the thin membrane of her wings. "And itchy."

"Really itchy, or just impatient itchy?" Reggie asked with a raised eyebrow.

"Really itchy. My skin feels dry, flaky, and I'm a little more jittery than usual. That could just be being cooped up, though. Claustrophobia's setting in." Aleksi had learned early in her life as a dragon that inactivity and being indoors for extended periods didn't settle well. Filtered air also didn't help. She needed sights, sounds, smells, and exercise. "Nothing like that retrovirus you gave me before." The previous therapy, the one that had made her non-infectious, able to be with Hutch without fear, had laid her flat on her back for a week.

"Yeah, that was kind of a shotgun." Reggie grinned and dropped the spent syringe in a bright red biohazard sharps container. "This is the sniper rifle. I can give you something topical for the itching if you want."

"No thanks. Nothing yet. The inactivity makes it worse. Maybe a trip outside tonight?"

"A walk around the grounds would be fine, I think. We can wrap you up in hijab." Persephone gestured to the door. "Let me show you something that might keep you occupied for a while. At least your mind, anyway."

"Sure."

Aleksi followed Persephone to her room—actually a suite nicer than any hotel she'd ever stayed in, with a comfortable living room, kitchenette with a fridge, a comfy bedroom, and luxurious bath. She would have traded it for a closet if she would have been allowed to go out at night, but Persephone had been adamant that they couldn't risk it. The phenotypic changes brought on by their genomic reversions would be unpredictable, and a catastrophic flight failure in downtown Boston would be...well...catastrophic. A dragon lying injured or dead on the street would yield more cellphone images than the Olympics, and even Persephone's family and the government wouldn't be able to cover them all up. They'd had enough difficulty covering up the few shaky seconds of footage of her being chased through the sky by David Gilford.

"Have a seat." Persephone waved Aleksi to the couch and started tapping on her tablet.

The big flat screen came to life as Aleksi sat down. "Movie night?"

"Not quite." Persephone had gone serious, shifting to her non-socialite persona, the member of a secretive and powerful family with more money and power than most governments.

Aleksi wondered which one was the real Persephone, or if there was a real Persephone. The woman lived a lie every day of her life. She'd married Hutch in an attempt to worm her way into the world of paleontology and cryptozoology. She'd told Aleksi that she wished they could have stayed married, that she'd had honest feelings for Hutch, but that keeping her family secret had become too difficult. Her devotion to family transcended her marriage, so she'd methodically put distance between them, and finally asked for a divorce.

Persephone booted up a file, and the screen lit up with a ridiculously complicated diagram. "This is the entire cascade of genetic and protein changes that we've been able to map so far. The four points of origin are the original infective RNA viruses from the sample. Those, of course, we've already eliminated, and are highlighted in red. The ones in yellow we're working on now."

About five percent of the cascade was highlighted yellow.

"And the rest?" Aleksi asked.

"We're mapping more, or rather my great-grandmother is. As you can see, the number of genetic alterations expands exponentially the deeper we dig."

"Is that supposed to be encouraging?"

"No." Persephone gave her a wan smile. "It's supposed to be *informative*. Frankly, we're spread thin, but we thought to get started somewhere and work out the rest in process. My great-grandmother's mapping, Reggie's working out the therapy plan, and I'm trying to cross check and carry on with our outside appearance as if nothing's going on."

"And you want me to help." Aleksi's eyes were drawn to the schematic, a labyrinth of genetic designations, protein codes, and biochemical messengers.

"Yes, but it's not as daunting as it looks." Persephone handed her the pad. "The coding key is right there. What we need you to work on is finding any crossovers between the cascades. You can see that they branch a lot, but we may have missed any number of gene switches or coding changes that interact between the pathways. If we miss a crossover, and treat you incorrectly, there could be complications."

"Like cascades reasserting behind your previous changes?"

"Exactly." Persephone sighed. "Quite honestly, Aleksi, you're more of a scientist than Reggie is, and *way* more than I am. Your help will be invaluable."

"But you can do things, have *done* things that I would have never dreamed possible," Aleksi argued.

"That's just capability, not expertise or talent. You're *brilliant*, Aleksi, whether you realize it or not. Nobody graduates *summa cum laude* from NYU and lands a PhD postgraduate position at Harvard without some serious brains." She sat down and put a hand on Aleksi's shoulder. "Hutch told me you were the most gifted student he's ever had."

"He's got a biased opinion of me." Hutch had more than that; he loved her, even as a dragon. That made him special in ways she'd never imagined possible.

"Maybe, but I've seen your work. My great-grandmother's read everything you've ever written. She agrees that you're brilliant, and if anyone in the *world* isn't biased, it's Gi-gi."

"And this will keep me busy." Secretly, Aleksi wondered if she was being humored, flattered into busy work. Still, the genetic puzzle of her transformation was fascinating. Teasing it apart would certainly occupy her mind.

"Yes, that, too."

Aleksi sighed and nodded. "Okay, I'll see what I can find."

"Great." Persephone got up and started for the door. "Call if you need anything. I'll take you for a walk this evening."

"Deal." The door closed, and Aleksi doffed her poncho. When alone or flying around the city, she preferred to wear nothing, the former for comfort and the latter for necessity. Six months as a dragon had purged the last of her modesty, and it wasn't like she looked human any longer, anyway. Lithe and muscular, her skin layered with fine golden scales, winged from the tips of her two long pinion fingers to her ankles, she looked more reptilian than mammalian. She brewed a coffee and started studying the schematic, learning their designations, following the pathways, color-coding them, and making notes.

One thing that had not been changed in Aleksi was her deep love of mysteries, puzzles in biology and evolution, quirks and secrets hidden in millions of years of camouflage, whether they were hidden in strata of rock, or junk DNA. In a matter of hours, she felt like she was seeing a pattern to the cascade, an elegant tapestry that wove disused codes into new expressions. Molecular von Neumann machines of genetic codes, making and remaking themselves, interacting and being reforged into compositions that were more than the sum of their parts. The tapestry painted a very clear picture in her mind.

*The monster*, she thought. *This is the monster hidden inside every living human being on the planet.* She tried to imagine a world full of dragons, the males aggressively driven to spread their genome and kill rival males, while females were genetically predisposed to protect their families. She couldn't, but one thing was clear: if the *Homo draconis* infection ever got out into the general population, it would mean Armageddon.

"Progress?" Persephone said from the door.

Aleksi snapped around at the unexpected entry, instantly on her feet, every muscle tensed. She hadn't heard her outside, hadn't smelled her, hadn't felt the vibrations of her footfalls or the door opening. She'd been so engrossed that a freight train could have run through the room and she wouldn't have noticed.

Persephone froze. "You okay?"

"Yeah, I...just..." Aleksi gave a little shiver, her wing membranes shuddering. The surprise had put her into fight-or-flight mode with the blink of an eye. "Sorry. I didn't hear you come in, and you startled me. I can't remember the last time that happened."

"I never thought Gi-gi's research findings were that fascinating." Persephone came all the way in, and Aleksi caught a whiff of fear from her. "You looked ready to rip me apart for a second there."

"I don't handle surprises well." Aleksi shrugged and nodded to the screen. "And this *is* fascinating. It's a lot more complex than I thought."

"Find any cross..." Persephone stopped to stare at the modified diagram Aleksi had compiled. "Holy shit!"

"I got kinda carried away, I guess, but color coding everything made it easier to see." Aleksi tapped the tablet and a color key came up. "So, I worked off of a standard color palate, with red, yellow, blue, and green as the four primary infective agents. Variations in those colors indicate some elements of crossover from other infective elements. Some have so many variants that the colors get too close together to pick apart easily, but it gives a broad idea how much interaction there is."

"A lot more than I would have thought." Persephone peered closely at the screen. "Do you mind if I send this to Gi-gi?"

"Not at all, but I'm far from done."

"It's all a work in progress."

"No kidding." Aleksi spread her wings. "Just like me."

Persephone's brow furrowed. "What do you mean?"

"I mean," Aleksi said, pointing to the screen, "if you think you can unravel *that* mess, you're way more advanced than you've let on."

"We *are*, but we'll bring you up to speed. Don't worry." Persephone gestured to the door. "Ready for a walk?"

"You kidding me?" Aleksi put the tablet down and hurried to the closet to pick out a robe.

Persephone had bought her several new hijabs, telling the salespeople that she was planning a trip to the Middle East. *Licensed to shop* was her motto. Aleksi put one on with long-practiced motions and followed her hostess out of her rooms, the Sanctum, through the wine cellar with its vast array of scents, and up the stairs to the garage. At the side door, Persephone made sure her hood and face scarf were secured, and then opened the door.

The night was clear, the lights of the city blocking the stars except for a few of the brightest. Still, the sounds and scents of three million human beings filled her like a heady draft of wine. She breathed deep, relishing the moment. The cacophony in her mind—the feel of grass under her feet, cool, complex air on her face, the thousands of tiny leaves quivering in the light breeze—enveloped her.

"Gloriousss," she hissed, hugging herself to keep from vaulting into the sky and taking wing.

"I'm glad you like it." Persephone matched her slow stroll across the lawn. "I've been thinking we should pipe in unfiltered outside air to help you with your claustrophobia."

"Maybe, if you could put a view from outside on the TV, too, that would help." Aleksi breathed deep. "I never thought I'd miss air pollution."

Persephone chuckled. "We're city girls, born and bred, both of us."

"True." Aleksi glanced at her sidelong and decided to change the subject. "Looking through the data got me thinking, Persephone. This thing, this latent monster, is in every human being on the planet. I know I've said before that it's dangerous, but..."

"But what?"

"I know you're secretive, and I understand why, but we should think of what to do about the first of David Gilford's victims. You said you think the government has her."

"Pretty sure of it, as a matter of fact, but we have no idea where."

"She's changing like I did right now."

"Yes, she is." Persephone stared her in the eyes. "Her name's Lori Watkins, by the way."

"Lori." Aleksi nodded; putting a name to the woman made the abduction more real, more urgent, more heartbreaking. "And it's likely that Buckmann's in charge of the project. They called her in when David broke containment."

"That's likely, yes."

"What do you think she'll do with this?" Aleksi raised one three-fingered hand outside her robe, flexing her claws. "With Lori?"

"I think they'll try to use her, analyze her." Persephone sighed. "They may think that a female subject will give them a psychologically stable experimental trial."

"And they may be right."

"Maybe, but there's no way to know." Persephone sighed in obvious frustration. "They're playing with fire again. They want to weaponize this; I'd bet my last dime on it."

"So would I. Well, your last dime, since I don't have any." Aleksi stopped and faced Persephone. "So, what do we do about it?"

Persephone blinked at her. "*You* don't do anything about it. You're in the middle of your treatment. You can't run out and—"

"I'm not running out anywhere. Don't worry." Aleksi turned and resumed walking, cocking her head as a distant siren wailed through the night. "Still, there might be something *someone* could do. They've basically kidnapped her and are holding her against her will."

"At least she's isolated. I don't think they'll be as stupid this time."

Aleksi snorted a laugh. "No, they'll ascend to a whole new level of stupid."

"What do you mean?"

"I mean they're not going to stop until they get what they want: an army of dragons."

"That won't happen, Aleksi. They know, Buckmann knows, what will happen if this infection breaks out."

"I hope so." Aleksi sighed and gazed up at the dim stars. "The world's still too beautiful a place to watch it be destroyed."

"That it is," Persephone agreed with a slow smile. "I'm sure someone somewhere is looking into the disappearance of Lori Watkins."

Aleksi squinted at her skeptically. "Oh? Who?"

Persephone shrugged, her smile intact. "Someone almost as tenacious as you are."

---

T his is the place." Tony Jasper put the POLICE placard on the dash and got out of the car. One of the few perks of being a cop was parking in yellow zones. His long-time partner, Marty Willis, got out of the driver's side and locked the doors. "Watkins worked here as assistant manager."

"If Blake finds out you're investigating this on her turf, she's gonna bite your dick off." Marty shot him a sour look. "And I mean that *literally*."

"Hey, we're just asking some questions. No harm in that. It's not like she's pursuing the investigation."

They'd gotten Lori Watkins' identity and the details of the attack from Blake, and the Boston Police Department had jurisdiction. Blake had been instructed by the powers that be to drop the investigation. But Tony and Marty worked for Cambridge Homicide and had received no such orders. Yes, they were outside their jurisdiction, but all the Boston Metropolitan Area precincts shared turf. He and Marty had found two of the rogue dragon's victims on an anonymous tip and had thought to try for a third. Their initial searches for information on Loretta Watkins and Charlie Fenwick had come up with nothing, yet another reason Tony thought the government had disappeared her. They'd wiped the slate clean; it was like Watkins and Fenwick had never existed. An unofficial inquiry to utility providers had yielded the address of an apartment in Lowell. Some careful questioning of their neighbors had yielded her former place of employment, but little else. Lori and her fiancé, Charlie Fenwick, had been fairly private people.

Jasper opened the door to the restaurant and grinned at Marty. "And my relationship with Detective Blake hasn't progressed to the dick biting stage."

Marty stopped and gave him another look. "*Way* too much information, Tony."

"Hey, you brought it up. I'm just giving you the facts."

He was seeing Detective Sergeant Anna Blake of the BPD, but so far it had only gone as far as drinks, talking, and some light flirting. He enjoyed her company, and she seemed to enjoy his. They had a lot in common. Both were cops, busy, single—she was divorced—and had desolate social lives. They were also both being careful not to get into something that might turn ugly. They worked in separate precincts, so there was less of a chance of work problems than between Marty and his husband, Charles, who worked in the Vice Division in Cambridge. They were, however, both homicide detectives, and work like that often caused friction in relationships, even cop-cop relationships.

A bright-eyed hostess greeted them with a smile. "Table for two?"

"Sure. A booth, if you've got one open, and we'd like to speak to the manager when they have a chance." He showed his badge, and her bright countenance fell. "No problems, just some questions about a former employee."

"Oh, sure. No problem. This way."

As they followed her to a booth, Tony took in the restaurant's theme: a casual sports-oriented place with too many flat-screen TVs for his taste. It was early, so the lunch crush hadn't hit yet, but places like this were always too loud to carry on a conversation. He and Marty sat, ordered coffee when the waiter came by, and perused the menu. Their waiter hadn't returned yet when a heavyset man approached the table. He wore a jacket and tie, the latter loose and the former tight around his bulbous frame. He also wore a worried expression.

"I'm Nate Berger, the day manager here. How can I help you officers?" He spoke with a deep north shore Boston accent.

"Detectives," Jasper said with a smile. "We want to know if you've heard anything about the whereabouts of Lori Watkins. She was an employee here."

"Yeah, I know Lori. She worked nights. She was nice. Knew her job and did it well. She didn't deserve what happened to her."

"You heard what happened?" Marty asked.

As far as they knew, the details of the incident had been utterly quashed, no news reports, no hospital reports, and barely a coroner's receiving report on Fenwick. About the same time Lori was whisked out of Mass General by two Men in Black clones, Charlie Fenwick's mutilated corpse had been taken from the city morgue by a hazmat team with Department of Homeland Security IDs. Security camera footage from the morgue had been confiscated, and the hospital camera feeds hacked. There was no official record of either of the victims anymore, but even the government couldn't delete people's memories.

"We heard Charlie was murdered. That's all. Some ganger mugging or something. Some Southie punks."

"And Miss Watkins?"

Berger shrugged. "She just didn't come back to work. We got a letter of resignation, signed and delivered by a lawyer with a court order to take all of her employment records. Corporate started to put up a stink, but then gave in." He shrugged again.

"Did you personally meet this lawyer?" Tony asked.

"Yeah. I'm day manager, so yeah. They weren't very polite."

"Did they look like either of these people?" Tony pulled the sketches he'd had made by the department sketch artist of the CDC and FBI people who had taken the other two victims.

Berger squinted at the sketches and pursed his lips, then shook his head. "Nope. Not even close, though that woman looks familiar. Maybe seen her somewhere."

"Any idea where?" Marty asked.

"Not off the top of my head, nope. Sorry."

"And you haven't heard anything about where Lori went?" Tony asked.

"Nope. Not a peep." Nate shrugged one more time for good measure. "We all liked Lori. She liked her job and knew the restaurant business. I wish she'd stayed, but..." One more shrug.

Tony produced a business card. "We appreciate the help, Mr. Berger. Please give me a call if you remember where you saw that woman, or if people start asking questions."

Berger took the card and smiled. "You mean like you guys?"

Tony tried to match the smile. "Yeah, like us, but without badges."

"Will do, Detective." Berger did a little mock salute with the Tony's card. "You have a nice lunch, on me. We got the best Reuben in town."

"Thank you, Nate." Tony closed his menu and sighed.

"Well, that was pretty pointless, unless you count Cop Rule One." Marty picked up his menu.

Rule One was, "Never turn down free food," but Tony wasn't ready to write off the effort as a loss. "I don't know. Someone got a court order. We might be able to track that down."

"What do you bet it was bogus?"

"Maybe, but that's a serious crime."

"So's kidnapping."

"Good point."

"Unless you're the government, and you call it '*detention*.'"

"Or quarantine. Remember, Lori was bitten by that..." Tony lowered his voice. "...that *thing* that they made."

"Exactly." Marty paused as their waiter returned.

"What'll it be, gents?" the young man asked with a smile.

"I'm told the Reuben is good," Tony said.

"It is! Fries with that?"

"Potato salad if it's no trouble."

"Not at all." The waiter scratched a note and turned to Marty. "And for you?"

"The Philly steak and cheese with fries."

"Got it." The young man scratched on his pad and hurried off.

"So..." Marty sipped his coffee, "my money's on the feds for Watkins."

"Ditto. If those...other people had taken her, she'd have been found in a hotel room by now." Finding the other two victims healthy and healed, though drugged, had been nothing short of miraculous. Wounds barely a week old were completely gone without significant scars. That meant someone out there had a cure for this infection, not to mention top notch medical capabilities. Tony had asked a physician friend about the scarring, and she'd said it was possible with really good plastic surgery skills, but that a week to heal injuries like that was amazing.

"Which begs the question of what the hell we're doing, other than risking our careers, of course."

Tony shot his partner a glare over his coffee cup. "I don't know, Marty, but I don't want to let it go. If the Feds have Watkins, and she's infected..."

"Then our *friend* won't be the only unidentified scaly object flying around Boston anymore."

"That's just it. Watkins is a civilian. Their last fuckup was a soldier, someone they thought they could control. They won't let Watkins out. They've *got* to know the danger of infection."

"Then why keep her?" Marty frowned. "Maybe they didn't. Maybe they...destroyed the evidence."

Tony shook his head. "No, they'd study her. They want to know why our *friend* is psychologically stable, if a bit touchy and scary as fuck, while their last experiment went whacko."

"Right." Marty nodded and downed his coffee. "Which really sucks for Lori Watkins."

"It certainly does."

They stared at each other for a moment, eye to eye, all but reading each other's thoughts. Tony and Marty had been partners for years and knew each other better than most married couples.

Finally, Marty smiled and said, "Just do it, Tony."

"You think she'll help?"

"I think she'll keep hunting until she finds Watkins, no matter who gets in her way, and she can go places we can't, do things we can't, and maybe, just maybe, if our *friend* finds her, she can…help her."

Tony nodded, pulled his phone, and started tapping out a text to the only person they knew who was in touch with the Dragon of Boston, Aleksi Rychenkna.

———————

## 2

**M**ary Buckmann stood behind Price and the new psychiatrist, Julia Olson, as the two physicians examined Lori Watkins. She'd watched the daily examinations through CCTV cameras for two weeks, as well as hours of footage of the subject pacing, reading, watching TV, sleeping, and even showering. Right now, she sat in a comfortable armchair with her feet up, enduring needle sticks, biopsies, and exams while Olson asked her leading questions.

"Can you describe these dreams in detail for me, Lori? I'd like to understand what you're going through."

"I don't want to," Lori slurred. She was heavily medicated—a titration of time-released ketamine and midazolam given in her food. Both drugs, hypnotic anesthetics with anxiolytic and amnestic properties, decreased inhibitions and made the subject complaint.

"I'd like you to, please, Lori. It'll help us treat you."

"B…blood. They're always about blood. I don't want to remember them." A tear slid down the side of Lori's face.

"Your blood? Are you injured in your dreams?" Of course, they knew from David Gilford and Derrick Penningly that people infected with *Homo draconis* had vivid dreams, and what those dreams entailed.

"No. Not mine."

"Whose blood?"

"Sometimes animals, sometimes people." Lori sniffed. "Sometimes Charlie."

"You have dreams about Charlie? Tell me about those, please."

"I…don't remember them. Just the blood…and the screams. His screams." Lori shook her head from side to side.

"Okay, Lori. I understand it's hard to remember, but talking about these things helps sometimes."

"Charlie's dead. He's really dead. Why do I keep seeing him in my dreams? He's gone."

"Memories play tricks on our sleeping minds, Lori. It's not uncommon. Perfectly normal. It's how we cope with grief."

"But you can't cure me. This…virus. What's happening to me? My fingernails were…long and sharp." Her eyes blinked open and she tried to raise a hand to look at her fingers, but the soft restraint came up short. Regardless, they'd cut her nails to the quick daily to prevent her from hurting herself again. "Was that real?"

Olson glanced over her shoulder at Mary, raising a questioning eyebrow. Mary nodded. They couldn't keep the truth from Lori for long, not all of it.

"Yes, Lori, that was real. The virus made your nails grow long and sharp. There will be some other changes, but we want you to know that this isn't abnormal. It's happened before to other people, and we're doing our best to treat you. You've got to understand that we're trying to help you."

Lori nodded. "What's happening to me?"

"It's the sickness, Lori. You remember the fever, right?" Lori nodded. "It's causing some physiological changes. It's why you're having the dreams, too. I'm sorry, but we can't stop them. We need you to know that this isn't going to kill you. You'll be fine, just different."

"Different?" Lori blinked at them. "How different?"

"Very different, but not in a bad way." Olsen patted her arm. "I think we're done here for now. You just rest. Are you hungry?"

"Yes."

"We'll get you something yummy, then. Would you like the TV on?"

"Please."

Olson turned on the TV and handed Lori the remote. Mary turned and left the room, examining the two guards in passing. Both were hard as nails, military and covert ops rated, and they'd been thoroughly educated in what to expect from Lori as she changed. Mary took some solace in their steady eyes, fingers resting firmly on the trigger guards of their weapons, vigilant and ready. She also took solace in the two-inch-thick steel door to Lori's room. Even David Gilford couldn't have broken that down.

Outside, Mary peeled off her protective gear and waited for Olson and Price. The featureless concrete walls of the facility's sub-basement were painted a light blue, but the cheery hue offered little warmth. Lori's room had a much warmer décor, with as many of her personal effects as they could get from her apartment. So far, their attempts to keep the woman calm and cooperative were working, but only with the addition of medications.

*A dragon with PTSD*, she thought with rue. *That's all I need.*

The two physicians arrived in less than a minute, and she faced them as they stripped off their gear. "Well?"

"Physically, she's fine," Price began. "Changing faster than the others, but we assume that's due to the huge dose of active HD virus. The genetic cascade is fully underway. There's no stopping it."

"And psychologically?" Mary asked Olson.

"Frankly, she's a mess; traumatized, terrified, and she's lost the only person she was close to. I don't think she remembers much of her boyfriend's death, but the genetic memory dreams have picked up on some latent or residual images. She hasn't mentioned anything resembling David Gilford, so that's a plus."

"How so?"

"If she did, if she sees herself eventually changing into something *like* him, the...creature that murdered her lover, it might destabilize her mental condition."

"How badly?"

Olson shrugged. "No way to know. We have no background information on her previous mental state, but she has no official record of instability."

"Whereas the other female subject had serious social anxiety disorder, and is now perfectly stable mentally," Mary added.

"Yes." Olson shrugged again. "Except for Rychenkna's disorder, they're remarkably similar, really. Both young, healthy, intelligent women of education. They both had goals, bright futures, and both underwent a psychological trauma with the loss of someone close, and also lost their careers."

"One other difference," Price put in, and they both looked to her. "Support. Rychenkna had emotional support."

"Hutchinson," Mary said with a nod. "We'll have to fill that role, ladies. I want us to give her everything she needs to feel loved, wanted, and safe. Any time she's awake, someone needs to be ready to step in and be with her, even if it's only to talk, watch a movie, or play cards. Whatever she wants, whatever she needs, we give her."

"Yes, Doctor," they both said.

"Can we taper her off the meds? If she's on amnestics, she's not going to remember us helping her."

"Yes. We'll shift to anxiolytics without amnestic properties," Olson said. "I wanted to give her something that would expunge the memory of her self-mutilation."

"Good choice. Reassure her that these changes are normal. Her senses are sharpening." Mary glanced at the door and lowered her voice. "Limit conversation within her hearing. And tell her that if she wants privacy, we'll give it to her. We're monitoring her for her own safety, but she's not a specimen under observation."

"*Tell* her, or actually remove the surveillance?" Olson asked in an equally hushed tone.

"Just tell her. The cameras in the bathroom are undetectable. We can install similar ones in her bedroom if she wants the other ones taken out."

"Okay."

"Good. Any unexpected changes in her condition at all, or any events like last night, you notify me, day or night. Got it?"

"Yes, Doctor," they both said.

As Mary strode to the elevator, her phone vibrated in her pocket. The facility had integral cellular hubs on every floor for full coverage, even six floors below the street and surrounded by enough concrete and steel to withstand an airstrike. She nodded to the two guards at the elevator and one pushed the button for her. She stepped aboard, pushed the button for the B2 floor, and pulled her phone.

"Well, I'll be a son of a..." The very last person in the world that she expected to hear from had sent her a text. "Aleksi, what are you up to now?"

Mary pulled up the text, shielded the screen from the elevator camera, and read: "Where is the woman attacked by David Gilford? Please, no more dragons."

Mary Buckmann gritted her teeth and pocketed her phone without answering.

---

S eems ironic to just box these back up after all your work." Quinton Neilson helped maneuver the heavy, fossilized bone bed specimen into an Ethafoam mold fitted into a polycarbonate crate and nodded to the technician. "Okay, down slowly."

"More ironic than you know," Hutch agreed, as the tech thumbed the control that lowered the two hundred pounds of rock into the crate. "Where are they going?"

"BU science department. They've got a nice display case in the entry hall of the new building."

"Good. At least someone will see them." Hutch ran his gloved fingers over the fossilized bear bones, beautiful in their own way. "I'm going to miss them."

"I'm not." Vince Takemo, one of Hutch's two newest grad students, and the one who had done the lion's share of grunt work cleaning up and taking samples from the specimens for their research project, handed over the foam-lined lid. "I've had enough rock dust for a while."

Quinton furrowed his brow and all but glared at the younger man. "And you're in the paleosciences department *why?*"

"Sorry, I'm more of an evolutionary biology geek than paleoscientist, Doctor Neilson. No offense."

"None taken." Quinton's mien softened, and his eyes shifted to Hutch. "To each their own forte. Some people love revealing the secrets buried in these old rocks."

"That's true, but we've gotten all we need from these, and it's good to know someone's going to appreciate them." Hutch knew Quinton was alluding to Aleksi, but he wasn't going to rise to the bait. The curator of Harvard's Museum of Comparative Zoology had been hit almost as hard as Hutch by the loss of the mystery specimen and Aleksi's disappearance. Of course, Quinton didn't know what had really happened to Aleksi. "We've got enough data to keep us crunching numbers for a year."

As they fitted the lid onto the crate, Hutch's phone vibrated in his pocket. It was his regular phone, not the burner he kept inside his jacket pocket, the one that only had one contact. He pulled the phone and blinked in surprise at the picture of the young woman in green witch makeup on the screen. He hadn't heard from Julie in weeks. He excused himself and took the call.

"Hey, Jules! How's the Big Apple?"

"Hey, Hutch! Totally crazy! Sorry to call in the middle of the day. You busy?"

"Always, but never too busy for a call from the wicked good witch of Worchester." Julie laughed at that. She'd played the farcical part of the green-skinned Ozwitch in a play before she'd gotten an offer from a New York production company to produce her own romantic comedy on Broadway. It had been the break of a lifetime, and she'd broken off their casual physical relationship to move to the city. They'd helped each other through a rough emotional patch, but they'd both known it wasn't love. On top of that, Julie had asked an inordinate number of questions about Aleksi. They'd been roommates before Aleksi's transformation, but Julie's lingering interest had always made Hutch suspicious. "What's up?"

"So, I wanted to apologize again for running out of Boston like the place was on fire, but chances like this don't just drop out of trees."

"Stop it. You had to take it, Jules."

"Yeah, well, anyway, I got all my transfers to NYU done, and we've got an opening date for *Up and Down*. I wanted to ask you to come down for opening night. It's not until December, so plenty of time. I'd love you to see it, and…well, I'd like to see you, too. Just to talk things over, you know."

*Talk things over?* That sounded strange, but he couldn't turn her down. "Sure! I'd love to come down. Send me the date. We'll paint the town!"

"Great! I'll send you the date. Thanks, Hutch! It…means a lot to me."

"Looking forward to it!" Again, she sounded strange, but a phone conversation in a lab wasn't the right time to ask what was wrong. "See you later, Jules. Break a leg!"

"Thanks!" The call ended and he stared at the phone for a heartbeat. Julie sounded troubled, despite her unbelievable opportunity. Maybe that was part of what bothered Hutch; Harvard Drama graduate students didn't get offers from New York production companies to produce their very first play on Broadway. It just didn't happen. But it had. "Too good to be true," he mumbled, wondering if the old adage wasn't all too accurate.

"Problem, Hutch?" Vince asked.

"No, no problem." Hutch put the phone away and shook off the icicles forming along his spine. "So, get with Beth and give me some numbers by the end of the week. We've got a proposal to finish."

"Will do, boss!" Vince waved and left the basement lab.

Hutch followed him out. He was late for his office hours—more like office minutes these days considering his four grad students, six grants, classes, meetings, and outside obligations as an expert witness and consultant on half a dozen environmental issues. He also had an appointment waiting for him and hated to keep them waiting. After climbing the stairs to the second floor and navigating through the connecting walkways to the Northwest Science Building, he found his appointment standing outside his office door. They certainly weren't there to talk to him about science.

"Tony! Marty! Sorry I'm late. What's up?"

"We need to chat, Hutch." Tony nodded to Hutch's closed office door. "Not in your office. Can we grab a coffee?"

"Well, I'm supposed to have office hours, but..." Hutch could see from their faces that this was serious, and they only had one thing in common: Aleksi.

"Consider this a professional consultation," Marty said with a crooked smile.

"All right, then. Let's hit Buckminster's for a coffee."

"Great." Tony gestured Hutch to lead the way. "Sorry for taking your time, but this isn't something we wanted to talk about over the phone."

"Okay." That meant Tony was worried about being overheard or maybe a tapped phone line. That, in turn, meant DHS was involved. When they'd exited the building and started down Oxford Street toward Buckminster's, he asked the only question that mattered. "Tell me this isn't about our mutual friend."

"Not directly, no. It's about one of the women injured by...the other person like her. She's gone completely missing, and we're trying to figure out who's responsible."

Hutch reached for the door to the coffee shop and looked askance at Tony. "You probably know a lot more about her than I do."

"Maybe, but there's a lot about her *condition* that you know more about than we do."

"From personal experience," Marty added.

"Right." That was true enough. Hutch new more about Aleksi's condition than almost anyone. They picked up their coffee and sat down at a table. "So, what do you want to know?"

"First, we found the two victims from Gilford's second attack in a Cambridge hotel room on an anonymous tip. They were fine, though drugged. They woke up in the hospital with almost no memories of the attack, what happened to them, or their injuries. The first victim, the woman who survived the attack, Lori Watkins, was taken from Mass General by people who *said* they were with the government. She hasn't been seen or heard from since, and all her work records were confiscated. Her apartment was emptied and her lease broken."

"And BPD was told to end their investigation of her boyfriend's murder, and to quit looking for her," Marty added.

"So, you're saying the second two victims were cured, but the first disappeared." Hutch didn't want to tell them that Aleksi had received treatment from some mysterious people that had resulted in her not being infectious anymore. "Sounds like two different groups at work here, otherwise the first woman would have turned up cured, too."

"That's what we thought." Tony sipped his coffee and cleared his throat. "Which leads me to think that the government took her. They don't have a cure for this thing. We know that from what happened with their *last* little experiment."

"Which would also mean they have an infected victim somewhere, and she's changing," Marty added.

"And infectious," Hutch finished for them. "So, what do you want me to do about it?"

"Two things, actually." Tony grinned mischievously. "We're not really supposed to be investigating this, so us going to DHS with kidnapping charges in hand is a non-starter. We *can*, however, ask you to ask some questions, and maybe make some suggestions to them."

"Suggestions?" Hutch arched his eyebrows.

"Yeah, like stop making dragons before they end the fucking world," Marty quipped.

"They won't listen. They didn't before."

"True, but you know a lot more about how this would play out if the infection broke out. If you hit them with a doomsday scenario, maybe they'll wise up."

"I can do that." Hutch had done a lot of epidemiology modeling on the *Homo draconis* infection, and even the best-case scenario was grim.

He also had Mary Buckmann's direct number. She might listen to him. "What else?"

"Maybe tell our mutual friend about this, too. She found the last one like her. Maybe she can find Lori Watkins."

"Doubtful, if the government has her hidden away somewhere." Hutch also wasn't going to tell them that Aleksi was currently undergoing gene therapy to revert her condition and was probably in no shape to hunt down another dragon.

"Still, if anyone should know about this, *she* should," Marty countered.

"I can't argue with that." Hutch nodded and sipped his coffee. "And if a miracle happens and she *does* locate this Watkins woman?"

"You tell us who has her and where. We still might not be able to do anything to help her, but there's *someone* out there who can treat her, at least make her not infectious like they did those other two women."

"Okay, Tony, I'll do what I can, but the most I can *suggest* to the government is to be more careful this time, and they're probably already doing that. If they can't cure Lori Watkins, they'll just study her with the hope that they'll eventually find a treatment." Hutch shrugged again. "I don't know if we should even *try* to stop them."

"Well, please send the wakeup call anyway." Tony nodded to Marty and they got up. "Sorry to put you in the middle, but you're our only contact."

"No worries." Hutch grinned and shook their hands. "At this point, I'm kind of getting used to being in the middle."

"Thanks, doc," Marty said with a grin. "And give our mutual friend our best. If she needs anything, just let us know."

"Thanks." Hutch didn't know what they could do for Aleksi, but having friends in the Cambridge Police Department couldn't hurt.

---

L ori paced her room like a caged wolf, her bare feet scuffing the carpet, long, curved toenails catching whenever she turned. She gnawed at her nails, or rather her claws, but they grew back fast. The track she'd worn in the carpet was as far from the door and the two glowering guards as she could be. They made her tense, with their visored helmets and strange looking guns. She could smell the oil, feel the electric hum of the weapons—*Some kind of stun-guns?* she wondered—see the droplets of sweat on their upper lips, and taste their fear. She scared them. Hell, she scared herself.

"These dreams of Charlie," Doctor Olson continued. "What do you think they mean?"

"I thought that was your job, to tell me what my dreams meant." Lori flicked Olson a glare. The psychoanalysis was bothering her more than the daily needle sticks and physical exams, though not as much as the changes. Every day she woke to new horrors, her own flesh mutating before her eyes. The meds helped, and she'd lost count of the days, but it couldn't have been much more than a week since she'd first discovered her changes, her claws, her freakishly keen senses.

"I know what *I* think they mean; I want you to tell me what *you* think."

"I have no idea what they mean. They're horrible, terrifying. It's like I'm the one killing him, tearing him limb from limb." Lori started to flex her hands into fists and caught herself before her claws pierced the skin. "I wish they'd stop. Can't you give me something to make them stop?" *Lord knows they're already giving me enough medications; one more seems simple enough.*

"There are some medications that we can try, but they're just treating the symptom, Lori, not the cause." Olson tapped her tablet without looking up. She, at least, didn't seem terrified of Lori. "You understand the difference, right?"

"I think so. Like giving a pain killer instead of fixing what's causing the pain."

"Exactly. These dreams of Charlie, they're different than the others, the ones where you're flying or hunting. Those, we *think*, are what we call inherited memories, or genetic memories. They're not from your own experiences, but from the infection you've contracted."

Lori stared at Olson skeptically. "How can an *infection* give me nightmares?"

"Well, this infection is very different, as you've already figured out. It awakens latent genes in your chromosomes. Genes that we didn't know were there because they were in fragments and didn't do anything. That's where the memories and your nightmares come from."

"And these awakened genes did *this*?" She stopped and held up a hand, flexing her claws out, extending her elongated third and fourth fingers, stretching the thin membrane forming between them, down her arm, all the way to her ankle. "That's what's making me into some kind of monster?"

The two guards tensed without moving. Lori could feel their unease, sense it like a vibration in the air. Their pupils dilated slightly, and muscles around their lips flexed. She narrowed her eyes at them and felt her lip curl back from her teeth.

"Easy, now, Lori." Olson warned, snapping the moment. "Focus on what we're talking about, not them. They're here for your protection."

"They're here for *your* protection, you mean. From *me*."

"For *everyone's* protection, then. Just relax and think about our conversation. I want you to try to stop thinking of what's happening to you negatively. You're not becoming a monster. You're human, and you always will be, only different."

"Different..." Lori resumed pacing, forcing herself to breathe and parse the scents in the room: the sweat, stale cigarette smoke, bad breath, body lotion, antiperspirant, and chewing gum. *Too much*, she thought, squeezing her eyes closed. "You have no *idea* how different."

"We actually do, Lori. You're not the first person to contract this infection, and we know you're going through a kind of sensory overload right now. It's expected. You'll learn to deal with the extra information, like blind people develop sharper hearing and more sensitive touch to read braille." Olson tapped her tablet and the big screen built into the wall came alive with a pastoral scene. The sounds of birds and wind filled the room from hidden speakers. "Just work on your breathing, and try to immerse yourself in the scene. It's peaceful, isn't it?"

Lori glared at the screen. "It's fake."

"Yes, but it's beautiful. Think of it as someplace you'd like to be and imagine yourself there."

Lori knew Olson was trying to help her, so she concentrated on the scene, on the beauty, the waving stalks of grass, the sounds, the muted colors. She closed her eyes and tried to place herself in that beautiful scene, but the scents of fear, sweat, oil, electricity, and the sounds of shifting feet, twitching muscles, heartbeats, stomach rumbles, and the background hum of the building and streets above outed the lie.

"I can't. It's not real. I can't smell it, feel it, taste it. It's just a picture and some sounds." She opened her eyes and fixed Olson with a level stare. "I'm feeling like I'm in a cell, a cage, with nothing to do to keep myself from going insane. I need some fresh air, real sunlight."

"I'm sorry, but we can't let you outside, Lori. You're infectious."

"Yeah, I know." They'd told her a hundred times they couldn't let her out. She was a prisoner here, no matter how they justified it. *Dangerous, infectious, monstrous.*

"We can give you whatever you want to keep you occupied and entertained, Lori. Whatever you can think of. Food, music, movies, exercise, meditation, yoga..."

"Yoga?" She shot Olson a sideways look. "*Really?* You think that'll help?"

"One of our previous...patients found that exercise helped."

Olson's hesitation was slight, but real. It made Lori wonder what word other than "patient" she might have said. *Subject? Victim? Specimen?*

Lori sighed and resumed pacing. "I'll try anything. I like to cook, if you could set up a decent kitchen for me."

"You've said everything but meat tastes funny. Are you sure you want to *cook?*"

"Cooking's like meditation for me, even if I'm not eating it." She resumed her pacing. "Anything to take my mind off what's happening to me. I'm feeling trapped, claustrophobic, cut off from people, the world, everything's too close, too confined."

"I'll see if we can set up a kitchen in here. We can bring in some more people for you to talk with, socialize with. Board games, cards, or watching movies?"

"Sure. Anything." She stopped as one of the guards shifted, suddenly tense. "You know what's bothering me more than anything is *them*." She pointed one clawed finger. "You think I'm dangerous; *they're* the danger here with their guns and body armor."

"They're here for—"

"They are *not* here for *my* protection, Doctor. You know that, I know that, and *they* know that." Again, her lips parted, pulling back from her teeth of their own volition. "They couldn't protect you from me anyway!"

The guards shifted again, hands flexing on their weapons.

"Stop doing that!" Lori snapped, hands spread wide at her sides, claws out. "Put them out in the hall or something. They're driving me nuts!"

"It's okay, Lori." Olson stood slowly and held out a hand, palm toward the guards. "We'll work something out. Just calm down and breathe."

"Telling me to calm down with soldiers holding guns in the room is like telling someone to hold still while you cut into them with a knife!" Lori breathed deep and seethed. "I breathe and I smell their fear of me. I can hear their hearts racing, taste their sweat, feel their muscles tensing. Get them out of here before I stick those *fucking* guns up their asses!"

Lori whirled away and stalked to her bedroom, slamming the door behind her. There, however, the confines were even closer, the lack of scents more profound. The pillow smelled like Charlie, and her clothes smelled like her own rage. She took off the loose pajamas and dashed to the bathroom, slamming that door as well. A monster stared back from the mirror: yellow eyes, fine scales at her temples, flattened nose, her teeth sharper, her cheekbones more angular. She slapped on the hot water tap and stepped into the shower, leaning into the scalding spray. She ran her hands through her hair, and it came out in clumps, one more horror piled on all the others.

Lori Watkins clenched her fists until the water ran red and cried her anguish into the cascading waterfall, her tears lost in the torrent.

## 3

———

Mary sat at her desk facing Price, Olson, and her security chief, Terry Harris, each with tablets in their laps. Their third weekly meeting wasn't going well. Her three department heads couldn't seem to agree on anything.

"She's progressing much faster than Gilford did. We think this is due to the large dose of active HD viral RNA." Price tapped her tablet and four graphs appeared on a big wall-mounted screen. "Strength, reflexes, sensory acuity, and skeletal structure are all way ahead. We're twenty-five days post inoculation, and although she's changing faster, and was unprepared for these changes, she appears to be as mentally stable as he was at this stage. I see no reason for the guards inside the room if they're bothering her."

"Tell that to Amy Richards and Jim Vincent." Harris tapped his own tablet. Pictures of two mutilated bodies blinked up to replace the graphs: a young woman and a man, the former riddled with bullets, the latter decapitated. "They might be alive if the guards were inside the room when Gilford went ape-shit."

"David went ape-shit because they were strapping a bomb around his neck and he smelled the explosives," Olson countered. "He reacted to a perceived threat, exactly like Lori's reacting to a perceived threat every time the guards in her room so much as twitch." Her eyes shifted from Harris to Price. "And Lori isn't *nearly* as stable as Gilford was at this stage. She's self-mutilating, crying, lashing out, and is still having dreams of eviscerating her fiancé."

"Taking the security out of the room is not going to calm her down and will put our people in danger!" Harris insisted.

"I disagree," Price said more calmly.

"The only way to find out is to take them out," Olson suggested. "If she calms down, great. We can't just keep pumping her full of drugs. She's suffering from survivor's guilt, paranoia, claustrophobia, post-traumatic stress, and grief. Gilford had none of those, and *still* went berserk when he perceived a direct threat."

"Gilford *was* suffering from claustrophobia. We had an easier time keeping him busy with simulations and exercise." Price shrugged. "He knew how to follow orders, at least."

"About her meds," Mary interjected, trying to push the conversation in a new direction. "We haven't exhausted all our options there."

"She's already on six different mood-altering drugs," Olson tapped her tablet. "Clonazepam as an anxiolytic, prazosin to alleviate her PTSD-associated nightmares—which isn't working very well—paroxetine and fluoxetine for depression, asenapine, a mood stabilizer and antipsychotic, and carbamazepine. We've had to slowly increase dosages over time due to tachyphylaxis. There are plenty of options, but we're already running into incompatibility issues. It's a pharmacologic minefield."

"But she's compliant and cooperative, for the most part," Price said.

"If you don't count all the times she's put her claws through her palms," Harris countered.

"That's not non-compliance, that's *psychosis*. She's punishing herself for surviving when her fiancé didn't. She may not remember the attack, but she's reconstructed it in her mind until *she's* the one killing him!" Olson took a deep breath, visibly calming herself. "She needs fresh air and to move around."

"Taking her outside is *not* an option!" Harris snapped.

"No, it's not, but decreasing her stressors is." Mary tapped her tablet and scrawled her signature on the order. "Put the guards outside the door. Everyone who goes in gets a panic button; the observation team in the comm center, too. If Lori shows aggression to whoever is in there, the guards go in and take her down." She nodded to Olson. "If she shows signs of calming down a little, taper off her meds."

Price and Olson nodded, seemingly satisfied with her decision. Harris glowered.

"Also, let's try some VR and see if we can keep her distracted. Games, simulations, exercise, food...what else?" Mary looked from face to face.

"Massage?" Price suggested.

Olson shook her head. "She'd never tolerate anyone touching her. Lori's self-image is in the toilet right now. She thinks she's a monster."

"She is a—"

"Lori Watkins is *not* a monster!" Olson snapped, glaring at Harris. "She's scared shitless of what's happening to her, and anyone would be." She looked to Mary. "You've *met* the other *Homo draconis*. From your own report, she's stable and perfectly sane when she's not faced with a threat. *That's* our goal. We have a subject similar to Rychenkna in many ways. Lori may be changed, but she's still human. If we treat her like a monster, she'll become one."

Price raised a hand to interject, and Mary mentally thanked her. "How about a hot tub with jets. She takes enough hot showers."

"That might help. I'll ask her what she thinks," Olson said.

Mary turned to her security chief. "Harris, no suggestions?"

His eyebrows arched, his dark forehead wrinkling up like a rug. "Not exactly my bailiwick, Doctor, but you might consider letting her stretch her legs in a bigger space. She may be human, but she's becoming a predator, too. You can see that in her eyes. You don't lock up predators and expect them to be content. Whether she knows it or not, she needs to hunt."

Physician, psychiatrist, and biologist all traded considering looks. "We don't have a gymnasium here, but you may be onto something. We have some larger spaces."

"We could set them up with VR and run a sim for her, see if she likes it," Olson said. "I wouldn't suggest anything violent. I'll ask Lori if she'll try that."

"Do that." Mary glanced at the time and nodded. "Thank you all for your input. Please remember that we're working *together* on this. That's all."

They left, and Mary got up to pace. She flipped on the live feed from Lori's room. A tech was playing a game with her, teaching her to juggle, which Lori mastered easily. The tech laughed and praised her skill, adding balls to the cascade one after another until Lori was keeping eight in the air at once, her clawed hands flashing like a martial artist's. She'd learned to keep her two long pinion fingers folded back out of the way, using a three-fingered grip for most tasks.

"Amazing," Mary muttered, remembering the footage she'd seen of Aleksi taking down armed assassins it a subway station. "No training, and she's flawless."

The potential applications for this were wide-ranging and invaluable. Lori was their prototype, but there were many female candidates who might volunteer for this. Only a fool threw away such a weapon. If Lori remained psychologically stable, the only barrier to their success was infection.

Mary went to her desk and sent an email to her research department. They'd been working non-stop for almost eight months on the *Homo draconis* infection. She drafted instructions for them to redirect their efforts from looking for a cure to simply eliminating the infectious elements. At this stage, Mary didn't particularly *want* a cure. She wanted a dragon she could send out into the field without risking the end of the world.

As she sent the message, her phone vibrated with a text message. Serendipitously, it was another message from Aleksi. "Where is David Gilford's first victim? We can cure her. Please, no more dragons."

Mary didn't believe for a moment that anyone had a cure for HD and ignored the message.

P ersephone glared at the phone, but it stubbornly remained silent. Aleksi was in no condition to banter with Buckmann, so she had taken over. She had long experience in persuasion and didn't intend to give up, but she found the woman's silence frustrating and worrisome. When people flat out refused to talk, that usually meant that they'd already made their own decisions and didn't want anything to cloud that.

She rolled up from her bed and stretched, vertebrae popping in sequence as she twisted. The sun was setting outside. Her sleep had been fitful and plagued with strange dreams lately. The former was due to Aleksi's treatment regimen. The results were promising, but the patient was having difficulty both physically and mentally. To that, Persephone could finally relate.

Her other phone chimed, and she read the text from Reggie. "Time for another shot."

She cringed and tapped, "BRT." She pulled on a shirt and jeans. The denim felt rough on her skin, but the shirt was three-hundred thread count Egyptian cotton and caressed her like a soft breeze. She put on a pair of slip-ons, checked herself in the mirror, tried to straighten her hair. *Hairline's receding, too... Great. Time for another new look soon.* Persephone sighed and started downstairs.

The palm-pad reader at the door to the Sanctum balked with a "Read Error" message.

Persephone sighed and keyed in a long sequence. "Override and re-initialize on voice print, Persephone, Amsterdam, Brussels, Chicago, Denver."

"Accepted," the pad displayed. Then, "Ready to re-initialize. Apply print."

She pressed her palm to the panel, and it lit up green, then finally it read, "Accepted."

She keyed in her access code, pressed her palm one more time, and the door popped open. She turned left and went to Gi-gi's room. Inside, her great-grandmother lay on her couch, eyes flicking over multiple screens of genetic data while one more followed Aleksi as she roamed around her rooms.

"She looks restless," Persephone said.

Reggie nodded. "Worse than ever. I offered meds, but she turned them down. She's twitchy as hell." He pointed to her arm. "Sleeve up, please. Treatment number twenty." He raised a small syringe in his other hand.

"You're really turning into a mad scientist, you know." Persephone rolled up her sleeve and held still as he applied a tourniquet.

"I'm perfecting my evil laugh." He slapped her inner arm and tucked her wrist under his armpit. A quick swab with an alcohol pad, and he popped the cap to the needle and slipped it into her vein with barely a pinch. A tug loosened the tourniquet, and he pushed the plunger. Reggie had a deft touch.

Persephone felt a tingle and a momentary flush, but it passed quickly. After twenty injections, she was getting used to it, and it was nothing compared to what Aleksi was going through.

"Good?" Reggie pressed a cotton swab to the tiny wound and dropped the needle into a sharps box.

"Fine." Persephone took the swab and pressed it hard, then pulled it away. The tiny V shaped mark was already closed. She flicked the swab into the trash and pulled down her sleeve.

"How do you feel, great-granddaughter?"

Persephone turned to face Gi-gi and shrugged. "Overall, strange, but good. Sharper senses, fewer aches and pains, more flexible, and stronger. I recommend it for every pre-menopausal woman." She flexed her polished nails out of their sheathes and grinned. They seemed well-manicured fingernails when retracted, but they were really weapons. She had to file them daily to keep them short enough to pass, though she'd seen some women with much longer nails. Persephone had been going through selective genetic modification for three weeks now, but the changes were minor and largely invisible. "Might be hard on the male population, though."

"And the side effects?" Gi-gi asked, unamused with her quip.

"The contacts bother me, but I'm getting used to them. I could live without the hair loss, but a wig will cover it up easily. I've lost weight, and my shape is...well...a little disappointing." She patted her breasts and hips, both flatter than before. "I'm sick of wearing a padded bra. I could claim I had a breast reduction, I guess."

"We could give you implants, if you'd like." Reggie grinned maliciously. "Something in a thirty-eight D?"

"Shut up." She lashed out with a nail to poke him in the chest. "This isn't exactly *fun*."

"Sorry, Seph." He rubbed the spot, wide eyed. "And I wasn't joking. We can give you your old shape back, if you like."

"Sorry, I'm a little short tempered. Hormones, maybe. I don't know how this thing's affecting me, but it's nothing I can't control."

"And the dreams?" Gi-gi asked.

"Yes, I'm having them, though not so violent as the ones Aleksi's told us about. Flying, hunting, like that, but not slaughtering anyone." She shrugged. "I've had worse, honestly."

"We'll monitor you closely for any changes we can't keep hidden. Since we're only giving you a few selective alterations, you *should* still be able to pass for you. That is vital for your role."

"My *role*?" Gi-gi's insensitivity often irritated Persephone. The woman's heightened intelligence had made her less emotional, more calculating.

"Yes." All the screens froze, and Gi-gi's lavender eyes swiveled to fix Persephone. "You'll continue as our primary interactor with society, politics, finance, and all the family affairs that maintain appearances. You'll *also* be our protector, if necessary. The government's still very interested in both Aleksi and the specimen, not to mention our research. They're dangerous in the extreme, ignorant but powerful, and cunning. We must be cautious, and ready to respond."

Persephone nodded. "Well, I didn't think I was going through this for *nothing*."

"Good." Gi-gi turned back to her screens, and they resumed motion.

"Anyway, I'm way more worried about Aleksi than I am you."

Reggie crooked his finger for Persephone to follow him out of Gi-gi's room. "She's not complaining, but you can see that she's anxious."

"I'll talk to her," Persephone said. "Maybe take her for another walk. That seems to help."

"Just be careful. I don't think she's violent—well not any more than usual—but I think she's hiding something." He put a hand on her shoulder. "And I think you're hiding something, too. You're touchy. You sure you're all right?"

She resisted the urge to brush his hand away. "Physically, I'm fantastic, Reg. I feel twenty years younger and sharper than ever. Aside from the dreams, cravings for meat, and being...a little uncomfortable in my own skin, I'm just a little jumpy and short tempered."

"Yeah, that last part I noticed." Reggie rubbed his chest. "You damn near broke the skin."

"Sorry." She cringed. "I'm still getting used to this."

"Well, don't let on to Aleksi," he said in a low voice. "She'd freak if she knew."

"You *think?*" She gave him a sour look. "No worries, Reg. I'm fine."

---

Aleksi roamed around her suite, desperate to find something, anything to occupy her mind. For the first time in her life, she found it difficult to read, to concentrate enough to focus on anything. She'd studied the genetics of her transformation until it began to take her thoughts in dangerous directions. It seemed an insurmountable task to repair all the changes, to make her human again. They'd barely scratched the surface with over fifty different reversion therapies, and the side effects had her feeling like she was coming apart at the edges, fraying. And, in fact, she *was*. Her wing membranes were thinning and peeling, retracting and sloughing at the edges. She itched so badly that even the soft poncho she usually wore felt like sandpaper. Her long finger bones ached horribly. Headaches, joint aches, stomach and digestive problems—some undoubtedly stress-related—plagued her day and night. Sleep was all but impossible; the hypnotic audios that used to sooth her insomnia didn't help anymore.

Worse than the physical symptoms, she felt the old specter of her social anxiety disorder returning full force. That unease, lack of confidence, doubt over every decision, left her feeling adrift and alone. She remembered her old self, the loner, a self-imposed exile more comfortable with books and her pet iguana, Iggy, than people. She obsessed about everything that she was losing, had already lost: her life, her love, her education, her career... The unknown specter of what and who she would be when this was finished, if it was ever finished, loomed over her like a burgeoning storm.

A knock at the door brought her whipping around, her heart hammering in her chest. She forced down the panic, cleared her throat, and said, "Yes?"

Persephone came in, bouncy and smiling as usual. "Hey. How are you feeling?"

"Honestly, not good." Aleksi turned away and resumed her roaming search for something to distract her. She didn't feel like talking or even being around Persephone right now. The woman had always made her feel inadequate. She was just so goddamned perfect. "I can't focus, and I'm feeling like crap."

"How about a walk outside." Persephone went to the closet and picked out a robe. "The fresh air will help. We can talk it over and maybe find a way to help."

"I..." Aleksi hesitated, unsure, uneasy. The thought of being outside didn't have the allure she remembered from only a week ago, and she didn't feel like talking with anyone, being psychoanalyzed. Memories of psychologists prying into her feelings when she was young felt like walking on broken glass. Persephone was trying to help, acting friendly, but Aleksi knew it was an act. Persephone's whole life was an act. Everyone put on an act when they wanted something from you. "I don't know. I don't think..."

"Oh, come on. Try it. If you don't like it, we can come back in." Persephone held out the robe. "Please, come for a walk with me."

Aleksi bit her lip, forced calm, and nodded. She didn't trust herself to speak, and it terrified her that the thought of going for a short walk outside was triggering a panic attack. *Is this what I was like before, scared of everything and everyone?* She reached out a shaking hand and took the robe.

"Thank you," Persephone said, as if Aleksi had done some great favor.

Aleksi nodded jerkily and donned the robe, pulling the hood over her head and affixing the veil, the motions so practiced that she didn't have to think or worry about them, even if the material did feel abrasive on her flaky skin. Familiar tasks were easier, making coffee, fixing a meal, making the bed, doing dishes. Anything that required thought, or worse, decisions, felt like pressing needles into her flesh.

Strangely, wrapped in the heavy cloth, Aleksi felt slightly better, a barrier between her and the world. She recalled warm sweaters, comforters, huddled on the couch with Iggy, safe, and felt like smiling. Maybe she could find comfort like that again.

She followed Persephone out of her suite, through the wine cellar, and up the stairs. Her mind wandered to more memories, Julie, her roommate, the men she'd brought over, the teasing from them, and watching her with Hutch. *Hutch…* She both longed and dreaded being with him again. If she became the woman she once was, the socially inept, anxiety ridden recluse, how could he still love her? He'd fallen in love with the Aleksi in transition, the confident, strong, passionate Aleksi.

Worry surged up in her chest.

*I won't be that woman anymore. He won't love me anymore!* She stopped and stared at the door leading out into the grounds, a deer in the headlights.

"Aleksi?"

Aleksi jerked around, wide eyed, caught in mid panic. "I… I'm sorry." Embarrassment warmed her face and she looked down, fighting the urge to clench her hands into fists. She couldn't without impaling her palms. She wrapped her arms around herself instead, squeezing tight to keep from shaking. "I…don't know if…this is a good idea."

"We're not even outside yet, Aleksi. It's safe. There's nobody out there. I promise. Just fresh air, grass, and trees." Persephone opened the door and held out a hand. "Come on. Breathe the air. It'll help."

Aleksi seriously doubted it would help anything, and balked at taking Persephone's hand, but nodded and stepped through to the outside. The low light dilated her eyes, every leaf, every blade of grass distinct. A thousand sounds pricked her ears, the hum of the city, millions of people, their scents, rotting garbage, sweat, the sweet aroma of roses from a nearby park. It all filled her head until it felt like she would burst. She remembered reveling in the deluge of senses, the hyper-awareness of her surroundings. Now, the cacophony seemed invasive, intrusive, an assault. She froze, trying to parse it all out, sort through it all, assess every single one for any threat, any danger, anything that could hurt her.

"Aleksi, you're shaking. What's wrong?"

Fingers brushed her shoulder, and she jerked around, stumbling back a step, clumsy, panicked. "D...don't!" The urge to flee fought with the reflex to lash out. "I... It's too much."

"Too much?" Persephone didn't seem scared, but still held out her hand where she'd reached out to touch her. "What's frightening you? There's nothing here that can hurt you. I promise."

Aleksi forced a deep breath, but that only brought a million more scents into her mind: birds, mice, squirrels, people, and Persephone, familiar, comforting, but slightly different than the olfactory imprint in her mind. Again, Aleksi forced down the panic. "I'm...having problems. Everything's frightening. I know it shouldn't be, but... It's like before, when you knew me before, in the restaurant. You scared me then, so beautiful and intimidating, cruel and taunting, powerful because you were rich." A familiar but alien anger threatened. "You held my career in the palm of your hand, and you knew it. You used it, or tried to."

Persephone gaped at her. "I'm sorry, Aleksi. I didn't know you then, and you're right, I teased you on purpose. I was lonely and jealous that Hutch had you for a graduate student. You have every right to be angry with me for that, but it was a long time ago." She reached out her hand, open and empty. "Your social anxiety's coming back, isn't it?"

Aleksi bit her lip hard enough to draw blood and nodded a quivering *yes*.

"And your senses are as sharp as they ever were, so everything seems threatening. Even me."

Again, the jerky nod. How did she know so much? "I'm scared, Persephone. What if...I'm stuck like this? A coward with the senses of a dragon? What if...Hutch doesn't..."

"Shhh, Aleksi, don't go there." Persephone took a small step forward, slow, tentative. "It's not going to happen. Hutch loves you. Nothing's going to change that."

"How can you *know* that?" Aleksi shook her head, hating herself, the panic, the fear, the worry. A tear slid down her cheek and she hated that, too.

"Because I've *seen* him with you, Aleksi. I *know* him. I've never seen him like that with anyone. Not even me, and I was *married* to him for two years." She smiled sadly. "And I'm still a little jealous of you."

"*Jealous?*" Aleksi barked a harsh laugh, half sob. "How can you be? I'm a fucking *mess*! A dragon scared of her own shadow!"

"You're caught in between what you are and what you used to be, Aleksi. It's not going to be easy. I'd hoped we could induce the physiologic changes first, but the psychological ones are harder to nail down. Neurochemistry is a nightmare to unravel." She took another half step closer, her fingertips now only an inch from Aleksi's shoulder. "But I *promise* you one thing: you don't have to be frightened of me. I'm here for you. Our family is strong, powerful, and smart. We're here to *protect* you. You're *one* of us now. We're *family*."

Aleksi sniffed and nodded. "I know, but...what if... What about..."

"Shhh." Another tiny step, and Persephone's fingers closed on Aleksi's shoulder, warm through the thick robe, solid, real. "You're obsessing about things that won't happen, Aleksi. I *promise* you we'll get through this. You'll be with Hutch again when this is all over. There are ways to treat your anxiety until the transition's finished." Her other hand rose to grip Aleksi's other shoulder. "Let us help you."

Fighting the urge to flee, to break loose, to run, fly away, lash out, Aleksi forced herself to nod. "Thank you."

Persephone smiled and nodded. "Good. Now do you want to walk with me, or go back inside? Your choice. No pressure at all."

*Decisions...* Panic seized her again. Would Persephone think her a coward for wanting to go back inside? "I...don't know."

"Never mind, then." Persephone must have felt her terror or heard the fear in her trembling reply. "Let's go in and watch a movie. Something light and funny. We'll drink some wine and have snacks. A girl's night in. How's that?"

Another quivering nod. Aleksi never thought that the confines of the Sanctum would sound comforting, but it did. "That sounds good."

So, she allowed Persephone to guide her back inside, down the stairs to the Sanctum, and into her familiar rooms. Aleksi breathed deep of the virtually sterile air, and her panic eased a trifle. Persephone bustled about, popping the cork from a bottle of wine that probably cost more than Aleksi's tuition for one semester, and picked out two glasses.

"So, what do we watch? Romantic comedy, stupid humor, feelgood movie, Monty Python?" Persephone handed her a glass and plopped down on the couch beside her. "Oh! Snacks!" She pulled her phone and tapped once. "Reg, we're having a night in to take the edge off and need appropriate snacks. Something meaty and yummy from the kitchen?"

"Sure, Seph. Give me ten minutes. Julian can do a badass carpaccio."

"Perfect!" She poked the phone, dropped it on the couch, and raised her glass to Aleksi. "Here's to girl's night in."

"Thanks." Aleksi tried to smile and sipped her wine. It was good but had a slight bitter aftertaste that surprised her. The second sip was better. "You pick the movie. Anything's fine." The last thing she needed was one more decision to worry about.

Persephone picked a feel-good classic, and they settled in. Aleksi began to relax, her worries easing, if not disappearing entirely. She wondered if it was the wine, the movie, or the company. She didn't

really fear Persephone, but she did find her a little overbearing sometimes. Life just seemed so simple for her, so preordained. But she'd
been born into a powerful family and all but *assigned* her life. Maybe
that was a kind of prison, too. Exactly like this room.

Reggie delivered a huge tray of very tasty tidbits, and they ate and
drank. The tension eased from Aleksi's muscles one fiber at a time,
until she started to get sleepy.

Halfway through the movie, Persephone stirred her awake with a
gentle touch. "Hey, you ready for bed?"

"Huh? I didn't...realize I was sleepy." Aleksi sat up and blinked.
"Sorry."

"Don't be. It's good to see you relaxed." Persephone got up. The
wine bottle was empty and the tray of treats, too. "Nothing like good
food, good wine, and good company to chill you out." She held out a
hand and Aleksi took it, wobbling a bit as she stood. "The wine hit you
hard."

"Exhaustion." She went to the sink and drank some water. "I
haven't been sleeping much."

"You will tonight." Persephone tidied up and started for the door.
"Don't worry, Aleksi. I'll talk to Gi-gi about your neurochemical
balance. We'll get this straightened out. Go to bed and rest. You
need it."

Aleksi nodded. "Thank you."

"Hey, like I said, we're family." Persephone smiled and left, closing
the door quietly.

Aleksi stared at the door for a while, listening, but she heard no
voices. She wondered for a moment if Persephone had slipped something into her wine but decided she didn't care. She had no choice but
to trust her new family now.

*No choice...* It felt oddly good to admit that. It was out of her hands;
her treatment, her future, her life, even Hutch. The cards had been
dealt and would fall where they would fall.

Aleksi went to her bedroom and laid down, pulling up a warm
blanket, curling her knees up, her head a little muddled, but calm. As
sleep took her, she remembered a long time ago, a lifetime ago,

waking with a fever in a disheveled little apartment, covered with blankets, fed and comforted by people who cared for her: Bob and Julie, Hutch and Lonnie, now Persephone and Reggie. She had to trust them.

They were her only hope.

*Hope...* The double-edged sword had long ago pierced her heart.

# 4

T he files on Mary's computer scrolled past slowly, fifteen
separate personnel documents, each one detailed, deep, and
impressive. Mary had only put a few criteria into her
search: female, combat training, covert ops rated, over forty years of
age, and a clean psych profile. Fifteen results out of all five branches
of the military. There were more options, of course: DHS, FBI, CIA
and a few shadier organizations within the government. Still, fifteen
was a good start.

A recorded conversation between Aleksi and the woman who had
stolen Mary's identity came back to her, and their experiences with
David Gilford reinforced her solidifying theory. The *Homo draconis*
infection turned men into monsters, drove them to spread the infection, to kill any non-related males and eliminate their offspring.
Females were slightly more stable, certainly violent, but more protective, especially with regard to women, children, and loved ones.

Their theories on the evolution of this condition supported this.
There had to be a reproductive advantage for the *Homo draconis*
changes to have arisen in the first place, not for the infected individuals themselves, but for genetically related ones. It was all about
family. In a pride of lions or great apes, the dominant male served

only two real purposes: protect the pride and procreate. *Fighting and fucking*, Mary thought with rue. *The only two things men do well...* The females hunted, reared the young, and protected them from rogue males.

They'd put Lori through a battery of tests to help verify this theory, exposing her to thousands of videos and images while recording her psychological and physiological responses. Any stimulus that indicated a woman or child in danger elicited a rise in heart rate and blood pressure, and a torrent of brain activity. Even without any close relatives, Lori felt the urge to protect. That was what they needed, but they also needed someone they could control, someone who would follow orders, someone who would *want* to follow orders.

Mary was looking for something specific.

She needed someone like David Gilford, older, worn out, dissatisfied with diminishing prospects, looming retirement or a sedentary assignment. She needed someone who would be willing to undergo a permanent change, someone who would be willing to become a dragon.

That was a very short list indeed. Most of these women had family attachments—if not children of their own, then nieces and nephews they were close to—and that was a non-starter. They needed someone without ties, without dependents or connections. Someone without any future but their work.

A cold realization settled into Mary's mind as she scrolled down, rejecting one candidate after another: *Someone like me.*

Mary had never wanted more out of life, never wanted a family, had few friends, and certainly didn't want a man in her life, or at least not anyone permanent. She'd thought about what it would be like to undergo the *Homo draconis* transformation, what it would feel like to be strong, fast, invulnerable...violent. Mary wasn't a violent person, or at least hadn't ever acted out on her violent impulses. There were always consequences to consider when it came to impulses, and she had learned a very long time ago to mistrust her baser instincts.

Giving into impulses opened you up to abuse, ridicule, disciplinary action, black marks on your record, bruises, torn dresses, screaming parents, and shame.

Mary realized that she'd stopped reading. The words meant nothing; only her memories remained vivid. The night of her high school prom revisited her once again, the horror of the assault when she'd said no to the boy's advances, then the added horror of her father, the ridicule, the name calling, the open-handed blow that had flattened her…

*No*, Mary realized. *No, I would not be a good dragon. I'd probably slaughter every male on the planet.*

She sighed and returned to her list, refining her search criteria: no history of sexual assault, stable formative home life, stable psychiatric evaluations, no family, and few emotional attachments. Yes, they would have to be very careful in choosing the next dragon. But there was one more hurdle they had to clear before they went there.

"Until we can make a subject noninfectious, it's too dangerous."

---

The trouble is, we have no neurochemical baseline. We have her original genome, but…" Reggie rubbed his eyes and sighed.

"But altering her genome in the sequence that is required by the cascade seems to have reset her neurochemistry, or at least altered it significantly, before changing her enhanced sensory acuity." Gi-gi flipped between several screens on her monitors, graphical representations of dozens of neurochemicals changing over time. "We have her neurochemical balance prior to our intervention, but not her original."

"We can't just keep giving her benzos," Persephone insisted. Two days of doctoring her food and drink with industrial dosages of clonazepam has induced sleep but did little to alleviate Aleksi's underlying anxiety. She did little but lay huddled in bed. "Eventually, she's going to become inured to the dosage."

"We can try escitalopram and D-cycloserine. It's the cocktail of choice for social anxiety disorder."

"That is certainly an option," Gi-gi said. Then she added, "Or we could attempt to manufacture the neurochemicals in deficit and administer them directly to her intracranial fluid."

Persephone gaped at her great-grandmother. "You want to drill a *hole* in her head?"

"That would be a necessity, yes. We can't administer them epidurally. The flow of CSF is inadequate to distribute the neurochemicals throughout the brain."

Persephone looked at Reggie, but he shrugged and said, "We should probably ask Aleksi's permission before we go to that extreme."

"In her current state of mind, she'd never agree." Persephone turned back to Gi-gi. "Let's try the escitalopram and D-cycloserine first, but I want to be up front with her about the meds we're giving her."

"Very well, but be careful," Gi-gi warned. "There's no way to predict how she might react. An angry dragon is quite likely less dangerous than a *panicked* one."

"*Undoubtedly* less dangerous," Persephone agreed. "I'll talk to her alone. If she goes ballistic, I have a better chance of surviving."

"Yes, but we'll be ready if things go poorly," Gi-gi said.

"There's one other thing to consider before we start this ad-hoc treatment, Gi-gi," Reggie interjected. "We know other subjects have proven psychologically unstable. With a sample size of only three, we can't be certain that their instability was solely due to their sex."

"The evolutionary rationale supports that theory, however," Gi-gi countered.

"Yes, but that's theory, not practice," Persephone countered. "We're going to *actually* start mucking about with her brain chemistry. The other possibility is that Aleksi's inherent social anxiety disorder is the *reason* she's a psychologically stable *Homo draconis*."

"That would be bad," Reggie said. "Don't suggest that to Mary Buckmann; she'd round up every person with SAD that she could get her hands on."

"We will *not* be telling Mary Buckmann *anything*," Gi-gi stated flatly.

"I think Reg was being ironic, Gi-gi," Persephone said. "But I agree with him in one respect. We need to tread carefully. Aleksi's in a fragile mental state. You should have seen the panic in her eyes when we stepped outside. I thought she was going to bolt."

"Agreed. We must not let that happen, not in her current state."

Persephone nodded. "Then give me the pills, and I'll tell her what we're planning. We can keep up with tranquilizers initially, then taper off to see how she's doing."

"Proceed," Gi-gi said, giving her official approval to the plan.

"Okay." Reggie went to their drug cabinet and retrieved two small bottles of pills. He handed them to Persephone. "They're time release, so one each every twelve hours."

Persephone nodded and took the bottles. "No time like the present, I guess."

Gi-gi touched a control and a view of Aleksi's bedroom flicked up to a screen. "She's currently in her bedroom, but her breathing patterns indicate that she's not sleeping."

"Good. I'll tread carefully." She nodded to them both and left Gi-gi's room.

The walk down the hall to Aleksi's door seemed very long. She knocked loud enough to be heard and opened the door.

"Aleksi? It's Persephone. I'm coming in." She stepped inside and closed the door behind her. "Aleksi?"

There was no reply, but she heard the rustle of blankets from the bedroom. Persephone strode to the door and tapped. "Aleksi? Can I come in?"

"Mmmmm." Her voice was muffled, probably into a pillow, but Persephone took it for a yes, and opened the door a crack. Aleksi lay curled in bed with her back to the door, covered with a sheet and blanket.

"How are you feeling today?"

"Crappy. I don't feel like company." Her voice was still muffled, but audible. She sounded groggy, but not angry.

"I'm sorry, but I need to ask you something. We want to try to treat your anxiety with some medications."

"You mean *more* medications, don't you?" Aleksi didn't roll over. "I know you're giving me something."

Persephone tensed. "Yes, we are. Clonazepam to calm you down. It seems to at least let you sleep, but we can't just keep giving you tranquilizers. This would be two medications that are for social anxiety disorder. If they work, we can taper off of the tranquilizers, and you should feel better."

"How...long?" The question came out haltingly, trembling with fear.

"How long would you be on the medications? We don't know exactly, but until the physiologic changes catch up to your brain chemistry. Once your sensory input eases up, you should level out."

"Weeks? Months? *Ever*?" Panic edged her voice.

"A few months at the longest, Aleksi, but we'll know if the meds are helping in a few days. We can adjust dosage and ease up on the tranquilizers then if it's working."

"And if it doesn't?"

Persephone wasn't going to mention an intracranial injection yet. "Then we'll try something else. We have other options, but we've got to keep moving forward with your treatment."

A long pause, and Persephone could detect a tremble beneath the blankets. She couldn't tell if Aleksi was crying or quivering in terror. Finally, slowly she nodded.

"Okay."

"Good. I'll get you a glass of water." Persephone hurried to the kitchenette, filled a glass from the tap, and returned. Aleksi hadn't moved. "You'll need to sit up to take these."

After a pause, she nodded and moved, struggling with the huddled blankets to press her back to the headboard. Her color was ashen, a yellowish gray rather than the vibrant gold of her usual hue, and the whites of her eyes were bloodshot. One shaking hand emerged from the blankets, the longer fingers thin and shaking, fluttering her flaking and peeling wing membrane. Persephone handed over the glass and quickly shook one pill from each bottle into her hand.

"Okay, here." She held them out.

Aleksi stared at her hand for a moment, the glass shaking in her grasp, setting up concentric waves in the water. Finally, she took the pills, put them in her mouth, and drank down half the glass.

"See. Not so hard, was it?" Persephone took the glass back.

Aleksi's eyes rose up to meet hers for a moment. "Please, go away." Her voice shook, and tears spilled down her cheeks.

"Okay. If you need anything, just call." Persephone backed out of the room and closed the door.

She took a deep breath and let it out slowly to calm her own singing nerves, then left the suite. She didn't know why, but seeing Aleksi like this was breaking her heart.

---

*S*he flies through canyons of concrete, steel, and glass, the city below teeming with prey. Scents of them, their fear, their sweat, their breath, come to her in an electrifying, mouthwatering deluge. Faces look up as she flies over, and she knows them. Her parents, her pastor, her friends from school... Then there is one that stands out like a beacon. Charlie! She lands, and he's in her arms, warm, alive, shaking like a leaf in her grasp. His voice pleads in her ears, "Please...don't kill me, Lori. I won't hurt you. I promise. Just don't kill me." She draws back, horrified at the terror in him. Then she sees the blood. His chest is torn open, muscle and bone ripped wide by claws... by her claws. There's something warm and pulsing in her hand, his heart, still quivering with the last of his fading life. Charlie is lying at her feet, eviscerated, dead by her hand, and Lori brings the warm meat to her mouth.

*L*ori lurched up from the nightmare with the taste of blood still in her mouth, Charlie's blood, his quivering heart pulsing between her teeth. She vaulted from the bed, claws tearing the sheets, wings billowing, the thin bones of her two longer fingers slamming into the bathroom door frame. She almost made it to the toilet before she threw up. Vomit spattered the floor and wall, the reek filling her nostrils as she retched her stomach dry.

"Lori? Are you all right?"

She retched again and spat. "Hell *no*, I'm not all right! Do I *sound* all right to you?" She lurched up and turned the faucet on, clumsily laving water to her face with her mutated three-fingered hands. Her claws brushed her cheeks, and she jerked them away. *Monster! Murderer!* No matter how many times she rinsed her mouth, she still tasted blood.

"Lori?" This voice came from the outer room instead of the speakers, and someone tapped at her bedroom door. "It's Doctor Price. Can I come in?"

"Only if you want to clean up puke!" Lori tried again to wash her face and rinse her mouth, managing better this time. Her hands were shaking. She spat out the vile taste and looked at herself in the mirror. The dragon looked back, her wide mouth full of sharp teeth, teeth meant for tearing meat. Her eyes were red from the water, and her scales shimmered in the bathroom light. The smock-like garment she wore was spattered with vomit. She pulled it over her head and flung it aside, turning away from the damning mirror before she could see herself. The winged monster horrified her.

"You were sick." Price stepped aside as Lori strode past, out of the bathroom, through her bedroom, and into the living room. Price looked tired and smelled of stale coffee and bad food.

"Figured that out, did you?" Lori went to the mini-fridge and pulled out a soda, anything to get the taste out of her mouth.

"I'm sorry. Another nightmare?"

"Yes, another nightmare." Lori tipped the bottle into her mouth, swished the sweet, fizzy liquid around and forced herself to swallow. Her touchy stomach clenched but settled down. "Blood! That's all I dream about anymore, and I'm *sick* of it!"

"I'm sorry, Lori. The medications don't seem to be—"

"I don't want you to be *sorry*! I want you to fix this!" She spread her wings wide and clenched her claws on the soda bottle. The thin plastic crumpled, her claws piercing it. Soda splashed to the floor. "You're a *doctor*! Give me something to take these dreams away! I want to sleep, just one night, without seeing Charlie ripped to pieces!"

"Someone's on the way with medication, Lori. Please calm down." Price stood with her hands out and empty, her non-threating stance. Fear wafted off of the woman in clouds.

"Calm down?" Lori gritted her teeth and flung the crushed bottle into the trash. "Tell me, Doctor, would you be able to calm down if you'd just murdered and *eaten* your fiancé? Could you calm down if there were always two soldiers outside your door ready to shoot you?"

"I understand that it's difficult for you, Lori, but we're trying to help. Please, let us help you."

"*Help* me, then! Do *something* for Christ's sake! I'm going *crazy* in this cage!" She stalked past her again and slammed the bedroom door. It hit hard enough to rattle the hinges and split the frame. Lori went to the bathroom and turned the shower on hot.

The room still reeked of vomit, but she needed to get clean, needed to wash off the blood, even if it wasn't real. Hot water helped, infusing her tense muscles with soothing warmth. The steam filled her nostrils, overwhelming the stench, dampening the sensory overload as the hiss of the shower drowned out the voices, the sounds of boots on concrete, of rustling uniforms, clicking weapons, humming electricity. She let the heat, steam, and white noise surround her in an insulating cocoon, blocking her off from the world.

Thoroughly numb, inside and out, Lori finally turned off the water. After toweling dry—also difficult with wings—she stepped out into her bedroom to find one of the techs, the young woman named Barbara who had taught her how to juggle, standing in her bedroom door with a plastic cup and a bottle of water.

"You okay, Lori? I was sent to bring you something to help you sleep." Her eyes were wide and a faint tremor rattled the pills in the cup.

"Fine now, just bad dreams. Thank you." She took the pills and washed them down with water. She could smell Barbara's fear through her protective jumpsuit. They were all scared of her. They had every right to be. She scared herself. "Tell Price I'm sorry. I know she's trying to help, but I'm losing my mind. I had a bit of a meltdown."

"No harm done. I'm sorry you were sick." She took the bottle back and nodded to the bed. "Go ahead and lie down, I'll tidy up the bathroom."

"Sorry for the mess."

"No worries." Barbara smiled behind her face shield, and it almost looked genuine.

Lori lay down on the bed and curled up with the extra pillow cradled to her chest. She listened to Barbara work, the scuff of her plastic booties on the tile, the swish of the towel cleaning up vomit, the toilet flushing. The smell of cleanser wafted through the room on the sterile air. She closed her eyes and tried not to think, to hear, to smell, to feel.

*Please, no dreams... Please...just one night alone...*

Eventually, the drugs took hold and sent her spinning down a deep black pit. She soared down on her wings, spiraling on the starlit darkness. At the bottom, Charlie waited for her, his bloody chest lying open and empty, his dead eyes fixed upon her in silent accusation.

## 5

utch stepped into the little Greek restaurant and scanned the noisy lunch crowd to no avail. He was late; parking around the hospitals was impossible, and he'd had to walk several blocks. The place was packed, and he couldn't spot the people he was there to see.

As he pulled his phone to send a text, a tall black woman with long braids stood and waved from the back of the restaurant, her smile flashing like a lighthouse. Hutch grinned and started working his way through the crowed dining room. Lonnie greeted him with a hug, and Jim Bornstein stood to shake his hand.

"You're looking good, Hutch!" Lonnie sat and pushed a chair out for him with her foot. "Life treating you well?"

"Crazy, but not bad. How's working in the real world?" He nodded to Jim. "Is he teaching you anything?"

Lonnie blew out her cheeks and shook her head. "I think my head's going to explode. I never wanted to get into medicine, but it's fascinating."

"And you've given us a real brain teaser to work on, Hutch." Jim waved over a waiter. "We've ordered already. Mama's does a great spinach pie."

"That sounds perfect, and an iced tea, please." The waiter nodded, his eyes never straying far from Lonnie. After the fellow left, Hutch nudged her under the table. "You cutting a wide swath through the medical school now?"

"Nah, residents are a bunch of jerks." She grinned at her boss. "No offense, Jim."

"None taken. You're right, most *are* jerks." He grinned at Hutch. "Lonnie's teaching them humility."

"Hey, someone's got to, right?" Lonnie leaned back in her chair, her predatory smile lighting up the room. "Anyway, what's up? Sorry to say we haven't cracked your mystery yet, but it's crazy complicated."

"Tell me about it." Hutch fell silent as the waiter delivered his iced tea, then said, "As a matter of fact, I wanted to tell you that some progress has been made on that front by an independent research team."

"Really?" Jim sat up like he'd been poked with a cattle prod. "How much progress?"

"Well..." Hutch grinned, lowered his voice, and leaned forward, even though there was no chance of being overheard in a room full of a hundred people all carrying on conversations at high volume. "Aleksi's not infectious anymore."

They both gaped at him and simultaneously asked, "How?"

"I don't know how they did it, and Aleksi can't tell me. These people are secretive, but they have *mad* biotech skills. They impersonated a DHS agent right down to her bad hairdo last winter, and it wasn't makeup or prosthetics. It was flesh and blood. They abducted the woman, and somehow copied her onto someone else in a matter of *days*. I talked to the impersonator face to face, and later, the person she'd impersonated, and I swear they were all but physically identical."

They both just stared at him.

Jim swallowed audibly and muttered, "That's incredible."

"That's what I said, but trust me, it's true." Hutch fixed them both with a level stare. "I don't know who these people are, but please don't start spreading this around. I only wanted to tell you that it's possible."

"We've kept our mouths shut about this for half a year, Hutch. We're not about to go blabbing now." Jim traded a glance with Lonnie, and she nodded. "We're actually making a lot of spin-off discoveries from what you gave me. Nothing like a cure, but real progress in finding dormant genes. These infectious RNA strands are nothing more than keys that unlock a chain reaction of hidden gene expression."

"Good." Hutch took a deep breath and let it out. "Now for the bad news."

"There's bad news?" Lonnie asked with arched eyebrows. "Why does there always have to be bad news?"

"Because there's balance in the universe, Lonnie." Jim nodded to Hutch. "What?"

"A little over a month ago, a person infected with this...thing got out and went on a bit of a rampage. People died, and three women were injured and infected."

"What the hell?" Lonnie's eyes widened further. "Not *Aleksi?*"

"No, someone else. Someone who was *voluntarily* infected by the government. He's dead, but two of the women he infected were scooped up by this group Aleksi's working with. They woke up a week later virus free and healthy. The first victim, however, has completely vanished. She was taken from the Mass General ER by people flashing government ID's. We think they have her."

"And this was a *month* ago? Hutch, by now she's—"

"I know, Lonnie. So do the people Aleksi's with, and the two Cambridge Homicide detectives who helped take out Derrick Penningly. The government hasn't admitted they have her yet, but I wanted to ask you two, as professional researchers, what you think I should do about it. I've been asked by Detective Jasper to plead with the DHS to do something about it, but other than asking them to hand the infected woman over to Aleksi's friends—which they won't do—I don't know what they *can* do. They're still pissed about the kidnapping and impersonation. I can show them what'll happen if this infection gets out in the open, and let me tell you, it's catastrophic, but again, that's nothing they don't already know."

"They want a weapon," Jim said, his countenance grim. "That's why they infected a volunteer."

Hutch nodded. "I think so. The thing is, I don't know if they're desperate enough to *use* that weapon at the risk of an outbreak. They've already taken that risk once, and it blew up in their faces. At this stage of the game, warning them seems a little redundant."

"You could offer to broker a trade," Lonnie suggested.

"A trade?" Hutch looked at her skeptically. "What kind of trade?"

"This infected victim for the infection cure," Lonnie said.

"And that would give them their weapon." Jim shook his head. "That'd be dangerous. What they would do with a bunch of soldiers like Aleksi..."

"Sure, they'd make a secret flying Delta Force or something, but *think*, Jim." Lonnie reached across the table and put a hand on his arm. "This is the *government*. They're not going to settle for nothing. They'll risk it with infectious soldiers, and then we're talking Armageddon." She nodded to Hutch. "How bad would it be?"

"A full-fledged outbreak?" He sighed and rubbed his eyes. "Total world population reduced to about fifty million inside a year if it went unchecked. The last subject showed clear intent on spreading the infection. It's some genetic imprint or behavior, I think. He didn't know why he was doing it, but he did." Hutch shrugged. "Evolutionarily, it makes sense in a world with low populations of genetically related individuals like tribal societies."

"Which is what Earth will be if this breaks out," Lonnie added.

Hutch could only nod.

"My God," Jim said, his face slack.

That, of course, was the cue for the waiter to bring their food.

Unsurprisingly, none of them were particularly hungry.

---

Aleksi lay in a fetal position on her bed, covered in blankets, her eyes tight shut, shivering not with cold, but with abject terror. She couldn't move, couldn't breathe, couldn't speak through the constant assault of non-stop panic. Every sound, scent, and tremor in the air frightened her. She ached all over, every joint, every inch of her skin itching, her nails stabbing her when she flexed her hands, her stomach empty and roiling.

*I can't do this. I can't do this anymore!*

Her thoughts had been spiraling for two days. She hadn't slept a wink, too scared to sleep. Sleeping meant being vulnerable. They'd come for her in her sleep, drug her, tie her down, and cut her open. The medications weren't working, and she couldn't make herself tell anyone, couldn't admit it. They'd know she was a coward. They would hate her for failing, kill her to eliminate their mistake, like euthanizing a lab rat in a failed drug trial.

The slim shred of her mind that remained coherent insisted that her fears weren't real, that Persephone and Reggie were trying to help her, but that voice of reason drowned in a sea of unrelenting terror. She remembered a therapist as a child—in retrospect, the woman had been a quack, a school nurse with an undergraduate degree in psychology—telling her, "Just don't worry about things so much." Telling an anxiety ridden child not to worry was about as effective as telling fire not to burn your house down. This was the same; her cognizant mind had no way to convince her that her fears were unfounded.

Aleksi knew only one thing for certain: she couldn't continue to live like this. She couldn't be this cowardly creature. Hutch would loathe her, Persephone would laugh and ridicule her, and Reggie would only stick her with needles, try to fix her, experiment on her. They would tie her down and cut her open to find out how they'd failed to cure her. She could feel them coming, smell their fear, their anger...

*No...no...no...no!*

Aleksi opened her eyes.

Her bedroom was dark, silent save for the hum of air conditioning, but she knew someone was there. They were lurking outside her door with needles and scalpels and chains. She had to get away, to hide, but where?

One trembling claw pulled down the blanket covering her head. Her dragon eyes pierced the darkness easily. She turned her head slowly, every sense straining, scanning the room for them. She expected a shadow looming over her, but there was nothing there. She didn't believe it. They *were* there. She *knew* they were there, even if she couldn't see, smell, taste, or feel them close by. She had to find someplace to hide where they couldn't get her.

Aleksi moved slowly, inch by excruciating inch out from beneath the covers, the air electric on her hyper-sensitive skin. Exposing herself grated against her raw nerve endings, but she had to find someplace safe. Nothing moved in the room. She gritted her teeth until her head pounded with the pressure and slipped one foot over the edge of the bed. It took all her nerve. She expected a clawed hand to flash out from beneath the bed at any moment to grab her and drag her down. But she had to move, had to hide. It wasn't safe here anymore.

Her foot touched the floor, the distant tremble of electric motors, traffic, footfalls, terror transmitting up through her bones. Aleksi moved like a viscous liquid in winter, weight settling on her foot, flowing out from under the blanket into the open.

*Where? Where can I go? Where can I be safe?*

The answer rang through her mind like a death knell: *nowhere*. There was nowhere she would be safe. The doors out of the Sanctum would be locked. She was in a cage, a prison. She couldn't escape. Her only hope was to find a place she could hold them at bay, defend, someplace with a door she could secure against them. Someplace small.

Aleksi edged around the bed, flowing from foot to foot, her clawed toes retracted to keep from snagging the carpet and making noise. The bathroom door beckoned. She slipped through, the cool tile on her feet eliciting a shiver. Easing the door closed, turning the knob so it wouldn't click, she scanned the tiny room, but there was nowhere anyone could hide. Only one way in and out. They would come for her, she knew they would, but here, maybe, she could keep them at bay long enough.

*Long enough for what?*

She didn't have an answer. Deep in her soul, Aleksi knew she would never leave this room. They would corner her here, take her, cut her open... Memories of a thousand dissections raced through her mind, skin sliced open, pinned back, organs removed one at a time. She saw herself flayed alive, heard her screams, felt the knife parting her skin.

Pain pierced her, igniting her imagined terrors. Her claws were bloody. She screamed and whirled, searching for her attacker, but there was no one. She was bleeding, six raking gashes across her stomach. Someone had cut her. *They're here!*

Aleksi flung herself back into the corner of the shower, slamming against the tile to slide down in a quivering heap. Her bloody claws raked down her forearms, tearing another scream from her throat. She watched her blood flow and couldn't stop it. They were here, inside her, and they were cutting her open.

"HELP ME!" she screamed, but there was no one to hear, only the terrors in her mind, laughing at her, cutting her skin open to reveal the human she had once been cowering within.

As Aleksi gasped for breath, a cloying sweet stench filled her lungs. She howled out her anguish, her terror, her loneliness, and darkness closed in to swallow her whole.

———

You sure she's out?" Persephone cinched the strap of her gas mask tight and put her hand on the door to Aleksi's suite. She raised a forestalling hand to Reggie. He held a syringe in one hand, but she would be the lead as they invaded the dragon's lair.

The earpiece chirped. "She appears to be unconscious. Her breathing's regular and slow. The sevoflurane is holding steady at five percent, oxygen level in the air is at eighty percent."

"Okay. We're going in. If she so much as twitches, you let us know." Persephone hated the idea of knocking Aleksi out with anesthetic gas, but there had been no other option. She'd been hurting herself, clearly in the midst of a psychotic break.

"Affirmative." Gi-gi's voice sounded as passionless as usual, cold and calculating. "Proceed."

Persephone turned the knob, and they went in, closing the door quickly behind them to keep too much gas from escaping. A faint, sweet odor invaded the seams of her mask. Sevoflurane was the fastest acting anesthetic gas available and had the added bonus of being difficult to overdose. As the patient fell unconscious, the breathing slowed, and, as less of the gas was taken into the lungs, the dosage in the bloodstream diminished. The patient's level of consciousness rose, respiration increased again, increasing the dosage. A steady equilibrium was established quickly, and in an atmosphere of high oxygen content, there was almost no chance of hypoxic injury.

*Let's just hope dragons sleep deeply*, Persephone thought as they crept to Aleksi's bedroom door. The knob turned easily, and the hinges worked silently. They knew she was in the bathroom, but Persephone also knew how fast Aleksi could move. If she fully awoke, she could be through the bathroom door and at their throats in a heartbeat. They'd been lucky she had chosen to retreat to the bathroom rather than try to escape the Sanctum, or hunt everyone down and slaughter them.

Persephone's heightened senses hummed at a fever pitch. She could feel Reggie behind her, hear his heart hammering in his chest. The mask blocked the more subtle scents, but the dark room seemed as bright as day to her eyes.

"I can't see, Seph!" Reggie hissed. "I've got to turn on the light."

"Fine." Persephone moved to the bathroom door, listened, and put a hand on the knob. "Do it."

The room flooded with harsh light, and Persephone's vertical irises snapped to thin slits to adjust. She held up a hand again to keep Reggie at the bedroom door. He nodded. She listened at the bathroom door, picking up slow breathing and the tap-tap of something dripping on tile. The doorknob turned slowly in her hand, and she pushed.

Inside, Aleksi lay curled in the corner of the shower, her back wedged against the tile, knees pulled up to her chest. Her head lolled forward to rest on her knees, but her arms were clenched in her own claws. Her forearms were torn open, claws lodged deep in the muscle, blood dripping to the tile.

"Oh, God." The sight of Aleksi like this, fetal and bleeding, ignited a fire in Persephone's gut. Guilt washed up like a tide to envelop her. She'd promised Aleksi that she was safe, that nothing could hurt her. They'd never thought that they'd have to protect her from herself. She rushed to kneel at her side, reaching to pull the claws from her flesh. "She's down, Reg! She's bleeding."

"Let me get some ketamine into her, and we'll get her to the treatment suite." He knelt beside her and straightened one bloody arm. "Give me some pressure on the vein. She's hypotensive."

"From blood loss, or the anesthetic?" Persephone squeezed Aleksi's upper arm. Her dragon eyes fluttered, and a low sound came from her throat.

"The anesthetic, I hope. The ketamine should help." He popped the cap off the needle and slipped it into the vein. "It looks worse than it is, I think."

Aleksi moaned, and her head moved, lips twitching. Persephone held steady while Reggie injected the anesthetic, ready for any purposeful movement from Aleksi. Aside from a few more muscle twitches, she didn't respond. When Reggie pulled the empty syringe, Aleksi heaved a breath and went completely limp.

"There, she's *really* gorked now." He checked her pulse at her neck. "Gi-gi, you can flush the gas out of the room. We'll get a gurney and—"

"I've got her, Reg, just get the doors for me." Persephone cradled Aleksi's head and nodded him back.

"Let me straighten her legs for—" As he pulled Aleksi's legs gently straight, more blood spilled on the floor. Her stomach bled from six ragged tears. "Shit! These are deep, Seph! We need to get her to the—"

"Get the doors!" Persephone slipped her arms under Aleksi and lifted her easily, a feather in her grip.

Reggie opened doors for her, and Persephone carried the bleeding dragon to the treatment room, leaving a trail of blood the whole way.

They had a table ready, and Persephone laid her gently down. Their younger cousins, Ed and Carrie, were already there to help, wearing surgical gowns and gloves. Ed put an oxygen mask over Aleksi's nose and mouth and tilted her head back while Persephone peeled off her gas mask. The lingering scent of sevoflurane clung to everything, muted by the overpowering scent of blood.

"Has she eviscerated?" Gi-gi asked over their earpieces.

"I don't think so. Don't bother me right now." Reggie slid an IV into Aleksi's forearm and taped it down, working fast. "Seph, open that pack and press the underpad inside to her stomach. I've got to explore the wounds. If she didn't penetrate her abdomen, we can just stitch her up. If she did, I'll have to do an ex-lap. Carrie, glove and gown me. I don't have time to scrub. You're assisting."

"Sure."

While Persephone opened the sterile pack, unwrapped the thick, plastic-backed pad, and pressed it to Aleksi's torn stomach, Carrie unpacked a surgical gown for Reggie and put it on him, then gloves, then a mask and cap. Ed attached a pulse oximeter, and the monitor started beeping with Aleksi's pulse. The oxygen saturation number came up, reading 100%.

Carrie pulled a big tray over and peeled the cover to reveal a complete emergency surgical kit. Reggie delved the sterile contents and slapped an adhesive pad to Aleksi's leg. An electrical lead clattered to the floor from the pad. An electrocautery wand came next, its plug also falling to clack on the hard linoleum.

"Okay, Seph, pull back, and I'll see if we have any bleeders. Plug me in to the Bovie unit under the table."

Persephone pulled the pad back and reached under the table to plug in the cauterizing wand and the grounding pad. It beeped a discordant note as Reggie tested it. The smell of cooking meat filled the air as he touched the cautery to the wounds, smoke swirling toward the ceiling.

Persephone backed away to watch them work.

Carrie looked her up and down. "You should wash up. You're all bloody."

Persephone looked down and caught her breath. She hadn't realized that her hands and shirt were both smeared red. "Right. Thanks."

She washed up and put on a mask, but by now it was pretty redundant. Aleksi would be receiving a massive dose of antibiotics. She tried not to clench her hands as Reggie touched the cauterizing wand again and again to the wounds. They shifted to her lacerated arms after a time, but there was less damage there.

"There, bleeding's under control, and I don't think the abdominal wall was violated. We'll swab her down with iodine, and I'll have a close look."

They did, saturating sterile gauze pads with dark red solution and working outward from the edges of the wounds. When Aleksi's abdomen was painted thoroughly, Carrie adjusted the harsh overhead lights to illuminate the gashes and Reggie inspected the damage under a pair of magnifying lenses. Persephone muttered a silent prayer under her breath.

"All right, I think she only did muscle damage." Reggie stood up straight and sighed. "*Really* lucky. We can stitch her up and hope for the best. Three-oh Vicryl first, Carrie."

"Good," Gi-gi said over their earpieces. "Persephone, if you're not needed in the room, I'd like to speak with you."

Persephone would rather have stayed, but Gi-gi's tone brooked no argument. "I'll be right there."

She paused to peel out of her stained shirt and pull on a scrub top, then made her way to Gi-gi's room. Her great-grandmother lay on her inclined bed as usual, watching half a dozen monitors. Two of them displayed the surgical suite from high angles. Persephone crossed her arms and waited.

"We were very lucky," Gi-gi finally said.

"I know." Persephone didn't know if Gi-gi was referring to Aleksi's relatively minor injuries, when she could have eviscerated herself, or their own survival. She could have rampaged through the estate like a fox in a hen house.

"I want your opinion, great-granddaughter."

"On Aleksi, or us?"

The data screens froze, and she looked at Persephone. "On *Aleksi* first. Why did this happen?"

"She had a complete psychotic break. I have no idea why, but her social anxiety seems to have escalated to full blown paranoia at the panic-attack level. I hope that she won't remember it when she wakes up. Our treatment of her anxiety failed completely, obviously, but again, I don't know why or how."

"Obviously." Gi-gi's wizened lips pursed momentarily. "Unfortunately, we're at an impasse in our treatment. Chronologically, her neurochemical balance was one of the first things altered by the initial infection. Consequently, those changes must be the first ones we correct. We cannot alter the genes that govern her enhanced senses before we change her neurochemistry. We have only two options: directly infuse neurochemicals into her intracranial fluid without knowing her baseline neurochemical balance or reverse our therapies completely. There's nothing we've done that we can't undo."

"She's not in any condition to make an informed consent to either of those procedures, Gi-gi."

"Correct, so we must make the decision for her."

She made it sound simple. It wasn't, and her passionless logic infuriated Persephone. "*We* did this to her, Gi-gi! She tried to rip out her own guts, and she did it because *we* couldn't do what we promised to do!"

"That's true, but irrelevant to our course of action, Persephone." Those lavender eyes fixed her without a hint of emotion. "You can't let your feelings interfere with our decision here."

"Why not?" Persephone stabbed a finger at the screen that displayed Reggie stitching up the fine-scaled skin of a deep laceration. "*Her* feelings certainly played a part in her decision to try to take her own life! How can you make a decision about a young woman's life without trying to understand what she's feeling?"

"Her feelings were not genuine, great-granddaughter. That was psychosis, albeit brought on by our failed treatment of her condition. Feeling sorry for her won't help us decide what to do next."

"It's her decision to make."

"She's not in any mental state to—"

"I *know* that!" Persephone gritted her teeth. "We have to reverse our therapies. Once she's herself again, we let *her* make the decision about how to proceed."

"Very well." Gi-gi turned away, and the data feeds resumed.

"But there's a third option we need to present her with," Persephone said.

The screens froze again, and Gi-gi turned to face her. "What option?"

"Euthanasia." Persephone pointed to the screen again. "If she doesn't want to live as a dragon for the rest of her life, or risk going through this again with another treatment regimen, we can give her a painless escape."

"I don't believe she'll choose suicide. She still has people who care for her, people she can help, a reason for living."

*And she still has Hutch,* Persephone thought. He was her best reason for wanting to live. "Maybe, but it's her decision to make."

Gi-gi nodded. "Very well. We'll begin reversal when she's out of surgery. Please tell Reggie that Aleksi is to be kept sedated and under restraints until we deem it safe."

"I will." Persephone left Gi-gi's room and started upstairs. She needed a shower. Somehow, scrubbing her hands hadn't seemed enough. She didn't know if she'd every truly feel clean again.

# 6

---

S he's in full-blown tachyphylaxis." Price pulled up a drug dosage chart on the big screen in Mary's office, numerous colored lines, all ramping up in ascending curves, some diminishing to be replaced by new colors. "The more we give her the more she needs."

It wasn't anything they didn't know, and Mary didn't like what she was seeing. Even with the increasing doses of antidepressants, mood-stabilizers, serotonin reuptake inhibitors, and sleeping medications, Lori was still having recurring nightmares, phobias, and violent outbursts. She hadn't hurt anyone yet, but Mary could sense that it was only a matter of time. Thirty-one days from her inoculation, Lori was fully transformed, dangerous in the extreme, and a psychological train wreck.

Mary felt like they were trying to diffuse a ticking time bomb. "Options?"

"We still have a few weapons in our arsenal," Olson said. "Her metabolism is...challenging, and her PTSD is persistent. We can try some of the more atypical antipsychotic medications, tricyclic antidepressants, low dose cortisol, some other combinations, but I'd like to monitor her liver enzymes. She's got a lot of meds on board. I'd also like to try more psychotherapy. The drugs aren't solving the problem, just treating the symptoms."

"All psychotherapy ever did for David Gilford was make him angry," Price warned.

"Well, exercise and virtual reality aren't working for Lori. I'd like to do some rescripting therapy, sleep dynamic therapy, or VR-induced hypnosis." Olson shrugged. "It can't hurt, and we might root out the mechanism of her survivor's guilt."

"Do you think her recollections are clear enough for that?" Mary asked. "She's persistent about not remembering the attack."

Olson shrugged. "I think she can remember more with hypnosis. Her phobias reside in her subconscious. We have to bring them out in the open so that her reasoning mind can deal with them."

"Stirring up memories of her fiancé's death will be dangerous," Price warned.

"Being in the same *room* with Lori is dangerous," Olson countered. "She hasn't hurt anyone yet, but we're running out of options."

"Maybe we need to simply call it a loss and start from scratch," Price suggested. "Instead of trying to fix something that's broken, start with something that's *not* broken. We've got candidates that—"

"Not some*thing*, Doctor, some*one*!" Olson snapped. "Lori is not a *thing*!"

"I know that! It was a figure of speech." Price's eyes went flinty. "Lori's psychologically damaged, possibly beyond the point of recovery. Trying to deal with her psychoses is dangerous. We know female *Homo draconis* are more stable than males. Why not start with a new subject?"

"I'm not ready to abandon Lori," Mary said. "I'll consider recruiting a new subject, line up candidates and put them through screening, but we have a bird in hand. We also still can't block the infective elements of HD. We should at least try to—" Her phone vibrated on the desk, and she snatched it up. *If this is another text from Aleksi, I'll...* But it wasn't a text. It was a call from Doctor Hutchinson. She held up a hand to Price and Olson. "I've got to take this. One second." She accepted the call and said, "Doctor Hutchinson. How are you?"

"Hello, Doctor. I'm doing well. I'd like to speak with you in person, if possible. There have been some developments."

"Developments with Aleksi?"

Across the desk, Olson and Price tensed, eyes wide. Mary supposed her own were pretty wide at the moment.

"Yes, but nothing's wrong. It's easier if I speak to you in person. I want to show you some population models I've been working on, and...discuss options."

*Options?* That sounded promising. "Okay, Doctor, I'm up for discussing options. Where would you like to meet?"

"How about Peet's Coffee south of the Harvard campus?"

"That's fine. When?"

"I'm open from three to five."

"Three this afternoon, then. I'll be there."

"See you there."

The call ended, and Mary stared at her phone for a moment. "Well, *that's* interesting."

"You think he's being honest or pulling your chain?" Price asked. "He's never given us anything on Aleksi before."

"I don't know what he's got up his sleeve, but he won't betray Aleksi. There's only one way to find out." She tapped up a screen on her desk and opened a line to her covert field asset supervisor, a clerkish man named Benson. When his face resolved on the screen, she said. "I'll need a covert escort this afternoon. Someone who won't stick out like a sore thumb in a coffee shop."

"One or two?" he asked, his expression flat, emotionless.

"Maybe two. One inside and one outside. I'm meeting with Doctor Hutchinson."

He nodded. "Understood."

"I'll get the details to you." She broke the connection, curiosity niggling at the back of her mind. *What do you have up your sleeve, Doctor Hutchinson?*

Aleksi swam from the depths of a deep black pit, floating to the surface on a buoyant bubble. Memories of a nightmare, fear, being stalked by something invisible, pain, and blood returned to her subdued consciousness. She tried to move and couldn't. Something soft but strong held her down, constricting her chest, hips, legs, and wrists. Fear electrified her, and she opened her eyes. Persephone and Reggie stood beside her bed, but she couldn't move. She was tied down.

Her nightmare fears of vivisection bubbled up like acid, but before she could react, Persephone spoke.

"Hey, sleepyhead. How are you feeling?" The calm reassurance in her voice eased some of Aleksi's terror, but she suspected it was a sham. Persephone was good at putting on false fronts.

"Why am I tied down?" Her words came out slurred, and she realized she was medicated. An IV ran into her arm from a bag. Her muscles flexed of their own volition, and thickly padded straps creaked.

"I'm sorry for that, Aleksi, but you were hurting yourself. The meds we were giving you to calm down your anxiety didn't work. You tipped over the edge, and we had to intervene."

"Hurt myself? I don't remember—" She craned her flexible neck to look down at herself. A drape covered her from hips down, but her arms and abdomen were swathed in bandages.

"It's probably better that you don't remember." Persephone rested a hand on her shoulder. "Aleksi, we woke you to talk to you about the therapy. Can you remember? You worked on the genetic cascades that we were trying to correct."

"*Were?*" A new fear trundled through her. "Why '*were*'? Aren't you still?"

Persephone shook her head. "We've isolated most of the sequences that altered your neurochemistry, and there's a problem. Those were some of the first changes you underwent from the initial infection. They're linked closely with more elements of the cascade. Your augmented senses came later. We can't revert your neurochemistry without effecting hundreds of other things, and you can't tolerate your old neurochemistry combined with your augmented senses. Your social anxiety sees everything you sense as a threat, and you sense a thousand times more now than you used to. We also don't have your baseline neurochemical balance, so we can't treat that directly, at least not with any accuracy."

All the details of what Persephone was saying got a little muddled in her drug-addled mind, but one thing came clear. "I'm *stuck* like this?" The straps groaned as her muscles seized.

"Not like this, no. We're reverting all the changes we made, so your neurochemistry should be back to your *Homo draconis* normal soon." Persephone shook her head slowly. "I'm sorry, Aleksi, but we can't continue our genetic therapies, not without doing psychological damage."

The double-edged sword of hope twisted in her chest. She would always be a dragon, would never be human again. All her anxieties thundered in her ears, mocking her hope, her love, her life. She'd lost everything.

"No...no...*no!*" The restraints on her wrists groaned, pain biting deep as small bones ground against one another.

"Aleksi, *relax*. You've still got Hutch! He still loves you! Remember that!"

But it was just another lie. Hutch couldn't really love a dragon. Even though the memories of the days they'd spent together lingered, his tenderness, her tortured mind couldn't believe it. The anxiety, the worry, the fear wouldn't let her. She bucked against the straps, the tortured muscles of her stomach and forearms stabbing her.

"I can't...*live*...like...this!" She jerked her right arm back against the soft restraint, and something popped in her hand. Pain lanced up her arm, and a scream tore from her throat.

"Reggie! Give her something!" Persephone put a hand on her arm. "Aleksi don't!"

But Aleksi couldn't hear through the roaring in her ears, the agony that would never end. There was only one way to end it. She clenched her eyes tight and *pulled*.

The bones of her thumb popped out of joint, tendons wrenching free, agony lancing up her arm. Aleksi jerked her hand free from the restraint. But the pain didn't matter, she had her hand free. Her claws slid free of their sheaths, and she reached up to her throat.

"Aleksi!" A grip like iron encircled her forearm, keeping her claws from piercing her flesh.

Aleksi opened her eyes to find Persephone's hand on her arm, the tendons standing out like cables on her forearm. Aleksi strained to wrench free but couldn't.

"How..." But her thoughts spiraled into a muddled tangle as Reggie pushed a syringe into her IV line. She stared into Persephone's eyes, and saw something she'd never seen before. "What did you...do..."

Before the answer coalesced in her mind, she fell into darkness.

---

When Hutch entered Peet's Coffee, Mary Buckmann was already there waiting for him. She sat in a corner table as far back from the windows as she could get, her back to the wall, a large coffee and a Boston Globe on the table. She met his eye and nodded but didn't offer anything more.

*Suspicious*, Hutch thought, but he couldn't really blame her, though he'd have to be monumentally stupid to do anything drastic in the middle of the day in a public place. She undoubtedly had people watching.

He waited in line at the counter, and Brandy, a barista he knew, had his usual waiting for him with a smile.

"There you go, doc, just how you like it!" She smiled and accepted his card.

"I must be getting predictable in my old age," he quipped, then added to himself, *Hopefully not too predictable.*

"Oh, shut up!" Brandy handed him the receipt with a faux scowl. "I saw you with that knockout drama student a few weeks ago. You can't fool me."

*Busted*, he thought. He laughed and left her a good tip. So, rumors of his short but intense relationship with Julie had gotten out. They'd never tried to hide it, but he didn't need the scuttlebutt. "Thanks, Brandy."

"Later, doc!" She took the receipt and winked at him.

*Great...* Hutch made his way to the table where Buckmann sat and took a chair. "Doctor. Thanks for coming."

"Doctor Hutchinson." She folded her paper and glanced at the counter. "Does Aleksi know you're seducing coeds?"

"Excuse me?" If they were having him followed, they might know about Julie, but the comment was way out of bounds. "I'm not *seducing* anyone, Doctor, and if that's how you're going to be, I'll take my options elsewhere!" He started to get up.

"Sit *down*, Doctor Hutchinson." The muscles of her jaw clenched. "I'm only concerned with what might happen if Aleksi found out about your other relationships. I don't think she would be very understanding."

"My social life is none of your business."

"*Everything* that either directly or indirectly touches on the *Homo draconis* situation is my business, Doctor. That includes you pissing off the only stable subject we know of by consorting with young women. Now, sit down. You called this meeting. Tell me what you want to say."

Hutch gritted his teeth but sat down. *Fine! Two can play this game.* "I called you because you're fucking around with something that could end the human race, Doctor Buckmann. I may be able to help you, but that's your call. Being an ass is *not* the way to engender my help."

"I'm not here to be your friend, Doctor. Tell me why you called this meeting."

"Lori Watkins."

He saw her twitch, but then she tried to cover it with a quizzically raised eyebrow. "Who?"

"Don't be coy. The Boston police know who took Lori, and I know what's happening to her." He didn't want her to know that Tony Jasper knew about the infection. "I'm probably the only person in the world willing and able to *maybe* help you not create another David Gilford."

"All right, I'll admit that we're taking care of Lori Watkins. What are you offering?"

"Two things." Hutch withdrew a jump drive from his pocket and slid it across the table. "These are the best population models I could create using all the data at hand. I've run it through about a hundred permutations, with variables for intervention, isolation, and even war. Please feel free to keep that and show it to your superiors. The *best-case* scenario is a cataclysmic fall in human population within one year."

"You're preaching to the choir, Doctor, but I'll have a look at this." She took the drive and slipped it into a handbag. "Rest assured, we're being careful. Now, what else."

"I'd like to know if you have a treatment for the infectious elements of *Homo draconis*."

"I'm not sharing our findings with you, Doctor Hutchinson."

"Then I can't help you." He picked up his coffee and started to get up again.

"Stop that!" She flashed him a glare and leaned over. "Sit down, and *listen*, Doctor."

"All right." He sat down. "I'm listening."

"I can't tell you about our research findings, but I *can* tell you that we're keeping Lori Watkins in a secure facility and using every means at our disposal to ensure that the infection is not transmitted."

"Which is a roundabout way of saying you don't have a cure." Hutch sipped his coffee and sighed. "Stop playing games with me, and stop insulting my intelligence, Mary. I needed to know if you'd cracked the infection because I know that there's someone out there who has."

"And how do you know that?"

"The two other women who were injured by David Gilford during his second attack were found in a hotel room drugged and infection free. They're perfectly healthy."

"How did you..." Her brows furrowed. "Detective Jasper."

"Yes."

"And how did he find them?"

"An anonymous tip. No way to trace the message."

Mary's jaw clenched again. "Okay, so, someone out there can crack the infective elements of *Homo draconis*. Are you saying you know who this is?"

"No, I don't know who it is, but I know someone who does."

Her eyes narrowed. "Who?"

"Aleksi." He enjoyed the surprise on her face. "She's no longer infectious, Doctor."

"How can you be sure of that?"

"You'll just have to trust me. I know it for a fact." He'd go straight to hell before he told Buckmann that he and Aleksi had been intimate. "I know also that you're not going to be satisfied with one subject in your little experiment. You'll put this into more soldiers, probably women, since you've learned your lesson with David Gilford. You won't let the fact that this infection could wipe out the human race stop you. You'll tell yourself you'll be careful, but you can never be careful enough."

"Meaning what, Doctor?" she asked, her surprise now transformed to suspicion and eagerness. She knew where this was going.

"Meaning that I've come to the conclusion that getting you the cure for the infection, and you people creating an army of non-infectious dragons, is slightly *less* risky than you creating an army of *infectious* dragons."

"That's probably an accurate assessment," she admitted. "So, how can you help us?"

"By asking Aleksi to convince her friends to trade their cure for Lori Watkins."

Her eyes narrowed again. "We're not going to deal with terrorists, Doctor."

"Spare me the flag waving, please. *Anyone* who has something you want and won't give it to you is labeled a terrorist."

"They infiltrated a government facility and stole a priceless artifact."

"Which is exactly what *you* did when you broke into my laboratories and stole the very same artifact from me, Doctor Buckmann." He sneered at her openly. "Maybe I should report *you* to the police as a terrorist."

"Do that, Doctor," she fumed. "See where it gets you."

"I'm sure it would get me thrown into a cell in Guantanamo." Hutch sipped his coffee and took a deep breath to settle his temper. "Now, can we please stop the pissing contest? These people stole something you'd already stolen from me, and they are better than you at biotechnology. Swallow your continent-sized ego for one second and consider your options. You either cut a deal with them and get everything you want, or you don't and you end up with nothing. I'm prepared to plead your case. Take it or leave it."

She stared at him for a long time, then said, "We would need proof they can do what you say."

Hutch shrugged. "A blood sample from Aleksi should convince you."

"It would."

"Then I'll see what I can do."

"Good." Buckmann stood, picked up her coffee and paper. "Tell Aleksi this, too, Doctor: Lori Watkins is fully transformed, and is psychologically unstable. Treating her to cure the infection won't help her mental state. If we can't help her there, I doubt they can."

*The arrogance*, he thought. Hutch had dealt with dozens of academics with the same attitude, and he knew exactly how to respond. "So, you know more about dragon psychology than Aleksi does?" He smiled thinly. "Good for you."

Her jaw muscles clenched, and her face flushed. Hutch just held his smile. Buckmann walked away without another word, and he picked up his coffee to leave.

"She seemed a little pissed at you, doc," Brandy said as he walked past the counter. "You dating her daughter or something?"

Hutch barked a laugh. "Oh, nothing like that. It was just an academic disagreement. You know how thin-skinned scientists are when their findings are questioned."

"Don't I ever!" Brandy rolled her eyes; she was a brilliant chemist in the masters program, and had gone through two advisors already. "Take care, doc!"

"You too." He raised his coffee to her and started for his office. Halfway there, he pulled his phone and said into it, "You hear all that, Tony?"

"Every word. She's a real reptile, Hutch!"

Hutch chuckled. "More like a cornered badger, Tony. I could handle a reptile. I have experience in that department."

Tony snorted a laugh. "True enough. You be careful now, doc. You need backup, sing out."

"Thanks, Tony. At least we know what happened to Lori Watkins now."

"Right. Another psycho dragon. Just what we needed."

"That's the truth. Take care, Tony. I'll be in touch."

"Later, doc!"

The call ended, and Hutch put his phone away. He idly wondered what would happen to him if Mary Buckmann ever learned he'd included a police detective in their supposedly private conversation. The answer he knew, had four walls, no windows, a thin mattress, and a stainless-steel commode and sink.

## 7

With Aleksi sedated and resting comfortably, undergoing the slow process of undoing the genetic changes they'd put her through, Persephone took the opportunity to catch up on her other life. Her own ongoing genetic manipulation had her edgy, craving meat, and longing for open spaces. Lunch at a sidewalk café with some art critic friends seemed the perfect distraction. Also, she'd promised Aleksi to keep in touch with Hutch in her name, and she planned to keep up her barrage of texts to Mary Buckmann, even though the woman had refused to reply to a single one of them.

In the house, they ran all communications through Gi-gi's virtually unhackable Wi-Fi network. Their calls ran through a constantly changing network of servers all around the world. Outside, they had to be more careful. Even though they'd modified Aleksi's phone with encryption, the cellular signal could possibly be traced and triangulated through towers. She never left the phone on for more than the few seconds it took to send and receive a text. So, while eating sushi, gossiping about the latest artists on the scene, and sipping wine, Persephone turned on the phone.

To her surprise, Aleksi had received one reply from Buckmann, and several sequential texts from Hutch. She read Buckmann's first, and her brow knitted in puzzlement.

It read, "We will accept Doctor Hutchinson's proposal."

*Hutch, what did you do?* Persephone pulled up his texts and scrolled to the top.

"Had a conversation with MB. Confirmed they have David's first victim, Lori Watkins. She's HD."

*Nothing we didn't suspect.* Persephone scrolled down.

"The threat of infection will not keep them from creating HD soldiers. Lori is psych-unstable, but they will get female volunteers. This risks humanity."

*Again, duh*, she thought scrolling to the next.

"Only one solution: convince your friends to give Buckmann the cure to HD infection. They get their army of dragons, but non-infectious. Dangerous, but not Armageddon. They will trade Lori Watkins for the cure. Need a blood sample to show them you're not infectious."

*Shit! So that's Hutch's proposal!* Persephone turned off the phone, pocketed it, and pulled her own. She shot a text to Gi-gi. "We have a problem, and perhaps an opportunity. Confirmed that DHS has Lori Watkins. She's HD, infectious, and psych-unstable. They want to trade her for the cure to the infection."

"Persephone? You have *two* phones?" One of her friends eyed her curiously. "What's up with that?"

"Resource management, dear." She smiled and popped another piece of raw Ahi into her mouth. "One simply does *not* give the same number to all of one's...*special* friends."

That got a laugh, and a round of comments about juggling multiple lovers. Persephone's phone vibrated and Gigi's reply appeared. "See me ASAP."

She tapped, "One hour," and pocketed the phone, raising her glass to her friends. "To past, present, and future lovers; may they never meet."

Crystal chimed musically, and they laughed and drank. Persephone paid more attention to her food and the conversation, trying to ignore the irony of her own virtually nonexistent social life of late.

An hour later, she parked the Jag in front of her home, handed her keys to their butler, Freddie, and trundled down the steps to the wine cellar. Inside the Sanctum, she ducked into the treatment room long enough to see Aleksi.

"How is she?" Aleksi lay on an upholstered reclining table equipped with a web of padded nylon straps. Her right hand was in a cast. Reggie had done surgery the day before to reattach the torn tendons of her injured thumb. An IV ran into her left arm.

Carrie looked up from her e-reader and shrugged. "Quiet. Reggie started the second reversal."

Progress was slow, but steady. "Thanks." Persephone closed the door and went to Gi-gi's room. "So, my ex-husband seems to have brokered a deal with Mary Buckmann."

Gi-gi didn't look away from her screens. "The answer is no. They cannot be trusted."

Persephone resisted the urge to sigh; they'd had this discussion before. "Their lack of trustworthiness is exactly why we should give them the cure. They won't let the risk of infection stop them from making an army of dragons."

"Giving them the cure will not only ensure that they *do* create an army of *Homo draconis*, but will give them insight to our capabilities. Exchanging Lori Watkins will expose us. It's too dangerous."

"More dangerous than a world-wide pandemic?"

"Humanity eradicated *Homo draconis* in the past, with less effective weapons and communications. If an outbreak occurs, they will do so again. This family will survive as it always has, through secrecy and caution."

"You're talking about *billions* of lives, Gi-gi. Humanity eradicated *Homo draconis* prehistorically. We have no way to know what the impact was on human populations or how they accomplished it. Have you modeled what would happen during an outbreak of HD with a world population of seven billion?"

"Yes." Still she didn't look away from her screens.

"And?"

"Doctor Hutchinson's models are quite likely accurate, barring any thermonuclear exchange."

Persephone gaped at Gi-gi. "You think they'd try to wipe out the infection with nuclear weapons?"

"That's one potential strategy. Regions governed by totalitarian regimes and areas with limited genetic exchange with the rest of the world would fare better. If *Homo draconis* was not eradicated, human populations would be reduced to less than fifty million, likely tribal societies of interrelated individuals."

"So, what you're saying is that you're willing to risk the lives of seven *billion* people to keep our secrets?"

"The risk is minimal." Finally, Gi-gi froze her screens and turned to Persephone. "The US Government cannot be trusted, but they are *not* fools. They will not allow an outbreak."

"They nearly had two with Derrick Penningly and David Gilford," Persephone pointed out.

"And they've learned from their failures. Lori Watkins will never escape; if they don't solve her psychological issues, she'll be euthanized."

"Then they start infecting *volunteers*." Persephone's nails slipped from their sheaths as if they had minds of their own. "They'll have their army whether we give them the cure or not!"

"Quite likely, but they'll take precautions to prevent an outbreak. Also, female *Homo draconis* don't seem to harbor the urge to spread the infection or kill non-related individuals. Aleksi was infectious for six months and didn't infect a single person."

"You have a sample size of *one* individual with a baseline psychological disorder to base that upon."

"Yes." Gi-gi turned back to her screens and put them in motion. "My decision is final. We will give *nothing* to Mary Buckmann."

Persephone cursed under her breath and left the room. She'd never before had the urge to murder her great-grandmother, but she had to admit, if she'd stayed in that room much longer...

*No*, she realized. *No, I wouldn't have.* Gi-gi was her family, and she harbored an intelligence that made the rest of them seem like idiot children. Persephone believed she was wrong in this decision, that it was based on faulty data, fear of discovery, and a lack of empathy, but she wouldn't go against her great-grandmother's orders.

She pulled Aleksi's phone and texted, "Sorry. No deal," to both Mary Buckmann and Hutch. She then turned the phone off and went to check on Reggie. She needed something to calm her nerves.

M ary stepped into the new director's office. "Thanks for seeing me, ma'am. I'm assuming you're up to speed on our progress, or lack of it, with Watkins." They could have done this by video conference, but the director's office was in the same building, and there were things that could be said in person that couldn't be said over even an encrypted connection.

"I am." She gestured to a chair and rubbed her eyes. The new director wasn't a physical scientist, but a cyber-security specialist and statistical analyst. She was brilliant in her own right, but often said biology made her nauseous. "Is there any real evidence to suggest future subjects would be more psychologically stable? We're oh for three."

"Yes. Rychenkna is psychologically stable."

"And she had social anxiety disorder prior to infection."

"Yes, untreated and poorly diagnosed. That seems to have been resolved by her transformation." Mary shrugged. "We're considering that her disorder might actually have *contributed* to her psychological stability post-infection, but we don't have any corroborating evidence."

"And we've had zero progress in neutralizing the infectious elements."

"So far, yes." Mary had already informed her of the conversation with Hutchinson. "We know it's possible. There's little doubt that Roberta Stewart and Sally McMaster were infected, and they're both fine. We've gotten blood samples from both of them, but analysis has revealed nothing unusual. Elevated white cell count, some strange antibody markers, but nothing we can use to reverse engineer the cure. We believe they were treated and released by the same people who impersonated me and are now working with Aleksi Rychenkna. Doctor Hutchinson reported that Aleksi's no longer infectious as well, though we have no concrete confirmation of this."

The director pursed his lips and glowered. "And this...organization has refused to offer this cure in exchange for Lori Watkins."

"Yes." There was nothing more to say. Aleksi's response had been disappointing, but emphatic.

"Do you think they'd take anything else in exchange?"

"I haven't offered anything else. What do you suggest?"

"Offer them the fucking *moon* if you have to, Mary. We *need* that cure. We can't risk an outbreak. We barely dodged that bullet with Gilford."

"Agreed." Mary pursed her lips. "So, anonymity, money, immunity from prosecution, a presidential pardon... Anything else?"

"Whatever it takes. Just ask them what they want."

"Understood." The notion of giving the people who had abducted and impersonated her a get-out-of-jail-free card didn't settle well with Mary, but she'd make the offer. "Is that all, ma'am?" She stood.

The director's eyes went flinty. "Just get that cure, Mary. Buy, beg, borrow, or *steal* it, but get it. Is that clear?"

Mary suppressed a smile. "*Crystal* clear, ma'am."

# 8

Once again, Aleksi awoke to the sensation of gentle restraint, like being wrapped in a soft cocoon. She tried to move and couldn't. Her head felt stuffed with cotton, sounds, smells, and sensations muddled. Flexing her right hand sent dull spears of pain up her arm. Her mouth was dry, and her stomach growled. She found that she could turn her head, and did so, but everything was dark.

"Aleksi?"

The voice, a woman's, sounded familiar, but she couldn't place it. Aleksi tried to speak, and it came out a dull croak. "Dark. Blind."

"We have the lights turned low. Just open your eyes."

*Open my eyes...* The thought didn't register. "Eyes?"

"She's too deep. Ease up a little more," the woman's voice said.

"Backing off a milligram. Give her a minute." This voice, a man's, also sounded familiar.

*A minute...* Aleksi wondered what a minute was for a while, and why they would want to give her one. She couldn't move and doubted she could take anything from them even if they offered it. Muscles flexed beneath the cocoon, stiff from sleep. Her right arm ached. She felt the need to stretch and suddenly yawned.

Her eyes opened, the dimly lit room swimming into clarity.

"Hey there." A woman smiled in her field of vision, and her name registered.

"Persephone." She cleared her throat and tried to lift her head. "My...mouth's dry."

"Here. We'll incline your bed." Something hummed, and Aleksi felt motion. The room moved, or rather, she moved. Yes, that seemed more likely. "Here's some ice chips."

A spoon rose up, and she opened her mouth. Cold bit her tongue, and she crunched the chips between her teeth. "Mmmm. Good."

"Here's some more." She took another spoonful, closing her eyes in bliss as the cool moisture washed the dry funk from her tongue. "How are you feeling?"

Aleksi blinked and thought about it. "Dunno. I can't move, and my arm hurts." A memory of a nightmare, or maybe not a nightmare, swam up from the cotton still packed around her mind. "Did you cut me open?"

The woman smiled. "No, Aleksi. You had an episode and hurt yourself. Do you remember?"

She thought about it for a moment and shook her head. "Nightmares. I thought someone was after me."

"Yes, that's what you thought. Your anxiety went a little wild. That was three days ago. We're treating you. You should feel better soon." Persephone turned and said, "I think we can ease up a little more. She needs to eat."

*Eat... Food...* Yes, that sounded like a good idea. She ran her tongue over her lips, and her stomach growled again.

Slowly, ever so slowly, the cotton receded some more. Senses sharpened and thoughts cleared, but her head ached a little. Anxiety, fear, dread, terror all lurked at the edges, seeping inward, and she felt herself tense, her teeth grinding, muscles straining against the restraints. She clenched her eyes tight to block out the fear.

"Stop!" she growled from between clenched teeth.

"Stop what, Aleksi?"

"No more... I don't want...to feel that way!" She quivered beneath the restraints. "Afraid..."

"A titch more midazolam ought to take that away."

Slowly, the fear eased, and she could breathe again. She blinked and gasped a deep breath, nodding to Persephone. "Better. I can... think at least."

"Good. Here's some more ice chips." Persephone spooned ice into her mouth, and Aleksi crunched them up. "How much do you remember about what happened?"

"I remember hurting my arm, but not...before." Aleksi crunched more ice and flexed her aching hand under the restraints. "You stopped me."

"Yes. You weren't thinking clearly, Aleksi. I had to stop you. We can talk about it when you're well."

"But...how."

"How what?"

"How did you stop me? I remember you grabbing my arm, and I couldn't move it. How did you do that?"

"Oh, that!" Persephone laughed and waved it off. "Hysterical strength. You'd just about torn your thumb off breaking free, and I—"

"Bullshit! I may be drugged and half crazy, Persephone, but I'm not *stupid*." Aleksi breathed deeply, taking in Persephone's scent through her mouth and nose. It was familiar, but slightly different. "You've done it, haven't you? You're...changed."

"I knew you couldn't fool her," Reggie said with a sardonic smile.

Persephone ignored him. "Yes, Aleksi. I've had some specific genetic changes. No cascades, but we've inserted discreet elements of the *Homo draconis* genome into mine. Strength, reflexes, eyesight, olfaction." She raised a hand and flexed, her painted nails unsheathing half an inch. "Some other minor surprises."

"Why? Why would you *do* that?" Aleksi tried to keep the disgust out of her voice and failed.

"It's nothing drastic, Aleksi. Nothing I can't keep hidden. It's for our protection."

"Protection from who?"

"From Buckmann and her machinations. There have been developments. They've admitted that they have Lori Watkins, David Gilford's first victim. She's fully transformed and contagious. They want the cure, and Gi-gi refuses to give it to them."

"They'll never stop hunting me." Aleksi started to shake under the restraints.

"Shh, Aleksi, just relax. You're safe here." She gripped her shoulder warmly, claws retracted. "We'll talk about this when you're better. We need to put some weight on you. You're malnourished with only IV nutrition. Are you hungry?"

Aleksi forced herself to breathe and nodded. Her stomach felt like a black hole.

"Good, because dinner doesn't look very appetizing. It tastes pretty good, but...well, we needed to make it easy to digest." Persephone picked up a Tupperware bowl and a spoon. "It was a shame to put a steak through a food processor, but that's what's on the menu." She scooped up a spoonful of reddish paste and said, "Open wide."

Aleksi did, and she had to agree with Persephone's assessment. It tasted good, but the texture wasn't right. She swallowed quickly and took another bite. Her stomach, at least, seemed happy about the meal.

---

Just watch the image and concentrate on the sound of my voice, Lori. Watch the patterns, how they evolve and change, how they move. Relax your muscles, your feet, and hands, your toes and fingers. Focus on the patterns and breathe with the rhythm. Nothing else matters except the image and my voice..."

Lori tried to do as Olson said, but concentrating only on her voice and the video of a line drawing that evolved in interesting geometric patterns proved impossible. As with all of the virtual reality sessions, she found them two-dimensional. Lori lived in five dimensions, and the visor and earphones only blocked out input and gave her false stimuli that didn't match her other three senses. She could smell

Olson, could feel her breathing, could have listed what she had for breakfast, how she drank her coffee, who she was sleeping with—more than one person actually—and that she used Avena body lotion, had polished her nails the day before, and was premenstrual. The pretty lights and soothing voice were only distractions from reality.

"This isn't working, Doctor."

"Deep breaths, Lori," Olson continued. "Just let yourself drift. Just listen and—"

"I *said* it isn't working!" Lori pulled off the visor/headphone rig and dropped it beside the ridiculously comfortable lounger. The chair was designed to dampen vibrations, one more straw of sensory deprivation piled onto her back. She lurched up and stalked toward the kitchenette. "It's only making me tense."

"You're not even trying, Lori." Olson sighed and rubbed her eyes. "This exercise is critical. We need to get to the source of your anxiety, and hypnosis will help us unlock your memories."

"I understand that, but even after a month studying me like a bug under a cup, *you* don't understand *me*!" Lori pulled a meatsicle from the freezer—a frozen block of hamburger on a popsicle stick—tore off the wrapper and crunched off a bite. Cold-meaty-deliciousness filled her mouth, the scent of the beef thawing on her tongue filling her sinuses. She closed her eyes, chewing in bliss, and had a snippet sensation of meat, blood, and bone between her teeth.

"Then *help* me understand. Why can't you concentrate? We've gone to great lengths to block extraneous sensory input."

"That's part of the problem. You can't, and even if you could it would only be infuriating!" Lori bit off another bite and crunched. "I can feel your heartbeat, Doctor. I can smell the oatmeal you ate this morning through the toothpaste you brush your teeth with. I can *taste* the sex you had last night in the back of my throat. I can sense the goddamn *garbage* truck up there tipping a dumpster!" She pointed to the ceiling. "They take the garbage at ten a.m. Tuesdays and Fridays. The air conditioning cycles every forty seconds. The cleanser they use in the bathroom tastes like a public pool. And worst of all, those two *jerks* outside the door can't stop fidgeting like a couple of sorority chicks at a frat party!" She stabbed the half-eaten meatsicle at the door.

"Then we'll have to do better." Olson stood and tapped her tablet. "I'd like you to try an immersion chamber. The water will dampen vibrations and block scents and tastes. It should allow you to—"

"Doctor, you're not *listening* to me!" Lori crunched the last of her meal and flipped the denuded stick into the trash. "Blocking my senses isn't the answer to *anything*! It only makes my anxiety worse! I need to breathe real air, see real sky, feel *real* sensations."

"I know you're feeling claustrophobic, Lori, but we can't let you outside."

"Then set up someplace full of plants and animals and shit that makes *sense*!"

"What's not making sense, Lori? Your rooms are as comfortable as we can make them." Olson's voice brimmed with frustration, but it flickered like a candle in a burning house compared to Lori's.

"Listen...to...me!" Lori fought to keep from clenching her hands, from driving her claws into her palms. "This place is sterile! The air smells like nothing. Everything I eat and drink is pre-packaged and virtually tasteless! Bring me some real food and let me cook it myself! Give me a cat or dog or a goddamn *hamster* to play with! And most of all, get those two fucking *goons* away from my door!"

"The guards have to stay there, Lori. We can't—"

"You can't risk me *hurting* anyone! I know!" Lori gritted her teeth. "You think I can't fucking hear you when you talk about me down the hall? You think I don't know *exactly* what those two bitches outside are thinking?"

"Lori, you're imagining things. I need you to calm down and—"

"I'll calm down when you get Judy and Alice the *FUCK* out of here!" Lori strode to the door and scratched an oval in the concrete with a claw at head height. She poked eyes and scratched a frowny mouth. "This is Alice. She likes to chew gum, spearmint, and she's got a rash on her ass that she keeps scratching." She took a step to the other side of the door and scratched another oval. "This is Judy. Her feet hurt, she's menstruating, and she smokes too much. Both Judy and Alice are terrified of me, but it's their job to shoot me if I show too much aggression." Lori whirled to face Olson. "Don't tell me I'm fucking *imagining* things!"

"I'm sorry, Lori. I didn't mean to insult you." Olson put her tablet down and clenched her hands in front of her. They were shaking, and her fear wafted from every pore of her skin. "I need you to calm down now."

"You're afraid of me." Lori couldn't keep her lips from curling back from her teeth. "You think I'm a goddamn monster! You're afraid I'm going to rip you apart and eat you!"

"No, I'm not, Lori. I just want you to—"

"Don't fucking *LIE* to me!" Lori whirled and slammed a clawed hand down on the kitchen counter, fracturing the plastic. She tore the broken piece off and flung it at the door. "Let me the fuck out of here or I swear I'll tear the goddamned *walls* down!" She ripped off another chunk of the counter and smashed it into the door. It scratched the paint, but that was all.

"Lori! Calm down right *now*!" Olson backed away, her eyes wide. "Stop breaking things! You're going to—"

"Don't tell me what I'm going to *do*, Doctor!" Lori raged, claws unsheathed, senses bristling. She heard the earpieces of the soldiers outside squawking orders, felt their weapons powering up, sensed them moving. She stepped away from the door and pointed at it. "Tell those two that if they open that door, I'll tear them to pieces!"

"Lori! Don't! You have to calm down!"

Lori heard the order, "Take her down! Do it now!"

"It's too late, Doctor." Lori set her clawed toes into the floor, spread her wings wide, and tensed like a coiled spring. "They're coming in to shoot me, now." She felt the heavy bolts clack free of the door frame. "I didn't want to hurt anyone!"

The electric motor that opened the door engaged, and she lunged.

Two weapons cracked simultaneously, each throwing a widening net of fine metal mesh. They were only ten feet away, but the nets spread too wide for Lori to evade. She swept her claws like scythes to knock the nets away, but the instant she touched the metal fibers, electricity lanced through her.

Fifty thousand volts constricted every muscle in her body in less than a second. She convulsed in mid lunge, a scream dying in her throat, and slammed into the door frame, then the floor. Darkness closed in, and she tasted blood.

9

———————

**M**ary Buckmann was desperate for a win. Lori Watkins lay in a pharmacologic stupor, restrained, monitored, and under guard. The director had refused to allow another subject to be inoculated with HD, even though they had four volunteers lined up, fully briefed, willing, and ready. Now, with everything to gain and nothing to lose, she took the director at her word.

*Buy, beg, borrow, or steal... Time to go on the offensive.*

She had offered all she could to this mysterious organization through Aleksi, but the answer had been a flat, "No. They don't trust you." Well, Mary couldn't blame them, but she wasn't about to take "No" for an answer.

She stood in her communications center, watching screens, listening to the chatter between her team members, the communications specialists, and tactical officers. The anticipation of the pending operation warmed her stomach and tingled along her nerves. It felt good to be doing something proactive.

"Spotters, report," Mary ordered.

"Spotter One, no movement," the first reported.

"Spotter Two, confirmed. Nobody home," the second said.

"Insertion team, you're a go," Mary said into the mic. She focused her attention on the body cam video feeds from the two insertion team operatives. The feeds from the team's body cams flashed with red borders as the op went live.

"Going in now," the senior of the two reported.

Mary watched them step out of their van and walk across the parking lot toward a pair of glass doors, feeling like she was playing a first-person video game.

The two specialists, disguised as IT contractors putting in a new Wi-Fi system, entered the condominium office and presented their work order to the condo manager. The company was real, but the service call was fabricated. The woman read it, looking bored, nodded and said it would be no problem. The leader was given a swipe card for the elevator. The manager made a copy of the work order and filed it.

"File a note to recover that copy," Mary said, and Benson acknowledged it.

Mary's team leader showed the manager a key they'd been given by the resident—false, of course—and took the elevator up to Doctor Hutchinson's floor. Mary's IT specialists had hacked the condo's simple security system and transposed the video from the hallway on Hutchinson's floor to the one two floors up where they were supposed to be doing the work. To the manager, if she bothered to watch the monitor, it appeared the contractors were going exactly where they were supposed to go. The lock of Hutchinson's door yielded to their expertise, and they were inside in seconds.

The door clicked closed behind them, and the lead operative said, "We're in."

The sound of rattling metal came over the speaker. "What was that?" Mary asked as the two video feeds jostled. Whatever it was had startled her people.

"A big lizard in a cage in the kitchen," one said, his body cam confirming his claim.

"That's Rychenkna's pet iguana. Start your sweeps."

Hutchinson was their only connection to Aleksi, and Aleksi was their only connection to the terrorists. There had to be something here they could use.

The two video feeds showed one of the operatives beginning a careful physical search, starting in the office, his gloved hands opening drawers and closet doors. There was a computer station there, but it plugged into a laptop Hutchinson must have had with him. The other operative unzipped his toolkit and took out a broad-spectrum radiometer. The device would detect anything in the spectrum within the apartment and localize the source. They hoped to hack into Hutchinson's Wi-Fi hub and access everything that went through it. He fired it up and started a casual sweep, then stopped.

"Ma'am, we may have a... Yes, there's a strong radio source here, and more Wi-Fi than there should be." He turned and read his screen. "Four Wi-Fi transmitters, one receiver, and a *really* powerful radio transmitter. This place is wired."

"Shit! Who the hell..." Mary's mind spun, then clicked on the answer. *Of course, they're watching him!*

"Orders, ma'am?"

"Localize the radio transmitter!" Her heart hammered in her chest. This might be the break they were looking for, but it was also a dangerous one. If this mysterious terrorist organization was monitoring Hutchinson's apartment constantly, even when he wasn't there, they might be watching Mary's team at this very moment. They could very easily, and not metaphorically, be poking a sleeping dragon with a stick. "I want the exact frequency, and I want to know if it's receiving more than Wi-Fi, and on what frequency!"

"Got the transmission frequency." The view jumped again as he turned a circle, the direction finder on his radiometer zeroing in on the source. He opened a closet to find a washer and dryer. "It's behind the dryer. One, I'm going to need a hand."

"Coming." The other operative hurried in, and the pair muscled the drier out from the wall, lifting instead of simply dragging it to keep from scratching the hardwood floor.

"Enough," the radiometer operator said, pulling a flashlight and crawling over the appliances. The beam caught a small square device in the dusty shadows. "No wires. This is high end." He reached down and picked it up in a gloved hand. "No labels or indicator lights. Covert. Really nice."

"Crack it," Mary ordered.

"Yes, ma'am." The operative worked fast, a power driver spinning out the four tiny screws holding the cover plate on. He pried it open and scanned the interior with his camera.

To Mary, the inside of the device looked like a maze of mysterious electronic components, the board labeled with tiny letters and numbers like secret code. Fortunately, she had specialists for this sort of thing.

"Got it!" a tech in the comm center announced. "It receives pings on VHF band. I have the frequency, ma'am!"

"Insertion team, button the transceiver back up, put it back, and get out. We've got what we came for."

"Affirmative!" The operative replaced the cover, secured the screws, placed the unit exactly where he'd found it, and two of them moved the dryer back. They were out the door in less than five minutes.

*Damn, it's nice to work with professionals*, Mary thought. "Monitor that VHF frequency for the pings, and get two direction finder teams on it. I want units in the field to triangulate the moment we get a signal!"

"On it, ma'am!" The communications officer started giving orders.

Mary made sure her team got out without trouble and called off the surveillance. Then she made a call to Captain Harris.

"Yes, Doctor?" he answered.

"We have a pending field op. This could be the people working with Rychenkna, so I want two full SWAT teams, one insertion, one outside. We'll have a location soon."

"I'll have them ready in twenty minutes."

"Make it ten." She broke the connection and went back to the communications officer. "Anything?"

"Two teams are going out now and scanning. We should have something soon."

Mary waited, trying to remain calm. "Nothing?"

"Nothing yet. The incoming signal isn't constant. More likely command pings every so often. They should..." He stopped and pressed a finger to his earbud. "We have a ping!"

"Excellent! Triangulate and zero in!"

"Working on it." The communications officer typed furiously. "Initial analysis points us to Back Bay. We're zeroing in."

"Good!" Mary called Harris again, and didn't wait for him to answer. "I need your people rolling now!"

"Out the door in five, ma'am."

"Excellent! Send them to Back Bay and patch the team leaders into the comm center. I'll have a precise location soon. Get up here."

"Yes, ma'am." He disconnected, and two minutes later two more body cam images flicked up to screens in the comms center.

"Team Alpha Victor checking in," one announced. The image showed the front seat of a van as the team leader climbed aboard. A driver in SWAT gear got in behind the wheel. He panned to the back of the big SUV to show six more soldiers aboard. "We're rolling."

"Team Beta Victor checking in." The other image was only seconds behind. "Out the door in one minute."

"Excellent!" She tapped her communications officer on the shoulder. "Get me that location."

"We'll have it soon, ma'am," the communications officer assured her.

"Good." Mary stepped back to let the man work and clenched her hands behind her back. A slow grin spread across her mouth. "I've got you now, you bastards!"

---

Persephone awoke from the most glorious dream—Sex and steak tartar, what could be better?—to the sound of her phone going berserk. She lunged out of bed to grab the noisy thing and realized what that particular ring tone meant: all hands on deck; general quarters; imminent mayhem.

The only message on the phone read, "Sanctum NOW!"

She threw on clothes and ran. When she entered Gi-gi's room, Reggie and half a dozen more cousins were there, too. A telling scene played on the monitors: scenes of Hutch's condo, two men in workmen's clothes moving the dryer, then finding the Wi-Fi radio transceiver Persephone had put there.

"How fucked are we?" she asked, earning looks from everyone, including Gi-gi.

"Unsure, but they found, disassembled, and analyzed our transceiver. We weren't monitoring this video, but the camera motion sensors activated while Doctor Hutchinson was still at work. This happened ten minutes ago."

"If they analyzed the transceiver..."

"They know the frequency of our transceiver ping, and may have triangulated our location." All the screens froze, and Gi-gi gazed at them. "We have no time. Take Aleksi, the specimen, everything irreplaceable, and go. Tell the staff they're dismissed with severance. I'm putting our failsafe protocols into motion now." Her ancient fingers moved on the remote and a red on black screen lit up.

Only two words were displayed: "System Armed."

Persephone's stomach dropped to her toes, and the dragon within her took control. "Everyone, we are scrambling! NOW! All irreplaceable samples, Aleksi, and any unique works of art have priority. GO!"

Her cousins ran from the room.

"I'll need your help with Aleksi, Seph!" Reggie shot over his shoulder as he dashed out.

"I'll be there." The door closed, and she turned to Gi-gi. "We can take you. Ten minutes."

"No. I'll see to it, my dear." The ancient lips quirked in a smile. "You've become quite something unique, great-granddaughter. I'm glad I lived long enough to see you come to your fullest."

"I love you, Gi-gi." Persephone gripped her arm, tears stinging her eyes. "*Au revoir, mon cher.*"

"*Au revoir, mon amour,*" Gi-gi said. "Now go!"

Persephone turned and ran. She found Reggie in the treatment room unfastening Aleksi's restraints. A gurney sat beside the bed, but Persephone intervened.

"Just get her IV, and make sure it doesn't come out!" She grabbed a trauma kit, ripped it open, snatched the scalpel from within, and slashed Aleksi's bonds. Reggie seemed to be moving in slow motion. "MOVE! I'm lifting in one, two, three!"

"Slow down, Seph! I can barely understand you!" He moved like he'd been dipped in molasses.

"You speed up!" Aleksi felt like a feather in her arms. "Keep up with me!"

Reggie ran behind holding the IV bag and an emergency ditch kit of medical supplies. They raced up to the garage where the cousins were loading vehicles with everything from art to biomedical samples stored in liquid nitrogen. They put Aleksi in the back of an SUV, hung her IV, confirmed it was still flowing, and dashed back downstairs.

"You'll need a lift for this!" Reggie opened the door to a storage room. It had already been ravaged by the cousins, but the original dragon specimen had been too heavy for them to lift.

"Get the gurney! I've got this!" As Reggie dashed out, Persephone sidled up to the sample. It sat in a plastic case lined with foam and weighed about four hundred pounds. She centered her weight, unsheathed her claws, and jerked the case off the table. She caught it, feeling the strain in every sinew of her arms, shoulders, and back, and lifted with her legs. When Reggie came in with a wheeled cart, she simply put it down in place and snapped, "Go!"

"Jesus H, Seph, I didn't know you could—"

"Neither did I. Now shut up. We don't have time."

They rumbled into the wine cellar, to the emergency elevator, and waited ten excruciating seconds for the door to open. To Persephone, the ride up one floor felt like a lifetime, but when the doors opened, only one of the four SUV's was already leaving. Two of the others were buttoning up, packed with everything they could get quickly, fortunes in art, unique precious stones and jewelry, and biological samples. There was space beside Aleksi for the specimen. They slid it in and slammed the door.

"You drive, Reg. I don't trust myself right now."

"Good! I'm not sure I trust you, either!" He dashed for the driver door.

"Carrie! All the staff?"

"They're already gone! No questions. They'll be fine! Go!" She was sliding a van Gogh sheathed in a hard plastic case alongside several other paintings.

Persephone got in the vehicle with Reggie, and they tore out of the garage. She looked back over her shoulder at the sleeping dragon in the back, and prayed to God they wouldn't get stopped for a traffic ticket.

---

Quite a place," Harris mumbled as the SWAT teams approached the gate. "A shitload of cameras. They'll know we're coming."

"Do we have aerial surveillance?" Mary asked.

"We just got a drone in place. No activity. The house is buttoned up tight."

"Information on the owners?" she asked her comm officer.

"A rich family named Terris. Not much more yet, but there's a ton of information on them. They're socially active and politically influential."

"Of course they are." The name Terris tweaked something in Mary's mind, but she couldn't remember what it was, and right now it wasn't a priority. She turned back to Harris. "Any sign of security measures?"

"Other than metric fuckton of cameras and motion sensors, no." He looked at her. "You want to go in hard or soft?"

"Try soft first."

"Roger." He touched his mic. "Alpha Victor, we try the soft sell. They've already got eyes on you."

"Affirmative, sir." The team leader turned as the driver lowered his window and poked the button on the intercom box.

"Department of Homeland Security. Open the gate."

"This security system is active. You are not authorized entry. You are being recorded. Please vacate the premises."

"On the authority of the US Government and the USA FREEDOM Act, we have authority to search these premises. Open the gate!"

"This security system is active. You are not authorized entry. You are being recorded. Please vacate the premises."

"No joy, sir," the team leader said.

"Cut it," Harris ordered.

The team leader gave the order, and two soldiers jumped out of the vehicle. One covered the other as the first tested the gate with a potentiometer and then applied a pair of bolt cutters to the chain that operated the gate. He then pushed it open, and they both got back in the SUV. The two vehicles raced up the drive to the front entrance and disgorged their occupants. One group approached the front door, while the other dispersed and took up perimeter positions. Harris kept up a steady conversation with his people, integrating what they could see from the drone.

"No vehicles," Harris said to Mary. "None visible from outside, anyway. Perimeter reports a big garage in the back. Locked."

"Perimeter, hold position for containment. Alpha Victor, go in." They were here; Mary knew it in her soul. They would find the people responsible for her abduction and impersonation, and they would get the cure for the HD infection. Both were here. But to get what she needed, they needed to take this place and its occupants intact. "We don't want a blood bath, commander, we want information."

"Understood." Harris keyed his mic to the team leaders. "Priority one is information and prisoners. Fire only if fired upon. Repeat, only if fired upon. Confirm."

"Confirmed," both team leaders said, relaying the orders to their people.

Alpha Victor approached the front door. The team leader put three men on either side of the door and assigned one to try it, standing back to provide his body camera a good view. The soldier tried the handle, shook his head, and stepped back.

"Locked, sir."

"Blow it," Harris replied.

"Demolitions, blow the door," the team leader said.

His team reorganized, one stepping forward to slap small charges to the latch and hinges, while the others took flanking positions. The demolitionist activated the radio detonators, stepped back, and said, "Fire in the hole! Three, two, one..."

The hinges and latch disintegrated into splinters of wood, masonry, and metal. The two flanking teams stepped up, wrenched the door away from the portal, and covered the entrance high and low. Laser light flicked through the smoke and dust.

"Negative contact, sir. The entry hall's empty," The team leader reported.

"Advance. Search and clear the ground floor."

The team leader made a motion with his hand, and his team went in. The moment they passed the threshold a blaring electronic voice issued from nowhere, freezing them in their tracks.

"Attention! Attention! You have trespassed on private property without a warrant! Authorities have been notified! Leave immediately! If you do not leave, countermeasures will be implemented! Attention! Attention!" The recorded warning continued to loop.

"Smoke and mirrors, commander," Mary said. "We have authority. Proceed."

"Ignore it!" Harris told his team. "They're rattling your cage! Clear the ground floor. Split into squads of four and give me telemetry!"

"Yes, sir!" Another screen lit up with body cam video, and they advanced, clearing rooms as they went.

They found sitting rooms, a coat room, closets, a dining room and kitchen—with clear evidence of a hasty departure—a small theater, servants' quarters, two stairways up, and one down. One team also found a cavernous garage, completely empty. There was an elevator here, and one door that opened after explosive persuasion to stairs leading down.

"I think they flew the coop, ma'am," Harris said to Mary.

"Search it. Every nook and closet. This is more than just a rich family mansion, commander. I *know* it!" Mary clenched her hands behind her back until her knuckles popped. "One team up, one down. There's *something* here!"

"Yes, ma'am." Harris sent the first squad down the stairs, and the second squad up.

Mary tried to watch both teams simultaneously. The warning announcement kept droning on, but the squads ignored it. The second team found bedrooms, offices, and a conference room. The first found a basement filled with boxes and out of season decorations. They also found a locked door.

"Blow it," Harris ordered.

Hinges and lock disintegrated in short order, and they found themselves in an amazingly well-stocked wine cellar.

"So far, they don't look like terrorists, ma'am."

"Then why is nobody here?" Mary didn't like the warning in Harris' tone, and she shot him a glare. "*Nobody* looks like a terrorist until they fly a plane into a building, commander. They ran. That isn't the action of an innocent person. Continue your search."

"Yes, ma'am." Harris relayed the order, and both teams continued.

The team in the wine cellar found an elevator and a door that opened into a stairway leading up. These matched up with what they'd found in the garage. They continued their sweep, clearing row after row of wine racks, thousands of bottles of rare vintages, a fortune.

*Whoever lives here has some serious cash*, Mary thought.

Then they found one more door.

This one was different, however; a solid armor plate with a thick frame built into the granite blocks of the foundation. There was no latch, but beside it, a palm-print scanner and a keypad stood nestled in a steel frame. This was clearly above and beyond anything a private citizen would have in their home.

The team leader had his specialist look it over and gave his report to Harris. "Armor grade steel, high tech identifying system. This is the shit, sir."

"Do they look like terrorists yet, commander?" Mary gloated.

"I'll admit, ma'am, they look *suspect*." Harris switched to the command frequency. "Can you safely blow it?"

"Dems, give me your best assessment."

"It's set in rock, not reinforced concrete. Five minutes with shaped charges and it's scrap, sarge."

"You copy, captain?" the team leader asked.

"I copy. Blow it." Harris informed his other team what was happening and told them to finish their sweep upstairs.

"Keep in mind that Aleksi Rychenkna might be standing behind that door, captain. Deploy your people however you see fit, but she took down four SWAT soldiers *before* she was fully transformed."

"I saw the footage, ma'am." Harris bit his lip and nodded. "Second squad, head downstairs. First squad, hold detonation until second squad arrives for backup."

Mary breathed easier; at least Harris was listening to reason.

The second squad arrived, and they all took secure positions. The demolitionist already had his charges set, so he simply backed away, gave the warning, and triggered the radio detonator.

This explosion was slightly more spectacular than the previous ones, but it was still well-controlled. The air filled with rock dust, and the heavily armored door fell flat to the floor with a tooth-rattling thud. A number of wine bottles were hit by flying rock and shattered, flooding the floor with dark red vintage. Red targeting lasers lanced through the dust, but nothing emerged. No people, no dragon, no terrorists.

"Advance by twos. Flanking positions!"

The team advanced in pairs, each watching the others' backs. The video feed showed a simple hallway on the other side. It looked like every hotel Mary had ever stayed in, each door sporting a card swipe and a keypad.

"Two doors right, five left, sir," the team leader said.

"Station two here watching the right. Send the rest left. Clear as you go," Harris ordered.

"Affirmative."

Six soldiers went left while two stayed at the shattered security door, their weapons trained to the right. The larger team blew each lock as they went, kicking doors open to reveal a residential suite, a meeting room, a laboratory, and a medical treatment room. In the medical suite, a cushioned bed dominated the space. Padded restraints hung from one side, the ends cut.

"They took a patient out of here in a hurry," Mary surmised, though she had no idea who that patient might have been.

The last door was set in the end of the hall. A charge was placed on the lock, the team stepped back, and it was blown to shrapnel.

The moment the advancing team cleared the dust, Mary knew they'd hit pay dirt. A high-tech medical bed dominated the center of the room with an oxygen generator beside it. A single occupant lay upon the cushioned surface. The periphery of the room was lined with bookshelves, cabinets of dark wood, and flat-screen monitors. Several monitors hung suspended from the ceiling where the figure in the bed could easily see them. Upon two of the monitors, Mary saw their own team viewed from the hallway outside and from the room itself.

One other monitor only showed two words in red on a black background, "System Armed."

The figure on the bed turned their head to face the intruders, and the red dots of laser sights wavered as they settled on it. Mary caught her breath.

"What the hell is *that?*" the team leader said.

Mary had no answer.

Lavender eyes stared at them from an impossibly wizened face, hairless, sexless, and seemingly lifeless save for those two piercing orbs. The lips—razor thin and lined with age—twitched once, and a hand like a desiccated mummy's moved on a remote control. The red on black screen changed, now displaying two new words.

"Detonation Initiated," blinked twice.

"Mother fu—"

Two of the screens in the communications center went immediately blank, cutting off the team leader's expletive. The view from the team leader outside the mansion jumped as the screen went white, then tumbled in an alternating view of sky, trees, and ground. The view from the drone a thousand feet overhead gave a more informative and devastating view.

The entire mansion ceased to exist, engulfed in blinding white flames. There wasn't a lot of force behind the explosion, but Mary could see the heat in concentric waves of distortion. Trees near the house burst into flames, and the nearer of the two SUV's tires exploded and caught fire, the paint peeling, armored glass melting. Harris bellowed orders to report, and for the perimeter team to withdraw. They needed no encouragement. Mary could hear screams from two of them who had been too close to avoid the searing heat.

"Deploy all available assets in the area!" Mary ordered, surprised to hear the calm command from her mouth. "Air support, medical, and security! I want that entire estate nailed down yesterday. I want damage control on the media before they even know what's happened here, and I want to know who the *hell* was behind this! I want records of who owned that place, who lived there, who did the maintenance, and who worked there. Pull everything you can! I want all these people found and detained this instant!" She gritted her teeth and seethed through them. Eight men were dead, and every bit of evidence had been burned beyond recovery. "Someone's going to answer for this!"

---

## 10

Tony Jasper sat at his desk in the Cambridge Homicide squad room, searching through financial records of three similar murder victims, when every cell phone and desk phone in the entire room simultaneously rang.

He looked up at Marty, his surprise and concern mirrored in his partner's face. "Something just hit the fan!"

"Sideways!" Marty already had his phone up. "All units alert, explosion in Back Bay. Took out a mansion. There are federal troops all over it, but BPD's scrambling everything they've got and are asking for coverage from Cambridge."

Tony had his phone up now, too, and scanned the same message, but there wasn't much more than an address. He minimized the screen on his computer and went to the department's mapping system. He typed in the address, and the map zoomed on the site. The estate dominated an entire city block, street views—*Thank you Google Maps*—showed a lofty mansion surrounded by high iron fencing. One command pulled up the records of the address.

"Terris. Why is that name familiar?"

"Beats me, but you should see the news feed, Tony. The house is a fucking crater."

Tony got up and went to look at Marty's screen. He'd pulled up footage from a local news helicopter. The formerly lofty mansion was an inferno, flames soaring a hundred yards into the air. "Jesus Christ!"

"That wasn't a gas leak, Tony." Marty tapped the screen where the info line scrolled by, claiming that a gas main had erupted beneath the house.

"With fed troops Johnny on the spot?" Tony pointed to the black vehicles and armed troops in DHS SWAT uniforms ushering fire trucks through the iron gates. "Bomb?"

"You *think*?" Marty shot him an incredulous look. "Question is, whose bomb? The feds' or the poor bastards' who were inside?"

"The place was owned by a family named Terris, which sounds familiar, but I can't place it." Tony went back to his desk and pulled up driver's license information on everyone at that address. He got eight faces and names. Two of them seemed familiar: a man with curly black hair, and an attractive middle-aged woman. "Where do I know these two from, Marty?"

Marty came around to squint at the screen. "Yeah, they look *way* familiar. Not the others, but those two…"

"Time to find out who Persephone and Reginald Terris are." Tony typed in a Google search on Persephone Terris and got a long line of hits: rich socialite, philanthropist, political donor, art collector, and… "Holy fuck, Marty! She used to be married to Dwayne Hutchinson!"

"Motherless son of a bitch!" Marty snapped his fingers. "That's it! That's where we saw them! The second murder scene! Those two women who we found in that motel room were taken by the FBI and CDC." He tapped the screen, once on the man's face, and again on Persephone's. "FBI, CDC."

"And she's Hutch's ex."

"And he's close to Aleksi."

"And the two victims were injured by someone like her."

"And *they* took them, and a week later, we find them in a motel room, drugged and cured."

Tony and Marty stared at each other, all the connections clicking together like falling dominoes.

"Oh, we have *got* to call Hutch!"

"If he's not already in federal custody." Tony picked up his phone and tapped Hutch's contact. It rang three times before Hutch answered.

"Yeah, Tony? What's up?"

"You need to turn on the news, Hutch. You're not going to *believe* this!"

---

H utch was in his car on his way home from a long day, and he didn't feel like playing guessing games with Tony Jasper. "I'm in the car, Tony. Just tell me."

"Nope. You'd crash. Just park and pull up Channel Ten. They're broadcasting the details now. Call me later." The call ended.

"Goddamn it, Tony." Hutch finished driving home, since he was only five minutes away, and parked in his spot. Still in the car, he pulled his phone and tapped up the Channel Ten news feed.

A talking head sat behind the news desk with aerial footage of a building fire over his shoulder. "...and with federal agents on the scene unwilling to talk to the media about how this explosion occurred, we can only wonder if a threat to national security might be at the bottom of the tragedy."

"And tragedy it is indeed, Bill." The other talking head took over. The screen behind them flicked to pictures of two people, both of whom Hutch knew very well. "The mansion was the residence of Boston socialite, Persephone Terris, and her cousin, Doctor Reginald Terris. They're both missing and may have been inside when the explosion ripped through their home. Neither is answering calls, and their phones are out of service, so we can only assume the worst."

Hutch stared uncomprehending for a moment, his heart racing in his chest. "Persephone?" He cut the news feed, pulled up her contact and called her, but as the news commentator had said, it came up with an out of service message. "Shit, shit, shit!"

He lunged out of his car and ran for the building. The elevator seemed to take forever, and his hand shook so badly that his key missed the keyhole twice before he managed to unlock his door. Inside, Iggy greeted him with the usual cage rattle, but Hutch barely heard it. He grabbed the remote and turned on the TV. When ten minutes of viewing gave him noting but repetitive conjecture, he called Tony back.

"So, you've seen it?"

"If you mean my ex-wife's house burning down, yes, Tony, I've seen it."

"It didn't just burn down, Hutch. It was an explosion. The feds are spinning tales of gas leaks, but that's bullshit."

"So, what are you not telling me, Tony? The feds were there when it happened? Did they blow up her house? What the hell happened?" Hutch's voice raised an octave with each question.

"We don't know exactly what happened or who caused the explosion, Hutch, but there's one more thing you need to know." Tony paused and Hutch heard him take a deep breath. "I thought your ex looked familiar, and the connection to the feds spurred my memory. We were at the scene with those two women who were injured by David Gilford, Hutch. They were whisked away by FBI and CDC agents, or so we thought at the time. They turned out not to be."

"I don't…"

"Hutch, just listen. The two who were posing as FBI and CDC were Reginald and Persephone Terris. Both Marty and I recognized them."

"Bullshit!" The denial came out of nowhere, harsher than Hutch had intended.

"Sorry, but it's not. And here's the kicker, Hutch. Remember, Marty and I found those two women later…*cured*. Now you say Aleksi is cured, too. She's *got* to be with them. The Terris' are the ones responsible for curing those two women and Aleksi. They've *got* to be."

"That's impossible, Tony! I was *married* to her for two years! You don't think I'd have gotten some clue that my *wife* was involved in something like this?"

"Maybe she wasn't when you were married to her, but her family's filthy rich. They'd have the resources to do this."

"I still don't believe it," he said, but the denial rang false. He recalled Persephone's fascination with cryptozoology, her willingness to fund their research into the specimen that eventually infected Aleksi and Derrick Penningly, and her seemingly incongruous questions about Aleksi later. "It *can't* be."

"Can't be, or you just don't *want* it to be, Hutch?" Tony wasn't being accusative, only pointing out the obvious. "You've got to at least consider it, because I guaran-damn-tee you the feds will be knocking on your door with questions."

"Yeah." Hutch swallowed hard. "Yeah, you're right. Even though I have no clue what the hell's going on here, they'll never believe me."

"That's true. Look, if you need help, just call, but I think your best bet right now is to tell the truth. Insist on a lie detector. You knew nothing about any of this."

"Thanks, Tony, both for the suggestion and letting me know." Hutch heaved a breath. "I'll try to find out if Aleksi was in the house when..." He couldn't finish the sentence.

"Just be careful, okay?"

"Oh, I will be. Thanks again, Tony."

"Keep me in the loop, Hutch."

"I will." Hutch ended the call, put down that phone, and pulled out his other one. He punched up Aleksi's contact and made a call. It rang and went to voice mail.

"Hey, I saw the fire on the news. Need to talk to you. Love you." He ended the call, taking a slim shred of hope from the simple fact that her number had not been out of service.

---

Aleksi woke, at least partially, struggling from the depths of sedation to the sensation of being carried. Hushed voices, fresh air, city sounds, scuffing feet, and a close, familiar scent. A heartbeat hammered against her shoulder, and warm arms held her.

"I told you to watch the IV!" The voice she recognized, too: Persephone, and she sounded stressed. The arms under her back and knees held her carefully but firmly, and Aleksi knew who was carrying her.

Aleksi struggled to open her eyes and blinked up at her.

"I'll get another one in as soon as you put her down. The propofol will... She's awake, Seph."

"Aleksi?" Persephone looked down at her and every muscle tensed. "Just relax. We had to move you. We'll be safe soon. Don't fight me."

*Fight?* That seemed an odd thing to say. Then Aleksi realized that she was unrestrained. She felt strange, muddy headed, but not sleepy. Her anxieties seemed at least subdued for now, though what Persephone had said struck a chord of fear.

"Not...sssafe...now?" she slurred. Her head was definitely fuzzy but was clearing slowly. She didn't feel particularly threatened. It felt kind of nice to be held like this; like she was a little girl again, cradled in her mother's arms.

"No, we're not safe. Soon. Just trust me."

"The midazolam will last a while. She should be okay."

Aleksi recognized Reggie, and there were others around them, younger, and they all seemed tense, worried, anxious. She could smell their nervousness, feel their heightened awareness, see their furtive glances into the surrounding semi-darkness. They were outside, walking down a narrow space between two buildings, a concrete sidewalk lined with shrubs on both sides, the buildings three stories tall, and the windows were dark. It didn't look familiar.

"Where...are...we?"

"Worcester." Persephone stopped and nodded Reggie forward. He descended a stair, and Aleksi heard keys rattling, and then a metal door creaking open. "Relax. We'll be inside in a second."

"Okay." Aleksi hugged herself, wrapping her wings around her shoulders. She felt less itchy, and her head was clearing a little more.

Persephone descended a stairway, turning sideways to get them through a door. It was darker inside, the air a little musty. The walls were blank, a narrow hallway. Persephone turned through another door into a homey space, not lavish, but comfortable, with a kitchen and a living area with couches, a TV, and a dining table.

"Here you go." Persephone put her down on a couch, and Reggie knelt down beside her. "We've got to get another IV started, Aleksi. You'll feel a pinch. Just relax."

"I'm...okay. Groggy but..." She watched the others bringing things into the room, crates and plastic cases, liquid nitrogen carboys, metal suitcases. She felt the prick of the needle and resisted the urge to jerk away. "Why...did we move?"

"We were careless, and Mary Buckmann is relentless."

"IV's set," Reggie announced. "Time for a lullaby." He reached for the crimp on the line.

"Wait." Aleksi put a hand on his, gently, resisting the vague urge to crush it. She knew they were her friends. If they wanted to hurt her, they'd already had every opportunity. They'd risked their lives for her. They were family. "I'm...okay for now. I want to know what happened."

Reggie and Persephone exchanged a long look. He shrugged and pulled his hand away from the IV crimp. "Your call, Seph, but I don't want to throw her into a panic. We're not equipped to handle that here."

Persephone nodded and motioned him back, then sat on the edge of the couch. "I'll tell you what happened, Aleksi, but first, you need to know that we're safe here. This is a hiding place we've set aside just in case something like this happened."

"Okay." Aleksi took a deep breath and let her building anxiety trickle away like melting snow. "So, we're safe. To tell the truth, I'm still a little wacked out on Reggie's meds, so it's hard to be upset about anything. Just tell me why we had to run."

Persephone nodded once. "Buckmann sent people to Hutch's apartment, and they found the surveillance equipment we installed there. We weren't monitoring it, but the transmitter maintained a connection with our equipment. Gi-gi caught the intrusion, but not before they tracked the signal. We got barely enough warning to get you and some irreplaceable things out. Buckmann sent soldiers into our home, and Gi-gi..." Persephone faltered, her face flushed and tears brimming in her eyes. "Our home's gone."

"Your great-grandmother?"

"There was no time, Aleksi." Persephone's tears spilled, but she didn't wipe them away. "Gi-gi was very fragile. There wasn't enough time to get her out, too. She knew her own limitations and ordered us to go. She stayed behind."

"Oh, God, I'm sorry, Persephone." Aleksi shook her head, her mind racing. This was all because of her. "You shouldn't have taken me out. You should have left me there."

"Aleksi, stop it!" Persephone put her hands on Aleksi's and squeezed hard. "This wasn't about you, this was about *us*, our family. Governments have been after us all over the world for centuries. We'll recover. We always do. And faster than they think we can." She released her grasp and looked around the room, at the other younger relatives bringing in boxes and equipment. "It'll take some time. We'll need new identities, all of us, right down to our DNA." She turned back to Aleksi and smiled sadly. "And you need to take the time to get better. Frankly, we *need* you."

Aleksi nodded, biting back on the rising guilt. They needed her, and she couldn't protect them as a psychological wreck. Then she thought, *Protection,* and that lead her to, "What about Hutch?"

Persephone furrowed her brow. "What about him?"

"Your house is destroyed and the feds were involved? He'll put two and two together. Even if he doesn't, Buckmann will think he knows something. They'll arrest him. They'll interrogate him!" Adrenaline began to burn away the pharmacological cotton smothering her mind.

Persephone blinked, and the faint lines around her eyes hardened, the muscles at her jaw bunching and relaxing. "Maybe, but I don't know what we can do for him, Aleksi. We're all being hunted. It'll be days before we can even go out in public."

"Warn him, then. Tell him the truth! He'll put it together anyway! You've *got* to tell him to run! Please!"

Persephone pursed her lips for a moment, then nodded. "I'll text him, Aleksi. We can't risk bringing him here, not yet, but we can warn him."

"Thank you." Aleksi sighed with the release of tension. She'd seen genuine concern in Persephone's face. "You feel it, too, don't you?"

"Feel what?" Persephone's brows knitted again.

"The urge...to protect." Aleksi nodded to the others still bringing in boxes and crates. "To protect your family, the people you love, Hutch."

Persephone smiled and nodded. "Yes, I feel it, Aleksi, and we will. Don't worry. Now get some sleep while we get all this sorted out. I'll text Hutch later."

"Thank you."

"You're welcome." Persephone opened the crimp in the IV, fluid flowed into Aleksi's vein, and she slept.

## 11

----

Fifteen minutes before Hutch's alarm usually went off, a strange one-time ring tone woke him. Both of his phones sat on the nightstand beside his bed, and with his head still muddled with sleep and dreams, he rolled over and stared at them. Had his alarm tone defaulted? Had he gotten a spam text? But no, the ring hadn't come from his regular phone. It had come from his Aleksi phone. But it hadn't been the message tone he'd assigned to Aleksi.

*A spam text?* he wondered. But as the fog of sleep dissolved from his mind, Hutch recalled his conversation with Jasper, the fire, the bomb, the feds. He sat up, turned on the light, and pulled up the message app. The number of the caller had been blocked. Curious and now fully awake, he pulled up the message.

"A is with me and fine. So am I. Feds are after us. Don't dial or speak in your home. Bugs. I'm not who you thought I was, but I do love you. P."

Hutch stared at the message for a long time, all of Jasper's conspiracy theories swirling around his mind like a thought-spam tornado. *P?* There could be only one answer. *Persephone? With Aleksi? She really is the one helping Aleksi?*

While his mind was still trying to engulf this epiphany, another text came.

"You okay?"

*What a question.* He texted, "Not really," and hit send.

"Sorry for the rude awakening," she replied, and he curled a lip at the double entendre. Then, "If B contacts you, tell her you know nothing. We have to disappear. Destroy this phone completely. Evidence."

He realized that she was right. Buckmann would probably come after him, but they'd get nothing. He texted, "Will do. When will I see you and A?"

"Couple of weeks, maybe. You won't recognize me. Take care."

He texted, "I will. You too. My love to A." He almost hit send, then added, "And you, too!"

Persephone didn't reply.

Hutch stared at the phone for another minute, still trying to parse out all the pieces of this puzzle. Persephone wasn't who he thought she was, had never been, had married him for ulterior motives. He recalled her family home, how he hated it, all the closed-mouthed staff, her cousins coming and going constantly, the locked doors and ridiculous security system. Aleksi was with her now, and they were on the run from the Department of Homeland Security. They were the ones who had impersonated Buckmann, infiltrated the DHS. Memories of an interrogation room, her familiar mannerisms, her walk, her knowing exactly how he took his coffee, calling him Hutch…

*Fuck!* He glared at the damning phone. *Persephone!*

Hutch lurched out of bed and stalked to the kitchen. Flipping on a light, he pulled out his biggest cutting board and the sharpening steel from the knife block. Cracking the phone open, he levered the battery out, then meticulously smashed every last component to bits, taking care to keep everything together. Iggy didn't like the noise or the fact that he was using the cutting board for something other than cutting up food for him, and he rattled his cage.

"You're not the first one to rattle my cage this morning, buddy. Sorry."

Hutch started to throw the shattered phone into the trash, then realized that Buckmann would search it. He scooped the tiny pieces of shattered electronics into a bowl and took them to the bathroom. There, he flushed them a few at a time down the toilet. *Search that, Doctor*, he thought, then realized they probably would, and flushed a few more times.

As Hutch stumbled back to the kitchen, his alarm went off in his bedroom. She'd texted right before his alarm. Then he remembered her warning about bugs in the apartment. *Of course she did. She didn't want them to think anything was different than my regular morning routine. Routine...*

Hutch went to the kitchen and started the coffee maker. By the time he had his workout clothes on, the pot was half full. He poured a short cup and put the pot back to finish, just as he did every morning. He then cut up some veggies and fruit for Iggy, made a breakfast shake for himself, and packed his work clothes and computer. He wondered if he should destroy his computer also, but Buckmann already knew he'd been corresponding with Aleksi. *It'll give them something to find.* He had emails to Persephone on that computer, too, but nothing damning.

He fed Iggy, drank his shake, poured the rest of the pot of coffee into a travel cup, and left the apartment. On the way to the gym, he wondered how far Buckmann would go. She would detain him for questioning, of course, but when he claimed ignorance, she wouldn't be satisfied.

*Leverage*, he realized. *She'll use me as leverage. And knowing Aleksi, it might actually work. But what the hell can I do about it?*

One thing eventually became clear: claiming ignorance wouldn't do him any good. The government could make up any charge they wished and manufacture enough evidence to make those charges stick. They would lock him up and publicly ruin him, both to coerce information out of him, and to push Persephone and Aleksi into doing something foolish.

*Not gonna happen*, he thought, but how could he stop them from arresting him?

*Easy answer*, he realized with a slow smile. *Get someone else to arrest me first.*

———

Tony Jasper had just settled in for work when a uniform walked up to his desk with a post-it note. He took it, and asked, "What's this?"

"Visitor." The uniform walked away without another word, clearly pissed at being relegated to the roll of messenger.

Tony read the note. "WM visitor, Hutchinson, in waiting A."

"Hutchinson?" *What the hell's Hutch doing here, and what's wrong with a phone call?*

"Whassat?" Marty's eyes came up from his desk.

"Hutch is downstairs. Wants to see me."

Marty scowled. "His phone doesn't work?"

"Dunno. Maybe he's still freaked out from yesterday." Tony was still pretty freaked out, truth be told. He stood and pulled on his sports jacket. "Dropped quite a bombshell in his lap."

"True." Marty started to stand. "Want company?"

"If you—" Tony stopped himself, thinking ahead. Hutch had come here in person for a reason. He had no idea what that reason was, but it might be better to have someone not with them who he could rely on for quick action. "On second thought, sit tight. I may need to call you in."

"Sure." Marty sat back down. "Eyes up for men in black."

"Right."

The quip had become their mantra with all the government entanglements surrounding the Aleksi situation. He wondered if that was why Hutch was here. Tony had told him to sit tight and claim ignorance, but something might have happened to spur him into action... or flight. The Boston PD was certainly stirred up and royally pissed at being excluded from the investigation into the explosion that had incinerated Hutch's ex-wife's house. Tony had phoned up his friend, Blake, to see if she could have a beer and talk over the event, but she'd been too busy. Most of BPD was pulling double shifts. They had APBs out on the entire Terris family, all the people who worked for them, and several other known associates. All apprehensions, to her ire, were to be turned over to DHS.

"Fucking feds think they own the whole world," she'd complained over the phone. "I told my people to nod and smile, but not to bend over too far picking up their shit."

He'd laughed at her choice of words and commiserated, asking if there was anything he could do to help. She'd begged off, taken a rain check on the beer, and told him to take care. "There's more to this than a gas leak, Tony. The feds are mumbling about terrorists. Watch your six, okay?"

"Always." He'd hung up and shook his head. *Terrorists...the new war cry of everyone in authority when their power is threatened.* There were real terrorists in the world, of course, but the accusation had become so knee-jerk, that "terrorism" had become the "cry wolf" of every government agency whenever they needed to requisition police assistance without any explanations. *Like "Communist" back in the fifties*, he mused.

He found Hutch waiting with the usual crowd of friends and relatives of witnesses or detained suspects. He looked haggard and carried a shoulder bag.

"What's up, Hutch?" Tony shook his hand and gestured to the door.

"I need you to take a walk with me, Tony." Hutch glanced up and down the hallway as they exited the waiting room. "I need to talk to you someplace private. Someplace without cameras."

"Let's go get a coffee." Tony could tell he was nervous, and frankly couldn't blame him, but acting nervous was as much a sign of guilt as running when someone yelled, "Stop!"

"Thanks."

They walked out of the precinct without a word and strode silently up the street to a favorite cafe, a tiny place tucked into an old apartment building owned by a retired cop. Tony waved to the barista, ordered two coffees and Danish as they passed the counter, and took a table in the back.

"So, what's with all the cloak and dagger shit, Hutch?"

"I'm worried about what Buckmann will do, Tony." Hutch glanced over his shoulder.

"Just chill. The more you look nervous, the more you look guilty." Tony paused as the barista delivered two coffees, cream, sugar, and two apple Danishes. When she'd left, he said, "I told you, just play dumb."

"Yeah, I thought about that, and I don't know if it'll do any good." Hutch lightened his coffee, took a sip, and eyed the gooey pastry.

"They got nothin' on you, Hutch." Tony took a bite of his pastry and chased it with coffee. He pointed to the other pastry, "Eat that. You look like you're about ready to fall down from malnutrition."

"*Thanks.*" Hutch shot him a sour glare, took a bite, and chewed, washing it down with another swallow of coffee. "But you know they won't be satisfied with that. They may not have anything, but that doesn't mean they can't *manufacture* something."

"You think they want to frame you for the explosion?" Tony furrowed his brow. "That's a stretch."

"Is it?" Hutch took another bite of Danish and shook his head. "Think about it. They don't care about me and might even believe I don't know anything about this whole thing, but they want…these people very badly. They'll use me for leverage, Tony."

"Maybe." Tony thought that the government might very well do exactly that. "And your girlfriend's got a temper."

"To put it mildly," Hutch agreed. "Which is what they're relying on. If our mutual friend does something rash, they'll take her or kill her. They might even get…other people to act rashly."

Hutch's reticence to use his ex-wife's name spoke volumes. "You think feds are tailing you?"

"Probably." Hutch pushed his plate away and drank coffee. "Maybe hoping I'll lead them to these people."

"Okay, that may be, and I wouldn't put it past them to use you as leverage, but what do you want me to do about it? If I put you in protective custody, it'll be like serving you up on a silver platter." Tony ate more Danish and shrugged.

"What about a safe house or something?" Hutch asked. "Don't you have places you keep witnesses when you don't want them to be found?"

"We do." Tony thought for a moment. Using department resources without authorization to sequester a witness wanted by DHS was a serious breech, but he didn't know for a *fact* that Hutch was wanted, or even that he was under surveillance. *Fuck it*, he thought, and pulled his phone. "I'm going out on a limb here, Hutch."

"I know, Tony, and I appreciate it."

"Oh, I'm not doing it for *you*. I just don't want our mutual friend to get upset. I've seen how much damage she can do." He punched Marty's number and put the phone to his ear.

"Your concern for my wellbeing is touching," Hutch mumbled with a flat stare.

"Whassup?" Marty answered.

"Hey, just coffee and Danish at Java Joe's. Want anything?"

"Hell yes! My usual. So kind of you to think of me."

"Hey, I'm the *good* cop, remember?"

Marty snorted a laugh. "No, I *don't* remember."

"*Nice*. I'll prove it to you. Call your hubby and tell him I've got a package for him here. A *big* package that needs to be kept *safe*."

"You sure?" Marty's skepticism could have been cut with a knife.

"Sure, I'm sure. Tell him he'll *like* this package. It's his favorite flavor. Pick it up out back. Tell him it's his early Christmas present. Call it a preventative measure. Vice cops, you know."

"You just don't want another male stripper for your birthday."

"You see right through me, partner." Tony hung up and took another bite of his Danish.

"Well?" Hutch asked, eyebrows raised.

"Relax and eat your breakfast, Hutch. The cavalry is riding to your rescue as we speak, wearing a Versace jacket." The look on Hutch's face was totally worth the risk he was taking.

Mary sat at her desk reviewing the body cam and drone footage from the Terris estate. She'd been running damage control and threat assessments all night long, and caffeine had stopped working hours ago. Her eyes felt like she'd poured sand into them, and her clothes felt itchy. She needed a shower, four hours of sleep, and a clean shirt, but wasn't likely to get any of the three.

She'd put out APBs on everyone and everything associated with the Terrises, and they'd apprehended a maid, a chef, and a butler who worked in the house. They all told the same story: Fifteen minutes after Mary had sent a team into Hutchinson's apartment, they'd been told they were being let go with one year's severance pay and needed to leave the house immediately. They'd done as told, and bank records confirmed that each had received a sizable deposit in their account. None of them knew anything about any secret rooms or lavender-eyed people in hospital beds in the basement, or so they claimed. They were being held, regardless. Two of the four family vehicles had been found. Persephone Terris's green Jaguar was in evidence now being gone over with a fine-toothed comb. They'd found hair and skin residue in the car and were doing DNA analysis. One black SUV had been found in Newton, parked on a side street, locked and alarmed. They'd towed it and were analyzing it but had found nothing.

*Nothing...* That was all they had found anywhere. Mary had gotten accusations from the Director, but she had thrown her superior's orders right back at her. "Buy, beg, borrow, or steal." She'd been given carte blanche, and there were no grounds for recrimination. The video proved that she had found exactly what she'd been looking for; the home of the terrorist organization that had kidnapped her, infiltrated the DHS, and stolen a priceless artifact.

Unfortunately, the house had been reduced to cinders. Chemical analysis had confirmed that the explosives had been thermite and white phosphorous, hot enough to reduce metal to slag and utterly destroy the electronics they'd seen in the basement. Analysis of the physical evidence was still pending, but there wasn't much left of the only person they'd found—if it indeed had been a person—or the eight men Mary had sent to their deaths.

*Not even enough to bury.*

She reviewed the high-resolution video of the figure lying on the hospital bed in the mansion's basement, the lavender eyes and wizened features. They only had a few seconds of this video, and it had been gone over frame-by-frame by specialists for enhancement and analysis. They had nothing, no conjecture, no hypotheses, no theories. Human, but altered in some way, was all that they could surmise.

"What the hell are you?" Mary froze the video and zoomed in on the creature's face, so lined with age that the skin looked like crepe paper. The thin lips quirked into the hint of a smile about a second before the explosion destroyed everything and everyone in the building.

*No answers... Nothing left...*

Mary's desk chimed for attention, and she stabbed the button to accept the call from the comm center. "Buckmann."

"Ma'am, the surveillance team assigned to Doctor Hutchinson has lost contact with the suspect."

"What? How?" She clenched her shaking fists below her desk.

"They reported that he went to the Cambridge Police Department, then walked with a cop to a nearby coffee shop. The cop came out a half an hour later, but Hutchinson didn't. When the agents went in, he was gone. One of the employees stated that he went to the bathroom, and they didn't recall him returning."

Mary bit off an expletive. "And who was the cop he went in with?" *As if I don't already know.*

"Detective Jasper, ma'am."

"Son of a..." Mary snatched up her phone and dialed Hutchinson. She received an out of service message. "Hutchinson's fled, probably with the help of the Cambridge Police. Put a bulletin out on Hutchinson and bring Detective Jasper in for questioning."

"Yes, ma'am." The screen went blank.

Mary got up and stalked over to the coffee maker, jammed her cup under the spout, and slammed a pod into the brewer. Tony Jasper had another thing coming if he thought he'd get away with interfering with a federal Investigation.

## 12

Tony had been in a lot of interrogation rooms, once or twice as the person being questioned. This one was higher tech than most, with an honest to goodness two-way mirror and unobtrusive sound and video recording devices. The door had no handle or knob, but a thumb-print scanner and keypad. The seats, much like those in every other interrogation room he'd been in, were hard and designed to be uncomfortable. All in all, he found the entire situation both annoying and entertaining. If nothing else, the look on his boss, Commander Fisk's, face when Tony told him he was being detained by DHS for questioning made his discomfort totally worth it.

He sat with his arms folded, his back to the door, facing the mirror, smiling just to unsettle the feds. Finally, when an hour had passed, Mary Buckmann came in. He watched her in the mirror but didn't stand.

"Detective Jasper, sorry to have kept you waiting, but we've been understandably busy."

"Doctor Buckmann, or should I call you Doctor Johansen?" She certainly looked like she'd been busy. Her face was a portrait of fatigue and stress.

"Buckmann, please. That project died with Derrick Penningly, as I'm sure you know, since you were the one who actually pulled the trigger." She sat down and put a file on the table before her.

"Yes, I was." She'd lied to him twice so far. He had no doubt that he'd been kept waiting on purpose, and he also knew that they had Lori Watkins. The Johansen Project might have changed names, but it wasn't over, not by a long shot. He smiled as she opened the folder— his complete personnel file from the department, no less. "So, did you call me in to clean up another of your fuckups, or was there something else?"

She smiled tightly at him. "We just need to ask you some questions, Detective."

"Fire away!" He grinned. "And call me Tony. I get tired of the whole 'detective, doctor' thing, don't you, Mary?"

"Very well, Tony. I will." She flipped to a page of text in his file. "At zero eight thirty this morning you met with Doctor Dwayne Hutchinson at the Cambridge Police Precinct, didn't you?"

"Yes."

"What did he want?"

"To talk."

"About what?"

"The explosion in Back Bay, yesterday. I'm sure you heard about it. Turns out his ex-wife's family owned the house, and she's missing. He's worried that she might have been inside, you see, and asked me to look into it. I have friends in the BPD, so he thought I might be able to find something out. Turns out, they've been excluded from the investigation." He nodded to her politely. "Excluded by *you*, Mary."

She had the poise not to deny that, at least. "And what did you tell him?"

"Exactly what I just told you, that the police had been excluded from the investigation and fed a bullshit line about a gas main."

"And how do you know it's bullshit, Detective?"

"Tony, please."

"Tony." The muscles of her jaw clenched. "How do you know the story of a gas leak was bullshit?"

"Because the blast and the fire were both wrong for a natural gas explosion. Also, there are these nice people with the Public Works Department who keep records and maps of every gas main in the city. It took all of twenty seconds to blow your smokescreen out the window, Mary. I'm sure the media will do the same in time, and then they'll know there's some kind of coverup."

"Very well. So, answer me this, Tony: why did you go to a coffee shop to talk instead of your office in the precinct?"

"Because Hutch looked like he could use a coffee, and the precinct coffee sucks. Besides, police make me nervous." He smiled his best *See? I can shovel the bullshit, too* smile.

She glowered. "And you ordered a Danish and coffee, then brought back some for your partner Marty Willis, yes?"

"Yep. He's a bitch when he doesn't get his sugar fix."

"You were there thirty minutes, Tony. It didn't take thirty minutes for you to tell Doctor Hutchinson—"

"Hutch. He likes to be called Hutch." Tony was having fun rattling her cage; it rattled easily. He could see the fatigue all over her, could smell it, in fact. She should have assigned someone less exhausted to do the interview. She seemed different than he remembered, less poised, more hard edges.

"...for you to tell *Doctor Hutchinson* that you didn't know if his wife was incinerated or not yesterday afternoon," she resumed, obviously irritated with his interruption. "What else did you talk about?"

"He was worried, Mary. I tried to help him not worry so much. That's what friends do for friends, you see? It's called *empathy*."

"Eight of my men were *killed* in that explosion, Tony! Where's your goddamned empathy for them?"

Tony hardened his eyes and dropped his smile. "I didn't know until this moment that *anyone* was killed in that explosion, Mary. It sucks that your people were killed. I'm sorry for your loss, and I grieve for their families. Now stop trying to put me on the defensive and ask me what you want to know."

"Where is Doctor Dwayne Hutchinson?"

He gave her a puzzled look. "I have no idea. He's got an office in

132

the Northwest Sciences Building on Harvard Campus. I've got his schedule in my phone, if you want to have a look."

"I know where his office is, and I have his schedule. He's vanished, and his phone's out of service."

*Thank you, Charles*, Tony thought with a shrug. "And you think *I* know where he went? Sorry, but I haven't a clue." And he honestly didn't. Charles had half a dozen safe houses in Cambridge. They'd deemed it best that Tony didn't know where Hutch was being kept, just in case it came down to polygraphs and waterboarding.

"We had two people surveilling Doctor Hutchinson when you took him for coffee, Tony. He never came out of that coffee shop. Where did he go?"

"I don't know, Mary. When we were finished talking, I picked up my order and left. I think he went to the bathroom. Coffee'll do that to you." Tony kept his face perfectly neutral, his tone utterly sincere when he added, "I had no idea you were tailing Hutch. I could have the Cambridge PD help look for him, if you like. We're pretty good at finding people."

Buckmann slapped the table hard with both hands, surging up out of her seat. "I *know* you helped him shake our people, Detective! I'm going to find him, and I'm going to find out how you did it! Then I'm going to have your fucking *job*!"

Tony blinked at her, honestly surprised at her outburst, but unimpressed. "You know, Mary, for this to really work, you need a *good* cop. All stick no carrot doesn't make it."

"We're not *cops*, Detective Jasper, we're the United States *Government*. If you want to keep your gold shield, you better tell me where the *hell* I can find Doctor Hutchinson!"

"Sorry. I can't help you, Mary. I don't know where Hutch is." He sighed and stood up. "Now, if we're done here, I've got police work to do. You know...*police* work? I'm currently investigating the whereabouts of a missing person. Her name's Loretta *Watkins*. Maybe *you* could help me with that."

Mary Buckmann's face went utterly blank. "Who?"

He snorted a laugh and pointed to the door. "Could you open that for me, please, Mary? I have a job to do."

---

Hutch paced the gaudy little ground floor apartment, beside himself with nothing to do. He had his computer but dared not use Wi-Fi. Marty Willis's husband, Charles, had warned him not to. He'd said that the government could likely track down his computer's IP address if he got online. The apartment was a safe house the Vice Department used to shelter witnesses who were at risk of tampering or being killed by pimps, drug dealers, or worse.

"It's safe here, Hutch," Charles had assured him with a sad sigh and a cringe as he surveyed the place. "Aside from the risk of nausea from the décor. Sorry about that. This place was leased by a local porn startup before they stepped over the line and we took it over. They had *dreadful* taste."

Hutch thanked Charles and assured him that it was fine, even though the purple crushed velvet wallpaper really wasn't his style. He decided he'd sleep on the couch, too, though that had probably been equally used by the apartment's previous tenants. So, he sat, read, watched TV, and paced.

Afternoon had worn on to evening when someone finally knocked at the door, the first five-note rap of "Shave and a Hair Cut."

Hutch tensed, though he didn't imagine federal agents would knock.

A key rattled in the door, and Charles came in bearing a huge Stop-n'-Shop bag. "Beware of pimps bearing gifts!" He smiled and closed the door.

"Just don't tell the neighbors I'm your trick," Hutch said.

"I would *never!*" Charles grinned mischievously and took the bag to the little kitchen. "*Client*, maybe, but never a *trick!* You don't have the look."

"Great." Hutch knew they had to be telling the department something about who he was and why he was being sequestered, but he didn't appreciate being cast as a john. Of course, he couldn't complain. They were virtually breaking the law for him. "So, what's for dinner?"

"Veggie wraps, noodles, libation, and some of those scrummy chocolate croissants from Au Bon Pain." He started unpacking. "Sorry, I'm not much good at shopping vegetarian. I had to stop myself from buying meat six times. Yogurt and granola for breakfast, bread, avocado, veggies, soup, fruit, and some fixin's for stir fry so I won't have to come by so often."

"Thanks, Charles. I appreciate it." It looked good, and he was hungry, but worry had murdered his appetite.

"You're welcome." Charles folded the bag and tucked it under his arm, then fished a phone from an inside pocket of his silk jacket. "And this." He handed it over. "Prepaid with cash and untraceable, so you can do some surfing. Use the Wi-Fi here with this phone only, but don't make any calls. Texts only. They may be tracking our phone calls. And turn it off when you're not using it, just in case."

"Thanks!" Hutch was dying with nothing to do. He powered the phone up.

"My pleasure." Charles showed Hutch the unlock swipe code and sighed. "I don't know how long we can keep this up. Buckmann brought Tony in for questioning. He said she didn't get anything from him, but she suspects he had something to do with your sudden disappearance."

"Well, we kind of thought she would, right?" Hutch connected the phone to the apartment's Wi-Fi and pulled up his favorite local news service. "Any other developments?"

"Nothing you can't read on the news, really." Charles flipped a dismissive wave. "The feds have dropped their stupid gas main story. They're now calling it a terrorist attack. Buckmann told Tony that eight federal agents were killed in the explosion." He frowned.

"God! *Eight?*" Hutch felt like a cold hand had grabbed him by the balls. "They're going to want to pin that on someone, Charles. Eight counts of murder."

"Yeah, and the war chant of 'terrorism!' is sauce for the goose. Probably good you vanished." Charles started for the door.

"And you'd go down for harboring a terrorist," Hutch added. "Hey, Charles, tell Tony—"

"Oh, stop it." Charles glared over his shoulder. "We're *doing* this. End of discussion!"

"Okay. Thanks Charles."

"I'll let you make it up to me." He grinned devilishly and opened the door. "You're already making Marty *wicked* jealous!" He laughed and closed the door behind him.

Hutch found himself smiling at Charles' flippant wit and mentally thanked him again. He put the food away and settled down with the veggie wrap, a beer, and the phone. It already had Tony's number as a contact, so he opened up the message app and typed, "Thanks for the phone. Any new news?"

The reply came in less than a minute. "Not much. Feds have locked down the investigation, calling it terrorism and national security. The media is tearing it apart. Your ex was their darling—rich, pretty, smart, and generous. Why terrorists would bomb her home isn't holding up without supporting facts, and feds aren't giving any."

"Any word on any of the Terrises?" Hutch texted.

"Nope. Feds have frozen the family's assets. Like $400M! Lawyers are contesting. Seems the family knows some judges. Helped get them elected."

Hutch smiled around a bite of his wrap. Persephone had indeed dabbled in politics. He typed, "Buckmann question you?"

"Yep. Got zilch. She sucks at it." Tony added a laughing emoji.

"Good. She ask you about P or A?"

"Nope. Just you. She's seriously freaked. Deaths in the explosion are on her. Not so cool and in control like she was with Penningly."

Hutch chuckled. "You don't know the half of it."

"Don't know what?" Tony asked.

Hutch thought about how much Tony knew about Aleksi, Persephone, and everything in between. But Tony had also saved his life with Penningly and agreed to hide him, risking his job. Hutch owed him. He typed, "B isn't the same person we met as Johansen. Someone impersonated her before. That's why she's so pissed."

"Impersonated? How?"

"Mad biotech skills. Flesh and blood copy. Don't know how."

After a pause, Tony replied, "Let me guess. Same People A is with now?"

"Bingo." Jasper was sharp, no doubt. Hutch decided to fill him in on the details that he would undoubtedly figure out on his own in time. "B wants them, and the cure. Tracked them down, invaded their home, and...boom!"

"Holy shit," Tony replied.

Hutch snickered and tapped, "That's what I said."

---

M ary found the evidence list from the burned estate dismal and depressing. Then again, just about everything that had happened in the last month had been dismal and depressing. Lori was in a chemically induced coma, Hutchinson had vanished, and Mary had lost eight people in the operation at the Terris estate and had fuck-all to show for it.

The evidence list read like her own epitaph: unsalvageable remains of computers, surveillance equipment, lab equipment, radio equipment, books, several thousand bottles of wine, jewelry, personal items... All of it was trash, melted or burned beyond recognition. The bodies of her eight soldiers and the creature they had discovered—Mary suspected it had been human but couldn't confirm it without data—were burned beyond even salvaging DNA. The creature had seemed human, more human than *Homo draconis*, but for all she knew it was something else entirely, some altered form of human. These people had a mastery of biotechnology that she couldn't fathom.

But she had top people working on this, the best forensic analysis specialists in the world. They were taking the pieces of slag apart under microscopes in hopes of salvaging something. Genetic analysis of the incinerated corpses had gotten nowhere, however; the heat had been too intense.

Mary's phone vibrated, and she snatched it off her desk. Any distraction from this morbid analysis of her failure was welcome, but anything related to her work would have come through the DHS communications system. Few people texted her personal number, and two of them she very much wanted to talk to.

Curiously, the contact was blocked, not Aleksi or Hutchinson. Then again, either one could be using a burner phone. She pulled up the text.

"You destroyed the only chance you had of getting a cure for the *Homo draconis* infection. Proof you can't be trusted with something so dangerous."

*What the hell?* This didn't make sense from Hutchinson, and it didn't sound like Aleksi. She texted: "Who is this?"

Excruciating moments passed, then she received, "The late Persephone Terris. If you let this infection spread, you endanger humanity."

*Terris! So, it's true after all. Hutchinson's ex-wife is part of this!* A text wasn't exactly evidence that would hold up in court, but it was enough for Mary.

On impulse, she texted, "Then help us."

The reply came immediately. "That ship sailed when you invaded my home."

Mary's temper flared. "And your ship sailed when you abducted and impersonated me!"

She received, "You got your life back, I won't."

Mary started to tap out an acerbic reply, when she remembered something from her conversation with Tony Jasper. "All stick and no carrot..."

She texted, "Give us the cure, and I'll call off the investigation."

"And you make an army of dragons? No deal."

"I'll give you Lori. She's psychotic and of no use to us. If we can't cure her, we'll have to euthanize."

The reply came after a short pause. "More blood on your hands."

Mary fumed, but she had no reply to that. She had a lot of blood on her hands. She put her phone down and made a call to her IT security head. Her face came up on her desk monitor.

"Yes, ma'am?"

"I've started receiving texts from Persephone Terris, or so they claim. I want you to analyze my phone and try to trace the source."

"I'll send someone up to get it immediately."

"And I need a mirror phone in case these people text again."

"Yes, ma'am. I'll have one on your desk in an hour."

"Thank you." Mary ended the call, again thankful for the good people who worked for her, good people she was letting down.

*And some not so good*, she thought, recalling the two field surveillance specialists who had lost Hutchinson. Outfoxed by a cop, they had been duly chastised and contrite. They'd been assigned to follow Tony Jasper and had given her some interesting information. He was, indeed, friends with a senior homicide detective on the BPD, Detective Sergeant Anna Blake. *Could Blake have helped him hide Hutchinson? Maybe...* But by all accounts, the relationship seemed to be only friendship. They met for drinks and talked about work.

A slow realization came to her: *It all boils down to Hutchinson*. With his ex-wife involved in this mysterious organization, and his former student the only psychologically stable *Homo Draconis* in the world, Dwayne Hutchinson was her lever. Apply pressure there, and Mary could move the world.

She tapped another contact on her desk comm, and Benson's face appeared. Her head of covert field ops looked exhausted. "Yes, ma'am?"

"We need to widen our net searching for Hutchinson. Put tails on Detective Blake, and Jasper's partner, Marty Willis. Someone helped him hide Hutchinson. I can feel it."

"I'll have people in place in thirty minutes, ma'am."

"Good. Thank you." Mary ended the call and leaned on her desk with her head in her hands, rubbing her temples. She needed sleep, but even more, she needed a break in this project. She had her entire career riding on this. Without the cure, making more dragons was a non-starter. She needed leverage to use against Persephone and Aleksi, and currently had none.

## 13

Aleksi accepted the spoonful of homogenized meat paste and swallowed quickly. She lay in an improvised restraint couch, a reinforced lounger fitted with padded nylon straps. In her current state of half sedation, half hyper-anxiety, they weren't taking any chances of letting her hurt herself again. Her claws had already shredded the armrests of the chair. Unfortunately, there was no knowing how long she would be like this. They didn't have the lab facilities here that they'd had in the Sanctum and couldn't continue the reversal of their genetic alterations without them.

Aleksi swallowed another bite, then shook her head when Persephone scooped another. "No more. I'm not hungry." She was, but her roiling stomach wouldn't take much more. Her constant state of panic barely kept at bay with medications had transformed her stomach into a roiling pit of acid.

"You need to eat, Aleksi." Persephone frowned and put down the spoon.

After four days of genetic and protein-alteration therapy to assume her new identity, Persephone didn't look at all like the woman Aleksi knew—thinner, more angular facial features, less curvy, more statuesque, her hair blond, her yellow irises hidden by icy blue contact lenses—but she still *smelled* like her. Their emergency hideaway had been equipped with all they needed to secure their new identities, but not a full biotech lab. Not enough to make Aleksi herself again. She lay trapped in a state of transition, a human mind riddled with social anxiety under constant assault by the senses of a dragon.

"I'll be sick." As if to confirm her warning, her stomach growled noisily.

"We can give you something to ease that." Persephone nodded to Reggie, also changed, though not quite fully yet. His curly black hair had been shorn short and dyed a dirty blond, his skin lighter, eyes blue instead of brown, cheeks less full, chin more pronounced. All of Persephone's cousins had taken on new features, looking now more Scandinavian than French.

"No more drugs," Aleksi pleaded. "I can't stay like this. Kill me or cure me, *please*."

"Stop that!" The muscles of Persephone's new face tensed. "You'll get better, Aleksi. We just don't have—"

"I *know* you don't have what you need! You've *told* me." The restraints creaked as she tried involuntarily to pull her arms up. "And I'm telling *you*, I can't *do* this anymore!" Her claws raked the hardwood frame of the chair, gouging out splinters.

"Reg, give her—"

"Touch that IV, and I'll rip your fucking arms off, Reggie!" Aleksi snapped through clenched teeth. "You need to *fix* me, not just keep me like a pet in a zoo!"

"We *can't*, Aleksi." Reggie sounded less threatened by her outburst than concerned for her.

"Then you're not *trying* hard enough!" Her arms strained until the padding pressed hard enough to bruise. "You have enough to change yourselves! Why not me!"

"That's different. These identities were set aside long ago in case of emergency. Your treatments were being manufactured as we administered them. Reversing them is just as difficult."

Aleksi gritted her teeth. They were missing something, and so was she. She knew it, but what was it? "Tell me what you brought with you from the house and what you have here. Everything! I'll figure it out myself!"

Reggie exchanged a look with Persephone, and she shrugged. "Go ahead. It'll give her something to do, and who knows, maybe she'll think of something we missed."

"Fine." Reggie sighed, pulled up a screen on his tablet, and started listing all the things they'd salvaged from the mansion, all the backed-up data they had access to, all the frozen samples of biotechnology, the original specimen, artwork, unique jewelry and sculptures, original manuscripts of ancient texts...

"Wait!" Something clicked in Aleksi's muddled mind. "You have the original sample?"

"Yes. It's irreplaceable. It was heavy, but we managed to—"

"And do you have the *cure*? The tailored retroviruses that you treated me with before?"

"Yes, we have those frozen, and can culture more easily enough."

A horrible, desperate laugh escaped Aleksi's throat.

"What?" Persephone put a hand on her arm, her features lined with concerned.

*She probably thinks I'm having a psychotic break*, Aleksi thought. *Or another one...*

"You've missed the elephant in the room! Infect me with the original sample, start the cascade, then treat me with the retroviruses. I'll be myself in three days!"

The two stared at each other, open mouthed.

"Fuck, she's *right*!" Reggie surged up from his seat and hurried to his improvised lab bench.

"Why didn't we think of that?" Persephone asked.

"Because we were concentrating on *fixing* her, not *rebooting* her!" Reggie pulled a rack of frozen plastic vials from a liquid nitrogen carboy, chose one, put the rack back, and wiped the frost free of the labeled tube. He held it up to Aleksi. "This is your backup copy, Aleksi. I'll have it in you in ten minutes!" He rubbed the tube between his palms to warm it.

"Backup copy... Ha!" Persephone grinned and squeezed Aleksi's arm. "Like you're a computer."

"That's me, a big, buggy operating system. Default to backup? Just hit 'Enter.'" Hope niggled at her heart once again. Then she remembered the three miserable days huddled on her couch after her original infection. "I'll spike a fever."

"Don't worry, Aleksi. We won't let it go that far." Reggie grinned and picked a bottle of something from the fridge, donned gloves, and transferred the thawed sample to the bottle with a syringe. "Also, your immune system is already familiar with this. About a day of feeling crappy from the initial infection, then a day of the retrovirus therapy. We don't need to let the infection reach every cell. Once the genetic cascade begins, we can kill the infective RNA, then kill the retroviruses, and you're done!"

Aleksi nodded, trying to stifle her anxiety, to destroy it with the hope he promised. She would never be human again, but at least she'd be sane once more.

Reggie injected the infective concoction into a small IV bag, swirled it, spiked it with an IV set, and spliced it into Aleksi's IV. The fluid flowed into her arm, the essence of *Homo draconis*.

Aleksi felt a cold flush, then pins and needles prickled her extremities. She shivered and closed her eyes. "Please, please, please..." she muttered beneath her breath, embracing the flicker of hope.

---

E very time we try to ease off on the sedation, Lori goes ballistic." Price flipped through screen after screen of graphs, drug dosages, vital physiologic data, blood enzymes, brain chemistry, and hormone levels. "We've tried a dozen different combinations and doses of every drug in our arsenal. She's requiring more and more sedation to keep her under, and her liver enzymes are elevated."

"She's spiraling." Olson rubbed her eyes. "We've failed. She's too far gone to undergo psychoanalysis, and it's too dangerous to risk waking her up, even in restraints. She'd hurt herself breaking free, then kill someone."

"Options?" Mary asked, though she knew what they were.

"Electroshock therapy, lobotomy, or euthanasia," Olson said.

Mary suppressed a surge of nausea. "How long before we're beyond the point of maintaining her sedation adequately?"

"Maybe three weeks, but nutrition is a concern, and her liver might fail."

"Continue the sedation and monitor her liver enzymes. We'll decide what to do if she goes into hepatic shock." Mary made a gesture that told them the meeting was over.

Olson and Price left without a word, both of them clearly depressed with their failure. Mary turned on the CCTV monitor of Lori's room. A nurse was tending her. They'd put in a nasogastric tube and were giving her nutrition. Lori moved without purpose as much as her restraints allowed, which wasn't much. Mary zoomed in, and saw her eyes moving back and forth rapidly beneath her lids.

*Dreaming, still...* Mary wondered what Lori would be if they fried her synapses with electricity or destroyed her prefrontal cortex with a steel rod. Euthanasia might be the kinder alternative. *But not yet,* she resolved. *Not until we exhaust every possibility.*

Mary went back to her surveillance reports, and the results were dismal. They'd found and impounded Hutchinson's car a block from the Cambridge PD, but found nothing in it to help them locate him. A woman was visiting Hutch's apartment every other day, but their interior video surveillance confirmed that she was only feeding and cleaning the cage of Hutchinson's pet iguana and occasionally watering plants. Following her had yielded nothing. Hutchinson had known he was going into hiding and had obviously arranged for his place to be taken care of.

Their extended surveillance had also yielded nothing. Detective Blake carried on all the duties of a busy homicide detective with no unusual activities. Willis, when not with Jasper, carried on an unamusing domestic life with his husband, a vice detective with the

Cambridge PD. Mary reviewed pictures of them together, both with Jasper and without. The couple ate out a lot, socialized with friends, and carried out their jobs. Jasper didn't go out much except to get drinks with Blake every few days, occasionally a meal, and they took turns picking up the tab. One report suggested that their relationship might be progressing toward intimacy, but that didn't mean anything to Mary.

She went through the list of Jasper's associates once again. Most were cops, but he had few close friendships. He had a sister in New York and one living parent in Wisconsin, neither of whom he'd spoken to in a month. Surveillance reported him texting a lot, and pulling his phone records revealed one new number in his usual list. The new number was for a prepaid phone purchased with cash only days ago. This might be Hutchinson, but could also be one of Jasper's informants or witnesses, or it could be work-related. Many of the numbers Jasper contacted were unlisted and untraceable. They tried pinging all of the unlisted numbers, but most were out of service when not in use. Mary's analyst suggested the numbers were confidential informants, not uncommon for a homicide detective.

On impulse, Mary called up Benson, her field surveillance specialist.

"Yes, ma'am?" He looked as tired as she felt.

"I'm following a hunch here: during hours when Jasper and Willis are working together, shift Willis' tail to his husband, Detective Charles Trenton-Willis, Cambridge PD, Vice Department. I want to know his movements."

"Yes, ma'am. We'll start tomorrow morning."

"Good. Thanks." Mary ended the call. It was a shot in the dark, but worth a try. At this point, anything was worth a try.

---

Persephone paced the living room of the ground floor of their new home, waiting for Reggie. The place wasn't what she was used to, but it was at least spacious and clean. Then again, *she* wasn't who she was used to. Every time she passed a mirror, she stared at the woman staring back with little recognition.

*Get used to it, Melanie*, she thought. Working on her new persona, her new face, hair, figure, walk, laugh, mannerisms, and voice had become her full-time job for the last several days. *You're not Persephone anymore*. She'd already memorized her past, her family history, her alternative life, all manufactured a long time ago. Third generation Scandinavian American, Melanie had inherited an embarrassing amount of money when her parents passed away. She had been a philanthropist and socialite in California until her husband died in a car accident—a genuine auto fatality that fit her profile with a little industrious hacking. She'd then moved to Boston for a change of life and to be near her only living family, Robert Ingram. It would take some getting used to, but it was something she'd been prepared for her entire life.

She felt the vibrations of someone climbing up from the basement and heard the stairs door open. Without knowing how, she knew it was Reggie. Maybe his gait, smell, or the sound of his breathing. The senses of a dragon were hard enough to get used to, and now she had a new face and body as well. At least she didn't have to wear a padded bra anymore, but she still missed her tits.

Persephone turned to face him as he entered the living room. "How is she?" She wasn't used to his new face either and constantly had to remind herself that this was her cousin.

"Better. Running a light fever but resting. I slipped something into her IV."

"And the HD cascade?" They'd only started the infusion that morning, but it didn't take long to initiate.

"Beginning. I'd like to give her until morning."

"Just don't let it get into her CSF."

His eyes narrowed. "Just don't tell me my *job*, Seph."

"*Melanie*. And you're *Robert*. Get used to it!" They were both tired and temperamental. She turned away and resumed pacing.

"Yeah, well, I don't know if I have to, now." He sighed and all but collapsed into an armchair.

She stopped and fixed him with a quizzical stare. "Why not?"

He eyed her and shook his head. "Think it through. Someone's got to take Gi-gi's place, and you're...well...not up to it."

Persephone felt the pit of her stomach drop away once again. Gi-gi was gone. She was still coming to grips with that reality; true grief hadn't yet set in. "Not until things simmer down. We need your skills right now, and the transition..."

"Right." He forced a smile. "Not exactly fun."

Neither of them had seen first-hand the transition that Gi-gi had undergone. The family kept meticulous records, of course, so they knew what to expect. Fifteen elders had undergone that transition over the past several centuries. Persephone's parents were gone, and Reggie's had refused and moved away to a family enclave in Portugal. Her other cousins were farther removed, and their parents were spread out all over the globe. They all had their own interests and projects. None of them would be pulling up roots to move to Boston to undergo the transition. She and Reggie were now the eldest active generation on the North American continent. They had everything they needed to put someone into transition, but the process took almost a year, and often resulted in unpleasant side effects, hair and bone density loss the least worrisome.

"Well, don't think about it right now. We get the family stable, settle in, find a nice place to live, and deal with the current situation. Then we can decide."

"Fair enough." Reggie—*No, Robert*—sighed and chuckled. "The *current situation*. We should probably put out some feelers. Find out what Buckmann's up to."

"Well, there's nothing in the news yet, so I doubt she's arrested Hutch." Persephone resumed pacing. "I wonder why not."

"Fear of Aleksi, maybe?"

"I hope she's learned her lesson there. God knows she's had enough warnings." Persephone wondered if people like Mary Buckmann ever took warnings seriously.

"If she doesn't take the warnings to heart, there *are* other things we can do to neutralize her." Robert gave her a sidelong look. "We've got enough resources to plant some incriminating evidence in her home, some drugs or porn. We're not Gi-gi when it comes to hacking, but Ed's no slouch. We could put sensitive materials on her private computer, even foreign secrets."

"Let's hold off on that for now, but it's an option." Persephone couldn't seem to stop pacing, and she was beginning to realize why. Feelings of claustrophobia were wearing on her. She hadn't been out for several days. "I'm pretty much settled into my new face, and I need to get out of here for a while. I may try some good old-fashioned stalking. Find out how Hutch is doing and maybe see if anyone's watching him. If not, I'll slip him a phone. I'll also check out Mary's apartment, see if it's under surveillance."

Robert barked a laugh. "You just want to take your new car for a spin, don't you?"

"*Maybe*." She grinned at him. "I'm a confirmed hedonist. Don't judge me."

"Not judging. Just jealous. You should start looking for a new place. Find a real-estate agent. Do some shopping." He waved her out. "I'm going to sleep for a few hours then take another titer of Aleksi's genetic markers. Go have some fun, but don't do anything I wouldn't do."

"That's *way* too restrictive, Cousin Robert." Persephone grabbed her keys, a micro-purse with her new ID, credit cards, and cash, and headed for the door.

The instant she stepped outside, she felt better. *Part of being a dragon, I suppose.* It was still early, but the sultry afternoon air hung on the city like a blanket. The two-block walk to a parking garage left her in a light sweat. Up three floors, she found her car right where it was supposed to be, delivered the day before. She poked the fob in her purse to unlock the Audi RS5 Coupe, pulled the cover off—*Royal blue, to match my eyes*—stowed it in the trunk, and got behind the wheel.

Plush leather upholstery hugged her ass like a lover. Persephone had loved her classic Jaguar, but she had decided that Melanie was more of a modernist. The RS5 was pre-leased, so it had a respectable amount of mileage and wear. A new car would have drawn attention she didn't want. The Audi would also do zero to sixty in about four seconds.

She touched the start button, and the engine purred to life. The sound and feel of the motor tugged at the corners of her mouth. Persephone looked in the rearview at herself. *Melanie's mouth...not a bad mouth, really.* She drove sedately out of the garage and got used to the superb handling and acceleration on the ninety-minute drive to Cambridge. The evening commute was starting, so she couldn't open it up, but she decided that she could learn to love this car.

First, she parked on Oxford street and walked up to the Northwest Sciences building. The blast of the building's air-conditioning ruffled her short hair, prickled her skin, and brought the scents of laboratories, offices, coffee, and people. She climbed the stairs slowly and turned down the hall. It was so easy to bound, to leap, to spring, but she had learned to restrain her movements. A few students and faculty walked the halls, chatting amiably or headed toward a late class or meeting, some getting ready to go home for the day. Hutch had office hours until five, and might still be in. Her stomach tightened at the prospect of seeing him.

Down the short hallway, two of the four office doors were open, but not Hutch's. There were five post-it notes stuck to his door, two from students, and three from reporters. He evidently hadn't been to his office today. She sighed, then heard movement behind her. Resisting the impulse to whirl, she turned to find a woman leaving the office across the hall.

Melanie caught her eye and smiled. "Hello. You must be Doctor Oliver." The name plaque on the door was a dead giveaway.

"Yes." The woman looked her up and down. "You another reporter?" She said "reporter" as if it was a lower life form.

"No, a friend of the family. Melanie Ingram." She held out a hand as Oliver closed her door. "I just wanted to pay my respects. Such a tragedy."

"Of course." Oliver shook her hand perfunctorily, and her upper lip twitched. "Reporters are all over the place. Doctor Hutchinson has taken a leave of absence."

"Oh. Well, maybe I'll give him a call, then."

"Don't bother." Oliver shouldered her bag and turned away. "His phone's off."

"Thanks," Melanie said, though Oliver was already gone. *Leave of absence, phone off? That doesn't sound like Hutch.* Of course, if he was being hounded by both reporters *and* Mary Buckmann, disappearing for a while might be a good solution.

She left the building and drove to his condo. His car wasn't in the lot. She drove around the block and parked on the street, searching for surveillance. She didn't see anything obvious, but that didn't mean they weren't there; Mary would be keeping tabs on Hutch. Melanie got out and strolled up to the building, practicing her new gait, less bounce, more languid. *Not much left to bounce,* she thought sadly. A bored-looking woman yawned behind the manager's desk in the lobby.

Melanie walked up and smiled to her. "Hello."

"May I help you?" The woman returned the smile.

"I hope so. My names Melanie Ingram. I'm looking for a place, and I thought something might come open here. I love the location, and the view from the upper floors is just killer."

"Lease or purchase?"

"Whichever." Melanie waved a hand. "Maybe lease first. If I like it, I can always make an offer."

"We have a couple of leases coming up soon. I could give you the contact information."

"That would be perfect. Thanks!" Melanie looked around the lobby. People were returning to their homes after work, tired, determined, weary. As she accepted two business cards from the desk clerk, a woman that she recognized walked in.

Lonnie Westinghouse strode across the lobby with a long, loose-limbed stride, not in a hurry, but with the sure gait of someone on a mission. Curiosity niggled at the back of Melanie's neck. *What the hell are you doing here, Lonnie?* She thanked the clerk and walked back out to her car. There she waited, fiddling with her phone, pulling up a real estate app just in case someone was watching with a long lens. She browsed listings, trying to decide where the family's new home would be.

Lonnie left the building fifteen minutes later, got in a late model Nissan, and drove away. Still curious, Melanie followed at a distance, watching her rear view for tails. They crossed the Charles on the Anderson Memorial Bridge, passed the sports complex, and wound through Back Bay toward the medical district. There, Lonnie turned onto a back street, parked in front of a nondescript building, and keyed herself in through the front door. Melanie parked half a block away and pulled up a person finder app on her phone. Lonnie wasn't hard to find with what Melanie knew of her. Gi-gi had compiled files on everyone within three degrees of separation from Aleksi. The app gave an address, phone numbers, email, and workplace. This was Lonnie's apartment, and she was working at Brigham and Women's. Melanie considered calling her or contriving to bump into her and ask about Hutch, using the friend of the family line, but decided against it.

*Where are you, Hutch, and why is Lonnie watching your place?* She recalled her last foray into Hutch's condo, that ill-fated placement of their video surveillance. Gi-gi had gotten Aleksi's number from that video, which had given them the opportunity to recruit her, but it had also betrayed them in the end. Then she remembered walking in and being startled by the rattling metal cage, and realization clicked.

"Lonnie's feeding Iggy." That meant Hutch had called Lonnie before he'd disappeared, which meant he'd left voluntarily instead of forcibly in the custody of federal agents.

"Wherever you are, I hope you're safe." Melanie put the car in gear and drove to an apartment building less than a mile away.

She knew this one well; she'd lived in it for weeks half a year ago. She wondered why Mary Buckmann hadn't moved, but it didn't matter. She drove past and parked a block away, deciding to go for a walk. It was past five, and she might get lucky and spot Buckmann on the way home. What she would do if she *did* spot the woman responsible for destroying her home and the death of her great-grandmother, Melanie didn't know...yet. Following her would be dangerous, but they might learn where they were keeping Lori Watkins. She just felt the need to see her in person.

Melanie strolled by the apartment building, watching for anyone paying her or the building too much attention. Mary might have people watching her place as well as a precaution. She spotted nothing unusual and crossed the street to the corner bakery. She ordered an iced tea and an éclair—*No guilt there. Melanie could use a few pounds*—and sat at an outside table, sipping, nibbling, and scrolling through real estate listings on her phone.

After a half an hour, she'd spotted no watchers or suspicious people, ran off one man who sat down at her table without asking —*Jerk*—and was just about ready to pack it in for the evening. She could still fit in some shopping and maybe a drink downtown.

Then Mary Buckmann walked up the street.

Melanie found herself rising from her seat, tea forgotten, before she realized she was moving. She crossed the street and walked the opposite direction as Mary, her gait smooth, relaxed, easy, but every nerve in her body playing a symphony.

*What are you doing, Persephone?* she thought. Then, *Not Persephone. I'm Melanie Ingram, and this is the woman who killed Gi-gi.*

Persephone Terris had never hurt another living soul and had certainly never taken a life. Melanie, however, might. Ten steps, and they would pass each other just before Mary turned up the stairs to her building. It would be easy, quick, and final. No blood, no fingerprints, no pain. One strike, and the woman who threatened her life, her family, Aleksi, Hutch, *everything*, would be gone. The threat would be neutralized, retribution served. There was a risk, yes, but it was minimal. There weren't any watchers likely, and Melanie would be around the corner before anyone even noticed the woman had fallen with a crushed trachea, shattered larynx, and pulverized carotid arteries.

Five steps, four; the world moved in slow motion. Melanie caught Mary's eye and let her gaze slide past. The woman walked like a block of wood with legs, no sway, no grace, no fun. Her clothes hung like a sack on a square hanger, no shape, no elegance, all business. *As if a touch of femininity would make her less professional.* Three steps. She remembered Mary's apartment, so sterile, functional, boring, lonely. Two steps, and Melanie's left hand formed into a weapon, fingers bent at the second joint, ready. One step, eye contact, and a brief look of curiosity in Mary's eyes.

Melanie started to take the last step, ready to kill, and a brief smile touched the other woman's mouth.

Melanie felt that smile like a spear, a touch of humanity from an inhuman enemy. Persephone had been her, assumed her identity, her life, her memories. All of Mary's past rushed in, her youth, her trauma, her trials and fears. She smiled back and walked past without dealing the lethal blow.

Her heart hammering in her chest, Melanie kept walking, rounded the corner, and unclenched her left hand. She'd half-expected Buckmann to turn and put a bullet in the back of her head, had been listening for the click of the pistol's hammer coming back. Melanie didn't know why she hadn't killed her, or why she'd felt such a driving impulse to do so in the first place. Now, however, with the adrenaline rush fading, the analytical Persephone inside her gave her the answer.

*You wanted to kill her because that's how dragons respond to threats. You didn't kill her because you're still Persephone Terris, or at least a part of you is.*

Persephone unlocked her car, flopped into the driver's seat, and closed the door. She gripped the wheel and stared at her hands for a very long time. *Am I a killer, or am I not?* she wondered. That answer, too, Persephone provided. *Yes, if need be, but you're not a murderer.*

Persephone started the Audi, pulled away from the curb, and headed for downtown. She needed a drink and some shopping. Yes, that always made her feel better about being herself.

## 14

The thump of a car door woke Hutch from a not-so-sound sleep. *Another john leaving a late-night tryst,* he thought, blinking at the light at the edge of the curtained front window.

Charles hadn't lied; this complex was a favorite for the sex trade, and the neighbor to Hutch's left kept up a steady stream of patrons. After six days, he knew the routines well. He wondered briefly how people kept up such activity, how they survived, how they had reached that point in their lives. The answers were probably as depressing as his own situation, however, so he adjusted his position on the couch and started to close his eyes.

A shadow moved past his window, then another in the same direction. Something clicked outside his door.

Adrenaline surging through his veins, Hutch leapt up the instant before two successive impacts took out the dead bolt and chain of the door. He was halfway to the kitchen as four figures in black, weapons leveled, barged through the shower of splinters.

"Stop! Federal officers!" one shouted, but Hutch knew they wouldn't shoot him. They needed him too badly to shoot, and he had nowhere to go.

He did, however, have one thing to do before they took him. He flipped on the garbage disposal switch and dropped his phone down the drain.

The sound was horrifying, and evidently enough to provoke his assailants. Something popped like a cap gun, and electricity lanced through him, stiffening every muscle in his body. He collapsed, and his chin hit the edge of the kitchen counter on the way down. His knees hit the floor, and he toppled backward; the impact jammed the tiny darts deeper into his back, but the pain was lost in a sea of spasming muscles. Rough hands lifted him, and the sound of grinding plastic was cut off.

The electrocution ceased, but every muscle in his body still spasmed. He could barely move, hardly breathe. The taste of blood filled his mouth, and he hadn't the ability to swallow.

Someone flipped him over, and something pressed hard between his shoulder blades. A zip tie constricted his wrists and was tightened down hard.

He tried to curse, but it came out as a slurred and blood dribbled from his mouth.

"Get him out of here and call the forensics team in," the officer in charge ordered, and they lifted him and dragged him out to the parking lot.

Hutch's bare feet scraped the sidewalk, but he barely noticed the abrasions. His tongue began to throb in his mouth, and he managed to spit out more blood.

They stuffed him into the back seat of an SUV, the zip tie biting his wrists. Armed guards crowded him on each side, and one of them put a black cloth bag over his head as the vehicle tore out of the parking lot. They were several blocks away when Hutch finally regained the ability to speak. He doubted the stream of profanity he slurred to his captors would ever come up in court.

Mary pressed her thumb to the ID pad of the lock, tapped in her code, and the steel door clicked open. She stepped into the interview room and eyed Dwayne Hutchinson in the mirror as she closed the door behind herself. He sat handcuffed to the steel bar in the center of the table, facing the mirror. His eyes were red and his face puffy from trauma and a sleepless night. She'd read his medical report and the field officer's report but felt no pity for him. Getting tasered in the act of destroying evidence earned no pity.

"Good morning, Doctor Hutchinson." She rounded the table, put her files down, and took her seat. "I'm sorry for the rough treatment, but our field officers had no way to know if you were armed or dangerous."

He glared at her closed mouthed. He had a bruise on his chin.

"We're still tracing the lease on the room you were found in and are considering pressing charges on Charles Trenton-Willis. You know Charles, I'm sure. Marty Willis' husband?"

Hutchinson just stared at her.

"Come on, now, Doctor. He's been delivering you groceries for several days. His fingerprints are all over the apartment. He colluded with Tony Jasper to hide you from us. Obstructing a federal investigation is a serious crime. I could have both of their jobs by the time they take their morning coffee."

He sneered at her now. "That won't hold up, Mary, and you know it. I wasn't charged with anything; there was no APB on me. I wasn't even requested to come in for questioning. There was no reason anyone would consider me part of a federal investigation." He spoke with a lisp from the injury to his tongue. It had taken three stitches to close the laceration.

"Then why were you hiding in a Cambridge Vice Department safe house?"

"To elude *reporters*," he said flatly. "My ex-wife was quite popular with the press and a number of politicians. Her death has created quite a stir in the media. I was tired of questions and decided to take a leave of absence from work until they lost interest. Charles was simply doing me a favor."

That was bullshit, and they both knew it, but the fact was, he was right. Mary hadn't put an all-points-bulletin out on him with local law enforcement. Their search was being handled wholly within her project. Still, she had pressure she could apply.

"I questioned Tony Jasper as to your whereabouts, and he withheld information. That's obstruction. He told Trenton-Willis to hide you from us; that's conspiracy. I can charge them both right now."

"And I can't stop you, but it's pointless. Tony never knew where I was."

"And why not?"

"So he could *honestly* tell the press he didn't know where to find me."

She snorted in disgust. "Come on, Doctor, you know that's ridiculous. I can have you on charges of treason in a heartbeat, and here you are spinning fantasy tales. You must know the trouble you're in."

"*Treason?*" He returned her disgusted snort. "And what *exactly* have I done that's treasonous, Mary?"

"Whatever we *decide* you've done, Doctor." She gave him a cold smile. "Your ex-wife is a terrorist. She kidnapped and impersonated me, infiltrated a federal facility, stole information and physical evidence, and is responsible for the deaths of eight federal agents. We have DNA evidence to back those charges up. If we so choose, you'll be charged with treason as her conspirator. That's eight charges of conspiracy to commit murder, just to begin with."

"That's ridiculous! There's absolutely no evidence to suggest I knew anything about what Persephone was doing outside her public life."

"No?" Her smile wouldn't have melted a snowflake. "I'm sure we can find plenty."

His glare returned. "Or…"

"Or what, Doctor?"

"This is where you say, 'Or we can make those charges go away if I cooperate.'" His glare evolved into a blank stare. "What do you want from me?"

"Cooperation, Doctor." Mary flipped open her file and pulled out and eight-by-ten glossy photo of Persephone Terris, then another of Aleksi Rychenkna, this one slightly blurry from a body camera atop the Prudential Tower. "We want the location of Persephone Terris and Aleksi Rychenkna."

"So you can blow up their *new* house?"

"The explosion at the Terris estate killed eight of my men, Doctor! We were conducting a lawful search with all due process. That was a terrorist attack!"

"Bullshit. You invaded a private home with soldiers. Did you have a warrant for that invasion, Mary?"

"We did, Doctor. When national security is at stake, FISA courts grant warrants very quickly." They actually hadn't had the warrant in hand until after the fact, but FISA courts were also cognizant of time constraints in terrorist situations and were willing to cover DHS's ass.

"National security?" He barked a laugh. "The same bullshit line every totalitarian government uses to trample the rights of its citizens whenever they like! They had something you wanted, namely the cure to the *Homo draconis* infection, and they wouldn't give it to you. You decided to take it by force, and got your asses handed to you. Now you're trying to use me as leverage to get what you couldn't by brute force. Pardon me if I don't give a flying *fuck* what you want!"

"You're refusing to cooperate with a federal investigation, Doctor. I can—"

"I know *exactly* what you can do, Mary."

"Then cooperate with us! We know you've been in contact with Terris and Rychenkna. Where are they?"

"You've been in contact with both of them, too! Does that make *you* a terrorist?"

"Tell me where they are, Doctor, or I'll charge you with conspiracy to commit treason!"

"I don't fucking *know* where they are, and quite frankly, I wouldn't tell you if I did!"

"Then I'll just have to use you as bait." Mary closed her folder and stood. "Your career is over! Your *life* is over! I'm charging you with everything I can think of, and I'm informing the media and Harvard of what you've been up to!"

A cold, malicious smile spread across Hutchinson's face. "You're baiting a *dragon*, Mary. You know what Aleksi will do. You know that female *Homo draconis* are genetically driven to protect their loved ones."

"I'm counting on that, Doctor." Mary rounded the table and started for the door.

"You're insane, Mary. She'll rip you apart! You, personally! Don't provoke her! I'm warning you!"

She unlocked the door and pulled it open, then looked back at him. "I don't accede to threats from *terrorists*."

"It's not a threat, and I'm not a fucking terrorist! I'm *warning* you! She'll rip your fucking heart out!"

Mary closed the door and leaned back against it, breathing hard. That had gone just about like she'd expected. Hutchinson would never betray Aleksi. There was, however, the very credible threat of Aleksi Rychenkna to consider.

As she strode for the elevator, she spoke into the mic sewn into the collar of her jacket. "Comm center, this is Buckmann. The Johansen Project is on security lock down. All personnel associated with the project are to remain on site until further notice. If anyone needs to go out, they do so under full security escort, no exceptions! Communications director to my office, ASAP!"

She would make good on her promise; Dwayne Hutchinson's life was over. He'd never see the outside of a cell again for the rest of his life. There would be repercussions, of course, but with luck, they'd bag this whole terrorist organization with him as bait.

---

Tony had barely sat down at his desk with his first cup of coffee when Marty walked in with Charles. One look at their faces told him something was very wrong.

"What?"

"We need to talk." Marty glanced around at the virtually silent squad room, the windows, then back to Tony. "Someplace *quiet*."

"Okay, I'm up for some exercise." He stood, transferred his Glock from his desk drawer to his holster, and donned his jacket. "Lead on."

Charles led them out to the hall, then to the stairs. In the stairwell, they interrupted two uniforms engaged in a quiet discussion, but at the sight of three detectives, they took their conversation elsewhere.

Charles descended to a landing between floors and leaned back into the corner. "Hutch is gone."

"Gone, gone, or dead gone?"

"I don't honestly know. I got a call early this morning from the landlord. The safe house was broken into during the night. The door was *professionally* destroyed; two hits with a mini-ram, one on the dead bolt, the second one on the chain." Charles shrugged. "The place had been thoroughly tossed, and the kitchen sink was torn apart. I spoke with the neighbor, and he said he heard someone bust in and shout out something about federal agents."

"Fuck." Tony gritted his teeth. "How did they find him?"

"I've no idea. Maybe they hacked our phones, or just plain followed me." Charles looked miserable. "I'm sorry, Tony."

"Well, it's no stretch to guess who took him." Tony ground his teeth. "We'll probably find out soon enough if we watch the news, but I want to dig a little deeper into Mary Buckmann. It won't likely do us any good, but maybe we can find some dirt."

"So, you're going from playing with fire to juggling grenades?" Marty made a face. "You're not *seriously* thinking of taking on DHS."

"Not officially, no, but we may be able to leak some things to the media to rattle their cage."

"Well, if you want to set up incriminating photos with prostitutes,

I'm your pimp, but otherwise leave me out of it, okay?" Charles sighed. "We're in for some blowback from the chief, regardless."

"True." Jasper looked to Marty. "You two should distance yourself from this. Buckmann's already all over me like white on a KKK rally. As far as you know, Hutch was in our safe house as a favor to avoid reporters. We've got plausible deniability if the feds come after us."

"And what are you going to do?" Marty asked with narrowed eyes.

Tony grinned. "Me? Oh, I think I'll ask for some help from friends in low places."

"Like the Boston PD?" Charles asked.

"Just for information. I may put a bug in Blake's ear about this, but I don't want to get her involved. The Loretta Watkins abduction happened on her turf, and she's still sore about having the murder investigation pulled out from under her. If I tell her I've got an informant who knows DHS took Lori, and the fed in charge is named Mary Buckmann, I'm sure word will spread like wildfire."

"Hell hath no Fury," Charles said with a smug smile.

"Exactly."

"Speaking of hell and fury, do you think our mutual friend knows about Hutch yet?" Marty's skepticism had been replaced by worry.

"If not, she will soon." Tony sighed and rubbed his eyes. "And then, all hell's going to break loose, and there's nothing we can do to stop it."

# 15

"Hey, sleepyhead." Persephone—the new, blond, lanky version—walked into Aleksi's downstairs bedroom with a plate in one hand and a big flip-top bottle of green liquid in the other. "Feeling up to a real meal?"

Aleksi stretched her wings stiffly and yawned. Once her anxiety had waned, they'd removed the restraints and put her to bed. The room was small and a little stuffy, but it had an honest-to-God window that opened into a sunken well on the street side of the house. The glass was painted black, but it let in outside scents and sounds, less claustrophobic even than her subway lair had been.

"As long as that's not Gatorade." She couldn't get over the differences in this new Persephone; thinner, more angular, and fairer, but she also moved differently, less bouncy, more fluid. She wondered if that was an affected change in her persona or part of the *Homo draconis* modifications.

"Nope, a special concoction of Reggie's guaranteed to replace every depleted electrolyte and vitamin in your body. The steak is for nutrition. You've lost weight." Persephone sat beside the bed and handed over the bottle. "It tastes better than Gatorade, I promise."

"It better." Aleksi took it, drank, and nodded. "Not bad." She took the plate and breathed in the aroma of raw meat, her mouth watering. "God, that smells good."

"You must be feeling better."

"Weak and shaky, but sane, and not feverish." Aleksi cut a piece of beef and slipped it off the fork with her teeth. She chewed in bliss, and her stomach gurgled happily. "Thank you, by the way, for trying. *And for saving my life.*"

"We aim to please. How's your hand?"

"Sore, but I can move my thumb." She demonstrated.

"And your anxiety?"

"About normal. I think claustrophobia's bothering me now more than anything else. At least the window opens. I can *smell* the world outside." She ate another bite and washed it down with a swallow of Reggie's brew, assessing Persephone's manner. She seemed a little too solicitous, as if hiding something behind a false front of politeness. "So, what's with the bedside manner? Some new catastrophe?"

Persephone grimaced. "Sort of. I just want to make sure you're ready to hear it."

Aleksi's stomach clenched. "Tell me."

"They've taken Hutch, Aleksi." The muscles along Persephone's more angular jaw clenched. "I should have killed that bitch, Buckmann, when I had the chance."

That didn't sound like Persephone, vindictive and petulant, yes, but homicidal, no. "When did you have the chance?"

"I staked out her apartment two days ago. She showed, and I walked right past her, two feet away." Persephone's hands flexed, and her polished nails extended half an inch. "I should have trusted my instincts. I was ready to do it, *could* have, and would have gotten away clean, but…"

"But you didn't because you're not a killer." Aleksi cut a piece of meat and ate it, surprised that her nerves were so steady, and that she understood Persephone's actions so well. "If it's any consolation, I know *exactly* how you felt, and why you didn't do it."

"I suppose you do." A smile flashed, this one genuine. "Yeah, I figured it out, too, but…if I had done it…"

"They'd have put someone else in charge, and probably *still* arrested Hutch." Aleksi ate another bite. "How did you find out they have him."

"It's all over the news. They've charged Hutch with treason, conspiracy to commit murder, obstruction of a federal investigation, and a whole host of lesser bullshit charges. It hit every news service in Boston this morning, and Harvard has already reacted as you might suspect. He's been suspended, his grants frozen, his students told to find other advisors. That's all pending trial and conviction, of course, but DHS can make up as much 'evidence' as they need."

Aleksi felt herself tensing and forced her muscles to unclench. She ate, and thought, and forced calm. "They're trying to flush us out."

"That's pretty much what we thought."

"She'll offer to trade Hutch for the cure."

"I thought about that, too, but the answer's no. We can't trust them to keep their word. They get the cure, and we've got an army of dragons hunting us."

Aleksi nodded; Persephone was right and she had thought this through. "What can we do to help him without getting caught, killed, or worse, captured?"

"Well, since, as you pointed out, killing Mary Buckmann won't accomplish much, probably not a lot. Without Gi-gi, we're hobbled. She was our brain, and she's gone."

Aleksi heard the hidden pain there and sympathized. "Do we know where they're holding him?"

"No. I could have stalked Buckmann, but it would have been risky, especially considering my mood." Persephone got up and started to pace the small room. "God, I wanted to kill her, Aleksi! How do you keep those impulses under control?"

"You did. You tell me."

Persephone stopped and stared at her. "By remembering that I'm Persephone Terris. This...other thing that I am is like a second skin. It's just a disguise. I'm still me underneath."

"And you're not a killer."

"I thought about that, too, I mean *really* thought about it, and killing isn't the issue." She took a deep breath, and Aleksi could see the tension under tight control. "It's murder. If I, or you, or Reggie, or the other cousins were under an immediate threat, I don't think I'd hesitate, but with Buckmann just walking down the street, it would have been murder. But now they've got *Hutch*, and it's harder to resist."

Aleksi nodded and took another bite of her steak. "Can I ask you a personal question?"

Persephone blinked at her in mild surprise. "Of course."

"Do you still love Hutch?"

Persephone paused, looked down, then back up to meet Aleksi's eyes. "Yes. Not the way you think, but...well, maybe a *little* the way you think, but yes. He was my husband. I'll always love him. If that makes you angry..."

"It doesn't." Aleksi ate another bite of steak and washed it down with more of Reggie's concoction. The flavors didn't match very well. "Do you have anything better than this to drink? I'll finish it, but it really doesn't go with steak."

Persephone smiled again. "I think I can rustle up a decent bottle of old vine Zinfandel."

"Thanks. And bring two glasses. I hate to drink alone." Aleksi remembered all the nights she'd drank alone and realized that it had never bothered her before. Now things were different; she had someone she *wanted* to drink with. "And we've got some thinking to do."

"Sure." Persephone started for the door.

"I think I may know someone we can ask for help, someone with resources we currently don't have."

Persephone stopped at the door and looked back askance. "Oh, who?"

"Sergeant Jasper with Cambridge Homicide."

Persephone gaped at her for a moment, then laughed out loud and shook her head. "Oh, that's just beautiful."

"You know him?"

"Oh, yes, my dear. I know Tony Jasper, and I think he would be the *perfect* outsider to bring into our confidence, at least to a peripheral degree. He already knows about you, and he's friends with Hutch."

"Excellent!" Aleksi grinned and took another bite of raw meat.

"I'll be right back. Keep those ideas coming, dear. We'll get Hutch out, one way or another."

Persephone left, and Aleksi continued eating and thinking. She would need her strength if they were going to take on DHS.

---

J asper's desk phone rang yet again. He glared at it, but it kept ringing. *Should let it go to voicemail...* The damned thing had been ringing off the hook, mostly reporters wanting an inside scoop. His friendship with Hutch had been no secret. Tony half expected every call to be DHS asking him to come in for questioning again. It rang a third time, and his OCD wouldn't let him ignore it.

He snatched it out of the cradle and said, "Detective Jasper."

"Hello, Sergeant. My name's Ingram. I'd like to arrange a meeting with you in person, if you have the time."

The woman's voice sounded calm and sincere, but her words had tabloid journalist written all over them. "I don't give interviews with the press, Miss Ingram. I'm sorry, but—"

"I'm not with the press, Sergeant. I have information for you of a... personal nature. Information about a mutual friend."

That perked up Tony's ears like a bird dog with a pheasant in their sights. "All right, Miss Ingram, where can I meet you?"

"I'd like to go for a drive. Less chance of being overheard. I can pick you up in front of the Cambridge Police Department in ten minutes."

"All right. How do I spot you?" Tony opened his desk drawer and pulled out his Glock, tucking the phone to his ear with his shoulder as he checked the weapon and holstered it. Across their desks, Marty's eyes met his with a question. He held up a finger.

"Watch for a blue Audi with a blonde behind the wheel."

"I'll be waiting." The call ended, and he checked for a callback number. The caller's number was blocked.

"Who was that?" Marty asked.

"A woman named Ingram." He stood and pulled on his jacket. "I thought she was a reporter, but she said she had information for me." He left out the 'mutual friend' part.

"She didn't say what it was about?"

"Nope, just said she had information for me and wanted to meet. Picking me up in a few minutes."

"Want a tail?" Marty started to get up.

"No, thanks. New CIs are twitchy. I don't want to scare her away."

"Suit yourself." Marty sat back down, looking more worried than ever. "Careful."

"Hey, I'm the *good* cop, remember? Nobody ever fucks with the good cop." He grinned and headed for the elevator.

"Wrong on both counts, Tony!" Marty called after him. "You're the full-of-bullshit cop, and they're always the ones who get shot in the ass!" That got a round of laughter from the other detectives in the room.

Tony laughed and pushed the call button. "Then I'll have to be careful, and thankful that I wore my Kevlar boxers." The door opened, and he stepped in.

"Way too much information, Tony!" Marty called out as the doors closed.

Tony rode down, wondering about this out-of-the-blue confidential informant. The term 'mutual friend' was one he and Marty used with Hutch when they were referring to Aleksi, but how would this woman know that? Maybe she didn't, and this was something else entirely. Maybe she was a reporter and was just luring him into her car where he couldn't walk away. Or she could be legit. They did have other cases, after all, and people did occasionally contact the police with information. But the call had come directly to his desk, not through the department switchboard. She also spoke like she knew people might be listening. That told him she was being cautious.

He strode out onto the front steps of the precinct and hooked his thumbs in his belt. Leaning on the third step balustrade, he watched the traffic for a blue Audi. Precisely ten minutes after the phone call ended, a royal blue Audi coupe rounded the corner, swerved across the opposing lane of traffic, and pulled up to the curb. As Tony started down the stairs and across the sidewalk, the driver's window lowered and an attractive woman with short blond hair and sunglasses smiled at him.

"Thank you for coming, Sergeant."

He nodded and smiled. "This better be legit." Tony rounded the back of the car, glancing down to memorize the license plate in passing, and got in. He'd check the plate later. The interior of the car was even more impressive than the exterior, with custom seats and dash. "Nice ride."

"That's what *all* the men say," she quipped with a smile as her window rose. "Fasten your seatbelt, please, Sergeant."

Tony reached for his belt. "Call me—"

The Audi darted away from the curb like a bullet from a high-powered rifle, pressing Tony back into his seat as they jinked across the oncoming traffic lane and accelerated.

"Jesus Christ, lady!" He clicked his belt and shot her a look. "You in a hurry?"

"Not particularly. You were saying?" She shot him that sideways smile again and took a hard right without signaling.

"I was *saying*, call me Tony." He settled in and watched her. She checked her mirrors twice in one block, then took another hard left. "You're checking for a tail."

"You're astute." She nodded and took another right. "Do you have a phone?"

"Yes."

"Please turn it off completely. They may ping you to track us."

"*They?*" Tony pulled out his phone and shut it down.

"The people we pay taxes to." She made yet another turn, this one so short that it earned her a horn and a finger from an oncoming car. "I believe you know Mary Buckmann."

"Yes, we're acquainted." *Well, that nails down what this is really about,* Tony thought. "She's a very determined woman."

"And so am I, Tony. And you're friends with Doctor Hutchinson."

"Yes." Tony tried to split his attention between the road and her. He didn't recognize her at all, and he was tired of answering her questions. "Who's the mutual friend you were referring to?"

"Aleksi Rychenkna." She shot him a level stare for a heartbeat. "She, I'm *sure* you've met."

"A few times, yes." *Who the hell is this woman*, he thought, wondering if she might be a plant by Buckmann.

"The last time was the night you ended Derrick Penningly."

"You know a lot of details about me and my friends, Miss Ingram."

"Melanie, please, and yes, I do. Aleksi and I are *very* close. We're also very close to Hutch." She smiled again, and took off her sunglasses, revealing icy blue eyes. "She's not a happy young woman right now, and neither am I."

"I'm not very happy about what's happening to Hutch either, but there's not a lot I can do about it."

"Isn't there?" She glanced at him again, one pale eyebrow cocked. "What they're doing to him is designed to draw us out into the open. They're destroying his life to get to us."

"Yeah, that was what he was afraid of." He eyed her again, his brain gnawing on her identity like a dog with a bone. The words coming out of her mouth all but said, "I'm Persephone Terris," but she looked nothing like the woman. "We were hiding Hutch in a safe house, but they found him. You know Buckmann has Lori Watkins, right?"

"Yes. Hutch told Aleksi as much. Buckmann offered to trade her for the cure to the infection, but giving the government the keys to an army of *Homo draconis* would be catastrophic. We refused their offer."

"Okay." That all but confirmed that this was a member of the Terris organization, but Tony remained more than a little suspicious.

Melanie shot him another glance. "Lori's not doing well, and they'll probably kill her if they can't control her, which they can't. They don't understand people like Aleksi."

Tony nodded, and something Hutch told him niggled at the back of his mind. With all Hutch had said to him about these people's biotech capabilities, that they'd kidnapped and copied Mary Buckmann to infiltrate DHS during the Penningly investigation, he was beginning to think he knew who this woman really was. But he didn't know if he should let *her* know that. Secretive people could become dangerous when their secrets were outed.

"So, what do we do about this clusterfuck, Melanie? I've dug into Buckmann as deeply as I can, and there's not much I can do but piss her off by leaking sensitive information to the media and telling them I got it from her. That won't accomplish much other than costing me my job."

"True, and the police don't get to investigate the Department of Homeland Security."

"Exactly." He eyed her critically, could see the determination in her chiseled features, the way she gripped the wheel, her long fingernails pressing into her palms. "What are you planning to do?"

"If we can find out where Buckman's holding Hutch, we'll try to get him out."

That sounded insanely dangerous, but there was one other loose end to consider. "And Lori Watkins?" he asked.

"Unfortunately, Lori's secondary. Buckmann may be holding them both in the same facility. If they are, and we can learn where, we'll try for them both. That, of course, would be quite a lot more challenging."

"It sounds like a shitstorm waiting to happen, actually."

She barked a laugh and took the Audi around a corner hard enough to press Tony's shoulder belt into his collar bone. "You have a way with words, Tony. We'll have to be careful. We're not without resources, but the loss of my home has set us back." That sealed the fact that he was actually talking to Persephone Terris. "We'll need help."

"I'll do whatever I can that won't get me arrested, Melanie, but do you mind if I ask you something?"

"Please do."

"What will you do with Hutch if you *do* manage to get him out?"

"We have the ability to change a person's identity, Tony, as I'm sure you've figured out by now. We'll take him in and give him a new life."

Tony thought about that for a moment. "Does he know that?"

"No, but Hutch doesn't have many options right now." Melanie took one hand off the wheel and put it gently on Tony's leg without looking at him. "And we're the only family he's got."

Tony looked down at her hand, the long nails, perfectly manicured but more pointed than most women wore. Her hand felt warm through the material of his pants. Her touch didn't feel like a threat, but he somehow felt uneasy.

"All right, Melanie. I'm in. You need help. Just let me know how and when. I've got friends in BPD and can create a nightmare of police presence anywhere you like with one phone call."

"Perfect." She pulled her hand away and delved the side pocket of her door. She came up with a phone and handed it to him. "This is encrypted. It can't be hacked or traced unless you call an open phone with it. Please don't do that. It has my contact in it, and one other. That's all you should need. If you're ever at risk of being arrested by DHS, destroy it as completely as you can."

"All right." Tony took the phone and tucked it away. "What next?"

"Next, I thank you *sincerely* and drop you off wherever you'd like."

"You're welcome. Anywhere within a block or two of the precinct is fine."

"Okay." She made another gut-wrenching turn and smiled at him. "I don't know how to repay you for this, Tony. We've got plenty of money, but..."

"Forget it." He laughed and smiled. "Let me drive your car sometime."

"Why, *Tony*!" She gave him a sultry glance. "Was that a come on?"

"God, no!" He laughed. "I was serious. This *is* a sweet ride."

"Then I can do better than let you drive it." She stopped at a red light and fixed him with a piercing stare. "You help me get Hutch out of there, and I'll fucking *give* it to you."

Tony's jaw dropped. "Um...I don't know how I'm going to explain that, but..."

"Oh, come on." The light turned green, and she hammered the gas pedal. The Audi shot forward with barely a chirp of the tires. "You're a resourceful man. I'm sure you can think of something."

## 16

I need to go out." Aleksi stared at Reggie and Persephone, her arms folded and her wings wrapped around herself. "Nothing personal, but this place is driving me crazy."

"We certainly can't stop you, but we *can* warn you to be careful." Persephone exchanged a glance with her cousin, and he nodded.

"And we can help you. We can make sure the coast is clear when you come and go. Take your phone and call when you're coming back."

"And stay low and away from Logan. Gi-gi picked up some chatter from the air traffic controllers about unidentified radar contacts a few months ago. They think they're drones, and some might be, but if Buckmann gets a fix on you..."

"I'll be careful." Aleksi grinned and picked her phone off the table. "Duct tape?"

"Right." Reggie retrieved a roll from under the kitchenette sink. "A thousand and one uses!"

"Right." Aleksi doffed her poncho, peeled off an eight-inch strip, and taped her phone to her thigh. She'd been itching to get out for days. After four days of exercising to rebuild muscle and eating like a starved wolf, she finally felt physically up to it. "Don't worry. I've been doing this every night for the past six months."

"But DHS has never hunted you quite like they are now, Aleksi. Partnering with us has put you on their most wanted list."

Aleksi grinned. "That's what I get for hanging out with the bad kids. Don't worry. I just need to stretch my wings and clear my head. I'll be back before dawn."

"Promise you won't do anything that'll draw attention," Persephone persisted. "No stalking stalkers or beating up bullies."

"You take all the fun out of being a dragon." Aleksi made a face and stuck out her forked tongue.

"Yes, I'm *such* a spoil-sport." Persephone wrinkled her nose. "Seriously. Be careful."

"I will be." Aleksi nodded to the door. "So, clear the coast?"

"Right." Reggie opened the door and climbed the short stair up into the alley between the buildings. Aleksi heard him shuffling around for a few minutes, then he said, "Clear. A few lights in the neighbors' building, but—"

"Back in a few hours, then." Aleksi climbed the stairs, scented the air, took in the view, and leapt.

Her wings caught the air, and she soared upward, easily evading the light from the apartment windows. She banked around the corner of the building and climbed, stalling at the southeast corner to land on the roof. She perched there for a moment, listening for any sign of discovery, clawed fingers and toes gripping the cornerstone like a gargoyle atop a cathedral. Silence, save for traffic and general city noises. She scented the air and scanned the eastern horizon. The area was wooded, urban, without the soaring skyscrapers of the city, but she could see the glow of Boston miles to the east. The sight drew her like a moth to a flame.

*People...Why am I so drawn to people?* After twenty years of social anxiety and avoiding human contact, these urges to be among humans never ceased to intrigue her. She wondered if someone without her underlying social phobia would be the same, or even more drawn to observe, listen, stalk, and protect. She wondered about Lori Watkins and what she was feeling.

She couldn't imagine what the woman had gone through: her fiancé murdered right before her eyes, then the horrific transformations while being locked away in some sterile government facility, no sky, no smells, no people she knew, nobody to help and support her, nothing to do but dwell on her own torment. *No wonder she's having issues...*

Aleksi launched herself into the sky and headed for the city.

Skimming barely above the level of streetlights, weaving between trees and buildings, air filled with millions of scents, she felt free, alive, for the first time in a month. Music, shouting, traffic, the bright lights of a baseball stadium, the roar of the small crowd. *Humanity...* She reveled in the living, pulsating life beneath her.

Aleksi paused at the corner of a courtyard full of restaurants, clinging to the side of a building just above a floodlight, virtually invisible in the shadow. The tables were full, and waiters and waitresses wove around with trays of food and drinks. Couples and groups chatted, drank, laughed, and paid as much attention to their phones as each other. Aleksi watched, analyzed behaviors, read body language, and listened to their laughter and conversations. One couple sat at a small table across from each other, both of them staring at their phones, all but ignoring one another, thumbs darting across screens, the drinks and plates of appetizers between them forgotten.

Aleksi imagined their texts. Her: "So boring. Worst first date ever!" Him: "Should never have asked her out. Total snob." Her: "He's said like two words the whole evening!" Him: "She's probably texting another guy." Her: "I am so going to stick him with the check!" Him: "Maybe she's got a sister..."

The urge to swoop down, snatch the phones out of their hands, and shout, "Pay attention to each other!" surged up like a carnal desire. Of course, she didn't. Instead, she leapt into the sky and continued toward the city.

*Phones*, she thought as she wheeled around a hotel, scanning the windows, spotting a few people still at desks, working late, texting. *Everyone pays so much more attention to their phones than direct personal interaction. Why? Safer? Easier? Simple habit?*

She soared and dipped and wove her way east toward the city lights, through the small communities of houses, apartment complexes, parks, industrial areas, and shopping centers. Her thoughts wandered and then returned, as they always did, to Hutch. The media had eaten up the government's false narrative of his covert terrorist activities. They'd destroyed him utterly, and it made Aleksi's blood boil. Now, at least, it wasn't her fault. She could blame no one for this but Mary Buckmann.

*And maybe Persephone, a little bit.* She felt a twinge of anger but knew blaming Persephone for Hutch's plight would be like blaming the driver of a car for an accident that was someone else's fault.

On impulse, Aleksi found a perch on a roof and peeled her phone off her thigh. She turned it on and tapped in Hutch's number from memory. An out of service message played. She hung up and thought about calling Buckmann, threatening her, offering to make a deal, but Persephone had warned her against it. That was what they wanted, to draw her out into the open and trap her somehow.

She thought about visiting his condo just to catch his scent, feel his space, but she knew she couldn't. They would have it staked out. She wondered what had happened to Iggy. Would they have taken him, euthanized him, like they said they would euthanize Lori Watkins?

*They...*

The entire government was hunting her, a seemingly unbeatable foe, like trying to fight the rising tide with a mop and bucket. Aleksi's claws ground against the concrete of the building's cornice, frustration and anger vying for supremacy. Persephone, Reggie, and Aleksi had thought up dozens of scenarios for finding Hutch and getting him out, but all of them involved facing a force of heavily armed federal soldiers. They had to figure out a way to get in and get him out before they could fully respond, but she couldn't carry him while flying. DHS would have vehicles and helicopters and an army of snipers ready to chase them down and kill them all.

Aleksi launched herself back into the sky and soared toward the city. She needed a distraction, something to take her mind off of this insurmountable task. The first thing they had to do was find out where Buckmann was holding Hutch, but even if they did, that wouldn't keep them from moving him. Persephone thought it had to be somewhere near Back Bay, for she'd spotted Buckmann at her apartment at less than half-past five. That wasn't much of a commute for Boston during rush hour. She'd also arrived on foot, so she might have taken the subway.

Aleksi thought of her subway nook and considered visiting it for old-time's sake. She wondered if her two old phones were still hidden atop the power junction box, or if DHS had found them. But her old lair was probably being watched. *What a boring detail that would be*, she thought, almost feeling sorry for the DHS agents assigned to sit in a noisy, dark, disused subway tunnel waiting for a dragon. *Boredom and fear...* She grinned at the thought of scaring the shit out of them just for the entertainment value.

The horn-screech-thump of a car accident snapped Aleksi's wandering thoughts. She wheeled toward the sound a block away and spotted the two cars t-boned at an intersection. Both drivers were already out of their cars swearing at each other. One had his phone in his hand, the screen still lit.

*Probably texting and driving*, Aleksi thought, soaring past without a second thought. *Phones, once again. Stick someone's face in a phone, and they pay attention to nothing else.*

*Phones...* Aleksi pulled up and landed on a low office building, pulling her phone once again. She texted Reggie, "Can you locate someone's cell phone like the feds can?"

The reply came in minutes. "If the signal is direct, not rerouted or encrypted, yes."

"Buckmann's phone?"

"Her personal phone, yes, but..."

"But what?"

"She won't be so foolish. She'll take precautions."

Aleksi texted, "Not if she thinks she can find me the same way."

Reggie replied, "But your phone's encrypted."

"Not my old one."

"Use that and she can find you!"

Aleksi grinned and tapped, "Let her try. We'll have her location before she can find me."

"She'll suspect a trap!"

"Not if I tell her I've quit working with you. Pissed at what's happened to Hutch. Your fault. Maybe tell her I'll agree to out you if they release Hutch with no charges."

"Not a bad idea. Let me work on the details with Seph."

Aleksi tapped, "Fresh air clears the mind." She slapped her phone back onto her thigh and launched herself back into the air.

The plan began taking shape in her mind, and it felt good. Aleksi had experience stalking stalkers. If DHS had one fault it was their confidence in their own invulnerability. They'd think they were on the offensive, when they were really being set up. Send them on a wild goose chase, get Hutch's location, then swoop in.

Of course, the moment she broke into to a federal facility, the jig would be up. With CCTV cameras, motion sensors, steel doors, and hundreds of armed guards, they'd close in on her in minutes. And they still had to figure out how to get Hutch out.

*First things first, Dragon Woman*, she thought, swooping around another building barely above the streetlights.

The canyons of Boston loomed ahead, her hunting ground. Let Mary Buckmann think she had the upper hand, that she could trap a dragon. Once they found Hutch, Aleksi would teach her what a real predator could do.

---

I can't believe you were actually *friends* with this guy and had no clue." Blake sipped her beer and shook her head. "I mean, a terrorist working as a Harvard Professor? It's like something out of a spy novel."

"Want me to tell you a secret?" Tony finished his beer and waved the empty at the bartender.

Blake eyed him sidelong. "Sure."

"It's bullshit."

She arched an eyebrow. "Bullshit how?"

Tony accepted the beverage from the bartender and pointed the neck at the flat screen above the bar. "He's their fall guy. They needed a win, and they went for the easy hoop. Hutch is no more a terrorist than I am." *Says the guy with the encrypted phone in his pocket handed to him by a dead woman.* "They paint him as some kind of an eco-terrorist nutcase and pin this explosion on him instead of taking responsibility for their own fuckup. The poor socialite Persephone Terris is killed by the vengeful ex-husband when he finds out she's on to his terrorist activities? *Really?* Not only that, but he blows up an entire mansion? How the hell did he manage that?"

"Terrorists have resources. Nutcases give them money." She shrugged and sipped her beer. "You sure you're not just defending him because you like him?"

"Oh, I'm *totally* defending him because I like him, just like I'd defend *you* from a bunch of bullshit charges because I like you."

"That's good to know."

"Why, you planning on doing something naughty?" He grinned at her.

She smiled at his obvious flirt. "Maybe I am. But tell me this: would you defend me if I *really* did something like that?" She pointed her bottle at the scene of the burning mansion that had been replayed on the news about ten thousand times in the last few days.

"No. If I *knew* you'd actually done it, I'd put the cuffs on you myself."

"Hmmm, that sounds interesting," she said with a sideways smile. "But how are you so sure Hutch didn't do that?"

"Let me tell you another secret." He leaned close, and she did too. She smelled nice, kind of a coffee-beer-woman-cop scent that he found erotic as fuck. He whispered, "I have it straight from the horse's mouth, but off the record, that eight federal agents were inside that house when it went up."

"Holy shit!" She stared at him from an inch away. "Who told you that?"

"The horse in charge of the operation that put those men in the house." He put a hand on her knee. "They went in after the *real* terrorists and got blown to hell. Now they're pissed and need a fall guy."

Her eyes widened. "*Jesus*, Tony, that's…"

"I know." He backed away and pulled his hand off her knee. "It sucks rocks."

"So, you're saying this Terris woman was the *real* terrorist?"

"That's what the horse told me. They're trying to use Hutch to flush them out, but it won't work."

"Why not?"

"Because these people aren't stupid."

"Being a terrorist in the first place is stupid." Blake finished her beer and put the empty down hard on the bar. "They're fucking criminals."

"Maybe." Tony sipped and eyed her. "Or maybe they only pissed off the government and earned the label 'Terrorist' for no good reason."

"There has to be a good reason." She nodded to the flat screen again, the picture of Persephone Terris dressed to the nines, bejeweled and coifed, her hand resting on the arm of a state senator. "How does someone like *that* piss off the government?"

Tony knew exactly how they'd done it, but he couldn't very well tell Blake. "Well, that picture alone might be part of it. Political influence, money, blackmail, favors, playing the game better than they do."

"You don't have a very high opinion of the federal government."

He snorted a laugh. "And you *do*?" He sipped his beer. "Remember when the feds swooped in and took the Watkins woman and all the evidence from both of those murder scenes without so much as a 'thank-you-very-much?' Remember last winter when they scooped up everything that had anything to do with the Penningly murders before we could so much as raise a finger?"

"I remember," she growled, lowering her eyes. "National security…"

"Right. Every time they want something we've got, they claim it's national security, or terrorism, or a fucking *plague*." Tony pulled his wallet, but Blake beat him to the punch, pulling two twenties from a pocket. "Hey, it's my turn."

"No, it's not, it's *my* turn." She slipped off her barstool and eyed him. "And if there's ever going to be a 'your turn' you have to promise me something, Tony."

"Name it." He stood and adjusted his belt.

"Promise me you're not a part of this shit." She nodded again to the flat screen.

"A *part* of it?" He shrugged, not wanting to lie to her, but knowing he couldn't tell her the whole truth. "Not more than knowing Hutch isn't a terrorist and being seriously pissed at watching his career being flushed down the toilet because some tight-ass government fuck has a hard-on. They're ruining a good man because they need to use him. His life is fucking over because they need a *lever*."

"All right. That's honest." She buttoned her jacket and smiled at him. "Tuesday, then? Your turn."

"Tuesday. Unless something comes up."

"Let me know." She started for the door.

"I will." Tony took a step and felt the encrypted phone vibrate in his pocket. "I'll see you later, Anna. I've got to hit the head."

"Later!" She waved without looking back.

Tony went to the bathroom, picked a stall, sat down, and pulled the phone. The text read, "We think H is within half an hour commute of B's address. How fast can you get a shitload of cops and news vans to an address within that circle?"

He thought about it, about Blake, and what she now knew. One call to her would bring down all hell and high water. He tapped, "10min," and sent it.

"Good," came the reply. "We'll give you a few hours warning. A few days from now."

"Okay," he replied and pocketed the phone.

Tony got up and left the bar, grinding his teeth at the indirect lie he'd told Blake. "So much for not being a part of this shit."

Hutch had to admit, he'd imagined worse than this. The cell didn't have any windows, but it was bigger than he'd thought it would be; ten feet square and eight feet high. No bars like a classic jail cell, but a sliding steel pocket door set in a cinderblock wall. The lighting was recessed and monochrome blue-white LED, which gave him a headache, and the mattress was barely three inches thick, but it was clean, air conditioned, quiet, and he hadn't yet been physically abused.

Mentally, however, it wasn't exactly torture, but close. He had nothing to read, no music, no entertainment, no stimulus whatsoever. Most people would find solitary confinement with semi-sensory deprivation a form of torture. Hutch did yoga, tai-chi, calisthenics, and meditated. He kept up the regimen as much to irritate his captors —whom he knew were watching his every move—as for his own physical and mental wellbeing. Five days in, he was still sane, well-fed, his injuries mostly healed, and healthy. He was not, however, happy.

Once a day for an hour they took him to an interrogation room, handcuffed him to a table, and turned on a TV to show him the news stories about himself. They'd painted a credible picture of a brilliant if somewhat obsessed Harvard professor gone bad. Behind the façade, Dwayne Hutchinson was an ecoterrorist, sociopath, seducer of young students—they'd even dragged Julie's name into it and had pictures of them together—and vindictive ex-husband. Persephone had left him when she learned of his subversive activities, and when she'd threatened to expose him if he didn't stop, he'd set a bomb in her home that killed her and her entire family. There was even a rehash of Bob Tomlin's murder, and speculation that Hutch had murdered the student, and then Aleksi Rychenkna, when they learned his secrets.

The loss of his career and destruction of his good name, however, angered him less than the repercussions. The news media hounded his students, both former and current, and it broke his heart to see them on camera. Terry Price and John Alverez, both nearing their fourth year and close to defending their dissertations, were hardest hit by being set adrift. Both had their research funding frozen because Hutch was their advisor and held the grants, so they couldn't move forward. Both had also, on camera, staunchly defended Hutch, refusing to believe the charges and denying any knowledge of any subversive activities. The two younger students, Vince and Beth, had refused to comment, saying only that they were looking for new advisors.

Watching their academic careers threatened depressed Hutch more than his own situation. Four people's lives were being harmed, like collateral damage in a military campaign.

But he had to convince himself that there was an upside. Aleksi was alive and free, maybe even cured completely by now. Persephone was also alive, though her life, too, had been destroyed. He'd actually laughed out loud when an unfortunate reporter had tried to grill Lonnie. She'd torn him a new asshole—only verbally, of course—and brought up facts that nobody in the press had mentioned: the theft of a priceless specimen from his laboratory, the chain of murders perpetrated by Derrick Penningly, Hutch's record of defending the environment in court, which pissed off large corporations and conservative politicians, and his record of publications and successful students, now academic professionals doing good work all around the world. She'd flatly called the government's charges fabrication and speculated why they were ruining his career.

"Ask *that* question!" she'd snapped at the hapless reporter. "Why a brilliant professor with a spotless record is suddenly cast as a terrorist? Because they *want* something from him! Doctor Hutchinson is the finest man I've ever known, and you're helping to destroy him! Now get out of my face!"

Hutch smiled at the memory. He sat lotus on his bunk, trying to meditate, but it wasn't going so well. Too many memories, good and bad, sweet and painful, swirled around his mind. He concentrated on the sequential relaxation of his muscles, his own heartbeat, breathing, serenity, but he knew what they were doing to him was not without purpose. They wanted Persephone's family and Aleksi, and not only what they knew but to destroy them utterly. They knew as well as

Hutch did that Aleksi wouldn't stand for doing nothing while his life was being destroyed.

The thought of what she might do terrified him.

His door beeped and slid open. Hutch opened his eyes as two armed guards stepped in. He had no way to know what time it was, but he was still full from breakfast, and they generally didn't give him his TV torture session until after lunch.

"Up," one of them said, lifting wrist and waist chains. "Time for a walk."

"Walk where?" he asked, not moving an inch.

"Where we walk you, now get up or get tasered. Your choice." The man's hand rested on the taser at his belt.

Not relishing another close encounter with high voltage, Hutch got up and held still while one guard put the manacles on him and the other stood ready in case the prisoner did something foolish. They then marched him out of his cell and down the hall to an elevator, where two more guards were stationed. This was new, since the interview room was on the same floor as his cell. During his arrival, the elevator ride down told him he was five floors below street level, and that there were six. The elevator went up seven floors above ground, too, so this was a big building. He didn't, however, know where the building was located, other than in Boston. He'd seen nothing but the inside of a black cloth bag in transit from the safe house.

Holding him by the elbows, they pulled him aboard the elevator and one of them pressed the B2 button. They rode up three floors and got out. The décor mirrored the floor he was being held on, same drab paint, same featureless walls, same recessed monochrome lighting.

"All those tax dollars, and they don't even give you guys wall art or motivational posters? Talk about torture!"

The guards didn't respond, but he hadn't expected them to. They took him to a doubled door that opened with a card swipe from one of the guards. They ushered him in, and Hutch found himself in some kind of communication center. Why they would bring him to such a place other than intimidation, he had no idea, but he was pretty sure the room's central figure would explain his presence soon.

"Doctor Hutchinson, good of you to join us." Mary Buckmann stood at the center of a wide horseshoe of monitors and workstations manned by technical people.

"Like I had a choice," he groused as his escort brought him to her side.

"We all have choices, Doctor. Some are easier to make than others. You chose to come here with your escort rather than being tasered. I chose to ask you here rather than let you languish in your cell because you are, despite our best efforts, the world's foremost authority on *Homo draconis* psychology."

Hutch scanned the monitors and realized what she wanted from him. "Lori Watkins?"

"Yes." She turned and looked him up and down. "I want your opinion on her condition."

Skepticism knitted his eyebrows. "And I want you to drop all the charges you've trumped up against me, tell the world I'm not a terrorist, and that it was all made up."

"Throw in the location of your ex-wife and Aleksi, and we've got a deal, Doctor."

He gave her a disgusted look and held his tongue.

"I thought not." She motioned to the monitors. "As you can see, Lori isn't doing well. Despite our efforts to give her a comfortable, nurturing environment, reasonably familiar surroundings, and all the freedom we could, she's progressed into violent psychosis and has had to be sedated and restrained."

Hutch could see from three different monitors that the woman—a fully transformed *Homo draconis*—had been restrained, and he assumed the IV's attached to her arms were administering drugs. Supposedly real-time physiologic data scrolled across yet another screen. If it was real, she was tachycardic, breathing fast, and receiving oxygen.

The room she was in had been decorated like a bedroom, but the walls and floor were the same color as the ones in his cell. He had no way to confirm it, but Hutch had a feeling she was being kept right here in the same building.

"We've done everything we can for her, Doctor, but we've failed, and we don't know why. We'd like your opinion as to why her mental condition deteriorated."

He eyed her incredulously. "And what the *hell* makes you think I'd help you in any way?"

"Because if we don't do something to help her, we only have three very bad options, two of which will irreversibly damage her brain, and one that will kill her." She pursed her lips, her stare as cold as ice. "I'm imploring to your humanity, Doctor. For Lori's sake, help us."

"My *humanity?*" His temper flared. "Wow. You really are a piece of work. You ruin my life, my career, damage my students' academic careers, charge me with crimes I didn't commit, publicize a metric-*fuck*-ton of lies about me, and you want my *help?*" He grinned through gritted teeth. "*Fuck* you, Doctor Buckmann."

She smiled thinly. "Your ex-wife has a cure for Lori's condition, or so we're led to believe, and she's refused to give it to us." She pointed to the screen. "Lori is her fault."

"No, she's *your* fault, Mary, just like David Gilford was *your* fault! You could have let Persephone's people take Lori, and she'd be healthy and happy today like Gilford's other two victims. You chose to keep her like a lab rat in a cage, not for *her* benefit, but for *yours!*" He sneered at her in disgust. "Don't show me a victim of your own arrogance and greed and tell me it's *my* responsibility to help her. It's not. And you're wrong about my expertise. I'm *not* the world's foremost authority on *Homo draconis* psychology. Aleksi is."

"You once tried to broker a deal between us and these people, Doctor. Your goal was to safeguard the human race against an outbreak of this infection. Trust me when I tell you that our failure with Lori won't stop our efforts. We have volunteers lined up, ready to undergo the transformation. They'll be infectious, of course, but they'll be ours, loyal, and stable."

"Until one of them goes nuts and slaughters your people, escapes containment, and starts infecting innocents." He glanced at his two guards, but their faces remained set in stone. "Just like Gilford did."

"So help us get the *cure!*" She turned to face him fully, clearly livid but holding it in. "Help us find and secure your terrorist ex-wife. You can help us! Withholding that help is endangering the entire human race!"

Hutch barked a laugh. "You're holding a gun to the head of humanity and telling me, 'Do what we want or we pull the trigger.' Who's the real terrorist here?"

"The terrorists are the ones withholding the cure to that!" She jabbed a finger at the monitors displaying Lori Watkins. "They have it and they're keeping it from us!"

"Because they don't *trust* you!" Hutch shook his head. "And you better pray to God that they *do* have a cure, and that Aleksi has been given it. Because, if she hasn't, if she's still a dragon, she's going to make David Gilford's rampage look like a tea party!"

Mary Buckmann glared at him, waved at the door, and snarled, "Get him out of my sight!"

The guards grabbed Hutch's arms and propelled him toward the door. Ten minutes later, he was back in his cell, trying to calm down from the altercation. No matter how he tried, however, Hutch couldn't get past the image of Aleksi wading through a sea of blood to try to save him.

# 17

Two men walked beneath Aleksi five feet from her nose, their headlamps cutting swaths of illumination through the silent subway tunnel. She looked like a lump of canvas stuck to the ceiling, her wings flat, face averted, utterly still. They looked, sounded, and smelled like MBTA maintenance workers. She hoped they were. They didn't smell like guns, that oily metallic tang she'd grown so hyper-attuned to. If they were disguised DHS agents, they were a lot better at disguises than being observant.

*Once again, bad evolution*, she thought. *How did humans ever survive without learning to look up?*

The answer to that question, she realized, might very well be clinging to the ceiling of a subway tunnel at this very moment. If early pre-human hominids had *Homo draconis* watching over them from on high, the evolutionary advantage to scanning for predators from above would be minimal. Like a kid with a really nasty big brother, they wouldn't have to worry about bullies on the playground.

Aleksi waited until they'd gone, then dropped back down to the rocky ground between the rails. The trains didn't run in the small hours of the morning, which made maintenance work possible on the active lines. It also made skulking by dragons easier. Silence was her ally. Humans were noisy and clumsy. She'd heard these two from a hundred yards away.

She crept on toward her old lair, pausing every few minutes to listen, scent the air, and feel for vibrations through the ground and subway rails. There was work being done some distance away, but nothing she had to worry about.

Closer, less than a quarter mile now, she paused longer and tasted the air. Still nothing. She also started checking for hidden cameras, though Persephone had told her that truly covert electronic surveillance was virtually invisible. They had cameras and microphones in Hutch's condo, and Aleksi had never spotted them. Such devices could be detected with a radiometer, but she couldn't very well carry one along. Besides, if she missed a hidden camera, and they caught her stealthily recovering her old phones, that would only reinforce her ruse.

Hearing, feeling, seeing, and smelling nothing threatening, she advanced. She had no doubt that DHS had gone through her old lair with a fine-toothed comb, but if she was lucky, they hadn't found the two old phones she'd stashed on a power relay box outside in the subway tunnel. One was the first phone Persephone had given her, encrypted and untraceable. The other, however, was a regular prepaid model that Hutch had given her. That one could be tracked, and that was what Aleksi needed.

Closer, she smelled the faint residue of gun oil, Kevlar, and quite a lot of human sweat. There had been soldiers here. The scents weren't fresh, but they weren't old either, and they sang along her nerves like static electricity. She remembered the first time she'd scented that particular medley, the night the first Doctor Johansen had sent assassins after her and shot up the Park Street Subway station. If they'd stationed people to ambush her, they'd learned nothing about what it meant to hunt a dragon.

Lowering herself to fingers and toes, she crept along the juncture of the tunnel wall and floor. She moved with smooth, liquid grace, settling each clawed member into the loose rubble of the tunnel before applying her weight. Straining her senses yielded only vague input; they'd been here recently, but she couldn't tell if they were still. Ahead, the junction box where she'd stashed the two phones loomed out of the murky darkness.

Someone sniffed.

Aleksi froze. The sound may have as well been a gunshot, unmistakable, but barely above the background hum of the city above and from farther ahead than the junction box. They were either at the entrance to the disused subway station she'd used as a lair, or just inside the door. Either way, they were being quiet, and their scent was faint. Buckmann had someone waiting for her, but they weren't staking out the spot where she'd stashed the phones. That could mean they didn't know the phones were there.

*Or they found the phones, and now have a camera watching that spot, and they'll open fire the moment I step into position.* Aleksi knew she was being paranoid, but paranoid and alive was better than oblivious and dead. She also needed those phones.

Aleksi crept forward, utterly silent, a shadow in the darkness. Twenty feet to the junction box, she detected no sounds of the lurker; the sniff must have been an anomaly, someone stifling a sneeze perhaps. She resumed moving.

Ten feet. She heard an indrawn breath, slightly muffled. They were either wearing something over their face or were inside her lair. Five feet to the junction box, and she could see the door to her old lair, still bent where she'd smashed it open while fleeing David Gilford. Whoever lurked there was inside.

At the junction box, Aleksi stood and stretched out a hand to the nook where she'd hidden the phones. They were there. She clutched them carefully and put them both between her teeth, careful not to bite down too hard. She had duct tape on her leg, but peeling it free to secure the phones would make noise. Aleksi *really* didn't feel like being shot at tonight. She crouched down and crept away, listening to the faint noises of the ambush, wondering if she'd been recorded on low-light video. If she had, they'd let her go, and so much the better. Aleksi's plan hinged upon the theory that Buckmann wanted Persephone more than her.

Several hundred yards away from her lair, and close enough to a subway station to get a cell signal, Aleksi transferred her Hutch phone to her leg and turned on the encrypted one. Aleksi ground her teeth while it booted. She'd been doing that a lot lately. This situation with Hutch had her well and truly angry, and the dragon within her was sharpening its weapons, preparing to kill the people who threatened the one she loved. The logical portion of her mind knew this, but frankly, she didn't care. She'd warned them, warned Mary Buckmann personally. The blood would be on their hands.

The phone finally finished booting, and she called Persephone.

"Success?" Persephone sounded tense.

"Yes. They had someone there, in my lair."

"All well and good." Relief softened Persephone's reply. She'd been worried, of course. They could have done this with new phones, but Aleksi had disagreed. This would add credence to the deception. "We'll set the phones up tomorrow. We're still working on the cell tower hack. Be careful tonight, please."

"I will be. I'll call you when I'm close."

"Okay. Good hunting."

"Thanks." Aleksi ended the call, put the phone on vibrate, and taped it to her thigh. She then took a running start and flew. She had decided to spend the night watching Mary Buckmann's apartment. In the unlikely event that the woman showed her face with less than a dozen soldiers to protect her, maybe Aleksi would test the theory that Persephone had not.

Maybe she would cut the head off the snake and see if it grew a new one.

---

G ot it!" Persephone's younger cousin, Ed, kicked his chair into a spin. He sat at the downstairs dining room table, three laptops arrayed before him, each displaying a different screen of code. Two were scrolling steadily, while one showed a spiderweb network of cellular towers. "WOOT! We are *in*!"

"Undetected?" Persephone asked, leaning over his shoulder.

"Cousin Melanie! I am *offended*!" Ed shot her a sad-puppy face. "I may not be Gi-gi, but I'm not a noob. Besides, cell carriers are shit for intrusion detection. They have beefy firewalls, but zilch for counter hacking."

"Good. Let's test it." She pulled her encrypted phone and texted Aleksi's, "Turn on your Hutch phone. We're testing our system."

A minute later, she received, "On," and the phone number.

Persephone texted. "I'm calling you on an open phone in ten minutes."

"Okay," came the reply.

"Okay, Ed. You've got our burner number. This is Aleksi's." She showed him her phone's screen, and he typed it in.

"Got it."

"I'm going for a drive. Call me on my clean phone when you pick up the call."

"Will do." He waved and went back to work, setting up his system to detect the call.

Persephone climbed the stairs out of the basement and strode for the parking lot. In the Audi, she eased out onto the street, drove three blocks to a major cross street, and headed east. At four a.m. the streets were all but deserted, but she kept an eye out for bored police. It would be embarrassing to be pulled over for texting and driving. Five blocks along, she turned on her open cellphone, and connected it to the car's audio system. At a stoplight, she tapped in the number from Aleksi's text and made the call. It rang once.

"Double Dragon Chinese Take Out. May I take your order?"

Persephone snorted a laugh. "I'll have the sarcasm with a side of eggroll. How is your evening going?" The light turned green, and she drove on.

"Uneventful. I spotted three people watching Buckmann's apartment. They're good."

"Did they see you?"

"If they did, they had orders not to call it in."

"Or to shoot you."

"Well, if they tried *that*, I'd have mentioned it…and they'd be dead."

Persephone felt a cold chill up her spine. "Aleksi, I know you're worked up about this, but—" Her other phone vibrated in the passenger seat. "Hang on. Got a call." She tapped her other phone to take the call. "You got me?"

"You're eastbound on Pleasant Street, coming up on Main. Aleksi's on top of an apartment building two blocks from Buckmann's place."

"Nicely done! That was fast!"

"Well, I knew what to look for on both ends. It'll be harder to track Buckmann down, impossible if she's rerouted her phone through some government server farm."

"Nothing's impossible. We'll set up the connection between Aleksi's phones when she comes home. Get some sleep."

"Ay-firmative!"

The call ended.

"You hear that?" she asked Aleksi.

"Yes. It'll work, Seph. I know it will."

"Intuition?"

"Need," Aleksi said, and Persephone could hear it in her voice. "Necessity is the mother to invention, you know."

"Yeah, well, none of us are Gi-gi when it comes to hacking, but we've got a good chance. All we need is one break. Everything else is lined up."

"A vehicle?"

"Yes. Reggie's doing the disguise and body work. We'll blend right in."

"What did you have him do, mock up a cop van?"

They'd considered that. Jasper had promised a full police presence. But impersonating police would present difficulties. There was always a chance of running into real police and having to play the part. Reggie had come up with a much better idea. "No. Way better than that. Don't worry about it."

"And he'll have medical equipment inside?"

"This is *Reggie* we're talking about. He'll have everything short of an ICU inside."

"Good. We may need it."

Persephone bit her lip. "You planning on getting hurt?"

"No, but I'm going into a federally guarded facility. You can bet your sweet ass they have armed guards."

Aleksi had a serious case of nerves going, and Persephone needed to put her at ease. "Why *Aleksi*, I never knew you thought I had a sweet ass!"

A wry laugh came over the line. "You never quit, do you?"

"Darling, the day I quit making sexual innuendos is the day *after* they put me in the ground." Persephone cringed; it was the wrong thing to say, and she knew it right after it came out of her mouth.

"Well, let's try not to make that happen soon, then. I've grown fond of your sexual innuendos. All things considered, however, I like Hutch's ass *way* more than yours."

Persephone mentally thanked her. "So do I. Especially my new ass. It's too skinny. Not enough bounce."

"Promise me one thing, then."

"Sure!"

"Once we get Hutch out of there, you'll have to change his identity, right?"

"Yes."

"Fine. Just don't touch his ass."

Persephone barked a laugh. "I'd never meddle with perfection, if that's what you mean, but I might cop a fondle now and then."

"If you do…" Aleksi paused, and then, "…I guess I'll have to get used to it."

Persephone's jaw dropped. "Let's get him out first, then we can discuss who gets to fondle what, all right?"

"Deal."

"I'm heading home. Call me when you get close."

"I'm leaving Back Bay now."

"See you." Persephone ended the call and turned for home, mumbling a little prayer that this suicidal plan of theirs wouldn't get everyone she loved killed.

S o, I've made things simpler for you." Ed motioned Aleksi to take a chair at the dining room table.

"It doesn't *look* simple." Aleksi sat down and squinted skeptically at the mishmash of electronics. She could barely see her old Hutch phone amongst the circuitry and plastic.

"Hey, it may not *look* simple, but I assure you that it'll work seamlessly."

She heard Persephone's bare feet trundling down the stairs and turned. She came in wearing a Halo-Kitty t-shirt and jeans, her short blond hair sticking up all directions. She wasn't wearing her contacts, and the yellow irises and vertical-slit pupils took Aleksi aback for a moment. The scent of soap wafted in with her, and her eyes were red and dark-circled. They'd all tried to sleep, but, like Aleksi, she guessed that Persephone hadn't gotten much.

Persephone stopped and stared at the electronics-strewn table. "Jesus, Ed, it looks like R2D2 had sex with a CB radio!"

He shot her a glare. "You wanted it fast and good; *pretty* wasn't part of the work order."

"Noted, but she's got to carry..." She stepped closer. "Oh, that's her old one."

"Yes. This is the decoy, or rather the bait for Buckmann's triangulation." Ed picked up the other phone, the encrypted one. It, too, had been modified, but appeared only vaguely mutated. "This is the one she'll carry, and I've bluetoothed it to an earpiece speaker-microphone that she can use to switch carriers without dropping either call." He picked up a small earpiece with a spring wire mic. "Try it on."

Aleksi took it and fitted it to her ear. The wire looped over and around her ear, the tiny mic at the end resting flat against her cheek. She shook her head sharply, and it stayed put. "It fits. Show me how it works."

"There's only one button, and that only turns it on and off." He showed her by poking the button, and the screen of the encrypted phone lit up. "The rest is voice activated."

"Okay, what do I say?"

"So, this phone is actually *two* phones. You can switch between them by saying 'Carrier One' or "Carrier Two." Carrier one is the one that'll only connect with your old phone through this." He tapped the mess of electronics. "Anyone you call on that will have no way to know you're not at the same location as your Hutch phone. I've stripped its contacts list to two numbers: Hutch's original phone, and Buckmann's."

"Hutch's phone's out of service," Persephone said. She hadn't taken a seat, but paced the floor, her nails clicking against one another. She wasn't handling the stress well.

"I know, but it might not be destroyed. If he kept it, Buckmann might have it. If she does, and Aleksi asks to talk to him, she might give him his old phone and tell Aleksi to call it." Ed shrugged. "If we didn't have his number in there, we might get hosed. Just trying to think of all the possibilities."

"Good thinking." Persephone continued pacing. "What if they call back right after Aleksi calls them. They'll track it down before we're ready."

"That's easy. I'm rigging it so I can turn it off when we're not using it." Ed tapped the encrypted phone. "I'll call Aleksi on carrier two when we're ready to make the second call."

"Perfect!" Aleksi grinned. "So, give me the voice commands."

"Sure. So, to call Buckmann, you say…" He bit his lip and picked up the encrypted phone. "Wait a second. I want to make sure we don't screw up and place the call now." He powered the phone down.

Persephone stopped and glared at him. "Yes, that would be *bad!*"

"I know, Seph. Just relax a little." Ed put the phone back down and opened his mouth to speak to Aleksi, but Persephone interrupted.

"I'll relax when this is *over*, and *not* before! Don't tell me to relax!" Persephone balled her fists, the muscles of her neck distended.

"Persephone." Aleksi stood and stepped between her and the table. She put her hands on the woman's shoulders, felt the trembling muscles beneath the thin fabric. "We're being *careful*. We know this is going to be dangerous. Unless you want to call it off entirely—"

"No!" Persephone dragged in a deep breath and let it out. "No, you're right. I just didn't sleep. That's all." She waved back to the table. "Go ahead."

Aleksi let her go and sat back down. She knew it was more than insomnia. Persephone felt the need to help Hutch, just as Aleksi did, but wasn't handling it as well. She nodded to Ed.

"Yeah, so, to make a call through your old Hutch phone, you say 'Carrier One, call Hutch,' or 'Carrier One, call Buckmann.' Like I said, those are the only two contacts you have."

"What if she wants me to call another number?"

"You can do that by voice, too. Just say the number out loud. You can receive calls on either line, too, but like I said, we'll be turning this thing off when it's not in use." He tapped the electronics nightmare with a finger. "If you *do* get a call, you'll get one beep through your earpiece for a call from carrier one, and two beeps for a call from carrier two. To pick up, say 'Answer call' and the carrier number, and you'll be connected."

"Okay. And if I want to make a call on the other line?"

"Yeah, just say 'Carrier Two,' and whoever you want to call. I've put Persephone, Reggie, me, and Tony Jasper in there, but I think we'll do a conference call when we go in." He looked up at Persephone. "I think Seph wanted to talk to Jasper, when the time comes."

"I do," she agreed. "But it's good to give Aleksi the number, just in case something happens and I'm unable to make the call."

They all knew what she meant by that, and they all equally hated the prospect of one of them being hurt or killed. Denying that possibility, however, would be dangerous.

"And your escape vehicle? Is it ready?" Aleksi asked.

"Reggie says the mods will be done this afternoon. He wants to let the glue set on the appliques in case we get rain." Ed looked up at Persephone again. "We should be good to go tomorrow night."

"Excellent." Aleksi nodded to Persephone and added, "Maybe we should get some sleep."

"Good luck with that," she growled back.

Aleksi ignored the acerbic reply and tapped the conglomeration of bastardized electronics. "Where are you going to put this?"

"Haven't decided. Somewhere far away from here, of course."

"Yes. Maybe south of the city. Far enough that they won't be able to get there quickly. Quincy or Braintree." Persephone clicked her nails some more. "So, two calls to Buckmann, the first one short, just requesting that you talk with Hutch and sow the seeds of your discontent with us. That should get her people mobilized in the wrong direction. Then, before they get there, we make the second call. We should be able to get a vague location from a call less than thirty seconds long."

"Unless Buckmann's as paranoid as we are, and she's encrypted her phone somehow, or ran it through a server network."

"If she has, we're fucked," Persephone said.

"If she has, we cancel the operation and think of something else. I'd still like to talk to Hutch."

Persephone pursed her lips and shook her head. "That would be dangerous, too. If they find that," she jabbed a finger at Ed's electronic nightmare, "they'll know we were up to something."

"I don't think they'll find it without a signal, but I could put it in a nondescript box and put a self-destruct on the phone. If we get hosed, we melt it down."

"Good idea." Persephone nodded and sighed. "Anything else?"

"Nothing new. I've still got a little work to do, but this should be wrapped up by dinner time." Ed tapped the mess of wires and boards.

"I'd like to talk to you, Seph." Aleksi stood and started for her bedroom.

Persephone followed without a word. When she closed the door behind them, she broke her silence. "I know what you're going to say, Aleksi, and I know I need to calm down. I thought *you* were the nervous one last night, but now...I just can't."

"You consider having Reggie give you something to help you sleep?"

"Yeah, maybe tonight if I can't relax." She heaved a breath. "How do you do it?"

"I tell myself this will work and think of what we'll have when we're done." She shrugged, unwilling to add the 'if we survive' part. "So far, it's working. That's not to say I don't feel like ripping Mary Buckmann's head off, but I'm sleeping, at least."

"I got to thinking yesterday, and I can't stop worrying about what we're *risking*," Persephone replied. "This could go *so* bad *so* fast."

"It's because you're calling the shots. You don't have your matriarch doing the thinking for you." Aleksi stepped up and put a hand on Persephone's shoulder again. "Think of it this way: your great-grandmother probably never would have agreed to help Hutch in the first place. You get to do what *you* think is best."

"I know, and a part of me is saying that she'd be perfectly justified in walking away from this. She'd let Hutch rot in a cell, as long as her family was safe."

"Justified, maybe, but that doesn't mean she would have been *right*." Aleksi grasped Persephone's other shoulder and pulled her into a hard embrace, wings wrapped around her like a blanket. "The difference is, to you and me, Hutch *is* family."

"Yes, he is." Persephone trembled all over, a leaf in the wind. "All I can think of is losing everything."

"And all I can think of is gaining everything." Aleksi pulled her tighter. "This will *work*, Persephone. I promise you."

Persephone shuddered in her arms and fumbled under Aleksi's wings to hold her. "Don't make promises you can't keep, Aleksi. It hasn't worked well for me."

"Hey, you didn't promise to make me human again. You only promised to try."

"I wasn't thinking about that. I was thinking about Hutch."

"Hutch?" Aleksi pulled back and met Persephone's dragon eyes with her own. "What promise?"

"Oh, a whole shitload." She laughed a sad smirk. "That we would make our marriage work, that I was in love with him. You know, to have and to hold, 'til death do us part."

So that was it; Persephone was having regrets about what she'd lost, all in the name of her family. But there was an easy answer to that.

"But now you can keep those promises. We're going to get him *out* of there! We can be a family again."

"Really? Can we?" Persephone shook her head. "I don't think he'll ever trust me again."

"He will. You watch."

"How do you know that?"

"Because that's just who he is." Aleksi let go of Persephone's shoulders and grinned. "Now, go out tonight and have some fun. Tomorrow morning you can have Reggie mix you up something to help you sleep. Tomorrow night, it's game on."

"Right." Persephone heaved a breath and turned for the door, then looked back. "Thank you, Aleksi. I don't know how you do it, but… thank you."

"I've got a lot of experience in not getting what I want, Seph. A whole lifetime of it. This time, I will." She grinned her best dragon grin. "Just watch me."

# 18

Mary snapped awake with her phone vibrating in her pocket. She'd only lain down on her office couch half an hour before, but exhaustion had taken her into a deep slumber. Who in God's creation would be calling her at ten p.m., however, left her sleep-addled mind stumbling for non-existent answers. She sat up, pulled her phone from her pocket, and stared at the incoming number with zero recognition. It wasn't one of her contacts, and she didn't get spam calls—one of the minor perks of her job—so it had to be someone who knew her number. Also, it couldn't be anyone in DHS; she would have received a summons over the intercom for that.

She punched the answer icon and said, "Doctor Buckmann."

"You've made a big mistake taking Hutch hostage, Mary."

"Who the hell..." Recognition hit like a bullet train, bringing her bolting up from her couch. "*Aleksi?*"

"Yes. I warned you, Mary."

Mary touched the mic at her collar three times in quick succession, opening a direct line to her communications director. "I don't take kindly to threats, Aleksi." She held her phone near the mic so they would hear both sides of the conversation and prayed that whoever was monitoring had brains enough to start a trace.

"This isn't a threat…yet. I want to speak to Hutch."

"We don't negotiate with terrorists, Aleksi."

"Bullshit! You were ready to negotiate when you thought you might get the cure! Besides, I'm not…with them anymore. They couldn't deliver on their promises and wouldn't make a deal to save Hutch. I want to talk to him. I'm calling back in ten minutes, and I better get to speak to him."

"Or *what*, Aleksi?" She had to keep the woman on the phone as long as possible, even if it meant making her angry. Of course, it sounded like she was already angry.

"Or you don't get what *you* want, Mary. I know where Persephone Terris is. There's a paraphrase from an old book that reads, 'Do not meddle in the affairs of dragons.' You should *heed* that warning."

The call went dead.

Mary called the number right back, but it was out of service. Aleksi had turned her phone off so they couldn't track her. She swore under her breath. "Comms, tell me you tracked that!"

"Partially, ma'am. South of the city. Braintree. That's all we could get."

"Send an airborne team to Braintree now, and be ready to triangulate when she calls back!" Mary sat down to slip her shoes on. "And have a security bring Doctor Hutchinson to the comm center. I want him there in five minutes."

"Yes, ma'am."

She tapped her mic, tied her shoes, and headed for the comm center. It sounded like Aleksi was willing to make a deal, but Mary was skeptical that she'd betray the Terrises. Then again, the dragon had a temper, and they'd refused to give over the cure to help Hutchinson.

*Such devotion to a man,* she thought to herself in bafflement. *How can she be so attached to him? They aren't even the same species anymore.*

S omewhere north of downtown but south of the Charles. Sorry, but that's the best I can do on the first call."

"At least we got something." Persephone patted Carrie on the shoulder, and she put the van in gear and pulled away from the curb. Reggie sat in the passenger seat while Persephone stayed in the back. There was enough medical equipment in the back of the van to serve as a MASH. Reggie and Carrie were dressed to fit the disguised van, while she was not. "The game is on, everyone. Keep monitoring us, Ed. We're moving." They'd been parked half a mile from Mary Buckmann's apartment for half an hour waiting for Aleksi to make the call.

"So am I. I'll be downtown in five minutes. Call me when it's time for the next call." The rush of wind accompanying Aleksi's voice went silent as she ended the call.

"Everything else ready, Ed?"

"We're primed and ready, Seph. The downstairs looks like the opening hour of DEFCON." Ed had three of the cousins at his disposal, all competent in cyber security and intrusion. Again, they weren't Gi-gi, but the matriarch had trained them.

"Good. I'm going to text Jasper." Persephone opened her message app and pulled up Jasper's contact. She tapped, "Near downtown. Exact location in ten min. Get your shit together."

A moment later, she received, "My shit is ready to roll."

Persephone had to admit that she liked Tony Jasper. She closed the app and put her phone in a hip pocket of her fanny pack. While Reggie and Carrie wore sharp business attire, she was dressed for night-time invisibility. Matte black from head to toe, her hair covered with a snug cap, and her snug pull-over shirt equipped with a stretch turtleneck that she could pull up over her nose. She also wore a sturdy vest with tool pouches and clips for climbing gear and dark driving gloves. They didn't know yet where they were going or what Persephone's role would be, but she was ready for virtually any eventuality. Her job was to help get Hutch out once Aleksi found him. The only thing she didn't carry was a weapon. She didn't need one. Her weapons were integral, and right now she was having difficulty keeping them from puncturing the fingertips of her gloves.

*This will work,* she told herself. *This will work because it has to work. We'll get Hutch out, and nobody's going to get killed.*

That had been her mantra for the past thirty-six hours. Even her sleep, what little she'd managed to snatch, had been plagued with dreams of blood and horror. That was nothing new, but these had included Hutch and Aleksi. She'd awoken in a cold sweat, insisting to herself that her nightmares wouldn't come true. She wouldn't let them come true.

"Okay, I'm downtown," Aleksi announced, re-entering the conversation. "How are we doing?"

"Jasper's ready to go as soon as we have an exact location. Where are you?"

"On top of the John F. Kennedy Federal Building. Nice view."

"Stay low. They could be monitoring radar."

"If they have radar that can pick me up flying five feet from a building, I'd have been shot months ago. I know what I'm doing, Seph. Trust me."

Persephone gritted her teeth, but Aleksi was right. "Just being a mother hen. Sorry. Take a piss on the federal government while you're up there."

"Right."

"Four minutes to call time," Ed interrupted. "Where are you, Seph?"

"On Tremont, coming up to the park," Carrie answered before Persephone could open her mouth. "Traffic's pretty light."

"Find a place to park. You may have to backtrack."

"Okay." Carrie spotted an open space and pulled over.

"Three minutes," Ed said.

"No countdown, please. I'm edgy enough." Persephone was having trouble keeping her claws from piercing the fingertips of her gloves.

"Right. Just the OCD in me. I could play some music, if you like."

"Don't you *dare*. All I need is an ear worm." Persephone took a deep breath. "You won't be able to hear us when you're talking to Hutch,

Aleksi. I'll text you when we get a solid location on him. Your phone will vibrate."

"Good. I don't want to drag it on too long. Buckmann will get suspicious."

"Good." They fell into an uneasy silence, time moving at a crawl.

Finally, Ed broke the silence. "Time. Aleksi, your Hutch phone is live."

"I'll make the call. Thanks everyone, ahead of time, I mean."

"No need to thank us," Persephone said. "We're family."

"More than figuratively, in your case, Seph," Reggie added. "You're genetically closer to Aleksi than the rest of us now, anyway."

"That's right. I didn't think of that. Well, I better make the call. Take care, everyone."

The background of wind in Aleksi's transmission went silent as she switched carriers. Ed, of course, would be listening in as well as tracking Buckmann down. They'd know instantly if anything went wrong.

---

Tony switched from his message app to phone and tapped Anna Blake's contact. It rang twice and she picked up. "Hey, Tony. What's up?"

"Hey, Anna, I just had a very disturbing conversation with a CI, and I thought I should let you know. There may be an event on your turf tonight."

"An *event?*" Her tone transformed from casual to business in one word. "I'm guessing this isn't a rock concert type of event."

"Not even close." He'd thought long and hard about making this call and had rehearsed it a few times. "Remember that shit I'm not supposed to be a part of?"

"Yes."

"Well, I'm not, except that I have someone on the inside feeding me information." That was true, as far as it went, which made Tony feel a little better about what he had to say next. "I've got credible information that there's going to be some kind of event in the downtown area tonight, and I say event, because I honestly don't know what the fuck they're planning." Also true, mostly.

"Are you telling me there's going to be a fucking *terrorist* attack on downtown Boston, Tony?" She had advanced to full-blown *no bullshit* mode now.

"I'm saying I don't know exactly *what's* going to happen, but you may want to mobilize your shit-storm response team. I'm in contact with my CI. As soon as I know more, I'll call you. I'll start things moving on this side of the river, and we can come over if necessary."

"Okay. Okay, I'll make the call." Blake took a deep breath and hissed it out through her teeth. "This better be legit, Tony."

"I wouldn't call you if it wasn't, Anna. I swear to God." That, too, was true.

"Thanks for the warning. Keep me informed."

"Will do." Tony ended the call, then picked up his desk phone to call Commander Fisk. His job was now officially on the line.

## 19

Hutch had been sleeping soundly when the guards opened his door and dragged him out of his cell. They took him up to the same communications room he'd seen before. Buckmann was there, looking like she'd also been awoken from a sound sleep, her hair even worse than usual. She also looked ready to chew iron and spit nails, bristling with energy, and obviously in full command mode.

*Something's happened.* Hutch kept his mouth shut; he'd find out soon enough.

"Doctor Hutchinson, sorry to wake you, but we have an opportunity here."

*She wants something from me. Something new.* There was no challenge to figure out that it had something to do with Aleksi or Persephone, but the next words out of her mouth confirmed his suspicion.

"Aleksi called me a few minutes ago and requested to speak with you. It seems she's had a disagreement with the Terrises and is on her own again. She's going to call again in a few minutes. I'd like you to speak with her."

Hutch stared at her for a moment, trying to figure out if this was real or some ploy to get him to reveal information. "And say *what*, exactly?"

"Anything you like. She didn't specify. She just agreed to consider helping us acquire the cure to the *Homo draconis* infection from the Terrises if I allowed her to speak to you." She shrugged. "No tricks, no conditions. Just talk to her."

Hutch wanted to tell her she was full of shit but held back. The chance to speak to Aleksi, to tell her not to do anything drastic, loomed like a beacon in the darkness. He also wondered what kind of disagreement she might have had with Persephone. He might be able to find out, too, if this really was Persephone who had texted him, or if it was some kind of deception and his ex-wife was dead. Of course, they could use the call to try to find Aleksi, but she knew that. She had a lot of practice at staying hidden. She wouldn't have done this if she didn't have some failsafe means to keep from being found. From Hutch's perspective, there was too much to gain and almost no downside.

He nodded, "Fine. I'll talk to her."

"Thank you." Buckmann turned to a monitor. "We have about two minutes. Do you want anything while we wait? A coffee?"

He snorted a laugh and rattled the chains that encircled his waist. "No thanks. I don't think I can hold a cup."

She looked him up and down as if noticing for the first time he wore the restraints. "Uncuff his right wrist."

The right-hand guard applied a key to the cuff and opened it. Hutch smiled thinly at Buckmann. "Thank you *so* much."

"You're *welcome*." She matched his insincerity perfectly. "Let me be clear, Doctor: if Aleksi helps us get the cure from these people, I'll exonerate you completely, tell Harvard that you were working with us voluntarily, and you'll get your life back. I'll also discontinue our efforts to find Aleksi. You have my word. You have a lot to gain by helping us."

*And Persephone has a lot to lose*, he thought. *That's if she's actually telling me the truth.* But if she and Aleksi had really had a falling out, that might change things.

A cell phone vibrated, and Buckmann pulled it from her pocket. She glanced at the screen and nodded. "This is her." She touched the screen and answered, "Aleksi?"

Hutch heard a voice over the line but couldn't make out the words. His heart raced in his chest. *Just be careful, Hutch. Just hold it together.*

Buckmann said, "Yes. He's right here. I'm handing him the phone now." She held out the phone, and Hutch took it.

"Aleksi?"

"Hutch? Is that really you? You sound weird."

"It's me, Aleksi. I'm a little hoarse, that's all."

"Say something only Hutch would know."

"Okay, um...you asked me up to your apartment the night after we went out with Twain. I asked you if you were on something and turned you down."

"Ha, right. I was more than a little drunk."

"How are you, Aleksi? I'm worried about you."

"I'm my old self, Hutch. I just needed to talk to you. Things...didn't go so well with Persephone's family. They tried, but it only made things worse. Don't worry about it. I'm more concerned about you. You know what Buckmann's done, right?"

"Yes, I know." He could tell from the slight lisp in her voice that she was still a dragon. And he also knew what her instincts were telling her to do: protect him, save him, free him. Her instincts, in this instance, would only get her killed. "It doesn't matter, Aleksi. Look, they're listening in, and probably trying to track you down. You should just hang up and—"

"Hutch, I'm not going to forget you. Not *ever*! Don't even *think* it. If I can get the cure for Buckmann, she said she'd let you go."

"Don't trust her, Aleksi." He shot Buckmann a glare. "They'd have to admit they made up the charges if they ever released me. I don't see them doing that."

Buckmann glowered at him but didn't say a word to defend herself.

"They could make something up, tell the media you cooperated with them to bring terrorists to justice. If all they want is the cure to the infection, I can get it without putting anyone else at risk. They'll be able to reverse engineer it to make more, and they get what they want."

"An army of dragons."

"Yes, but *noninfectious* ones!" She heaved a sigh. "I know it's not a good solution, but it's the *only* one. It gets you out of there, *and* it keeps the human race safe."

He had to admit that she was right, but her solution also meant trusting Buckmann. "They'll never keep their end of the bargain, Aleksi. Give them the cure, and they have all the cards. They'll create their army and hunt you down."

"No, they won't, Hutch."

"Why not?"

"Because if they double cross me, I'll rip Mary Buckmann's arms off." Hutch could almost see the rictus dragon grin, the very real threat to cross the line Aleksi had never crossed. "She can't stay hidden forever. I'll hunt her down and anyone else involved in her little science experiment, and I'll slaughter them. I know she's listening, and I don't care. She should have learned her lesson with David Gilford. There's nothing she can do to keep me from finding her if she betrays me in this."

Hutch could tell from Buckmann's eyes that she was indeed listening in, but again, she held her tongue.

"There's another solution, Aleksi. Leave me here. They're not hurting me, and I'm catching up on my yoga and meditation."

"That's not an option, Hutch. They *are* hurting you. Your career—"

"It doesn't *matter*, Aleksi! It's not as important as *you* are. They're letting us talk so they can track you down!"

"Don't worry about that. I can fly away. They'll never catch me."

"It's not worth the risk, Aleksi! Even if they send me to prison, it's not worth you getting captured by these thugs."

Buckmann glared at him, but Hutch gave her the finger, though the gesture was somewhat hampered by his left hand being cuffed to the chains around his waist.

"Hutch, stop it. I can *fix* this! Nobody has to get hurt, and you can get your life back!" Aleksi's tone brimmed with guilt and responsibility. Responsibility for him.

"This isn't your fault, and it's not your problem to fix, Aleksi!"

"It is, and I *can*!" She insisted. "You just hold tight, Hutch. I'll call Buckmann back on this phone when I have the cure, then I'll leave it with the phone on where she can find it."

"And trust her to keep her end of the bargain? No, Aleksi."

"She has *real* incentive to keep her end of the bargain. All she has to do is remember the pictures of Derrick Penningly's victims. Remember the slaughter of their people when David broke out of their facility. Remember that, Mary, because if you double cross me, if you don't exonerate Hutch and give him his life back, every bit of it, you'll see all of that again."

"Aleksi, don't—" Hutch began, but the call went dead. He looked at the screen to no avail. Aleksi was gone.

"Status?" Buckman turned away from Hutch to the array of monitors and technicians.

"Solid fix! Braintree, just south of the train station. Pearl Plaza."

"Converge but do not engage!" Buckmann ordered.

"You lying *bitch*!" Hutch threw her phone down hard. It shattered into a hundred pieces, drawing the attention of everyone in the room. He started to take a step, but the guards were already on him. "She'll tear your people apart! You're blowing your only chance, Mary! Don't do this!"

"Get him out of here!" she ordered, and the guards dragged him out.

Hutch seethed, but there was nothing he could do with one hand chained and the other arm twisted behind his back. They frog-marched him to the elevator while his heart pounded like a caged beast against the bars of his ribs.

*But the beast isn't caged*, he realized, as the elevator doors closed and they started to descend. *The beast is free. Buckmann will double cross Aleksi, and she'll wreak havoc...because of me.*

G ot him!" Ed announced over their earpieces.

"Location?" Persephone lunged up to between the front seats of the van, eyes fixed on Carrie's phone in the nav cradle. Her nails pierced her gloves and the upholstery, but she didn't notice.

"Sending it to Carrie's phone now. We're texting Aleksi to let her know she can end the call. She's a badass, by the way. Buckmann's got to be pissing her pants!"

"Good." Persephone tried to relax, but she may as well have been trying to stop the rain that had begun to patter against the windshield.

A destination icon popped up on Carrie's phone, then a route and a duration. "That's close! Nine minutes!" Carrie put the van in gear and pulled out into the sparse traffic.

"Shit! Persephone, it's the O'Neill Federal Building!" The sudden terror in Ed's voice spoke volumes. "It's a fucking *fortress*, and I can't localize the call's location inside. They've got an internal network for cell traffic. There's no way—"

The connection crackled, and Aleksi broke in. "I'm en route. It's only three blocks. I'll be there in one minute."

"Aleksi, be careful. The building's like Fort Knox. We have to figure out what to do, not go off half-cocked!"

"I'm not going to barge right in the front door, Seph. Don't worry. Ed, get some schematics or floor plans or something. I need a way in that's not guarded or wired with alarms."

"We're on it," Ed replied.

Persephone's nails drove deep enough to grate against the metal frames of the seats. "Aleksi, it's a huge building, and we have no way to know where they're holding Hutch. We should consider aborting the—"

"Not until we have a *look*!" Aleksi snapped over the rushing wind. "I just need a way in! Give me that, and I can find Hutch."

"Without getting shot?"

"Just give me a minute for fuck's sake! I'm coming into view now. There's a taller building under construction right next door." Aleksi paused and Persephone imagined her swooping around towers, exposing herself to cameras and radar.

"They'll have security cameras, Aleksi!"

"You *think?*" Another pause. "Okay, there are two triangular sections to the building: a lower portion that's five or six floors, and a taller one that's maybe a dozen. I think it'd be safer going in the taller one. I can see some big air handlers and other stuff on the roof. The lower section has a huge skylight in the middle and a bunch of solar panels. There are cameras on the higher structure, but they're all pointing out or at the service door."

"She's right," Ed confirmed. "There's also an elevator machine space on the taller structure. It has a dedicated air handling system, Aleksi! You may be able to get in that way and access the elevator shaft, but it'll be tight. You've got twelve floors above ground and two below in the taller structure, six above and six below in the lower one."

"Let me get a look."

Persephone gritted her teeth. "Aleksi, you have to wait until we call in Jasper before you—"

"I'm only having a *look*, Seph! Calm down!"

"Give her a minute, Seph," Reggie said. "We haven't crossed the Rubicon yet."

"No, but our feet are wet," she shot back. Persephone pulled her claws from the seats and forced a breath, then another.

"The vent cover will come off, and I don't see any cameras or wires. I think we should try this, Persephone. If I can access the elevator shaft, I can search every floor by scent without exposing myself or setting off any alarms." The sound of something grating on metal came over the phone. "Text Jasper. I'm going in. Ed, I need you to guide me. There's a screen and a filter inside."

Persephone swallowed her heart and managed to speak without screaming. "Okay, we're a go. I'm making the call to Jasper." She pulled her phone and tapped up Jasper on her message app while Ed guided Aleksi in through the air duct. She sent, "O'Neill Building is the target! Go now!" and hit send.

Seconds later, she received, "Holy fuck! Okay. Cavalry on the way!"

"They're on the way, Aleksi. Wait until they arrive!"

"Fine." The sound of claws rending thin metal ceased. "I'm just looking at the duct. Not in yet. I'll wait for the lights and sirens to arrive."

In the moment of silence, Persephone's mind whirled ahead to her part of their job. They needed a way to get Hutch out. "Aleksi, is there an alley between the O'Neill and the building under construction?"

"Yes. That's on the low side of the building. It's narrow."

Narrow was bad. Aleksi needed some space if she was going to fall six floors with Hutch strapped to her and not crash. "How tall is the construction site next door?"

"Like a dozen floors higher than the O'Neill building."

"Okay. Do you think you could jump that gap with Hutch?"

"Yes, but I don't know if any of the cameras cover that side, and there are windows at that level. I'd have to smash through."

"Damn." Persephone's mind raced. "How about a construction crane?"

"Yes. There's one in the alley between the buildings."

"Excellent! And it'll reach the roof of the O'Neill?"

"As long as it'll rotate around that far, sure. It'll reach the lower roof near the middle."

"Okay, that's our way out. Ed, I want schematics of the elevators and stairwells in the O'Neill yesterday! I want floorplans of every floor above and below ground. They won't be holding Hutch in an office."

"That's just it, Seph, most of the building *is* offices," Ed confirmed. "Above ground, anyway. The plans for the levels below ground are classified. I have how *many* floors, and where the elevators and fire stairs are, but that's about it. Basic construction blueprints."

"That'll do," Aleksi said. "I can find him."

Persephone spoke through gritted teeth. "I hope so, Aleksi, because if you can't, you'll be trapped inside with the exits blocked by soldiers."

"You're such a fucking *optimist* tonight!" Aleksi growled back.

"Look on the bright side. We know where he is, and we've got a way in."

"It's the way *out* I'm worried about," Persephone countered.

***

The O'Neill building? Are you fucking *kidding* me, Tony?" Blake not only sounded incredulous but dumbfounded at the same time.

"There are very few things in this world I won't joke about, Anna, and a goddamn terrorist attack is pretty much on the top of that list." Tony tolerated a scowl from Marty as they got into their car. "I've already called Commander Fisk and unloaded. Cambridge PD is on the move." And Tony's job was on the line.

"And you trust this CI? I mean *really* trust them?"

"With my *life*, Anna. I'm sorry I can't give you any details, but I swear to you, this is legit. There's a credible terrorist threat on the O'Neill building! Personally, I'd rather respond to this threat and have it turn out to be nothing, than *not* respond and end up standing on the side of a crater in downtown Boston tomorrow morning that we could have prevented!"

A breath of silence, then Blake responded. "Fine, Tony. I'll pull the pin. Boston PD is moving, but I'm giving my commander *your* name!"

"Do that. My dick's already on the chopping block on this side of the river."

"I hope not," she said with a laugh. "I was hoping to make your dick's acquaintance someday."

Tony gaped like a gaffed fish, then cleared his throat. "Well, if it's not chopped off tonight, I'll see if I can arrange an appointment."

"Do that," she said with a chuckle. "Now I've gotta go. You just started an avalanche of shit, and I'm standing at the bottom of the hill."

"Yeah, I'm right there with you. My next call is to the O'Neill building. What's your ETA?"

"Maybe ten minutes at most for the big guns. We'll have patrol cars there in five."

"CPD's on the way. See you there!

"See you." The call ended, and Tony started pulling up the number for the Tip O'Neill Federal Building.

"You *sure* about this, Tony?" Marty asked as he pulled out of the parking lot and fired up the lights and siren.

"Yes," he said, sparing a look at his partner. "I'm more sure about this than I've been about anything since Derrick Penningly tore off the roof of my car."

"Fine, but if this doesn't pan out in some way shape or form, your ass will go down in flames."

"I know." Jasper found the number and dialed it. "Good thing I'm wearing fire-retardant boxer shorts."

Marty snorted a laugh and concentrated on driving. There were half a dozen black-and-whites along with them, and the street was lit up like Christmas.

The phone rang once and went straight to voice mail. "The Thomas 'Tip' O'Neill building is currently closed. Our normal operating hours are from eight a.m. to five p.m. Monday through Friday. Please call during those hours or leave a message after the tone. If this is an emergency, dial nine-one-one." A flat tone followed the message.

"This is Detective Sergeant Tony Jasper of the Cambridge Police Department, Homicide Division. I have received a credible threat of an imminent terrorist attack on the O'Neill Building from a trusted confidential informant. Cambridge PD and Boston PD are being mobilized. Please evacuate the building immediately." He ended the call and stuffed his phone into his jacket pocket.

"You really don't think they'll evacuate, do you?" Marty asked.

"Shit, Marty, I don't think they'll even *hear* that message until tomorrow morning, but at least I covered my ass."

"Right." They shot across the Charles River, blue lights strobing across the rain-swept water. "Why does shit like this always happen when it's raining?"

"Law of nature, I suppose." He stared out at the city he loved and gritted his teeth. "Or God just hates cops."

215

# 20

R eport." Buckmann watched the monitors with her hands clenched behind her back.

The triangulation of cellular signals from four different towers pinpointed the location of the call from Aleksi, but she doubted the dragon would still be there. She'd ordered her airborne unit to approach and reconnoiter from a distance. Four other monitors showed light-enhanced and thermal images from the helicopter's belly mounted camera and the helmet cam of the door gunner. She'd also given express orders not to engage Aleksi Rychenkna; after the catastrophe with David Gilford, they'd seen how poorly that would go.

"We have limited visibility but visual contact with the target area," the observer reported. "Negative contact with the suspect or any persons on the roof or around the structure. No movement. No heat signatures."

"Orbit at one thousand meters and report," Mary ordered. She turned to pace, and her shoe crunched on pieces of shattered plastic. "Comms, you made a clone of my original phone. I need the original back as soon as possible. Rychenkna will call back, and we need to be able to answer."

"Yes, ma'am. I'll have it in your hand in ten minutes." The man started tapping out an order on one of his screens.

"Also, I want a recording of that call on my desk system ASAP. Have voice analysis go over it. I want to know if she was lying to us."

"Yes, ma'am."

"Thank you." She turned to Benson, her field specialist. "Do we have any covert ground assets in the Braintree area that we can mobilize?"

"None, ma'am, and it'd take an hour to get them there in this weather. There's a snarl on the southern artery."

"Send a team anyway. If we get another call, I want someone nearby."

"A tactical team?" He glanced at her with a raised eyebrow.

"Yes, but put two plain-clothes operatives in with them."

"On the road in ten minutes, ma'am."

"Good." Mary started to pace again and bits of shattered cell phone crunched underfoot again. "And get maintenance in here to clean up this mess! Damn Hutchinson anyway for pitching a fit."

"Still no visible movement or heat signatures," the aerial observer reported. "There's some trash on the roof, but nothing else."

"Trash? What is it?"

"Construction materials, maybe. A tool box or old lunch cooler."

"No wires?" Since the explosion at the Terris estate, Mary had become paranoid of bombs.

"Too far to say. We can do a fly over if you want a closer look, ma'am."

Mary thought furiously; Aleksi wasn't there, probably miles away by now, but she might have left them something. "Yes. One low altitude fly over. Get as much on camera as you can. We'll have a unit there in an hour to inspect the site."

"Affirmative, ma'am." The observer relayed the order, and the helicopter banked in for a low pass. The best image they got from the roof showed a small lunch cooler beside a bucket of roofing scraps. "Looks like some maintenance worker left his lunch box, ma'am."

CHRIS A. JACKSON

"Looks like." She turned back to her communication specialist. "The call could have come from inside the building, too, right?"

"Yes, ma'am, but all the businesses are closed. She would have had to break in."

"Benson, tell the ground team to search for signs of break in when they arrive. Have them inspect the roof if they don't find anything." Recalling the police investigation of David Gilford's one and only successful covert op, she added, "Rychenkna leaves distinctive marks when she takes off and lands."

"Right away, ma'am."

Mary stepped out of the way as a tech arrived with a broom and dustpan. She watched the young man work, feeling like she'd missed something, but unable to say what that something was. She played the conversation back over in her mind again and again, and then shook her head. If only she could have talked to Aleksi after Hutchinson, she felt she could have assured her that they had no interest in punishing the professor any more than necessary. If Aleksi got her the cure, she would do as she promised. They could make up any story they liked, and the media would make a hero out of the man.

"Ma'am, we've got a call from building security. There seem to be several police cars arriving all around the building."

"What?" Mary whirled to stare blankly at the security tech. "How many?"

"More coming in as we speak. Ten units at least. Building Security's deploying people outside to see what's going on."

"Find out who's in charge. If this is a crank call, I'll have their balls on toast!"

---

The wail of sirens converging on the building sounded like music to Aleksi's ears. "Cavalry's here. I'm going in."

Ed came to her immediately through her earpiece. "Okay, beyond the HEPA filter, you should have about two meters of duct before the air handling fan. If you can cut through the duct wall, it'll put you in

218

the machine space. There's not a lot of room, but you should be able to get to the elevator shaft from there."

Aleksi tore the screen and replaceable HEPA filter out and bent the inner screen out of her way. She crawled into the space and pulled the louvered access panel back closed behind her. It wouldn't fool anyone under close inspection, but it might hide her ingress point from a helicopter. As she turned, the thin metal of the duct buckled under her weight with a loud bong, and she cringed.

"What was that?" Persephone asked over the earpiece.

"Nothing. Just the metal bending. Let me work."

"Not like the movies where people crawl for miles through ducts without a sound, huh?" Ed sounded amused.

Aleksi found a seam in the thin metal, inserted her claws, and peeled a piece back. That, of course, made even more noise, but the motors that ran the elevators and the air handling fan were running, too. She couldn't imagine anyone installing audio surveillance equipment in a machine space like this. Video and motion sensors, however, were distinct possibilities. The opening widened enough for her to peer through, her eyes piercing the darkness within easily.

"No cameras or motion sensors that I can see," she said. "Can you tell if I trip an alarm?"

"We're working on their security firewall now. We're into their utilities and safety systems, but the rest is harder. I miss Gi-gi."

"Don't we all," Persephone added. "We're coming up on the building now. There are police all over the place. God bless Tony Jasper."

Aleksi ignored their chatter and rolled down the metal wall of the duct like tin foil. The shearing metal made a tearing noise like ripping paper. When she had a hole big enough to fit through, she reached outside the duct, grabbed a support rod, and squirmed through, bending in ways few humans could match. Ed hadn't lied; there wasn't a lot of room inside. She slithered over electrical conduits, water pipes for air-conditioning, massive electrical motors and cable spoolers, and finally found a narrow catwalk around the elevator shafts. A metal stair led down to a service door, but that wasn't the route Aleksi would take.

"I'm at the shafts."

"Should be three of them. The shafts aren't separated by solid walls, so you should be fine. If an elevator starts up while you're going down, just move to another shaft."

"Okay, I'm going down." Aleksi started down, crawling head-first, her claws finding easy purchase on the steel frame supporting the elevators. Cables descended into the darkness in all three shafts. "Two of them are moving."

"The offices are closed, so it's probably security responding to the police arrival. They shouldn't go any higher than the ground floor."

"Great." Aleksi was beginning to think of Ed as her guardian angel. Then she had a horrible thought. "Will I lose our phone connection inside all this metal and concrete?"

"Nope. I'm already into their comm network; not their mainframe, but their cellular network. They have cell boosters all over the place. You should keep a solid signal."

"They won't detect a new connection?" Persephone asked.

"Shouldn't. The system's automatic for guests. About ten thousand new connections every day. We're a needle in a haystack, Cuz."

"Good." Aleksi stopped at the first pair of elevator doors and gripped the steel frame with her toes, leaving her hands free. Even though they didn't think Hutch would be held on an upper floor, she wasn't taking any chances. She inserted her claws into the gap between the doors and pulled them open just enough to scent the air outside. She breathed deep, searching through the myriad aromas for the one she sought: Hutch.

Nothing.

She released her grip and moved on. *Only seventeen more floors to go.*

S howtime!" Tony got out of their car before the wheels even stopped rolling. He would be the ranking CPD officer on site, but this wasn't his turf. The rain plastered his hair flat as he waved over a uniformed Cambridge sergeant in a rain slicker. "Fredricks! We coordinate with Detective Blake. Her turf, her call. We support and report. Got it?"

"Sure, Detective." The big man grinned, his white teeth glowing against his dark skin. "Shoulda brought your wellies."

"Right." Tony flipped up the collar of his jacket and scanned the scene as Willis joined him with an umbrella. "You came prepared at least."

"Always." Marty pointed to the building's main entrance. "There's Blake. Looks like she's chewing ass."

"Hope so." They started over, and BPD officers waved them through. He picked up Anna's no-bullshit tone ten steps away.

"And I'm telling *you*, Captain, that we have a credible warning of an imminent attack on this building! A Cambridge detective has a CI inside their organization. You *have* to evacuate the building!"

"With all due respect, Detective, that's impossible." The man put his hands on his hips and shook his head. He was backed by a dozen security guards, and there were more inside.

"How do you figure having a confidential informant inside a terrorist organization is impossible? How the *hell* do you think they bagged Bin Laden?"

"Not that, ma'am. I'm telling you it's impossible to evacuate the building. We have immobile assets inside. I can warn the section chief and inform the director, but there is no way on God's green earth that we can evacuate this building."

"Well, that just sucks, Captain!" Blake folded her arms and sighed. "At least let us search for explosives. We've got dog teams here."

"I can let you search the office levels, Detective, but only under supervision. I'm afraid the basement floors are off limits. We'll handle those ourselves." He waved his people forward. "My men will accompany your dog teams inside. That's the best I can do."

"Well, that's something, anyway. Thank you, Captain. We'll set up a perimeter. If this attack comes from outside, maybe a hundred cops will scare them away." She glanced around and spotted Tony standing only feet away. She nodded to him, then her eyes focused beyond him. "Well, shit! Who called the fucking *media?*"

Jasper turned to find several news vans pulling up outside the cordon of police cars. Lights, cameras, and well-dressed field reporters were already being disgorged. "Well, I wonder how *that* happened?" He muttered.

"You're really a bitch sometimes, you know that, Tony." Marty gave him his patented *you are so full of shit,* look.

"That I am." He grinned and yelled to Sergeant Fredricks to tape off the area, then turned back to Blake. "We'll keep the jackals at bay, Detective. You take care of business."

"Thanks, Tony." Blake turned back to the security captain, and Tony descended the steps to the cordon of police cars. He resisted the urge to look up into the rain-streaked sky, knowing that a certain dragon would be winging in soon.

Little did he know that she was already inside the building.

## 21

Mary turned to a monitor filled with Security Chief Harris's concerned features. "What the hell's going on outside, Harris?"

"Reports from building security state that Boston Police Department received what they're calling a 'credible threat' of a terrorist attack on the building."

"A *terrorist* attack? Who's in charge of the BPD?" Mary would bring an avalanche down on their heads with one call to the director.

"A Homicide Detective named Blake."

"Blake?" Mary ground her teeth. "This has got to be coming from Tony Jasper. Look at the outside camera feeds and find me Jasper. Bring him in and grill him. I want to know what the *hell* prompted this."

"They're insisting they have a credible confidential informant inside a terrorist organization, ma'am." Harris cocked an eyebrow at her. "If this *is* coming from Jasper, it may be real."

"This is the same asshole who sheltered Hutchinson from us, Harris. You think he'd call in a real threat?"

"He's a cop, ma'am. If he had an inside line, I think he would if there were lives at stake. They're insisting the building be evacuated, but we both know that's impossible."

"Hell yes, it's impossible." Mary clenched her hands behind her back so hard her knuckles cracked, visions of the Terris estate being engulfed in white flames looming in her mind. "Still, bring Jasper inside and find out where this is coming from. I want the name of his CI, and *exactly* what they told him."

"Yes, ma'am. Security is allowing the BPD bomb teams to the upper floors. They've got dogs."

"Fine, but no police come down here."

"Of course not." He nodded once again. "I'll keep you posted."

Mary paced and tried to think this through. She didn't believe in coincidences like this. Jasper could be pulling their chain in retribution for what they'd done to Hutchinson, but the very same night Aleksi calls? No, something was going on.

She turned to a tech. "I want to see Hutchinson's cell."

"Yes, ma'am."

After a rattle of keys, a monitor came up with four light-enhanced views of a cell. Dwayne Hutchinson lay on his bunk, but his eyes were open. He lay there staring into the dark, his hands folded over his chest. Mary ran through the conversation between him and Aleksi again in her head but came up with a blank. Aleksi was fifteen miles south in Braintree. The Terris family, however, could be right next door for all she knew.

"Get me a recording of the conversation between Hutchinson and Rychenkna. I want to listen to it."

"Yes, ma'am."

*Could this be real? Could Aleksi be Jasper's CI?* If she really did have a falling out with the Terrises, she might warn Jasper of an attack.

"Inform our security people that we may have a situation. Anyone not on duty is to report to the ground floor. External video feeds are to be monitored at all times. Anything twitches, we go into full armed response."

Her people put the order through, scrambling her off-duty security personnel. Mary resumed pacing and swore under her breath. *I'm missing something. I can feel it.*

---

J esus, I never knew there were so many police in Boston." Carrie turned onto Causeway Street and stopped for Reggie to get out and pan his shoulder camera around. When he got back in, she motored past the massed police cars and news vehicles as if searching for a parking place. There wasn't one to be had.

"Some are Cambridge cops." Reggie pointed down Causeway Street. "That's the alley. Drive past and pull a U-turn."

"If I get a ticket for an illegal U-turn..."

"I think the police have bigger issues on their mind," Persephone said.

Carrie drove past the alley, and Persephone glanced up the dark path. A barrier of chain-link and plywood separated the construction site from the ground floor of the O'Neill Building. Police stood at the corner behind a barrier of yellow tape, but they couldn't block the entrance to North Station there. They formed a cordon with some under the shelter of the subway entrance, but there were none in the alley itself. She pointed to the darkest stretch of the street.

"There. Turn around and park. You do your thing, and I'll get out the back."

"You sure you don't want us to go around the block?" Carrie asked.

"No, this is fine. I've got to get up to that construction crane." She would have some climbing to do, but the facing on the building wasn't complete yet. She would find a way up.

"Okay." Carrie made a U-turn, pulled over to the curb, and flipped on her high beams. "Showtime, Cuz."

Carrie and Reggie got out, the former with a microphone and umbrella in hand, and Reggie with his shoulder camera and a lighting rig. Carrie posed and Reggie turned on his lights. Between the van's high-beams and his lights, they would spoil the dark vision of any cop who happened to look their way.

Persephone cracked the back door of the mocked-up news van, checked for traffic, and got out. A quick glance around the corner of the van to check for people, and she cinched the straps of her pack tight, vaulted the six-foot concrete and chain link barrier, and dashed across the short distance into the construction site.

A dark maze of partially finished walls, stairs, steel, and glass festooned with construction supplies and equipment engulfed her. She worked her way through the labyrinth to the taller structure and found a stairway. It was a long climb to the top taking the stairs, and her legs were burning when she got there. The door to the roof was locked, which seemed ridiculous. Persephone gripped the handle with both gloved hands and twisted it hard. Something inside snapped, and the door swung open onto the rain-soaked roof.

"With me, Ed?" she asked as she traversed the cluttered roof to the crane.

"I'm here. Working on schematics for Aleksi. What do you need?"

"I need a crash course on how to operate a tower crane."

"I'll put someone on it."

At the edge of the building, Persephone squinted through the slashing rain, down at the O'Neill building and the alley far below. There were support girders from the roof to the crane, I-beams about ten inches wide. Swallowing her apprehension, she walked across the dizzying drop to the side of the crane, scrambled through the frame to the ladder, and started climbing. At the top of every section, the ladder opened to a small platform and another ladder. These, she supposed, kept people from falling more than a few yards if they missed their grip. They would slow her descent if she had to leave in a hurry, however. The climb used different muscles than the stairs had, so she reached the top without too much fatigue. There, however, she found the door to the control cab locked.

"First things first, Persephone."

She worked her way up over the control cab and started out along the steel catwalk to the very end of the crane's boom. The rain didn't help, but her gloved hands and rubber-soled boots offered sure grips on the slick metal. At the end, she stepped over the guardrail and clambered down to the cable itself. She'd never had a fear of heights, but the dizzying drop with absolutely nothing beneath her made her stomach lurch. At the massive pulley, she shrugged out of her pack, clipped a carabiner around the cable, and let it go. The pack fell to the weighted ball at the end of the cable and hung there. She climbed back up and traversed quickly back to the control cab.

The door to the cab had a glass panel, but Persephone assumed it was safety glass. Instead of trying to smash it, she extended her claws through the fingertips of her gloves and tore the rubber gasket out from around the window. The panel popped out with a little persuasion. She set it aside, reached through, and worked the latch from the inside. The cab had a single seat with toggle controls on each armrest, and a panel for starting up the main motor.

"Okay, Ed. I need some instruction."

"You're lucky that construction companies have shit for network security. The motor's electric and should have power. There is a main switch on the panel that powers the motor. It's key access, so you'll have to deal with that. The main switch should be under a transparent safety cover."

"Found it." She clawed the cover off and pulled her electronic lock pick from her fanny pack. It slipped into the lock easily, and she worked the controls. When the tiny LED flickered green, she turned it. Something clicked behind the panel, and lights came on in the cab. "Shit! The lights just came on in here. Give me a second."

Her claws made short work of lighting fixtures and plunged the cab back into darkness. She breathed easier. "Okay, that's better. Now, I assume I sit in this comfy chair."

"Yes. You have two toggles. The right hand controls the cable itself; away from you spools cable out, toward you brings it in. The farther you push and pull, the faster the cable spools. The left toggle is swing, just right and left with a dial around the base for braking. Forward and back runs the carriage in and out. It's pretty simple, really."

"Good. Let me get the hang of this." The federal building was lit up, but the tower crane was dark, and the sky pitch black. Even if someone did look up, they'd be light-blind, and wouldn't see the crane's arm. She started carefully experimenting, turning the crane slowly outward from the construction site, then running the pully carriage in far enough to keep from interfering with anything on the federal building's roof. "Who the hell puts solar panels on a government building, anyway? Aleksi, how are you doing?"

"I'm busy dodging elevators. All three are running now, and cops and security are exploring the upper floors. They've got dogs, so I skipped a few floors. Dunno if I ever told you, but dogs don't like my scent. If they pitch a fit, we're in trouble. I'm one level below the street. Hang on."

Persephone ran the cable down partway, then stopped. Someone might spot a cable descending to the roof on one of the security cameras. Unfortunately, there was nothing else for her to do but wait.

"Nothing on B1, going to B2," Aleksi reported.

"How are you doing on their mainframe, Ed?"

"Slow. We're flogging a dead horse here, Seph. It'll take us hours."

"But you're in their comm system and environmental controls?"

"Yes. I can even turn on their sprinkler system if you really want to piss on their parade."

Persephone grinned to herself. That would certainly cause a distraction. "Maybe later."

"Nothing on B2, and I'm out of floors," Aleksi announced. "I need to get to the other half of the building. It has more floors below ground. Get me to the other bank of elevators."

"Floorplan's up," Ed chimed in. "Go up one floor, then exit the elevator and go left."

"Opening the door wide enough to get out won't set off an alarm?" Persephone asked.

"I doubt it," Ed said, but he didn't sound certain. "If it does, we'll know right away."

"That's not very comforting," Aleksi said. Then she asked, "What's on B1? It smells funny."

"Looks like a lot of piping and air handling equipment for the lower levels, from the plumbing and electrical schematics, but watch your step. They might have guards and cameras. All the lower levels are key access only."

"I'm opening the elevator doors now."

Persephone held her breath, waiting for the sound of an alarm.

---

Aleksi clawed the elevator doors open barely wide enough to peer through. Until now, she'd only needed a gap of a couple millimeters to sniff the air, but now she needed to see. The hall was lit only by recessed safety lights, the main fluorescent panels dark. It smelled of oil and hot metal in here, like the bay of an auto repair shop. She could hear the hum of electric motors, pumps, fans, and felt an underlying vibration through her claws. A domed security camera stood out from the ceiling right above the center elevator in the bank of three. If someone was monitoring it, they might have already seen her peering out from the cracked doors.

"There's a CCTV camera on the ceiling here," she whispered into her mic. "One of the black domed ones."

"Can you see a brand name on it?"

"No. It's got a white beveled housing about five inches across."

"That's good. It's not one of the high-end Sonys. Probably a Lorex. Good that the government goes to the lowest bidder. The housing's aluminum. Can you reach it from the elevator?"

"From the top, yes, but if I take it out, won't it set off an alarm?"

"Probably. We should have given you a can of spray paint! Damn!"

"Well, I can't just sit here. Maybe if I—"

"Wait! Is that a drop ceiling, or solid concrete?" Ed asked.

Aleksi peered out and up at the panels of acoustic tiles. "A drop ceiling."

"The space above it is probably eighteen inches. If you can get in there, can you crawl along the supports?"

"Yes, but there's no access to it from the elevator shaft."

"But the camera's most likely panning the hallways, not the space between it and the elevators. They pan back and forth, not three-sixty. Is there a ceiling panel between the camera and the elevator?"

"Yes." Aleksi's teeth chirped as she ground them together. "So, you're suggesting I reach out from the top of the elevator door, pop out the panel, and crawl into the drop ceiling space without being seen by the camera a few feet away? *Really?*"

"Um...yeah. Can you do that?"

"I've no idea, but I guess we'll find out."

Persephone muttered a curse over the line but didn't object to the insane plan.

Aleksi maneuvered to an inverted position above the elevator door and pulled the doors open wide enough to slip an arm through. Listening to the tiny electric motor that controlled the camera, she reached out and placed three clawed fingertips against the ceiling panel as close to the center as she could manage. She pressed, and the panel tilted off balance. Cursing to herself, she extended her claws into the soft acoustic material and lifted again.

It came free of its bed with a slight scrape.

Aleksi froze and listened to the hum of the camera's electric motor rotating the lens back and forth without pause. She moved the panel aside and lowered it carefully, extricating her claws from the board. That left her about a foot and a half of opening to slip through.

Again, she listened to the rotating camera. It made its arc in about ten seconds, then stopped and reversed. If she moved when it was in the middle of its arc, the lens should be pointing away from the elevators, and she would have a chance of not being seen. She listened; the motor stopped and started again. She counted to four and moved.

Months of experience slipping silently through tight places paid off. She kept her wings folded back, gripped with her fingers and toes, and wormed up through the open panel. Her hip brushed the loose board, jostling it, but she was through in two seconds, latching onto the support frame bolted into the concrete ceiling. Just like Ed had said, she had eighteen inches between the drop ceiling and the concrete one. Plenty of room.

"Okay, I'm in."

"Wow! Excellent." Ed chuckled nervously. "So, turn left from the elevators and keep going until you find a solid wall."

Aleksi followed his directions, crawling along inverted like one of the alien monsters in that SciFi movie that had scared the crap out of her a lifetime ago. A twisting route took her from the taller half of the building to the shorter half. She lifted drop ceiling panels a few times to get her bearings. Eventually, she found the other elevator bank, this one also with a security camera mounted in front of the middle pair of doors. This time, slipping from the drop ceiling to the elevator went easier. She might have wrenched the doors open a little hard, but she was through in less than two seconds and closed them softly behind her. Thankfully, the elevator hadn't been on this floor.

"I'm in the shaft and headed down to the deeper sub-levels. Still no alarms?"

"Nothing on our end, and Reggie reports no change in activity on the street. Persephone?"

"All I can see is the roof. So far, it hasn't done anything." She sounded both bored and nervous.

"I'm at the doors for B2. Hang on." Aleksi inserted her claws in the door and pried it open wide enough to draw in air through her nose and mouth.

*Guns!* the scent screamed in her head, sending lightning arcing through her nerves.

She froze, senses heightened to a fever-pitch, attuned for threats. Two men stood very nearby, their breathing and heartbeats muffled but audible. One shuffled his feet, and something creaked, a strap or belt. *Guards*, she thought with a silent curse. *Shit just got real.*

Aleksi breathed in once again and tried to sort through the thousands of scents, difficult with the two men so close. She caught a familiar scent, the olfactory image in her mind clicking onto a memory. A woman in the dark under a concrete amphitheater dome in Boston Common Park, turning to face her, fear in her eyes; Mary Buckmann. She was on this floor. Aleksi's teeth ground together. Then she caught a bare whiff of that warm, spicy, Hutch scent that she knew so very well. He'd been here, but the scent was so faint that it felt like he'd only passed this way. Of course, she was at the entrance to an elevator, so hundreds of people had passed this way. From the lazy demeanor of the guards, she assumed she hadn't set off any alarms yet, so she let the doors gently close and moved farther down the shaft.

Between floors, she whispered, "I caught a faint scent of Hutch on B2, but there were guards at the elevator door. Buckmann's on that floor, too. Only four more floors left. I'm moving down."

Nobody replied.

"Anybody there?"

"We're here, Aleksi. No worries."

*No worries...* A bubble of sardonic mirth almost escaped, but she fought it down. Now wasn't the time for a fit of nervous laughter.

At the next two floors, she encountered guards at each elevator door, stationed identically to those above, but no scent of Hutch. She reported her findings and descended. As she cracked the doors to B5 and drew a silent breath, her head exploded with the scent she'd been longing for.

*Hutch!*

He was here, and the scent was strong. There were also, of course, two guards stationed at the elevator doors. She eased the doors closed and whispered. "He's on B5. Strong scent. But there are two guards at the doors and no way around them." She swallowed hard and made a decision. "I've got to go through them. Get ready. All hell's about to break loose."

"You can't use the drop ceiling to get past them?" Ed asked.

"No way. They'd hear me lift the panel and shoot me." She lowered herself to stand in the doorway, her clawed toes gripping the floor, and clutched the crack between the doors with her fingers. "If I'm fast, they won't have a chance. I'll take out the camera, too, but they'll know what's happening in seconds anyway. There's no other way."

"Okay. The stairwell is in the southeast corner if you need it. It goes all the way to the roof. The elevator doesn't."

"Got it." Aleksi took a deep breath, jerked the doors open, and lashed out with one clawed foot.

The blow caught the man in the small of the back, just off center. He was airborne before he had time to react or even scream, and hit the nearby wall with a crunch of body armor and bone. The other guard started to turn, his rifle coming up, but Aleksi grabbed the muzzle, pushed it away, and struck him with a clenched fist in the solar plexus. His body armor soaked up some of the blow, but he folded over. His finger seized on the trigger, sending a burst of bullets down the hallway.

*Well, crap! So much for stealth.*

Aleksi tried to wrench the gun from his grasp, but it was secured with a strap. Her jerk sent him into the wall headfirst. Fortunately, he wore a riot helmet, so the impact didn't splash his brains all over the place. Still, he crumpled to the floor, senseless.

The other guard was moving, barely, but still had his rifle. Aleksi took the time to rip the security camera off the ceiling, then pounced on him, grabbing the rifle and bending the barrel. He was struggling to breathe, but his eyes were open. Stark terror painted his face white. She pulled him up so their faces were an inch apart and hissed through clenched teeth, "Stay *down!*" Then she tore away his earpiece and holstered pistol and pitched them into the open elevator shaft.

"Every fed on the street just stopped and cupped their ear!" Reggie said over the line. "I think the shit just hit the fan."

"Move, Aleksi!" Persephone snapped. "I'm lowering the hook now."

Aleksi *moved*.

# 22

---

ecurity breach, level B5! Two men down, and a security camera disabled!"

"*What?*" Mary whirled to the security station. "B5 is Hutchinson! Show me!"

The brief video showed a guard flying across the scene to hit the far wall and crumple to the floor. Three muzzle flashes lit the screen, then, as the lens swiveled to track another image, a clawed hand loomed into view and the image went dark.

"Shit! That's Rychenkna!" A ball of terror ignited in Mary's gut. The dragon was here, in the building. *She's here for Hutchinson, not me!* At least she hoped that was the case. "Full alert! Lock every door and secure the elevators! Bring up every camera on that floor and warn Hutchinson's guards that—"

"She's taking out cameras as she goes, ma'am!" The screen flashed up in split view, a winged golden blur, then blackness, one after another. "Go*damn* she's fast!"

Visions of the video Mary had seen of Gilford laying waste to the facility in Waltham revisited her memory. Nineteen dead, including the former director. Still, she had to respond, and there was only one way.

"Get all teams down there, now!" Of course, two thirds of her people were on the ground floor dealing with the police presence. *Goddamn Tony Jasper*, she swore under her breath. This had been carefully coordinated. Mary winced as another camera went dead. "How the *hell* did she get in?"

"The team we lost was guarding the elevators. She may have come down the shaft."

"Damn it! Block the shaft. Put all three elevators in that bank to B1 and lock them there! Send our teams down the stairs. Alert the lower floors and evacuate all non-combat personnel up to B2. She got in, but she can't get out! Tell the teams on B5 that she'll go to Hutchinson. Ambush her there."

The comm tech sent the orders.

Another camera went dead, this one without even getting a glimpse of Rychenkna. *How the hell does she know where the lens is pointing?* Then one of the few remaining caught her at the far end of a hall as she came around a corner. Mary caught her breath. She'd seen plenty of video of Rychenkna, and even met her once, but she'd never seen her like this. The dragon barreled around the corner like a streak of golden lightning, wings billowing, claws gouging concrete, yellow eyes wide, and teeth bared. She banked up a wall with the momentum of her turn, chips of concrete flying as her claws scrabbled for purchase. The golden eyes fixed on the video camera, and she charged.

Mary imagined in that span of less than a second that this was what the soldiers Gilford had killed saw in the last moments of their lives. The dragon came so fast that the camera couldn't focus. A blur, the flash of claws, and the feed went dead.

*Dead...*

Mary swallowed hard. She'd thought she'd been hunting Aleksi in Braintree, and the converse had been true. They'd been set up. The conversation with Hutchinson was a diversion, a ploy. Somehow, they had found out where they were keeping him. Mary patted the pocket of her jacket where her absent phone had once resided.

"Get me Harris! IT, we've got a network breech! Implement cyber-security countermeasures. I think they tracked the incoming call to my phone. Shut down our internal cellular network. They may be using it."

"Yes, ma'am."

Her security chief's face came up on a monitor. "We're locking off the elevators and sending troops down the stairs, ma'am. They won't get out."

"Good. We've also got a potential network breech. Our comm system may be compromised, but we need it. Our cellular network may be how they found us. I'm shutting that down."

"Yes, ma'am."

"And get BPD the hell out of the building. They're lining up to be collateral damage at this point!"

"Already being done. The entire building's on phase one lockdown."

"Excellent!" Harris was showing initiative. "There's only one way out of there! We block that, and they have nowhere to go."

"Yes, ma'am. We're on it."

"And they've got to have assets outside. Rychenkna can't hope to fly out of here with Hutchinson. Get two airborne assets on site ASAP."

"Right. Making the call now."

She nodded and turned away. Technicians were carrying on low conversations with their networks, reporting camera outages, relaying her orders, and conversing with soldiers. A map of the floor showed the outages in red, more than half the floor. Hutchinson's cell was up on another monitor from the inside; he was up, staring at the door, his eyes wide, clearly terrified. He'd undoubtedly heard the gunfire. Another view came up on a monitor, the shaky image of a helmet cam, a leveled weapon, another soldier moving with him.

"Give me audio on that feed," she ordered.

"Yes, ma'am." One keystroke brought the audio up.

"Form up! Video feeds to the south is dead, but she could come from either end."

"Affirmative." The view panned, and Mary saw there were four soldiers, two facing one direction, two the other. She recognized the corridor. They were standing outside Hutchinson's cell.

"Does anyone else have helmet cams?"

"Only the unit leader, ma'am," The tech responded.

Mary glanced at the map of the floor. Like many detention facilities, it sported parallel corridors with cells situated back to back. Rychenkna had taken out cameras on the next parallel corridor. One feed still remained on one end of this one, but the other had been destroyed. The leader's helmet cam fixed on the end of the hallway. Wires dangled from the ceiling where the domed camera had been ripped away.

"Where the hell is she?" Mary whispered.

"No fix on the intruder, ma'am." The question had been rhetorical, but the information was welcome.

Mary knew Aleksi was here for Hutchinson, and the team had open fields of fire thirty feet in both directions. The trap was set. Even a dragon wasn't fast enough to evade that kind of kill zone. She felt a pang of remorse; the only psychologically stable *Homo draconis* in the world was about to be killed.

*But where the hell is she?*

Something cracked over the audio feed and the view whirled. The video camera from the end of the hall swiveled to track. The soldier's helmet cam showed a flash of white, jerked with an impact, then tumbled. A weapon fired a burst, and someone screamed.

"What the *fuck?*" the comm tech swore.

The helmet cam focused on a sideways view of the floor, legs and clawed feet. A soldier left his feet and flew into another. A clawed foot came down a few inches from the helmet cam, talons grating against the concrete floor. Another weapon fired, and the dragon spun low, wings billowing, under the spray of bullets, too fast to target.

The hall camera came to bear, and Mary saw what had happened. A broken ceiling tile lay in pieces among three of the four fallen soldiers. She'd come down from the drop ceiling.

The dragon gripped the weapon of the fourth soldier, thrusting the muzzle away as more bullets sprayed the wall, gouging out chunks of concrete. He reached for his sidearm, but she was too fast. A clawed hand closed on his forearm and bones cracked like dry twigs. He screamed.

Aleksi slammed him against a wall, claws embedded in the man's Kevlar vest, her bared teeth an inch from his face. The audio pickup caught her growled, "That wasn't very *nice!*" She released him and grasped his rifle, bending the barrel. He slid to the floor, cradling his shattered arm. One of the other fallen soldiers moved, and she tore his weapons away and flung them down the hall. "Now, if you want to *live*, don't fucking *move!*"

Mary swallowed hard as Aleksi's attention fixed on the live camera. Four combat veteran soldiers had been taken down in seconds. She'd known exactly where they were and how to get at them—this from a socially repressed graduate student. As Aleksi approached the camera and raised a clawed hand to destroy it, Mary longed for a platoon of dragons at her command. Maybe that, *only* that, would keep Aleksi from killing her as she'd promised. She turned to watch Hutchinson's cell cameras, impotent and, she had to admit, afraid of what she had set into motion.

"She warned me," Mary mumbled to herself. "She warned me, but I didn't listen."

---

We lost our connection to Aleksi," Ed announced.

"No shit," Persephone snapped. Listening to the screams and gunfire over the open line while sitting in this damned chair with her hands shaking on the crane controls had been bad enough. When everything suddenly went silent, she had to fight the urge to climb out and slide down the cable to help. "How?"

"They shut down their entire internal cellular network. Someone must have realized that we were using it. We can't reestablish the connection because the network's completely down, and Aleksi's too deep in the structure for an outside signal to get through."

Persephone's mind raced. "Okay, so we can't talk to her. Instead of concentrating on what we *can't* do, let's find something we *can* do. How do we help her?"

"Diversion?" Reggie suggested. "We might draw off a few of the security force."

"Most of the building security are still tied up on the ground floor," Ed said. He'd hacked into traffic cams and had views of three sides of the building. "Whatever force Buckmann's using, they're not standard security guards, anyway."

"No, they're probably special ops soldiers." Persephone bit her lip, again resisting the urge to burst into the building herself. *Think, Persephone, think! Use your damned brain!* "Buckmann can't have that many. We'll just have to trust Aleksi to handle this on her own. Save the diversion for their escape."

"If there *is* an escape," Reggie said.

"There *will* be. There *has* to be." Persephone kept her eyes trained on the stairwell door to the roof hundreds of feet below. "They may know Aleksi's inside, and they may even think they know what she's capable of, but they've also got to be pissing their pants right now. Gilford tore apart one of their facilities from the inside trying to escape."

"They've meddled in the affairs of dragons," Ed said.

"Yes, they have." She breathed in and tried to calm her singing nerves. "Keep pinging Aleksi's phone. When she gets above ground level, we should get a signal."

"Will do," Ed assured her.

"Until then, we wait."

---

Hutch backed to the far side of his cell as bullets pinged against his door, thankful for the first time for the armored barrier. Of course, only one thing could elicit such a response from his guards, and that irrevocable fact caused him more concern than the prospect of being hit by a stray bullet.

"Aleksi... God, no." As screams and dull impacts reached him through steel and concrete, he imagined her beautiful golden skin bullet riddled and bleeding, his fault. She was coming here for him. "Please, don't..."

There was silence for a heartbreakingly long few seconds, then a grating sound came through his door. Metal groaned, then, with a twang, the cell door flew open. The harsh blue-white lights gleamed off of golden scales, wings, and vibrant yellow eyes.

"Aleksi!" He took a step, but she was faster. Her wings enfolded him, warm, living, and unriddled with bullets. Outside the door, however, several soldiers lay on the floor. "What have you done?"

"Nothing I didn't have to do, Hutch." She released him, and her eyes flashed around the cell. "Nothing they didn't force me to do. I haven't killed anyone yet. Now, let's get the hell out of here."

She pulled him into the hall, and he paused to look down at the fallen soldiers. They all seemed to be breathing, though a few were bent in ways that human bodies generally didn't bend. "Aleksi, you shouldn't have done this. It's a *trap*. This is exactly what they wanted, why they took me in the first place."

How she'd managed to take them down without killing any of them he had no idea, but he admired her restraint. How she'd gotten in here in the first place mystified him, but she was here. Still, getting out would be an entirely different story. He considered picking up a rifle or pistol, then decided against it. With Aleksi at his side, guns seemed a little redundant, and would only risk one of the soldiers considering him a big enough danger to shoot.

"Then Mary Buckmann is a fucking idiot." She pulled him down the corridor. "I warned her. She should have known better than to try to trap a dragon."

"They're also probably *listening* to us!" he hissed, low enough for her to hear, but hopefully not loud enough for the microphones in his cell to pick up.

She stopped and turned to him, pulling him close, pitching her voice low also. "If I make her mad, she won't be thinking clearly. Now, we have to get out of here, and I just lost my connection to my family, so we're on our own."

"Your *family?*"

"*Our* family. Persephone's family." She gripped his hand and tugged him along. "You have to stick with me and do what I say, Hutch. They're coming for us. I can hear them in the stairwell, and as far as I know that's one of only two ways out of here. Okay?"

He nodded, taken aback by the tempered steel in her tone. "Then. Let's go." He followed her quickly through the hallways, his mind racing. "How the hell did you *find* me, anyway?"

"Buckmann's cell phone." She flashed a cringing smile and squeezed his hand. "Sorry, but I called you to track you down."

He'd wondered about the real reason for her risking discovery to talk to him, but she'd misunderstood his question. "No, well, yes, but... I mean this is a *big* place. How did you find out where they were holding me?"

"Oh. Your scent." She paused at the corner to the hall with the elevators, cocking her head and breathing in deeply. She released his hand and raised one clawed finger. "Hang on a second. Stay here."

"Sure, but—"

Before he could finish, she darted around the corner, clawed toes scratching the floor. Fearing the worst, he edged forward, back pressed against the wall. When gunfire didn't erupt, he leaned to peek around the corner.

Aleksi stood over two soldiers lying on the floor. She clutched one by the collar, his pale face an inch from hers. He held a pistol in one hand, but her clawed fingers encircled the weapon.

"I told you to stay down," she growled in a most un-Aleksi-like voice. The plastic grip of the pistol cracked, and the soldier grimaced in pain.

"Aleksi! Don't kill him!" Hutch lunged around the corner.

She glanced at him, and her bared teeth sent a chill up his spine. "I won't, but I really *should*!" She wrenched the pistol from the terrified man's grip and tossed it down the open elevator shaft, turning her attention back to the soldier. "They tried to kill me."

"Orders!" the soldier stammered. "Following orders!"

"He's right, Aleksi." Hutch put a hand on her shoulder, felt the muscles trembling beneath her golden skin. "He's just a soldier."

"Fine. Then follow *this* order." She flung the man aside, but not so hard that he hit the opposite wall. "Stay down!"

Hutch breathed a sigh of relief and knelt to check the other soldier. He was breathing, but deeply unconscious. Aleksi leaned into the elevator shaft and looked up into the darkness.

"Damn! They've blocked all three shafts a few floors up." She turned and unsheathed her claws. "We'll have to take the stairwell." She glanced around and retrieved an unmangled rifle from down the hall. "Can you use this?"

"I suppose so, but I really don't want to kill anyone." He took the weapon. It was surprisingly light.

"Neither do I, but I don't want to be strapped to a table and cut open, either." She stared down the hall.

"Wait, Aleksi!" A thought that had been in the back of his mind for days bubbled to the surface. "You said you found me by scent. Could you find someone else?"

She turned to him. "If I know them, yes." she breathed in the air. "Buckmann?"

"No. They showed me a live video feed of Lori Watkins. They've got her sedated, and I think she was in this building."

"Hutch, I don't know if I can get *you* out of here. I can't carry an unconscious woman and—"

"They're going to *euthanize* her, Aleksi." He stepped up and put a hand on her arm, lowering his voice. "And they know we're on this floor. If we go to another, maybe we can get around them."

"I don't..." Her head jerked, and she tensed. "They're coming. Come on." She pulled him back toward the bank of elevators.

"I thought you said they blocked the shafts."

"They did. We're not going up. We're going down." She paused at the open door and peered over the edge.

"Why down?"

"Because I've scented the air on every other floor of this building and smelled no other dragon. If they've got Lori here, she's down there." She nodded to him. "Strap that over your shoulder and hold onto me. Be quiet. There'll be guards down there."

Hutch shut up and did as he was told, wrapping both arms over her shoulders to grasp her without choking. She then simply reached into the shaft, and his feet left the floor. Biting back a curse, he blinked in the comparative darkness. Light from the floor above gleamed off of steel rails and machinery at the bottom of the shaft.

Aleksi stopped at the three double doors to the lowest floor, perching easily on the ledge with two clawed feet and one hand. She inserted her claws into the gap and forced them apart a bare sliver. He felt her take a deep breath, then she released her grip on the doors and turned her head to whisper.

"She's here. Two guards at the middle door."

"Okay," he whispered back. "Put me down."

The floor to the shaft was only three feet below the doors, so she just stepped off.

Hutch released her and took the rifle off his shoulder. "Door number one, two, or three?"

Aleksi glanced at him, then at the three doors. "Tell you what; you make some noise against this door, and I'll go through the far one."

It made sense. "Okay."

"And stay low. They might shoot through the doors."

Hutch swallowed. "Okay."

Aleksi crept through the steel framework between the shafts to the far pair of doors. He could barely see her in the dark, but the faint light gleamed on her scales as she climbed up. Hutch waited a few heartbeats, and then crouched low and slammed the butt of his rifle against the doors above his head.

Voices reached him, and the clatter of metal. Then, in a flash, Aleksi was through the far doors. A crash, and a short burst of gunfire. *Please don't get shot, please don't get shot.* Hutch scrambled to the far elevator shaft and peered cautiously up over the lip of the open doors. Metal and plastic cracked, and a destroyed security camera clattered past the opening.

*Thank you.* He grabbed the lip of the floor and vaulted up.

Aleksi stood over the two fallen guards, glaring at another camera farther down the hallway. She glanced at him, then at the fallen guards. "Toss their weapons down the shaft. I'll be right back."

"They already know we're here, Aleksi."

"I know. I just hate cameras."

Hutch moved to comply as she dashed off to destroy more cameras. Each guard carried an identical rifle to his own, as well as a sidearm. Rolling them over to check their breathing, he noticed that they were women. He found the buttons on the sides of their rifles that ejected the magazine and tucked the two spares in the belt of his orange overalls, then tossed the rest of the weapons into the shaft.

When Aleksi returned, he pointed to the guards and asked, "Why women?"

"Because Lori's on this floor," she said.

"I don't..." Then Hutch realized what she meant. "Ah, because she's infectious."

"Right. Buckmann doesn't want another David Gilford." Aleksi motioned him forward. "We need to move. This way."

He followed, trotting to keep up. Aleksi destroyed every camera they found, but he had no doubt that they were tracking them and sending more soldiers. There was now only one way out of this labyrinth, and Buckmann knew it.

"Stop!" Aleksi hissed in a whisper, freezing and lowering into a crouch. She glanced back at him and pointed to the next corner. "Two more guards."

"They must be guarding Lori's room."

Aleksi nodded and crept forward on all fours, moving like a cat stalking a mouse. Hutch marveled for a moment at the muscles rippling along her back and legs. He knew her body intimately, of course, but he'd never seen her like this, all predator. He loved her, but sometimes she scared him. At the corner, she leaned down low and twisted her neck to peer around with only one eye. She pulled back and turned to him.

"Two at a metal door. There's another door right across from them, too, but these are different."

"The doors or the guards?"

"The guards. Their weapons are big and boxy, the muzzles square, and I can hear a high-pitched whine. I think they're Tasers."

"You want me to..." He hefted the rifle in his hands. "I mean, to distract them?"

Aleksi bit her lip, then nodded. "Just fire blindly around the corner. Don't try to hit them. I'll take them from the other direction."

He nodded.

"Count to ten, then shoot." She dashed down the other way and around a corner before he could tell her to be careful.

Hutch counted slowly to ten, then pointed the muzzle of the rifle around the corner, vaguely at the ceiling, and squeezed the trigger. A three-round burst jerked the weapon in his hands, and he nearly dropped it. Despite its light weight, the thing had a kick.

Shouts and the tromp of boots sounded from the hallway, then a crash and a scream. Something crackled like lightning and Hutch cringed. *Aleksi!* Another crash, and he raised the rifle to his shoulder and leaned around the corner. He didn't want to kill anyone, but he wasn't going to let them take Aleksi, either.

Two soldiers lay on the floor, one unconscious, the other with her arm bent the wrong way at the elbow. Aleksi stood with one of the odd rifle-like weapons crumpled in one hand. Hutch dashed up and checked the unconscious one. She had a pistol at her belt, too, so he took it and threw it down the hallway. Aleksi disarmed the other and dragged her over beside her fallen companion, then leaned down face to face.

"Now, tell me how to open that." Aleksi pointed to a heavily armored door with an electronic control pad beside it.

"Card swipe and code. We don't have cards." The woman spoke through clenched teeth, obviously in pain, but equally defiant.

"Bullshit! You're her *guards*! You have to be able to get in!" Aleksi's claws closed on the front of the woman's body armor.

"We did, but they took them when they saw you coming!" There was panic in the woman's voice now. "I swear! Search us if you don't believe me!"

"Fuck!" Aleksi dropped the woman and glared at the door.

"You can't break it like you did mine?"

"I don't think so. It's built to keep Lori in." Aleksi stepped up and applied her claws to the edge of the metal frame. Concrete crumbled, but even when she placed a foot against the wall and pulled, the metal didn't give. She let go and stepped back, heaving deep breaths. "No." She turned back to the conscious guard. "Who has the cards?"

"Doctor Olson took them, but they evacuated all the medical staff." The woman was trying to cradle her broken arm, but with the elbow bend backward she couldn't.

Aleksi looked at Hutch. "We don't have time to figure this out, Hutch. We've got to go."

"But what if we—"

Alarms blared and emergency lighting flashed yellow strobe light, cutting Hutch off. Then, astonishingly, it started to rain.

---

D amn, I hate waiting like this!" Persephone said through gritted teeth.

"Not much else we can do, Seph. They cut all external access to their network, too. We're locked out." Ed sounded as frustrated as she felt, but he didn't have the instincts of a dragon pressing on him to do something.

"Completely locked out? Even their emergency systems?"

"No, those are hard-wired to the police and fire departments. Regs, you know."

"Fire department... Shit! That's it! Regulations!" The idea blossomed in her mind like a supernova. "Trigger every alarm you can get your hands on, Ed! Do it now!"

"Fine, but why?"

"Because fire code regulations require that all electronic locks open in case of an emergency! It keeps people from being trapped in a fire!" Persephone flexed her claws in anticipation. "Besides, we will quite literally be pissing on their party!"

"Fantastic." After a short pause, he announced, "Done!"

But Persephone didn't need his pronouncement to see the results. Strobe lights flickered from every window, and she heard the echo of alarms through the hiss of rain outside. She didn't know what good it would do, but it was something.

"At least it's raining inside as well as outside, now."

# 23

---

T he *fuck?*" Aleksi squinted through the artificial rain up at the nearest sprinkler. "Fire alarm?"

"Why would they set off the fire alarms?"

"Maybe..." Aleksi turned back to the door, trying again to claw it open, but to no avail. "Fuck it! We've got to go, Hutch!" She reached for his arm, but he jerked away.

"Wait, Aleksi! Let me try something!" He waved at the two guards. "Get them away from here." He raised his rifle and aimed for the door.

"It'll ricochet, Hutch! It's armor plate!"

"The door is, but the wall isn't." He aimed obliquely and fired a round. The bullet gouged a sizeable chunk of the cinderblock wall away. "If I weaken the frame, maybe it'll come out."

"Fine! Just don't shoot yourself!" Aleksi grabbed the two guards and dragged them away.

Hutch backed away from the door as far as he could, leveled the rifle at the wall, and pulled the trigger. Concrete shattered, exposing the heavy metal casement and rebar within the concrete. The construction was new; Aleksi could tell from the color and smell of the chips. They'd installed the door especially for Lori only a little over a month ago. The concrete was hard, but it wasn't armor plate.

Hutch ran out of bullets, ejected the empty magazine, popped in another, figured out how to chamber a round, then started in anew. Three round bursts, controlled and accurate, peeled a trench of ruin around the door. After his third and final magazine ran empty, he dropped the rifle and waved away the rock dust.

"Try now!"

Ears ringing from the gunfire, Aleksi stepped up to the destroyed wall and started tearing at the fractured concrete. Rebar had been welded to the door frame, but the rebar was mild steel and the frame stainless. The welds were weak enough for her to break one at a time.

*Time... We don't have time for this!* She worked frantically, ripping and tearing, popping the metal rods free around the frame. Finally, when she was done, she gripped the edge of the door and pulled for everything she was worth. Metal groaned against concrete, but still the door didn't budge.

"Fuck!" She glared at the door, wishing that she could breathe fire like a mythological dragon.

"Wait! The top moved, Aleksi! It's the floor that's still stuck!"

Aleksi glared at him, then at the stubborn door. "One more try, then." She gripped the top of the frame, flipped up to place both feet against the wall above the door, and *pulled*.

Metal groaned and concrete popped like popcorn. The sinews of her back, shoulders, and legs strained, but she felt the thing moving. Aleksi screamed out her rage, her frustration, her anguish, and heaved.

In a shower of fractured concrete and tortured metal, the heavy door finally gave way. Aleksi leapt free as the thing fell like a toppling obelisk. It landed with enough force to shake the floor.

Through the dust, inside the room, a dragon lay upon a hospital bed, thickly padded straps secured around her, IV's suspended above, monitors displaying vitals, and cameras, cameras everywhere.

"Help me get her out of here!" Aleksi dashed in and started ripping restraints free and pulling IV's and telemetry leads.

"They said she was psychologically unstable, Aleksi. Maybe we should leave in the IV's."

"Lock me in a fucking room for a month, and *I'd* be psychologically unstable!" In fact, Aleksi had clear memories of her mental state degrading while locked away in Persephone's mansion, and that had been voluntary. "There's no way we can carry her with all this shit." Aleksi finished with the last restraint and checked Lori's eyes. The vertically slit pupils were blown wide. "She's out. Come on. You'll have to carry her. I'm going to be busy."

"Okay." Hutch lifted the dragon into a fireman's carry. "She's thin, Aleksi. She probably doesn't weigh more than a hundred pounds!"

"Malnourishment." She glared at the cameras, knowing in her soul that Buckmann was watching through the lenses. "That's what happens when you cage a predator. Come on!"

---

S hut down that goddamned alarm!" Mary bellowed over the shrieking cacophony. She wiped the water from her face and squinted through the spray at the monitors. "And turn off the sprinkler system!"

"No can do, ma'am!" a security specialist called back over his shoulder. "Every sensor in the building was tripped! Smoke, heat, radiation, all at critical levels. We can't lock it out."

Water cascaded off the panels, down the keyboards and monitors. "Will we lose our systems?"

"Negative!" another tech shouted over the din. "Everything's hardened. But we've got another problem, ma'am!"

"What *else* could possibly go wrong?" As if in answer, the sound of gunfire came over the pickups in Lori Watkins' room. "Who's firing that weapon?"

"Don't know, ma'am. Rychenkna took out the hall cameras. But the alarms have also unlocked all the stairwell doors. OSHA requirements. Escape routes have to be open."

"We've been *hacked* for Christ sake! Get Network Security on this now!" The gunfire ended, then started again. "And get people down to B6! They're trying to take Lori Watkins!"

"Let them!" Mary turned to find Captain Harris in the comm center, his face grim.

"What?"

"I said let them take her, ma'am. She's worth nothing to us, and she'll slow them down. Maybe we can box them in."

Realization struck; he was right. "Can we unlock that door remotely?"

"No, and I don't think it's necessary anyway." Harris pointed to the monitor. The concrete around the door was cracking.

"My God."

"They weakened the frame with gunfire," Harris said as the cracks widened and the frame of the heavily armored door rocked outward. Concrete crumbled, and the entire door and frame tipped out into the hallway. "They're in."

"Send Taser teams to the stairwell. I want them—"

"No Tasers, ma'am." Harris gestured to the ceiling. "Water and electricity don't mix."

"Shit!" Mary gritted her teeth. "Fine, then. Take Rychenkna down."

"Ma'am, in the confined space of the stairwell, that will be costly. She'll have the advantage."

"She's had the advantage at every turn, Captain! It's time to turn the tables. Use tear gas, flash bangs, whatever it takes! Take her the fuck *down*!"

"Yes, ma'am."

"And call in airborne support. Nobody gets out of the building!"

Harris shouted commands into his mic, then turned to her with a nod. "Two helicopters are already on the way. Every exit's covered."

"Good!" Mary watched impotently as Rychenkna and Hutchinson took Lori Watkins from her bed. "Call Doctor Price. I want to know how long Lori will stay sedated with her IV pulled."

"Yes, ma'am." A tech put the call through.

"If she gets free, ma'am…" Harris warned.

"I *know*!" Mary wiped the water from her face and swore under her breath. "Armageddon."

# 24

Aleksi paused for a moment at the stairwell door, senses straining. The blaring alarms and spraying water were both a curse and a blessing for her: they would interfere with the soldiers' vision, electronic gear, and hearing, but it did the same to her senses. Water would make footing treacherous, but more for the soldiers than Aleksi. She couldn't feel or hear anyone on the stairs, but she knew they were there. Water dampened the scents of sweat, fear, and gun oil somewhat, but didn't eliminate them completely.

She turned to Hutch. "They're on the stairs. Stay here."

"Aleksi, I don't want you to be shot! Let me go first! They won't shoot me."

"No." She smiled and brushed his cheek with the backs of her knuckles. "No, that won't work. I couldn't. That's not what dragons do."

He opened his mouth to say something, but she was through the door before he got out a single syllable.

*Six*, her senses told her. Then, even as she lunged for the stairwell's metal railing, she realized there were more. *Six close, six more higher up. That could be a problem, or an advantage.* More guns were bad, but the higher ones couldn't fire without endangering the lower team. Bullets would ricochet with deadly consequences in the concrete stairwell.

As she grabbed the railing, she heard a boot splash down on a step to her left and above. She kicked up, lashed her wings, and clutched the underside of the next level's stair for a moment. Two soldiers started to raise their rifles, but her claws dug furrows in the concrete, propelling her at them like a missile.

The lower one, the one she'd heard on the stair, she could barely reach. Her claws hooked the lip of his helmet, and her momentum flung him backward hard. Doing so flipped her legs up over her head, and the next flight of stairs came into view. Two more soldiers, their rifles already in line. The other lower soldier got off one premature shot that passed below her, the muzzle blast misting the cascading water into fog, the bullet's track a cone-shaped shockwave. Aleksi snatched the muzzle of his weapon as her flip continued. The strap securing his rifle came taut, and she lashed him around into the wall. As her feet and the soldier hit the concrete, and before gravity could send either of them to the floor, she flexed her legs and flung the stunned soldier up the stairway at the two descending with all her strength.

Both soldiers fired, and blood misted the air, but not hers.

Her bullet-riddled missile struck the lower soldier square in the chest, flinging him back into the upper one's legs. The upper soldier flailed forward, her eyes wide, her weapon forgotten as she tumbled over her two allies. Aleksi caught her by her vest and swung her around the corner of the stairwell into the first man she'd knocked down. He'd been struggling to his feet, and the thrown soldier caught him square in the back. Both of them flew down the stairs to smash into the wall below.

*Two more in this wave.*

Boots splashed down the stairs while shouts rang out about men down and shots fired. The noise told her exactly where they were. When the first boot came into view, Aleksi lunged up, grasped the foot in a clawed vice, and jerked the surprised soldier through the steel guardrail. Bone snapped as his other leg bent the wrong way, and his scream shivered the air. The other soldier leapt past the spot and fired blindly around the corner before he even landed, an impressive move, and not what Aleksi had expected. Two of the rounds missed by only inches, the third put a hole in one wing.

Aleksi dropped the screaming soldier, launched herself straight up, and bounded off the underside of the next flight. She slammed straight into the last of the six in the squad before he could re-aim his weapon. The breath left his lungs as her shoulder slammed him against the wall, ribs cracking beneath his body armor. With his face an inch from hers in a stunned grimace of terror, Aleksi took a heartbeat to listen for more from above.

*Two floors up,* she thought. *Plenty of time.*

"You *shot* me," she growled at the terrified man.

He tried to headbutt her with his helmet while reaching for his pistol, but the blow only caught the ridge of thick bone above her eyebrows. She crushed his hand around his pistol, and, as his mouth opened in a scream, she smashed that very ridge of bone into his face. He went down spitting blood and broken teeth.

Aleksi threw his pistol down the stairwell, and snapped the clip securing his rifle. She started to throw it away, then reconsidered. She didn't care for guns, but she needed a few seconds to make sure all the soldiers behind her were truly out of commission. She pointed the muzzle up the stairwell, hooked a claw around the trigger, pulled, and held it down.

The noise, ricocheting slugs, and cries of alarm were impressive.

When the magazine ran empty, she bent the barrel and dropped the weapon. As she turned back to check the others, however, the clatter of something metal falling down the stairwell pierced the ringing in her ears. Whirling, she spotted a green cylinder, a hex nut on each end and holes along the shaft, tumbling down toward her.

Aleksi moved without thinking. She didn't know what the little cylinder was, but it couldn't be good. Lunging up, she snatched the device out of the air and pitched it hard back up the stairs. She bounded off a wall and dove for cover, covering her ears an instant before the world exploded.

The muffled rattle of gunfire reached Persephone's ears through the open cab door. The sound seemed to be coming from the roof below her, but no one was visible.

"They're in the stairwell," she said as realization struck. "Ping her phone!"

"I've been pinging every thirty seconds," Ed replied.

*Thirty seconds in a fight is an eternity for a dragon!* Persephone opened her mouth to tell him to ping her again, then thought better of it. Interrupting Aleksi with a phone call while she was being shot at would not be a good idea. She took a deep breath and waited, her hands trembling on the crane's controls.

A helicopter roared past, its searchlight igniting to pan across the roof below. The feds knew Aleksi was coming up the stairs. Persephone squinted through the rain as the aircraft banked, and spotted a soldier in the open door, a long rifle aimed down.

"They're going to shoot her when she comes out! We've got to warn her!"

"She should be able to hear us as soon as she gets above ground level," Ed informed her, not for the first time.

Persephone gritted her teeth and made a decision. "Aleksi could climb from the basement to the roof in thirty seconds, Ed. Ping her continuously!"

"Okay, okay!"

"Thank yo—"

A reverberating explosion far louder than the gunfire rattled the roof door of the stairwell.

"Jesus! What the hell's going on in there? We heard that down here!" Reggie sounded half-panicked.

"They're using explosives. Probably grenades." Searchlights lanced up from the street. One swept across the crane, and Persephone ducked back, though a figure in black would be all but invisible. Another painted the helicopter, and the man in the door flinched back, shading his eyes. "Get ready for the diversion,

Reggie. The moment she comes out, all hell's going to break loose."

"Just give me the word, Seph. We're ready."

"Good." Persephone girded her frayed nerves and, for the first time in years, prayed. "Please, God, don't let them die. Please don't die. Please..."

---

The windows of the O'Neill building rattled with the concussive blast. Every cop on the street stepped back and looked up, and several raised their weapons.

"Holster those, you jackasses!" Blake snapped, glaring at her people. "The building's full of federal security! You shoot one, and I have fifty *miles* of paperwork up my ass!"

"What she said!" Tony echoed.

As chagrined cops lowered their weapons, Blake sidled over to Tony and Marty. "All we need is for some moron to start shooting."

"Got that right," Tony agreed.

"That was a flashbang, or I'm a choir boy," Marty said with a sidelong look at Tony. "*Something's* going on in there."

"That, too," Tony agreed. "But *weren't* you actually a choir boy when you were a kid?"

"Sure, but I gave it up." Marty flashed him a grin. "Being a cop's less dangerous."

Tony snorted a laugh.

Blake glared at them both. "Don't you two take *anything* seriously?"

"We're taking *this* seriously!" Tony shot back deadpan. "Does that mean we can't crack wise?"

"Yes, it *does*." Her glare remained undiminished, but her lips quirked into a brief smile. Then she turned to the towering structure and the helicopter orbiting overhead. "I guess your terrorist threat just became more credible."

"To tell you the truth, I'd rather have been wrong. If the shit hits the fan, there are too many bystanders." He looked back at the line of media vans. "Maybe we should move them back."

Another explosion shook the windows, and every cop flinched. None of them drew their weapons this time, however.

"Sounds more like a firefight than a bomb threat. Who in their right mind would attack a federal building?" Blake blinked at Tony and Marty. "Your CI was on the level, at least."

"Well, whoever they are, they're serious."

Blake nodded. "True that. Can't imagine them getting out alive, though."

Tony shared a grim glance with Marty. At this point, he couldn't imagine it either.

## 25

Even before Aleksi's ears stopped ringing, she'd checked the fallen soldiers and made sure they were all down for the count. Thankfully, they were all still breathing. She disabled their guns and snatched two more of the concussion grenades from their belts. If the feds wanted to play catch, she was ready.

As she bent the last of their rifles into a pretzel, the door to B6 cracked open and Hutch peered through wide eyed. "You okay?"

She could barely hear him over the ringing tinnitus. "Fine. Six down, six to go. I'm going up. Stay here. They're throwing concussion grenades, and I—"

Something clattered from above, sharp impacts of metal on concrete, but a different sound than the flashbang grenade. This sounded like a soda can full of sand. Still, she wasn't taking any chances. She shoved Hutch back and lunged up the stairs, bounding off landing after landing, claws grating on concrete. At the third landing, she saw it, a gray can falling end over end, trailing smoke.

*Tear gas!* They were attacking her senses; a flashbang to numb her hearing and blind her, now tear gas to obliterate her sense of smell.

Aleksi gasped a breath, caught the smoking canister, and opened the door to B4 long enough to throw it through. Boots splat-splatted down the stairs above her. Her eyes stung, her ears rang, and she didn't know how long she could hold her breath. She needed a moment to regroup, so she pulled the pins of both of the concussion grenades and threw them hard up the stairwell. They hit the wall of a landing at a steep enough angle to send them up the next flight. Aleksi bounded down to crouch at the bottom of the stairwell, huddled with her hands over her ears, eyes shut.

The two grenades detonated at the same instant, rattling her teeth in the confined space. She gasped another deep breath, then bounded back up the stairs, bouncing off of concrete walls like a superball with clawed feet. She caught the first two soldiers while they were still blinking and shaking their heads.

Claws lanced into Kevlar vests, and Aleksi braced her feet on the stairs and yanked them both downward with all her strength. They hit the door to B3 with a sickening crunch, but Aleksi was already moving. Gunfire flashed, and her ringing ears rang some more as bullets spalled off of the wall beside her head. She lunged at the shooter, pirouetting in flight around the muzzle flashes. Her blow caught him under the chin hard enough to snap his head back and send him choking to the floor.

Another blast of gunfire came blind from around the corner of the next flight, probably intended to keep her down. All it did was give her a target. She snatched the muzzle of the rifle and jerked the soldier into the guardrail. The startled woman's face met with the railing's two-inch galvanized steel pipe with a resounding clang. The soldier fell like a ragdoll and rolled down the stairs.

*Two more.*

At the B2 landing, she risked a breath. The tang of teargas still hung in the air, but the fire suppression sprinklers were washing it quickly away. Buckmann's command center was on this floor, and Aleksi had to suppress the urge to hunt the woman down and rip her arms off as she'd promised. Instead, she leapt again to clutch the underside of the next flight of stairs. Here, she flattened herself against the surface and froze for a moment, waiting for her senses to sharpen.

"My team's in pieces," one of the soldiers above said, obviously talking into a mic. "She used our own flashbangs! Send reinforcements now! We'll hold position at B2 landing, that's Bravo-two landing."

*Thanks for the update*, Aleksi thought with a feral grin. Did they really think she wouldn't hear them? Didn't they even know what they were hunting?

*Time to teach them never to hunt a dragon again.*

Boots splashed down the stairs, wet rubber squeaking on the nonskid tread of the steps. The muzzles of their weapons were aimed down the stairwell, the way any normal human would climb up. Aleksi, of course, wasn't normal or really human, and like most humans, they didn't look up.

*Bad evolution.*

As they started down the stairs beneath her, Aleksi dropped on them, one clawed hand on the back of each of their necks. She flexed hard enough to break the skin, but not bones.

"Drop your weapons, or you're dead," she hissed in their ears.

The rifles went limp, and hands raised. "Don't! Please!"

Aleksi smelled urine and felt a brief pang of sympathy for these witless men and women. They had no idea what they were up against.

"Pistols out and on the floor! Unclip your rifles and drop them. One wrong move and I snap your necks." She twitched her claws and felt tremors up and down their spines. "Do it now!"

Guns clattered to the stairs.

"Good!" Aleksi marched them down to the door of B2 and said, "Open it."

The soldier in her right hand reached out and worked the latch, pulling slowly. The hallway within was empty.

"Now, tell Mary Buckmann that I'm leaving this building with my family. If she tries to hurt them, I'll slaughter every last one of you and rip out her heart. Tell her that if *one* bullet is fired at the people I love, the blood's on *her* hands!"

"Okay, okay! We'll tell her!" the soldier squawked in a panicked tenor.

Aleksi shoved them through the door, slammed it, and looked around for some way to block it closed. Snatching up one of the fallen rifles, she smashed the hard, plastic stock against the railing. The plastic splintered. She tore the biggest piece free and jammed it under the door. That might hold them, but not for long.

*Now, Hutch.* She flew down the stairwell to the bottom, but the door was already opening.

"I can hear them coming from the other direction. They must have sent down an elevator!" He already held Lori in his arms.

"Good. Come on!" She pulled him through, snapped another weapon's stock into plastic kindling and jammed the door. "Hand me Lori and go up as fast as you can. The stairway's clear, but it won't be for long. I'll be right behind you!"

He handed over the limp dragon and started up three steps at a time. Twelve flights, and Hutch never slowed. *All that running*, she thought, unable to keep her eyes off his ass. Of course, panic and adrenaline probably enhanced his performance. At the second floor, her earpiece pinged twice in her ear.

"Accept call, carrier two."

"Aleksi! Are you okay?" Persephone sounded ready to explode.

"Yes. We're coming up. Three of us. We got Lori."

"They've got a helicopter circling with a sniper!"

Aleksi cringed, remembering how accurate their airborne marksmen were. She would have to be fast. "I'll take care of it. Is the hook ready?"

"Yes, right at the edge of the roof near the alley. I don't think they've spotted it. They're watching the stairwell door. Be careful! They're ready to shoot you the moment you step out."

"Yeah, they've been trying to shoot me all night. Get ready."

"We're ready."

At the fifth floor, she said, "Hutch! Hang on. I've got to hand her over. We've got company upstairs."

"Company?" Breathing heavily, he took Lori in his arms. "What kind of company?"

"A helicopter with a sniper. I'll distract them. You take Lori to the construction crane hook to the left side of the building. There should be a pack hanging from it. It has a harness inside. Put it on and latch onto the hook. You'll have to carry Lori. We've got a van waiting in the alley. They'll lower you down to it."

"Um...all right." He didn't sound enthusiastic.

"Don't worry." She grinned a dragon grin. "It'll be—"

A crash from below cut off her quip. Reinforcements were coming. Evidently, Buckmann either hadn't gotten her message, or hadn't taken it seriously...again.

"Damn! They're coming. Give me five seconds, then go!"

"Okay." He swallowed hard. "Please don't get shot."

"You neither." She kissed him and flew through the door so hard it bent the hinges.

---

T he United States Government doesn't accede to threats from *terrorists*!" Mary glared at Harris and the two injured soldiers. A med tech and Doctor Price pressed bandages to their necks to staunch the bleeding. "Doctor, get these two to medical and test them for the HD virus!"

"Yes, ma'am." She motioned the tech to the door and handed off her patient. "You've got about five minutes until Lori's sedation wears off."

"This will be over in *two* minutes!" Mary turned to Harris. "They're in a box. Send troops up the stairs. The helicopter will pin them down. They've got nowhere to go."

"Rychenkna won't be stopped by one sniper aboard a helicopter, ma'am. Let me call in a gunship."

"I will *not* have an Apache shooting up downtown Boston, Captain! We have a second helo inbound."

"Yes, two minutes."

"And the street's full of police."

"Yes." He looked dubious.

"Well, let them earn their goddamn pensions for once. Tell

building security to inform BPD that the terrorists have freed a prisoner and are trying to escape with them. That is the God's honest truth! If Rychenkna manages to get Hutchinson and Watkins off the building, their SWAT teams have a shoot order from me."

He swallowed hard and nodded once. "That's a hell of a risk, Doctor."

"This whole *project* has been a risk from the very first day, Captain. Now, give the order!"

Harris turned and hurried to the security console.

Mercifully, the fire suppression sprinklers finally gave out. The alarms continued to howl, however.

Mary turned to her comm specialist. "Hook me up with the helicopter camera. I want to see what's going on."

"Yes, ma'am." He tapped and pointed to a screen. Through the rain-slashed air, a spotlight illuminated a metal door on the roof.

Mary opened her mouth to ask to be connected to the aircraft's intercom system, but at that moment, the stairway door burst outward and the dragon took wing. A muzzle flash lit the air, and the bullet dug a hole in the roof a foot behind Aleksi.

"Good *Christ*," the comm tech muttered as the camera and searchlight swiveled frantically, trying to track the target. The scene tilted as the pilot banked hard.

Mary stood speechless as the rain-blurred view flashed with muzzle flares from the sniper's rifle. Then a blinding flash lit the entire sky and half of their exterior cameras. For a moment, Mary thought it was lightning. Then the entire building shook. Several of her team shouted out reports of explosions, and screens resolved from the blinding flash to show a rain of glass and shattered windows. Then the helicopter camera caught a blur of something too fast to focus on. An instant later, the monitor went black.

"Get me the flight crew!" Mary ordered.

"On audio one!" The comm tech punched a key, but the only thing to come over the speaker were a man's shrill screams.

D iversion now, Reggie!" Persephone ordered as Aleksi burst out of the stairwell door.

"One diversion coming up!"

Persephone tried to watch everything at once: the stairwell door, for Hutch and Lori would be emerging any moment; Aleksi, as she fought for her life; and the tiny wedge of Causeway Street to her left and below. A strobe-white flash lit the fronts of the buildings on Causeway and Lomasney Streets opposite the O'Neill building, and a deafening report shook the tower crane and shattered windows. Reggie's diversion, four powerful but largely harmless fireworks, were supposed to send every cop and security goon scrambling for cover, allowing them to move the van into the alley without being seen. The explosions were a lot more powerful than Persephone had thought they'd be. She muttered a mental apology to Tony Jasper.

The helicopter banked hard, but whether it was an attempt to evade Aleksi, bring the sniper to bear, or in response to the explosions, Persephone didn't know. Then her attention shifted, for Hutch emerged from the stairwell at a run with a dragon in his arms. He ran heavily with the extra weight, but he rounded the array of solar panels and headed for the crane's hook.

"Come on, Hutch!" Persephone wished she had a phone connection to him and cursed herself for not thinking of that. She could have given Aleksi a second earpiece.

The helicopter roared past, dangerously close to the tower crane, so close that Persephone could see the terror on the pilot's face. She couldn't see Aleksi anywhere.

Below, Reggie backed the darkened van into the alley and stopped. The lift panel in the roof began to open, the interior lit with red light. He'd prepared for an overhead rescue but had hypothesized Aleksi dropping in with Hutch from above. That was supposed to have been what the harness was for.

*All the best laid plans...*

Hutch knelt to lower Lori to the roof, then lunged up to open the dangling pack. The harness was simple, but it took precious seconds for him to clip together the shoulder and crotch straps. He secured the tether to the hook, then knelt back down to lift Lori in his arms.

Persephone's hands quivered on the crane controls. *Up, then swivel, then down. Easy!*

Then the door to the stairwell burst open again, and SWAT garbed soldiers poured out. They scanned the sky first, then one spotted Hutch and raised a rifle.

"Aleksi! They're going to shoot Hutch!" Persephone pulled the lift control and turned the boom. Hutch rose into the air and swung out over the alley, Lori's limp wings billowing in the blustery rain. As Persephone flipped the control to lower them, a rifle fired. She scanned the rain-lashed heavens but couldn't spot the dragon anywhere. "Aleksi!"

The helicopter roared past again, banking the opposite direction, its belly facing her.

That was when Persephone saw the blood.

# 2 6

---

The instant Aleksi smashed through the door—right into the beam of a searchlight—a rifle bullet spalled off of the roof behind her. The sniper had been prepared for her, and he was good, but Aleksi moved like a golden bolt of lightning through the rain-streaked night.

Her wings lashed the air, and she banked hard, then back in a desperate evasive maneuver. She didn't have to look up to locate the helicopter; sound and her own shadow from the tracking spotlight gave her all the information she needed. Unfortunately, the sniper wasn't using a targeting laser, so she had no idea where he was aiming.

Something tugged at her left wing near her hip, and another rifle shot boomed out. The echo of the report, however, suddenly vanished in a blast of light and sound. Reggie's distraction shattered windows along two city blocks and sent news crews and police to their bellies. They all probably thought the building had exploded just like Persephone's house.

"Sorry, Tony," Aleksi muttered.

Thankfully, Aleksi was still over the roof, so her eyes were spared most of the blinding flash. She hoped the sniper had caught the flash full in his light-intensifying goggles. As she banked again to evade the searchlight, another shot zipped past, leaving a crease in her right arm.

*Maybe not.*

She barrel-rolled and snapped her wings full, stalling for an instant. The searchlight beam lost her.

*Yes!*

Aleksi billowed her wings and climbed, turning hard after the helicopter. The searchlight caught her again briefly, and the rifle flashed, but this shot missed by a wider margin. She jinked and rolled then snapped up into a climb. The helicopter banked hard, swiveling in the air to bring the rifleman to bear, but Aleksi dove, and rolled under the shot. A line of shattered raindrops streaked past her flat belly a hand's breadth from her flesh.

*That's the last shot you get, asshole!*

She rolled, folding her wings in a dive, and then snapped into a climb right under the aircraft. Her claws ripped the camera-searchlight mounting from the aircraft and pierced the thin aluminum skin of the helicopter's belly. The vibration of the motor felt like a frantic heartbeat through her fingers. The sniper, however, must have felt her hit, for a shot punched a hole through the aircraft's underside and her left wing.

*That fucker's persistent!* she cursed under her breath. It was time to teach him what a dragon could do.

Aleksi felt the rifleman's rubber soled boots clumping in a circle through the skin of the mechanical monster. She could sense his movement, feel him readying for another shot. *There, there, and...there!*

Another bullet pierced the craft's hull inches from her chest, and Aleksi freed a hand to punch up through the aluminum. The jagged metal tore her knuckles, but her claws closed on the sniper's sturdy boot, piercing deep enough to grate on bone.

She felt him scream through her claws.

Fearing another shot, Aleksi jerked with all her strength, ripping the man's leg down through the hole she'd made. Jagged metal tore at his pants and flesh. The rifle fired, but the bullet went wide. Aleksi snapped the man's leg, eliciting more screams, and scrabbled up and into the aircraft.

The sniper lay there, his rifle forgotten, gloved hands gripping his leg. A flight crewman reached for a sidearm, and Aleksi took the gun and three of his fingers away. More screams. Ripping the rifle away from the sniper, she threw the weapons out the open door. The pilot was screaming now, too, and the copilot turned with a pistol in hand.

*Really?*

Aleksi watched the muzzle, his finger tightening on the trigger, and twisted as the gun went off. The bullet holed her wing. She took the gun, broke his wrist, then took the sniper's sidearm as well. The weapons flew out the door.

The aircraft jerked hard, the pilot attempting to knock her out the door, but the claws of her toes were imbedded in the deck. She reached between the two pilots' seats, closed her claws on the pilot's shoulder, and growled in his ear.

"Fly away, or I'll fucking kill you all!"

He glanced over his shoulder at her, eyes wide, mouth agape. His crew was incapacitated, unarmed, and the dragon in his aircraft had her claws in the muscle of his shoulder. One jerk and she could send that arm out the door after their weapons. Realization struck, and he nodded frantically.

"Wise decision."

"Aleksi! They're going to shoot Hutch!"

*What?* Her mind stumbled. How could they shoot Hutch when she'd thrown their weapons out the door?

She pulled her claws from the pilot's shoulder and turned. The helicopter banked hard, and she saw through the open door the troops pouring out onto the roof. Some raised their weapons to the sky, but two had their rifles aimed across the roof. A muzzle flash lit the night.

They were shooting at Hutch lifting Lori in his arms.

"Aleksi!" Persephone screamed.

The dragon tore out of the aircraft, snapping her wings into a plummeting dive.

The crotch straps of the harness bit in hard, jerking Hutch and Lori off the roof. He didn't know who was running the crane, but he would have a few choice words regarding the abuse of his testicles when he met them.

He swung slowly out over the blackness of the alley, gulping at the sudden void beneath his dangling legs. Lori's limp wings billowed, catching the wind, spinning them like a top. She stirred in his arms, weakly, without purpose.

*Don't wake up. Please, don't wake up!*

As they spun, the roof opened up to his view, and he saw the soldiers pouring out of the stairway door. Most had their guns aimed at the sky, but two were aiming at him. He opened his mouth to curse, but the muzzle flashes brought him up short. Hutch had never been shot at in his life and didn't like the experience in the slightest, especially since he couldn't duck, dive for cover, or evade the deadly fire.

Something jerked, halting their spin, but he felt no pain. He'd heard that sometimes pain came slower, but he didn't feel like he'd been shot.

Lori twitched in his arms, twisting, her wings moving against the air, enfolding him.

*Don't wake up, don't wake up! Please don't wake up!* But as they began to descend, screams and gunfire erupted from the roof, bullets zipped past to shatter the windows of the partially constructed building across the alley, and Lori's eyes fluttered and opened.

"Lori! Don't struggle. We're getting you out. Just relax." They descended past the lip of the roof into darkness, and he breathed easier.

Her yellow eyes widened, her lips pulling up away from her teeth. She twisted in his arms, her claws pressing against his back. "They..."

"Lori, please! Don't fight me! We're helping you! We're getting you out!" Hutch held her tight. "You're safe!"

"*Lies!*" She twisted, and her claws pierced the fabric of his prison jumpsuit, then his skin. "Not safe! I'll *never* be safe! They made me murder *Charlie!*"

"Lori, please! I'm trying to *help* you!" Hutch gritted his teeth at the pain of her claws raking his back. He considered simply letting her fall. She had wings, after all. She might reflexively fly. But Lori was infectious and mentally unstable. Who knew what would happen if he let her go? He shifted his grip on her, hugging her close, and felt the warm slickness on her back.

*She's been shot!* he realized with horror.

"Lori, *please*, relax. I know it hurts, but we're helping you. You'll be free!"

Soft red light bloomed beneath them, and he glanced down into a rectangular hole in a van's roof. A man and woman within looked up at them. He didn't recognize either of them.

"No!" Lori twisted and flexed, clumsy and weak by dragon standards, but getting stronger by the second. "Don't make me do it!"

"Lori, I've got you!" Hutch held her tight, even as her claws dug into his back. "You're safe! We're trying to—"

Pain blossomed in his shoulder as Lori's teeth buried deep in the muscle. Hutch gritted his teeth against a scream, and not only due to the pain. Lori was infectious, just like David Gilford had been when he'd infected her...with a bite.

---

A t the sight of the soldiers firing at Hutch—the muzzle flashes catching the suspended pair like a camera's strobe, the jerk as bullets tore flesh, the blood—something within Aleksi shattered. Her heart, perhaps, or maybe her soul, she didn't know. She felt as if an egg within her cracked and opened, like a part of her she'd never known was being born into a world of agony. She knew what that part was; she'd been denying it, repressing it, holding it imprisoned within herself for half a year.

This time, she couldn't.

The dragon within her tore free of her tenuous control, filling her every sinew with rage.

Her wings lashed the rain-laden air, claws extended and teeth bared. Aleksi dove in a twisting spiral right at the knot of soldiers. Bullets streaked up at her, too many. Rounds punched holes in her wings, and pain lanced down her back. It didn't matter. Nothing but a killing shot would have stopped her.

She struck two of them with her outstretched claws, wings billowing to arrest her dive. Her bullet-riddled wings didn't perform quite as well as she had become accustomed to, however, and she skimmed the roof with her chest.

Screams and blood filled her wake. Her claws tore through legs like scythes through wheat. Two more men crumpled to the roof behind her, weapons forgotten, hands clutching horrible wounds, shattered bone white in the streaming light, arterial blood spraying.

Aleksi folded her wings and smashed into another soldier's legs, grasping and burying her teeth deep in muscle and bone. Blood, the glorious taste of warm, living meat in her jaws, fueled the dragon's rage. She dug her clawed toes into the roof and spun, flinging the torn soldier like a flail into two others. One leg came off at the knee as he struck, and all three went flying. A rifle fired, a ripping salvo of full automatic panic, and more pain shot through her like a bolt of lightning.

She sprang and slashed the air with a wing, spinning high, lashing out with claws. A man's face tore away, a gurgling spray of blood painting another shocked soldier crimson. They were too closely bunched to fire at her without risking each other, but fire they did.

Bullets tugged at her wings, but also struck another soldier. Screams and curses rang out from all sides.

A feral roar escaped Aleksi's bloody jaws as she tore through the remaining soldiers. Muscle, sinew, bone, and viscera painted the roof. Muzzle flashes illuminated her prey in stark, shocking detail, the wounds, the fear, the carnage and death.

Finally, it was over. The Dragon of Boston had broken free of Aleksi's self-imposed prison to ravage the ranks of those who threatened the people she loved. A voice, not hers, spoke in her ear, words that meant nothing. The blood around her had not only tarnished the roof of the O'Neill building, but her soul as well.

She was a killer, a murderer, a monster.

"I *warned* them," Aleksi muttered, looking down at her blood-stained claws, swallowing the taste of human meat. "I told them not to meddle in the affairs of dragons."

"Aleksi! Move!"

The horror in Persephone's scream tore through the shock of what Aleksi had done. Senses returned, pain, sound, scents, and the heart-thumping vibration of helicopter rotors slashing through the rain. A muzzle flash strobed through the night, galvanizing her into action.

Aleksi whirled instinctively to evade the next shot, but she saw instantly that the airborne sniper wasn't aiming at her. Another muzzle flash illuminated the tower crane, and sparks showered from the bullet's impact in the control cab.

"Persephone!" Aleksi launched herself into the sky, a cry of anguish tearing from her throat. "No! Get out!"

She received no answer. The line, or maybe Persephone, was dead.

## 27

A leksi, oh God..." Persephone stared in helpless horror as the dragon tore through the soldiers.

Aleksi had always held herself in check, always avoided killing, afraid of what it might unleash, both within herself and from people like Buckmann. She was the only psychologically stable *Homo Draconis* alive, and DHS treated her like a potential asset.

Until now.

Persephone wondered, as Aleksi tore, maimed, and killed the soldiers who had threatened Hutch, if either of those would continue to hold true. Would Aleksi still be herself when this was over, or would only the dragon remain? Would the government hunt her down regardless of the cost? Would they learn from their mistakes, or continue to deny that they were no longer at the top of the food chain?

"Persephone! We've got them!"

Unable to look away from the horrific spectacle, Persephone released the crane's controls. "Are they alive?"

"Yes, but... Shit! Get a syringe into her!"

That didn't sound good. "Reggie?"

"Busy here! Lori's kinda awake!"

"Awake?" That jarred Persephone out of her fascination. The fight was over anyway. Aleksi stood amid a litter of bloody carnage, staring down at what she'd done. "And Hutch?"

"Alive, but hurt. Now don't bother me!"

Persephone imagined things in the van were busy indeed, and they still had to get away. "Aleksi?" Persephone got up from the chair and craned her neck to peer out to the street. She didn't have a good view, but things looked quiet for now. She looked back to Aleksi, but her friend still stood there, obvious and in shock at what she'd done. "Aleksi, they've got Hutch and Lori. They're safe. You can get out of there. We're done!"

Still, the dragon didn't move. Persephone wondered if she would ever move again.

The roar of a helicopter jolted Persephone into motion. A search light swept the roof, the blood red and stark, the dragon's golden scales glittering, unmoving.

*She's a sitting duck!* Persephone slammed open the door to the control cab and dashed to the railing, thinking that Aleksi's phone might have been smashed. She cupped her hands around her mouth and screamed at the top of her lungs, "Aleksi! Move!"

A rifle flashed from the helicopter, but instead of the dragon, the bullet smashed through the control cab of the tower crane.

"Shit!" Persephone ducked reflexively and dashed for the ladder, another round clanging off of the gantry nearby.

They weren't shooting at Aleksi, they were shooting at *her*. She gripped the ladder handrails and dropped, pressing her feet to the rails to slow her descent. Another shot lit up the night, and the bullet careened off of the metal cage around the ladder. Something struck her hip, and pain lanced through her.

Persephone hit the first landing and staggered. Agony jolted through her hip, and her leg felt like it would fold. She reached down and felt sharp shards and blood, but a glance down showed her bloody plastic instead of bone. The bullet had hit her phone but had passed through and lodged in her hip. Her leg held her weight but trembled.

She hobbled to the next section of ladder and slid down as another bullet clanged against metal only inches from her head.

"Don't these fuckers ever learn?" She landed and lurched to the next ladder section. Another bullet struck the crane, this one a few feet away. Maybe they'd lost her in the darkness and rain.

Then the helicopter's searchlight caught her full on. She stared into the blinding light as the aircraft stopped in a hover only yards away. The sniper leveled his rifle at her, his face a study of concentration.

Persephone slid down, expecting the next shot the moment she landed. This one would certainly take her down.

But it didn't come.

The roar of the helicopter's motor changed pitch and the searchlight wheeled crazily. Persephone crouched and squinted into the rain, her light-blinded eyes adjusting in an instant.

Her jaw dropped open with a gasp of terror. "Oh, no..."

---

Hutch struck the edge of the van's roof opening with his hip as they plunged through, but the pain of the impact paled in comparison to the agony of his shoulder. Lori seemed to have latched onto him in a panic, and her teeth were grating against bone.

They hit the floor and crumpled into a heap of arms, legs, wings, claws, and blood—both Lori's and his own. He didn't know how badly she was hurt, but his own injury was far worse than a bone-deep laceration. She was infectious, and the HD virus was now in his blood.

*I am so fucked*, he thought as the blond man and woman reached down to help.

"Persephone, we've got them," the man said, unclipping the harness from the crane's hook.

"She's been shot, and she's waking up!" Hutch gasped through clenched teeth. He kept a firm hold on Lori. The damage was done; he was infected. If he let go of her, she might bite someone else.

"Yes, but... Shit!" The man whirled to the young woman. "Get a syringe into her!"

"Right!" The woman snatched a ten-CC syringe from a tray and flipped the cap off the needle. She jammed it into Lori's thigh and depressed the plunger.

Lori shuddered in Hutch's arms, her claws pressing into his back. The man and woman moved to pry her loose, but he shook his head. "I've got her. Just get us the hell out of here."

"Right! Drive, Carrie! I'll get the roof closed and take care of them."

The woman scrambled to the front of the vehicle, and the van lurched into motion. The blond man slammed a control on the roof, and the panel hummed closed. He crouched then and flipped a switch that changed the light from red to white.

Lori trembled in Hutch's arms, claws and teeth sending shocks of pain through him. He looked down at her, yellow eyes wide, panicked, teeth bone deep in his shoulder, blood flowing down his arm. A flushing tingle invaded his extremities. His head swam with sudden dizziness, and the world closed into impenetrable darkness around him.

---

Aleksi slammed into the side of the helicopter and ripped open the sliding door, her blood on fire with the dragon's need to kill. They'd shot Hutch and were trying to kill Persephone, her family, the only people in this whole fucking world she cared about.

"Shi—" the flight crewman screamed, reaching for his pistol, but his cry was cut off, along with his life.

Aleksi's claws sprayed blood and gobbets of meat across the cabin. The sniper started to turn, and stumbled back, right out the open door. The tether securing him to the deck came taut, and he slammed into the edge of the deck, flailing to find the skid with his feet and bring his rifle to bear.

Aleksi stomped on the rifle, reached down, and ripped the tether free of its D-ring. She then kicked the sniper under the chin, sending him sprawling back into the void.

A pistol went off in the confined space, and something struck her in the side. She whirled and lashed out even before pain registered. Her claws raked the gun and hand away in a spray of blood. The copilot started to scream, and the pilot hauled on the control yoke.

"I fucking *warned* you!" Aleksi raged, tears and blood streaming down her face. "But you *don't...fucking...listen!*"

With each final word, her claws slashed. The copilot's life ended in an impressive spray of blood that painted the interior of the windows. The other man screamed in horror as she tore his right arm off at the shoulder. His dismembered grip hauled the control yoke to the right, and the helicopter yawed. Her third blow stifled his scream and ended his pain and terror.

The aircraft spun out of control, spiraling in its death throes. Aleksi watched the partially constructed building sweep past, wondering if Persephone had survived. Then the taller tower of the O'Neill building flashed by, and the deck tilted alarmingly under her feet. Rows of solar panels and the huge square skylight loomed up, to the right, a swath of blood and torn meat at the stairwell entry.

For a moment, Aleksi considered riding the dying aircraft to its final demise. She'd killed. She was a monster.

*But not like Derrick Penningly or David Gilford*, something within her said. She'd killed to protect, not to feed.

As the roof flashed up at her, Aleksi whirled and dove out the open side door, wings billowing in the rainy night. Pain stabbed her side, and her wings were riddled with holes, but she didn't crash. She banked up and skimmed over the rows of solar panels, glancing over her shoulder to witness what she had done.

The helicopter smashed into the skylight, the main rotor scything through glass and steel, weakening the support frame enough for the aircraft to continue its plummet down into the main atrium of the building.

Aleksi cringed, hoping not too many people died when it hit. If the fuel tanks exploded, the fire would be catastrophic. She banked around once to peer down into the gaping hole. The helicopter had hit a suspended walkway some floors up from the ground, miraculously right side up, and stuck there. No explosion, only twisted metal, shattered glass, and blood.

"I told them," she said to herself, wheeling away and dipping low over the city.

She looked down at her side and saw blood, but she couldn't tell how much was hers and how much belonged to the soldiers she'd slaughtered. Landing on a convenient building, she took stock. Eighteen holes in her wings, two grazes, and a shallow bullet wound across her stomach that was still bleeding. Her back hurt, too, but she couldn't see how badly she'd been hit. She pressed a hand to the bullet's track and heaved a shuddering sigh. Her phone was silent, either off-line or damaged. She thought of Hutch and Persephone. Were they alive? She needed to know.

"Carrier two, call Persephone."

She received an out of service message. Persephone's phone was either off or destroyed. Aleksi stifled a sob and said, "Carrier two, call Reggie."

It rang twice before he answered. "Aleksi?"

"Yes. Do you have Hutch and Lori?"

"Yes, we have them, and we're on our way home. They're both injured, but stable."

*Injured but stable.* Well, that was far better than dead.

"And Persephone?"

"I don't know. I lost contact with her."

"Ed, are you on the line?" she asked.

"Yes. Sorry, but Persephone's phone is down. No signal at all to my ping."

Aleksi looked up into the sky, letting the rain patter against her face. *Please, please let her be okay...*

"Are you okay, Aleksi?" Reggie asked.

"No." The answer came automatically and had nothing to do with her physical state. The horror of what she'd done had begun to settle in. "No, I'm not okay."

"Tell us where you are, and we'll come pick you up."

"No." Aleksi heaved a breath, which turned into another sob. "I'll see you at home. End call. Phone off."

She stood there for a while longer, letting the rain wash the blood from her body. She didn't think any amount of water would wash it away from her soul.

"I warned them," she finally reminded herself. That was her only saving grace, the one thing that might save her. Mary Buckmann had learned what it truly meant to meddle in the affairs of dragons. Maybe they would learn. If they didn't...God help them.

Aleksi checked the gash across the side of her abdomen; the bleeding had slowed to an ooze, and she could move without making it worse. She checked her wings again, damaged, but no broken bones. They would keep her in the air. Reggie would stitch her up. There was only one burning concern left in her mind, but there was nothing she could do about it.

"Persephone..."

The Dragon of Boston leapt off the building and wheeled toward home.

---

Persephone limped away from the construction site and into Downtown Boston, her hip stabbing her with every step. She found an alley and stopped to listen. The sirens were still howling, fire trucks from every station north of South Boston responding to the crash. She gave a mental thanks that the aircraft hadn't exploded as they always seemed to in Hollywood movies.

"Well, I guess Boston isn't Hollywood." She leaned against a dumpster and tore off her stocking cap. "In Hollywood movies, the heroine doesn't get shot in the ass."

She struggled out of her utility vest and shirt—she wore a faded Red Sox tee beneath—unclipped her fanny pack and unfastened her pants. Hissing as she pulled them down over the injury, she stared for a moment in surprise. There wasn't that much bleeding, just a circle of tiny wounds from shattered bits of plastic around a larger puckered crater right above her hip bone. The shot had been a ricochet, thank God. A direct hit there would have probably killed her. Still, it hurt like hell, and she didn't feel like digging out the slug with her claws.

"Perfectly good pair of panties literally shot to hell!" She wiped off the blood with her cap and pitched it and her vest into the dumpster, then she pulled up her pants and fastened them with gritted teeth. "No more skimpy bathing suits, I guess."

Tucking in her t-shirt and tying her long-sleeve black pullover around her waist, she ruffled her damp hair up and set out for the bright lights of a nearby sports bar. The Sox were playing out of town, so the place was packed, but a number of people were outside, pointing and talking about the incident. Half of the screens inside were showing the O'Neill building from the street, the explosions of Reggie's distraction, and the helicopters flying overhead. Persephone went to the bar, ordered a double vodka martini, and forced a smile at the cute bartender. The woman returned in a heartbeat with the cocktail.

"Rough night?"

"You could say that. Hey, would you mind calling me a cab? I've had too much to drive, and my phone's dead." She put a little slur in her words for good measure.

The bartender smiled back. "I'm off in half an hour if you want to save the fare."

Persephone cocked an eyebrow. "You're sweet, but I'm dead on my feet tonight." She raised the glass to the woman. "Maybe another night."

"No problem." The woman pulled her phone and tapped the screen to summon a taxi. "Here in ten minutes."

"Thank you…"

"Betts." She held out a fist.

"Melanie." Persephone bumped the fist. "Nice to meet you, Betts."

"You too. New in town? I don't recognize you."

"I am, actually." Persephone sipped her martini—it was very good—and sighed. "Out from LA permanently."

"Divorced?"

"Dead husband."

"Oh." Betts' face fell. "I'm sorry."

"So am I." Persephone gave her a sad smile. The necessary lies were always the easiest. "Moved out here to make a new start."

"Good for you." Betts gave her a nod. "If you ever need a shoulder to cry on, I'm here almost every night."

"I'll remember that. Thank you." She fished a twenty out of her fanny pack and dropped it on the bar.

"Drink's on me." Betts waved it off and walked away to see to other customers, unaware that she'd just reaffirmed Persephone's faith in humanity. *Such a simple thing, faith...* She sipped her drink and mumbled a little prayer that Hutch and Aleksi were alive.

"Cab's here," Betts called what seemed like only seconds later.

"Thanks!" Persephone downed her martini, put her glass down on the twenty, and wobbled out of the bar, her unsteady gait unfeigned.

She told the cabbie to take her to an address in Back Bay where she'd parked the Audi, leaned back in the seat, and watched the city she loved pass by. When he pulled to a stop, she paid him in cash with a ridiculous tip and got out, trying not to limp.

Clicking her key fob and opening the Audi's door. She made sure to keep her shirt between her bloody hip and the leather upholstery as she sank into the seat. One touch fired up the engine. She drove home at a leisurely pace, resisting the urge to speed. Traffic was light, at least. Getting pulled over now would be disastrous, and whatever had happened had happened.

An hour later, she pulled into the off-street parking lot behind their building and spotted the van. Someone had already peeled off the stickers that had transformed it into a Channel 5 News van. She parked beside it and got out, gritting her teeth at the stabbing pain in her hip.

Breathing in the night air, she smelled blood, and not her own. Horrified of what she would find, Persephone dashed for the cellar door, her pain forgotten.

## 28

Aleksi landed on top of the safe house, crouching to listen and scent the air out of habit. She knew instantly that she was the first one back. She thought about going in or phoning Ed but decided to wait in silence. She'd find out firsthand what had happened.

The rain eased off, and she shook the water from her wings. Her injuries twinged, but all the bleeding had long since stopped. She pulled her wings around her and listened for the sound of the van, breathing in the night. *Please let them be all right... Please...* What seemed an eternity later, the mocked-up van pulled into the parking lot. The cellar door opened below, and Ed and three more cousins hurried out.

Aleksi checked for anyone else around and swooped down to land at the back doors of the van. They opened, and Reggie started in surprise.

"Jesus, Aleksi, you scared the shit out of me."

"Sorry." She squinted past him into the red-lit interior. "How are they?"

The dragon, Lori, lay strapped to a stretcher with an IV in her arm, and Hutch sat up in a padded seat, his shoulder swathed in bandages and his face pale. He blinked and smiled at her.

"Fine. Lori's sedated with a gunshot wound that isn't serious, and Hutch...well Lori kind of went a little crazy when she woke up."

"I'm fine." Hutch stayed put as Carrie maneuvered back between the seats and pushed the gurney with Lori out the back. The other cousins started peeling off the stickers that disguised the van and helped usher Lori toward the stairs. Carrie helped Hutch up and steadied his arm. He accepted Aleksi's help getting down, and his eyes took in her conditions. "Looks like you're worse off than me, but you managed to get here okay."

"I'm fine. Just a few grazes." Aleksi wrapped a wing around him and helped him toward the cellar stairs. "I haven't heard from Persephone yet, Hutch."

"I know. Reggie said they think her phone's out." He sighed and worked his way down the stairs slowly. "Look, Aleksi, I've got to tell you, Lori, she...bit me." He touched his shoulder. "Deep. There's no doubt that I'm infected."

"Don't worry. Reggie can block the infection before it settles in and starts anything." She guided him into the basement living area where they'd set up a treatment room. "Reg, Hutch needs you to—"

"Already thawing the retroviruses." He pointed to a recliner. "We'll get an IV in and start the treatment as soon as they're ready. Don't worry, Hutch. Chances are, we can catch it before the cascade begins."

"Chances are?" Aleksi scowled at Reggie. "What do you mean?"

"It's been over an hour, so there's no way to be sure we'll catch it in time. He's already running a fever." Reggie started an IV and began running fluids in. "There's no way to tell right now if the cascade's begun, and we're not set up to do any major genetic alterations. Eventually, we can fix anything, but I need to set up a lab for that."

"Which will take time," Hutch added with a sad smile. "Aleksi, if the cascade has already started, there's nothing he can do."

"Then we'll just have to find another lab! Maybe Jim Bornstein can—"

"I'm not going to drag Jim into this, and I can't show my face. The feds will have every cop in Boston looking for me."

"Then we'll go someplace else!" she insisted. "I'm not going to let that happen to you, Hutch. You *know* what this thing does to men!"

"Yes, I *do* know." He reached up and brushed her cheek with his fingers. "I'm not going to become another David Gilford or Derrick Penningly, Aleksi."

"You won't! They can fix it!"

"Not soon enough, and they can't keep me sedated while they set up a genetics laboratory." He gestured to Lori, breathing fast and twitching despite the heavy sedation. "We've *seen* what happens there. If I start changing...I want them to...end it."

"No!" She glared at him and grasped his hand hard, refusing the logic, the facts, the cold resolve in his eyes. "Over my dead body! I won't let them! Not after...everything that's happened." *Not after I became a killer to save you*, she didn't say.

"It's not *your* choice, Aleksi." He squeezed her hand hard. "It's *mine*. I'm not going to become something that *you* have to destroy!"

A tear slipped down her nose and dripped onto their clenched hands. "Goddamn you Hutch! I can't let you die!"

"Nobody's dying today."

They both turned to find Persephone standing in the doorway. Aleksi's heart leapt. She lunged across the room and grasped the woman in a fierce embrace.

"God, it's good to see you alive!"

"You, too, Aleksi." She sounded a little strained, so Aleksi released her. Pain contorted her features.

"I'm sorry! Are you okay?"

"I've got a bullet in my hip, but I'm walking." She flashed a smile and stepped past Aleksi to Hutch's chair. "I know I don't look like my old self, Hutch, but—"

"Persephone?" His eyes roved up and down. "You're..."

"A new woman." She leaned down and kissed him, then glanced back at Aleksi. "Now, enough talk about dying. Reggie will have the cure into you in five minutes, and I'm going to pull out all the stops to find a new home where we can set up a lab. We'll have it put together in a week, or my name's not Terris."

"But your name's *Ingram* now," Aleksi reminded her.

"Shut up, you." She glared and hobbled over to a chair. "Now, I know you're busy, Reg, but when you get a break, could you please dig a bullet out of my ass?"

"When I get a break, yes." He glanced at Lori, and Aleksi. "Looks like I've got a couple of dragons to patch up, too."

"Triage," Carrie cut in. "Get Hutch started while I look at Lori's wound, then we'll pull the bullet out of Seph, then stitch up Miss Swiss Cheese wings over there. Simple!"

"Right. Simple." Reggie drew something from a cryovial into a syringe and injected it into Hutch's IV. "There. You're cured. I'll have a look at your shoulder in a minute."

"It actually feels pretty good." Hutch lifted his arm with a grimace.

"Dragon bites heal fast," Aleksi held up a hand.

"Dragons heal fast in general, which reminds me." Reggie pointed to Lori. "I'm assigning you to be her guardian, Aleksi. She's been on God knows how many meds for about two months. She could wake up at any moment and go ape shit. You're the only one who can deal with her."

"You're also probably the only person in the room she'll listen to," Persephone added.

"Challenge accepted." Aleksi clutched Hutch's hand briefly and went to the gurney on which Lori lay. She pressed a hand to her forehead and examined her head to foot. Strangely, she felt a tug of emotion in her gut. She didn't know this woman, had never met her, but they shared one commonality: *We're the same species*, Homo draconis. They were, technically, related through the original dragon sample. For that matter, she and Persephone were similarly related, though to a lesser degree.

*My legacy*, she thought, wondering, hoping, praying that this would all work out.

"Don't worry, Aleksi," Persephone said, as if reading her mind. "We're family now. We take care of our family."

Aleksi nodded without looking at her, staring down at the familiar draconic features. She found them less monstrous now, even beautiful. For the first time, she saw what Hutch said he saw in her.

"Yes, we're family." She ran a hand down Lori's golden cheek. "We're family."

---

M ary Buckmann stepped out onto the roof of the O'Neill building and grimaced at the scene. Eight body bags were lined up in a neat row, and a medevac helicopter lifted off the roof with four survivors, all of them maimed in one way or another. There had been another dozen injuries in the stairwell, and eight more guards on B5 and B6. Add in the two airborne teams—four injured and four dead—and the grim total added up to twelve dead and twenty-eight injured.

*A fucking nightmare*, she thought to herself.

As if on cue, her new phone vibrated in her pocket. Predictably, the number was blocked. The text read, "I warned you. The deaths are on your hands, Mary. Think again before you threaten the people I love...for you are tender and taste good with ketchup."

Mary stared at the message for a long time, then deleted it. There was no real threat there any longer. The project was over, and if it ever did start up again, she wouldn't be a part of it; the director had told her as much not ten minutes ago.

"Not with a terrorist organization capable of *this* out there, Doctor. I'm sorry, but we're done with this project for now. Until we crack the infection problem, the *Homo draconis* experiment is on hold. I'm putting you in for a transfer. It'll be safer for you if you're out of Boston."

*And a terrorist organization is free to make their own army of dragons.* Mary walked over to the smashed skylight and squinted down at the wrecked helicopter. A hazmat team was off-loading the fuel, and medical personnel were hauling away the corpses. *An army of dragons, when one can do this.*

Her phone vibrated again, a call this time. She looked at the caller ID and let it go to voicemail. She had no desire to talk to Tony Jasper.

---

No answer." Tony ended the call without leaving a message. There was no point, and he didn't want what he had to say to Mary Buckmann recorded anywhere.

"Well, I imagine she's been a little busy tonight." Marty gazed up at the O'Neill building as the medevac helicopter took off. "Hell of a mess."

"And one hell of a credible threat! You need to keep that CI at all costs, Tony." Blake strode up with an exhausted scowl on her face. "The feds aren't talking, but there were four on that chopper that went down. I doubt any survived the crash. How the hell they knocked down a helicopter is beyond me."

"Who knows." Tony shared a conspiratorial glance with Marty. They knew what had knocked down the helicopter. "Some kind of secret weapon, I suppose. I wonder if they got their prisoner out in one piece."

"I don't know how, but those concussion explosions were obviously a diversion." Blake waved at the shattered windows across the street. "Not one injury, except for some hearing loss."

"And a shit-ton of soiled underwear," Marty added.

"Roger that." Blake glanced around, but most of the BPD and Cambridge units had already left the scene. The feds had been adamant that they could see to the details. The only flashing lights left were from one hazmat fire unit and four ambulances. "I think we're done here, Detectives. I'm officially off duty anyway, so can I buy you both a beer?"

"No thanks," Marty said with a shake of his head. "Three's a crowd."

"I'm game, but it's my turn to buy." He waved to Marty. "See you in the morning."

"See you, partner." Marty waved and headed for their car.

"So, O'Brien's?" Tony asked as they strode for Blake's car.

"Nah, it's going to be crawling with cops after this. I don't feel like dealing with the bullshit." She flashed him a smile and a shrug. "Been a long day."

"Where then?"

"I know a place not far."

"As long as they've got cold beer, I'm in."

"We can pick up a six-pack on the way."

Tony stopped in his tracks, his brow knitted in confusion. "Pick up a..."

Anna turned and gave him a look and a wink. "Yeah. My place. You're buying the beer. It's *your* turn tonight, and you promised to introduce me to that friend of yours."

He gaped at her.

"Close your mouth and get in the car, Detective Jasper." She fished out her keys and unlocked the doors.

Tony closed his mouth and did as he was told. As he clipped his seat belt, his encrypted phone vibrated in his pocket. He fished it out and pulled up the text.

"If that's work, you're off duty," Anna said.

"It's not. It's my CI checking in." He smiled at the text, tapped a reply, and sent it.

"Oh?" She cocked an eyebrow at him and pulled the car out into traffic.

"Yep. They just wanted to touch base."

"Good. Now turn that damned thing off."

"Yes, ma'am." He did, but the text ran through his mind on repeat, warming his heart.

It had read, "A, H, and LW all okay. Thanks. IOU one Audi AS5 Coupe. What color?"

On a whim, he'd replied, "Blue." He didn't know how he felt about accepting a gift from someone the government considered a terrorist. He didn't need or particularly want a flashy new car, either. He had almost everything he wanted right now. He had to admit, however, it was a sweet ride. Maybe he'd store it in a nice garage and save it for his retirement, take it out on weekends to drive through the Blue Hills with Anna.

Tony filed a mental reminder to delete those texts, but he'd do it later. He reached across the car and put a hand on Anna's, lacing his fingers with hers. "Thanks for believing me tonight, Anna. It means a lot to me."

"I'll let you pay me back sometime." She shot him a grin and squeezed his hand. "I accept chocolate in all denominations."

"Ha! Noted." He squeezed her hand back.

# EPILOGUE

Mary stared around her apartment at the few remaining boxes and sighed. "Next stop, El Paso." Her transfer had taken two weeks to go through, and the moving arrangements had taken another week. She'd done very little but deal with the fallout from the attack on the O'Neill building, pack all of her worldly possessions, and see to all the details of her upcoming assignment in that time. In the morning, she'd be on the road. "From chasing dragons to chasing human traffickers. Unbelievable."

Still, the posting would be admittedly safer, and she doubted anyone under her would get murdered due to her screwups. There had been few formal reprimands when everything settled. She'd taken the job they'd given her, followed protocols, and used her best judgment. Federal guidelines for dealing with terrorist threats, her superiors all agreed, hadn't been written with dragons in mind. Maybe they were being rewritten, but nobody had asked for her input.

*Dragons...* Mary sighed and rubbed her face. The last three weeks had been one of the few times in her life that she regretted not drinking.

She'd been given a full security detail to keep her safe after the incident, for all the good it would have done, but Aleksi hadn't made an appearance. Not even so much as a text. Mary supposed she'd let bygones be bygones; they'd both done things they hadn't wanted to do, and she'd been right about one thing: Aleksi had warned her more than once. The blood was as much on Mary's hands as the dragon's.

She went to the kitchen and opened the fridge, but it was empty. Everything had already been packed or thrown away. The moving van was already gone. The rest would fit in the trunk of her car in the morning. She didn't even have a box of crackers or coffee in the apartment.

It was late, so the corner bakery was closed. There was a bar and grill a block away, and she could use the walk. The first cool front of autumn had come through Boston, bringing crisp clean air. The forecast for El Paso was in the nineties for the following week, with humidity in the teens. That would take some getting used to.

As Mary strode for the door, shadows moved in the corners of her apartment. She froze and turned, gaping at the two yellow eyes glowing in the reflected light. Terror gripped her stomach in a vice, and her hand reached for the pistol under her jacket.

"Don't!" The eyes moved, and Aleksi emerged from the shadows, golden scales glistening, claws extended. A wide scar crossed her stomach, and her lips curled back from her teeth. "We're not here to kill you, Mary, but if you touch that gun, I'll reconsider."

"We?" Mary turned at the scuff of another clawed foot on the carpet to find a second dragon standing at her living room window. Mary's hand dropped away from her pistol. "Lori?"

"Yes," the other dragon said, her voice stirring memories in Mary's mind. "I had to see you before you left Boston."

"Why?" Mary glanced from one dragon to the other. Aleksi had said they weren't here to kill her, but they had every reason to. She'd caused them both a lot of pain.

"Because I wanted to tell you that you were wrong." Lori took a step forward, less fluid and graceful than Aleksi, but still the movement of a predator, a cat stalking a mouse, and Mary was the mouse. "You don't understand us and you never will."

"I've been wrong about a lot of things." She looked to Aleksi, and a flicker of hope kindled in her heart. "I did warn them about David and the danger of an outbreak."

"I know you did." Aleksi stepped forward, too, and more scars gleamed in the lamplight. She hadn't gotten through the battle atop the O'Neill building unscathed. "He wasn't your fault, but Lori..."

"I had no choice about Lori," Mary insisted.

"Bullshit!" Lori took another step, and Mary could see the rage in her eyes, the tense muscles, the claws ready to rip her heart out. "They *told* me about the other two women David infected. They're *fine*! They're *human*! All you had to do was let them take me, and I'd be human, too!"

"I couldn't do that, Lori," Mary said.

"Why not?"

"Because I wasn't *allowed* to. If I'd tried, I'd have been overridden and replaced. That's the way the government works. Checks and balances."

"Your checks and balances forced me to become a killer, Mary." Aleksi stepped up to her, close enough that one sweep of her claws would tear Mary open. "I warned you, and you did the one thing that I couldn't stand for. You took the man I love from me and destroyed his life." Aleksi's lips curled back from her teeth. "I *told* you that female dragons have protective instincts! I *warned* you!"

"Yes, you did. And you warned David Gilford. You told him to own it, learn to control the urges, and he couldn't. I should have learned from that, too. I didn't know what you would do."

"Well, now you do." Aleksi stepped past her to Lori's side and the two dragons regarded her. "I know you're leaving, that you've been reassigned somewhere, but you need to tell these people something."

"What?" Mary breathed a little easier; if Aleksi wanted her to deliver a message, that meant she'd survive this encounter. "Tell them what?"

"Tell them that their thinking is fundamentally flawed." She rested a hand to Lori's shoulder. "Your organization thinks only about advancing their own power base. A new weapon, a new tool, a new discovery only means more control, more intimidation, more brute force to manipulate the world, other governments, other people. You call people like Persephone Terris terrorists because they differ from that mentality."

"They killed eight of my—"

"No, Mary, *you* killed them," Aleksi raised a clawed hand. "Just like you killed those soldiers on the roof of the O'Neill building. The Terrises had something you wanted, and you tried to take it. If a burglar broke into this apartment to rob you, and you shot them dead, who would be at fault?"

She had a point, but one that the federal government would never accede to. "Telling DHS to give in to terrorist demands is a non-starter, Aleksi."

"What demands did they have other than to be left alone, Mary?"

She had another point, and Mary nodded. "I'll tell them, then, but it won't do any good. The Terris family will remain on the terrorist list. I don't have that much pull."

"No, but tell them this, too." Aleksi took Lori's clawed hand in her own and raised them together. "We are *family*, and we *protect* our family. We want nothing but to be left alone, in peace, but if you or *anyone* comes after us…"

"You have what they wanted, Aleksi; an army of dragons. They'll never stand for that."

"We're not an army, Mary. We're *family*. Get that through their heads. Ask them what they would do to protect *their* families. Tell them. Warn them. That's all."

"I will, but I can't guarantee any results."

Aleksi nodded and released Lori's hand. "Then we're done here."

As the two dragons turned to leave, Mary said, "Thank you, Aleksi."

She froze and looked back, yellow eyes narrow and gleaming. "For what?"

"For not killing me."

"We're not murderers, Mary. We never were." They turned and slipped out of the open window, silent and deadly, and more than a little beautiful.

Mary took a deep breath and let it out slowly. She'd do as they asked but had little hope that her warning would change anything. The government would look at the casualty reports and see a threat.

*That's on them*, she thought, turning away from her past for the last time. All she could do was deliver Aleksi's warning. She'd looked up the quote and discovered that it was a paraphrase from an old fantasy novel. She found it all too appropriate. She knew exactly what she would tell her superiors.

"Do not meddle in the affairs of dragons, for they are subtle and quick to anger."

---

Aleksi landed on the roof of the statehouse dome and breathed in the cool air. Winter would be here soon, and she couldn't wait.

Lori landed beside her, her claws gouging the gold finish. She'd picked up flying quickly, and reveled in the experience, but she was still learning the finer points of landings and staying hidden. She looked at Aleksi with a question in her eyes but didn't speak.

"What?" Aleksi folded her wings and cocked her head, listening to the city, breathing in the scents of a million humans.

"How do you do it?" Lori asked.

"Do what?"

"Keep from killing people who deserve it." She gestured back toward Back Bay and Buckmann's apartment. "If you hadn't been there to stop me..."

"You have to remember what we are, *why* we are, but also who *you* are." Aleksi rested a hand on the other dragon's shoulder. "You're Lori Watkins, not a monster, not a murderer."

"Easy to say..." But Lori nodded. She was trying, and that was all Aleksi could ask.

Lori's recuperation had been difficult but quick. Once the infective elements of her condition had been cured, they'd taken her into the hills of western Massachusetts and turned off her sedation. Only

Persephone and Aleksi were there when she woke up lying in a secluded meadow. The open space and kindred company quashed her claustrophobia and paranoia. Instead of fleeing or attacking, she'd started asking questions, and for several days they'd done nothing but camp out, eat good food, drink good wine, and talk. Lori was still dealing with PTSD, survivor's guilt, and the violent instincts of a dragon, but Aleksi had offered the one thing she needed: family. Flying helped, too. She was still twitchy, dealing with drug withdrawals and violent impulses, but she was stable and learning to cope.

"We only kill to protect the ones we love, Lori. Doing otherwise is the unforgivable sin."

Lori nodded down to the teeming masses of humans out on the streets for a Saturday night. "What about the ones who prey on the weak?"

"That's a more difficult call. For the most part, we have to hold back from killing. It's just too dangerous for us." Aleksi grinned. "That doesn't mean we can't scare the shit out of an occasional sexual predator, however." She still had Tony Jasper on speed dial and had delivered more than one rapist to BPD through his tips. "But above all, we protect our family. If we start hunting rapists, the government will start hunting *us* again, and that will put everyone in danger."

Lori nodded. "I never had one, you know. A family, I mean. At least not one worth a damn. I was trying, when..." Her eyes teared up.

"I know." Aleksi squeezed her shoulder. "If you want to try, we can ask Reggie to start reversing your condition. It's unpleasant, but you shouldn't have the same problems I did. It might work."

"No thanks." Lori smiled sadly and spread her wings. "This is who I am, now. I don't think I could go back to what I was."

"Well, keep it in mind."

"I will."

Aleksi's phone vibrated against her leg, and she peeled it free. She smiled at the picture on the caller ID, chiseled features, cleft chin, high cheekbones, and wavy black hair; he wasn't the Hutch she remembered at all, but the sight of him still made her heart race. She touched the screen to accept the call.

"Hey."

"Hey, Dragon Woman. When are you coming home? It's family dinner night, and Carrie's making steaks."

"Says the vegetarian," she chided.

"Well, I may fall off the wagon this once. Medical advancements, you know."

"Right." Reggie had informed Hutch that his family propensity for heart disease and colon cancer wouldn't offer any challenges to their expertise. In fact, Hutch had convinced the family to leak a few of their advances to Jim Bornstein. He and Lonnie were about to make a breakthrough in cancer treatment. "We'll be there in fifteen minutes."

"I'll open the wine."

Aleksi ended the call and taped the phone back to her leg. When she looked up, she found Lori staring at her, tears streaming down her face.

"What?"

"You're so lucky, that's all. Hutch is…so special." She sniffed and wiped away the tears.

"He is, but don't be sad about it. You'll find someone."

"Not likely."

"Don't bet on it." She clutched Lori's hand and gave it a tug. "You're beautiful, Lori. Some people can see past the scales and wings, and Persephone's got a big family. A few more new cousins are coming to stay with us, and she said they're dying to meet us. We're still human, after all."

"I keep telling myself that." Lori squeezed her hand. "Thank you."

"Come on, sister. It's family dinner night. I'll race you home."

Two dragons leapt into the sky above Boston, swooping and diving through the canyons of buildings and trees toward home—and family.

## THE END

# ACKNOWLEDGMENTS

Many thanks as always to my wife, Dr. Anne L. McMillen-Jackson, for her patience and support through this and all of my other works. Juggling multiple writing projects makes me hard to live with, and I'm not dead yet, so that attests to her saint-like level of tolerance. Also, thanks to John Hartness and the entire crew at Falstaff Books for their help, friendship, and professionalism. A lot of research went into this book for the treatments of many psychological disorders, and I'd like to thank all of the scientists carrying on research in this minefield of neurochemistry and behavior.

# ABOUT THE AUTHOR

Born and raised in Oregon, Chris met his wife and soulmate, Anne, while attending graduate school in Texas. Since then they have been gaming together since 1985, sailing together since 1988, married since 1989, and writing together off and on throughout their relationship. Most astonishingly, they have not killed each other during the creation or editing of any of their stories…although it was close a few times. Since 2009, the couple has been sailing and writing full-time aboard their beloved sailboat, *Mr Mac*. They return to the US every summer for conventions, always happy to sign copies of their books and talk with fans.

Find him on Twitter here: https://twitter.com/ChrisAJackson1

Or on Facebook here: https://www.facebook.com/chris.a.jackson.967

Check out Chris's books on Goodreads https://www.goodreads.com/chrisajackson or on https://www.jaxbooks.com/

## ALSO BY CHRIS A. JACKSON

**From Jaxbooks**

*A Soul for Tsing*

*Deathmask*

The Blood Sea Tales

Weapon of Flesh Series

The Cornerstones Trilogy
(with Anne L. McMillen-Jackson)

The Cheese Runners Trilogy
(novellas – also on Audible)

**From Shadow Alley Press**

*Pacifica* (Book 1 of the Alden Northcliff Saga)

**From Dragon Moon Press**

The Scimitar Seas Novels

**From Paizo Publishing**

*Pirate's Honor*

*Pirate's Promise*

*Pirate's Prophecy*

**From Privateer Press**

*Blood & Iron* (ebook novella)

*Watery Graves*

**From Fantasy Flight Games**

*The Deep Gate* (hardcover novella)

**From Catalyst**

*Crocodile Tears* (e-book novella)

# FALSTAFF BOOKS

**Want to know what's new & coming soon from
Falstaff Books?**

**Join our Newsletter List
& Get this Free Ebook Sampler
with work from:
John G. Hartness
A.G. Carpenter
Bobby Nash
Emily Lavin Leverett
Jaym Gates
Darin Kennedy
Natania Barron
Edmund R. Schubert
& More!**

http://www.subscribepage.com/q0j0p3